ALLISON & BUSBY
TWENTIETH CENTURY CLASSICS

What is it that makes us pick up and read a book again and again? The memory of that first immersion when everything but what we were reading pales into insignificance? When the book ate with us, walked with us, travelled with us, slept with us, and, when it was finished, we grieved as for the loss of a close friend. For us that book and what it had to say to us remains as true now as it did when we first connected with it.

There comes a time when we realise that we haven't seen it let alone read it for years, and when we try to get it in the bookshop find that it is out of print and there are no plans to reprint. Second-hand copies are in short supply so the book is lost to us. It is that sense of loss which stimulated me into starting up the Allison & Busby Twentieth Century Classics, reprinting old favourites which still speak to me as strongly as they did when I first picked them up.

These are not the books you are going to find in other series, the national classics which have been in print for ever; these are my favourites, books I think should be in print, books that I really believe you will want to read and enjoy, books that will speak to you as they have to me.

If I am right and these are books you enjoy reading then why not write to me with your own out-of-print favourites and I will see whether they too can be included in this new Allison & Busby Twentieth Century Classics list.

PETER DAY
Editor

THE
WIDOW

Francis King

ALLISON & BUSBY

This edition first published in Great Britain by
Allison & Busby
an imprint of Virgin Publishing
338 Ladbroke Grove
London W10 5AH

Printed in Great Britain by
Mackays of Chatham Ltd, Lordswood, Kent.

ISBN 0 7490 0024 4
The moral right of the author has been asserted

TO MY SISTER
PAMELA NICHOLAS

I
BEFORE

I

They quarrelled that morning, as they had so often quarrelled during the voyage out. On his side there were weakness and pain and, with them, the exasperating consciousness that, in some inexplicable way, someone had cheated him of the recovery which he had promised himself as soon as they were out of England and away from his doctors; while on her side there was an anxiety so obvious in spite of all her efforts at concealment that, intensifying his own anxiety, it had now begun to make even her presence intolerable to him. It was only that morning that he had found himself shouting at her: "Oh, don't fuss! Don't fuss so! Can't you leave me alone?"; and that morning, as she herself tearfully pointed out, she had said nothing at all. But it was enough for her to peer at the thermometer with that faint line appearing down the centre of her smooth, broad forehead as the corners of her mouth went limp, and then to give the thermometer a brisk shake and say with an equal briskness while she held it under the tap: "Well, that's an improvement on yesterday," turning her head at the same time to force him a silly, nervous smile. The terrible thing was that he knew her too well; she could hide nothing from him.

After that brief outburst, when he shouted at her not to fuss, the perverse desire to drag out into the open the fear which he could only just glimpse, cringing behind her smile, made him fling back the bedclothes to reveal his thin, hairy legs with the pyjama trousers rucked about the knees. Although he felt wretched and had decided, when he had first woken up, that he would spend the day in his bunk, her look of panic was enough to bring his feet down to the cold, slippery floor of the cabin, as he commanded: "Bring me my dressing-gown. Why are you staring at me like that? Hurry up!"

"But, Adrian, you're not going to get up, are you? Is that wise?"

"Of course I'm going to get up. Didn't you say that the temperature was an improvement on yesterday? Come on—hurry up! Or do you *want* me to catch cold?"

She brought the dressing-gown and put out an arm to steady him when he tottered on his way towards the wash-basin. "This damn ship!" he growled: but the sea stretched infinitely calm beneath their port-hole and the ship was moving with only the gentlest of vibrations. Once at the wash-basin, he began to cough and spit, not because he felt any real necessity to do so, but because he knew that this, too, would alarm her; but then he found he could not stop and he had to go on and on, while he felt her arm growing firmer and firmer about his wildly jerking shoulders. "Oh, damn, damn, damn," he exploded, tearing himself away from her.

"You see, you shouldn't have got up."

"Mind your own business. I'm—perfectly—all—right." When he had choked out the words, the coughing at last stopped. "Quite all right," he repeated, wiping his streaming eyes on the wrinkled backs of his hands. "Now where is my razor? . . . You didn't dry it properly last time," he grunted as she handed it to him. "Look at this rust. . . . I'll wear my white tussore suit." He could not bear the way she was gazing at him, still with that look of patient, frightened suffering which she had never succeeded in hiding. But she ought to hide it, he thought in a wild exasperation; it was her business to hide it. "Come on! Come on!" he cried. "And the white shoes. Get them out of the cupboard, Christine."

"But, darling, ought you to be getting dressed? If you want to go up on deck, can't you do so in your dressing-gown?"

"And be stared at by everyone? Thank you, no. . . . Anyway, aren't we docking after luncheon?"

"Yes," she said faintly.

"Well, I intend to go ashore."

"Adrian, no!"

"I'm sick of being cooped up on this tub. It won't do me any harm."

"But, Adrian, while you have a temperature—it's absolute madness."

It was then that they really began to quarrel. "Sometimes I think that you enjoy having me laid up in this—this coffin,"

4

he had accused her, looking venomously about their expensive state-room. "How do you expect me to get well, when I get no encouragement from you? Nothing but these lugubrious looks as though—as though I were dying!"

"Oh, Adrian! You—you were told to be careful—and you oughtn't really to have left England for at least another month——"

"These doctors are just so many old women. . . . They all said that I came out of the operation wonderfully, didn't they? Well, didn't they? Naturally, I am a little weak, but it doesn't do to give in to weakness. That's what you don't understand, never have been able to understand." He shaved himself jerkily, every now and again nicking his face with a muttered: "Damnation!" Then, "That's better," he said. "I don't look too bad." He peered into his own feverish eyes and then beyond them, at the reflection of Christine, seated on the edge of an arm-chair, her hands in her lap, while she still silently, sufferingly and reproachfully continued to watch him. "Have you nothing to do?" he wanted to shout, but he controlled himself, because that reflection, so remote and small in the mirror above the wash-basin, had all at once given him a sensation of remorse and tenderness that was almost a physical qualm. Slowly and breathing heavily, he began to pull on his clothes. At one point, a cuff-link fell from his fingers, and, as he slowly doubled himself over, his left hand gripping the wash-basin while his right groped blindly downward, she moved on to the very edge of the chair, in an agony of doubt whether to help him or not. Suddenly he tottered, taking two curious little shuffling steps backwards and then one forward as though in a tipsy dance; and that at last decided her. "Oh, don't, don't!" she jumped up to plead with him. She snatched the cuff-link off the floor and, clutching it in one fist, went on: "Can't you see that you're not well enough to be on your feet? Adrian—do get back to bed!"

"Would you kindly allow me to decide for myself how I feel this morning?" She had always been able to withstand his noisy explosions of rage, but his sarcasm never. "May I have that cuff-link? Thank you. Now suppose you find yourself something to occupy you. I know that you never read, but you must have some knitting that you could take with you up on deck."

Once again she sat down but, because she knew that it

annoyed him, she forced herself not to watch him as, with clumsy hands, he fumbled at his tie, his trouser-buttons and the laces of his shoes. She told herself that he was ill and probably in pain, and that none of the wounding things which he now never ceased to say to her had any real significance. But they were said, and they wounded. Then she thought, as she had lain awake thinking for most of the previous night, of what would happen if she lost him: until, panic-stricken, she deliberately forced herself to concentrate on other, more trivial anxieties. There was a prescription which she had somehow mislaid; and she had forgotten to pick up the book which was being kept for him in the ship's library. Superstitiously she had the idea that by entertaining, even for a moment, the fear of his dying, she would somehow make it easier for that dying to become a reality. Nor was she wholly wrong. He had always known what she was thinking and he knew it all now; and there were times when to see his own fear mirrored back at him as, in the past, she had mirrored his devotion, gave him a feeling of hopelessness and terror. What was the good of this struggle? he would then begin to think. Why keep up this pretence? But, a few seconds later, the forces of his will would rally as, to the amazement of his doctors, his physical forces had rallied after his operation, telling him that, of course, he was all right, already he was better; it was she who infected him with her spineless apprehensions and who, by doing so, actually retarded his recovery. Then he would burst out at her in frustrated rage as he had burst out just now.

Suddenly, in the middle of her reverie, Christine was aware of a sound which more than anything else—more than the coughing, the restless creaking in the bunk below her at night, or the feeble shuffle-shuffle of his feet as he walked—froze her with terror. This was a breathing which sounded like a series of low sobs that could not be controlled. For many seconds she listened, rigid on the edge of her chair, while she continued to stare out of the port-hole with eyes that nowadays had the strained look of someone who ought to be wearing glasses— although, in fact, she had all her life enjoyed exceptionally good sight. There was a low shore, a bundle of palm-trees, and above them a pinkish misty glare. She put her small hands to her mouth and then, no longer able to force herself not to look, slowly turned her head. He was once more standing at the looking-glass above the wash-basin, with a silver-backed brush held in each of his hands. From time to time he would make a feeble stroke at his head and then he would lower the brush and, leaning with his stomach against the basin, would stare at his own image. Before him, with the stopper still off, was the bottle of Floris hair-lotion, beside the other bottles of after-shave lotion, Caron lavender, bath essence, and, a little apart and so much more ugly, of the medicines which he always fretted against being made to swallow. Without replacing the stopper of the hair-lotion, he was now unscrewing the bottle of lavender and shaking it on to one of the silk handkerchiefs which he bought from the Chinese pedlars who so often came to their door. All his life he had been a dandy, but there was nothing soft about him; and his colleagues in the Indian Civil Service, though they joked about his appearance, all of them knew it. "Like a whisky ad. in *Esquire*," had been the normal comment when, half-admiringly and half-mockingly, people discussed him. But in that society it was impossible to ridicule a man who shot, played polo and swam better than most of his subordinates and all his superiors. There was a terrible pathos for Christine in the way in which, even when enfeebled by illness, these habits of a lifetime still persisted. He was now examining his hand-sewn shoes, holding them to the light that came through the port-hole. Then he went across to the bell and not so much pressed it as leant heavily on it.

"I don't think much of the way you've polished these," he said to the steward. "Have another try."

He came back to the wash-basin and once again gazed at his reflection. Feebly, he began to twitch at the suit which was sagging about his emaciated body: and it was the contrast between the beautifully tailored suit, less than three months old, and the frame on which it hung that at last reduced Christine to tears. She squirmed round and, in a futile effort to hide from him, buried her face in the back of the chair.

"Now what's the matter? What on earth's the matter?" he demanded, swinging round at her.

She could only continue to sob.

"Oh, stop it! For God's sake stop it!" It seemed to her uncanny that the words themselves and the tone of anguished appeal in which they were shouted at her were exactly the same

7

as those she had suddenly heard, one morning, when told to wait for him outside his room in the London nursing-home until the specialist had finished. Then, as now, she had been frozen in horror. But when she had been allowed to go in to him, Adrian had smiled at her and told her that he had passed a comfortable night and was feeling much better; and she had never dared to ask what it was that had drawn from him that terrified and terrifying cry.

"It's cheerful, I must say, to have you behaving as if you were at my funeral. Didn't I tell you to go up on deck, and leave me? Didn't I? He spoke to her back and shoulder because, although her sobbing had stopped, she still sat twisted round, with her face pressed into the chair. In a sudden rage he burst out: "Get out! Leave me! Leave me alone!"

It was fortunate for them both that at that moment their daughter Gwyneth came into the cabin. She was only just eighteen, but she looked older, with her glossy fair hair pulled back smoothly over her ears into a bun from which at least two tortoise-shell hair-pins could always be seen protruding. She had the same heart-shaped face as her mother, with high cheek-bones and a delicate, pointed chin; but her heavy black eyebrows, the firm line of her jaw and her expression of sulky, almost rebellious determination gave to her face both a strength and a charmlessness which her mother's face lacked. It was often said that Mrs. Cornwell, with her subtle pink-and-white colouring, her large pale blue eyes under the faintest of eyebrows, and her softly waved grey hair, was a pretty woman; but no one called Gwyneth pretty, only handsome.

Gwyneth glanced from her father to her mother, and then asked:

"What's been going on? What's the matter?" There was no answer, and she repeated: "Have you been quarrelling again?"

She never used any make-up but powder and as she now turned her flat, sallow face from one of her parents to the other, the light from the port-hole glistened on the minute beads of sweat on one side of her nose and on one of her eyebrows which her mother had so often suggested in vain that she should thin. She always held her large hands close to her side except when, as now, she wished to give to her words an emphasis which she seemed incapable of providing through her beautiful, but monotonously low-pitched voice. Then she would knit her fingers together, so that only the whitened knuckles showed, and rock them up and down.

"Mummy, what have you been saying to him? What is it? Why can't you leave him alone? You know you only upset him."

"I upset him? What have I done to upset him?" Christine sat up in her chair, rummaging in the pocket of her shantung suit for a handkerchief she could not find. "Why do you always turn on me? Why do you at once assume that I'm the one to blame? You don't seem to realize . . ."

"Oh, Mummy, Mummy, Mummy! Do stop it!" She knew that her mother was about to burst into fresh tears, and she had the feeling—part contempt, part pity, part embarrassment—with which this spectacle always filled her. "Stop it!" she repeated, and her locked hands were jerked even more vehemently. "What good does it do?" It was a question which she often asked, both aloud and to herself, when her mother insisted on having one of her scenes. For she herself, as she always admitted, was "no good" at scenes. "Look, darling, why don't you go up on deck? Larry is there and you can sit with him." Larry was Christine's step-son, the child of Adrian's former marriage to an American girl, the daughter of a missionary, who had died in giving birth to him. "I had always thought that the one thing I couldn't bear would be to have a stupid child," Adrian would say of this boy. "But I rather like Larry. And I don't find his inability to pass examinations as upsetting as I expected." Sometimes Adrian would also say how odd it was that the mother of his two clever children had been Christine, whereas the American girl, whose intelligence he exaggerated in memory, had mothered a fool like Larry. The boy was now in the Indian Army which Adrian, like most Indian Civil Servants, regarded with the same affectionate contempt with which he regarded his son.

"Daddy insists on going ashore. Do try to persuade him how silly it would be. He's not in a fit condition . . ."

"Oh for God's sake—mind your own business!" Adrian, seated on the edge of the bunk, had begun to put a new cassette into his Leica.

"Let me do that." Gwyneth took the camera and the cassette from him. "No wonder you complain that your film gets spotted." She tweaked out the silk handkerchief which he had

9

carefully arranged in the breast-pocket of his suit and began to polish the lens, saying as she did so: "If he feels well enough to go ashore, let him go ashore. It's for him to judge. You mustn't fuss him so, Mummy. It's the worst possible thing."

"That's what I keep telling her."

"There—that's better!" Gwyneth clicked the case of the camera shut, and handed it back to her father. "I read that article in the *Criterion* last night. I wonder if he's right about Annette. It's always seemed to me that Wordsworth only . . ."

Christine stood looking at them, with one hand on the knob of the door while with the other she clasped the sodden handkerchief she had at last found rolled into a ball, under her chair. She had wanted another kind of daughter, and so once had he. But whereas he had quickly reconciled himself to this shy, sharp-tongued, gauche, brilliant young woman whom they had found waiting for them at the docks when they had returned on leave after three years abroad—perhaps even preferred her to the conventional picture they had formed in their imaginations—for Christine it had remained a nagging disappointment. The daughter she was going to take back to India was to be pretty and ingenuous and together they would go about the London stores choosing the clothes which she should wear to ride with young subalterns in the morning on the *maidan* or to dance with them in the evening at Government House. Christine herself, though she had forgotten this, had been even more shy than Gwyneth when she was a young girl; and unconsciously she had fashioned in her mind the image of a daughter who would be no less pretty than she had then been, but without any of the timidity and the inhibitions which had prevented her from enjoying that prettiness. Gwyneth was to be like the daughters of all her friends, for conformity was of importance to Christine: but she was to be gayer than they, more attractive, better at tennis and bridge, more fashionably dressed, more graceful and daring on horseback. It was, therefore, a bitter shock when she discovered that Gwyneth was not merely incapable of supporting this rôle, but contemptuous of doing so. At first the girl had even announced that she was not sure that she wished to go out to India; and when Christine had said, "But, darling, it's every girl's dream," she had returned dryly: "Every girl's, perhaps—but certainly

10

not mine." In the end she was persuaded only by her father's illness, and the oddly formal and reserved, yet profound friendship which had grown up between them during his months in hospital. "India will change her," Christine would often say apologetically to her friends. "She needs bringing out of herself." But she herself believed it even less than they. When, on the boat, she had introduced her to young men who were either friends of Larry's or subordinates of her husband, Gwyneth had made it embarrassingly obvious that she was bored by them. She had even refused to go to any of the dances held on shipboard, preferring to play piquet with Adrian, to read to him, or to hold long conversations with him, during which she sat unbecomingly with her legs wide apart and her chin supported on one arm which was in turn supported on a knee. Apart from her father, her only friends appeared to be two or three of his elderly colleagues, themselves returning from leave, a middle-aged American woman missionary, and the plain, blue-stocking wife of a tea-planter who incessantly knitted and talked in a high-pitched complaining voice. None of Christine's own circle had seemed to please the girl.

"I shall be up on the boat-deck," Christine now said, as she turned to go; and she was furious but not surprised when neither of them answered her or even looked up.

Larry lay sprawled on a deck-chair, doing nothing. He was wearing shorts reaching almost to his knees, which were covered in freckles of the same khaki colour; a khaki shirt open almost to his navel, not out of exhibitionism, but because two buttons were missing; and a pair of clumsy sandals which revealed that one of his feet was smeared either with oil or with tar. He had an unlit pipe in his mouth, but, in his state of complete animal relaxation, he did not even chew on it. On the deck lay the Dornford Yates novel which he had carried around with him ever since the voyage had started: the jacket had become more and more stained and frayed, but it still marked the same place which it had marked when he had first come on board. He was not handsome, but his strength, good nature and air of physical well-being gave him an attractiveness of which he himself was entirely unconscious.

His sand-coloured eyelashes fluttered open as he heard Christine approach, and then he yawned twice, stretching his arms to their fullest extent and clenching his fists as though he

11

were about to swing himself on to an invisible bar in the air above him.

"Lazy boy," Christine said. "Do you ever do anything but sleep?"

He tweaked at the reddish hair which sprouted between his collar-bones and gave a slow, slightly crooked smile which revealed teeth that were discoloured with nicotine and were curiously small for one of his size. "Certainly," he said. "I played deck-quoits for an hour this morning. And before breakfast I had a work-out in the gym. Someone told me that to-morrow evening they are going to show a George Arliss film, The House of Something-or-other."

"Rothschild?" she suggested.

"Could be." He chuckled and pointed with the stem of his pipe at an elderly man in shorts who had just trotted past them. "That's his fifth time round. Unless I missed him while I was snoozing. They say that when we go ashore we should look out for the amber. Or was it jade? Anyway you can tell the genuine stuff by rubbing it on your sleeve and then if it picks up a piece of paper—a *little* piece of paper . . ."

"Amber," Christine said.

"Oh, amber, is it?"

There were times when, in exasperation, she wondered if he were not mentally deficient; and then she would find herself comparing him with Tim, her own son, who had, the previous year, won the top classical scholarship to his public school at the age of twelve and a half. It always puzzled her that Tim and Larry got on so well.

"Daddy insists on going ashore to-day. I tried to persuade him that it would be silly of him, but of course he wouldn't listen."

"How is the old boy? I suppose I ought to go down and see him."

"Gwyneth is there."

"Oh, she's there, is she? He would not now go, for Gwyneth puzzled him and made him feel uneasy: and though he was used to being puzzled, to be ill at ease was an experience rare for him.

"Do try to persuade him to stay in bed."

"You know he doesn't listen to me—does he? Still he's right in a way—I mean, about not giving in to things like illness."

12

Larry was never ill, except when he damaged himself in a game of polo or hockey, or suffered a particularly virulent hang-over. "Perhaps you fuss him too much." He realized that these last words were not what she wished to hear, and at once put out one of his large hands to pat hers clumsily. "You fuss all of us too much, you know—and spoil us."

Such demonstrations of affection both touched her and filled her with guilt. She had been a good mother to him and only those who were told ever knew that he was not, in fact, her son. But she had never been able to love him, even before Gwyneth and Tim were born, although she had made every effort to do so. Perhaps she had been too jealous of the dead American girl whose letters Adrian had kept for so many years until, suddenly, one day when they were spending their leave in Italy, she had found him putting a match to them in the empty grate of their hotel bedroom. Larry himself never asked about his mother; and when, on going to his preparatory school, he was given her photograph to take with him, he returned home at the end of the term mysteriously without-it. Adrian often told Christine that he was sure that Larry cared far more for her than her own children did: and that would never fail to annoy her.

The palm of Larry's hand felt disagreeably sweaty on the back of hers; but she had always found physical contact with him, even as a child, vaguely disagreeable.

Suddenly he said: "You're still scared, aren't you?"

"Scared—scared of what?"

"Of this—this thing that he's had."

It was disconcerting when someone normally so unperceptive to the point of stupidity and even, Christine sometimes thought, idiocy, all at once came out with a remark as full of insight as this. But it was not uncommon for Larry to produce such surprises.

"Yes," she hesitated, "yes, to tell you the truth, I am still nervous. Do I show it?"

"Perhaps not to others. But I know you so well," he replied. "Don't I?"

She had never supposed that Larry knew anything well, except how to fire a gun, hit a ball or ride a horse. Once again, as so often in the past, his sympathy, affection and kindness made her want to withdraw herself from him, and yielding to this impulse she now got up, went over to the rail, and rested her arms along it.

The town was dazzlingly near, its white houses seeming to melt together in the heat as she looked at them until they formed a single long, throbbing bar of light, floating between the hazy glare of the sky and the darker glare of the ocean. Suddenly she was conscious of the sweat trickling down her face and of the unpleasant way in which her underclothes were sticking to her, and then, a moment later, of a terrible weariness, like the first onset of an illness, which made her head sag over her arms and her arms themselves lean more and more heavily on the rail as if in an effort to support her whole body. Somewhere, deep inside the ship, a chain rattled and clanked; and at the same moment one motor boat, and then another and another, set the whole air vibrating. She had the sensation of a nightmare; but what elements of a nightmare could be found in the cheerful bustle and noise around her, as passengers gathered up on deck, laughed and shouted to the vendors jumping up and down in the rowing boats below them, clicked their cameras, jested and pushed each other, the sun glinting up all the time in burnished arcs from the black, churned-up sea? Yet the sensation of an evil dream was so violent that she almost cried out in horror.

Suddenly a large, sweaty hand had closed round her arm, and a voice was saying: "You oughtn't to stand in this sun without a topee. Come!"

"Oh, Larry . . ." she began. But, as always, she had nothing more to say to him. And so, listlessly, she followed him into the saloon, her handkerchief, still sodden with the tears she had shed in the cabin, pressed to lips which, for some idiotic reason, would not stop trembling.

II

Christine was sulking. As the others ate their luncheon she replied to their questions only in monosyllables, looking not at the person who had spoken, but either at the plate or out of the window, while she played with some morsel of food. When, after two or three such attempts to draw her into their conversation, Adrian and Gwyneth began one of those discussions which seemed intended deliberately to exclude her, and Larry contented himself with continuing to gobble down a steak in silence, his khaki shirt sticking to his massive back and shoulders and the sweat streaming down his face, Christine rose, placed her napkin slowly on the table before her, and made her way out. That none of them called after her to enquire where she was going once again intensified her fury.

Later, Larry came to where she was seated on the boat-deck to ask her if she was going to accompany them ashore.

"I suppose your father sent you."

"No. But he was wondering too. And so was Gwyneth," he answered in a clumsy attempt at diplomacy.

"Well, tell them both that I'm not going to leave the ship. I know when I'm not wanted."

He looked down on her for a moment with his small, green, not unkindly eyes, the rims of which were inflamed from the sun and too much bathing. Then he smiled: "That's silly," he said.

"It's not silly at all."

"You know they both want you. And I want you anyway."

"I'm sorry, dear." She was grateful to him, but she did not intend to yield, and so rob herself of Adrian's coaxings and apologies or of Gwyneth's remorse. If they wanted to spoil her day, let them spoil it—and suffer for it afterwards. "Anyway this glare has given me a headache," she said, putting a hand to her forehead.

He laughed: "Then why on earth sit out staring at it?"

"Yes. I think I shall go below, and lie down with an aspirin."

"Come, I'll take you." He picked up her bag and book for her, and when she still remained seated in her deck-chair, repeated: "Come!"

He made her lie down, rang for the steward to bring her a carafe of iced water, and then, as he attempted to shake out two aspirins from the bottle into his vast palm, somehow succeeded in making at least a dozen cascade on to the floor. "Oh, Larry!" she exclaimed petulantly; and her small beautifully shaped mouth became thin and ugly with irritation as she

15

watched him, her head turned sideways on her pillow, while he groped and rummaged on hands and knees. "No harm done!" he gasped. "But I don't think much of the way this steward dusts under the bed. Phew! That seems to be the lot."

"Thank you, Larry dear." All at once she felt grateful and tender towards him: not merely for his obvious affection and kindness but also, though she was unconscious of this, for making her feel less intellectually inferior to Adrian and Gwyneth by yet again establishing his own intellectual inferiority to herself.

After he had left, Christine did not remain for long on her bunk. She lay for a while on her side, with a hand under her cheek and her knees drawn up, listening to the noise of the passengers as they made their way down into the boats that would take them to the shore. At one moment she heard Larry shout out: "Whoa there! Whoa!" as though to a horse: and then, presumably addressing Adrian, "Give me your stick." After that the hubbub diminished, until a silence came like water slowly and invisibly welling up into the cabin from some profound source of loneliness and panic. She clenched her hands to her sides, turning over at the same time on to her back and staring up at the ceiling where a fly was, at that very moment, twitching on a mottled coil of fly-paper. She wondered if there were any passengers left on board, indeed if any of the crew remained; and partly out of curiosity and partly because she could no longer bear this sensation of drowning, inch by inch, in silence and solitude, she put out an arm and pressed the bell for the steward. After what seemed many minutes a man in stained dungarees and a singlet, whom she had never seen before, appeared in the doorway. Since she could think of nothing to say to him, she asked:

"Is the regular steward not on duty?"

"No, madam. He's gone ashore. Is there anything I can get for you?"

"No, thank you. I wanted to ask him about something he had promised to do for me."

She lay back for a while and then, as though suddenly remembering an urgent appointment, leapt off the bed, pulled her dress over her petticoat, tugged a comb through her hair, slipped her small feet into her court-shoes and went out on deck. After the gloom of the cabin she could hardly bear the dazzle, in spite of the sun-glasses she drew from her bag.

There were still some rowing boats below, with sweaty men, exactly like the one who had answered the bell, unloading what she supposed were provisions. They did not speak to one another except in isolated grunts or hoarse cries, with an occasional obscene ejaculation when a packing-case slipped from their straining fingers or they lurched against each other. Many of them were stripped to the waists, and their bodies had a curious, corpse-like greenish sheen against the golden brown of the bodies of the native coolies. Although they were so far below her, in that brilliant light she could see the smallest details with what was almost the clarity of hallucination: their grimed and chipped fingernails; the mole like a brown wood-louse curled up on the neck of one man, the extraordinary tattooing of Union Jacks, snakes, birds and women; even the sweat glinting down the spine of the coolie as he bent to heave up a cask.

The last of the motor-boats was chugging towards the shore, crowded with passengers, and Christine wondered how it was that it had taken so long, until she remembered that, as she had lain on her bunk with the clamour ebbing from her, she had been exasperated by the repeated staccato interruption of an engine grinding into action, back-firing two or three times, and then once again plopping and hiccoughing to a standstill. A blue-grey scarf of smoke was swirling out behind, parallel to the water, until, all at once catching the breeze which came in-termittently off the shore in tepid, lethargic waves, it disinte-grated into innumerable shreds and wisps, the fumes of which struck the ship many seconds later to cling there, sweetish and cloyingly nauseating like some cheap Indian scent.

She was about to retreat from this stench, when she saw, to her astonishment, that the little boat which had diminished to no more than a white triangle below the immense white oblong of the port had now veered round and appeared to be chugging, not away from the ship, but once more towards it. Sometimes, as a gust blew off the shore, it would be concealed in a cloud of smoke; but each time it would burst through this envelope to reappear closer, larger and yet more noisy. She screwed up her eyes in an attempt to focus better against the terrible glare of the sea; and as she did so, she was aware that all work had ceased on the boats below her.

17

"Why's she coming back?" "What's up?" "What's the matter with her?" She could hear their voices: but they seemed to be much further than that engine which now was hammering behind her eyes, in her throat and against her ribs.

At last she could see clearly: the majority of the passengers were all huddled together up at one end of the boat, while at the other end, separated by several feet of emptiness, five people were bending or kneeling over something that was hidden from sight. Among the five she suddenly recognized, with a pang, first the scarf, an unbecoming shade of electric-blue, which Gwyneth had tied round her head, and then Larry's bare, sturdy legs with the khaki shorts above them. Adrian was not visible.

The boat slowed and with hoarse shouts, which were almost like the yelling of some wounded animal, from the grey-haired sailor at the tiller, it slewed round towards the open hold. The face of someone kneeling was momentarily upturned to say: "Here, give us a hand," and Christine saw that it was that of the young ship's doctor. Two of the men in grimy singlets, one of them tattooed in red and blue from his wrists to his arm-pits, hesitated and then went forward to help to pick off the floor of the boat something which Christine still could not see. The other passengers were most of them looking back towards the port from which they had come, speaking to each other, if at all, in abrupt snatches of dialogue. Christine saw a dangling arm, a foot, swaying between the two vast pairs of shoulders to which the sun gave that curious greenish sheen; and then, her dazed stupefaction all at once turning to an active horror, an open mouth with a black stain all down the one side.

She began to run, trying to find her way down through the echoing corridors of the vast liner from the first-class to the hold. She saw a door with "Steward" on it and hammered on that; but there was no answer. Later she found herself trapped in a pantry, permeated by the sweet-sour smell of dishcloths hanging up to dry, one of which, as she ran out again, brushed her face with a nauseating clamminess. She clattered down one companion-way but then had to run up another. In the third-class some small children were squatting in the corridor, playing marbles; as she raced past she accidentally knocked against one so that as she hurried on she could hear his diminishing wail and the rattling and scrape of a marble zigzagging along the polished floor behind her. The lower she went, the hotter it became.

Then, at last, she had emerged on to the deck where the men were working; and she even saw one of the two who had helped to carry Adrian. "Where is he?" she demanded. "Where have they taken him? Where can I find him?"

At first they looked at her in amazement; then, slowly, they realized to what she was referring and one said: "He's been taken along to the sick-bay, that's where they've taken him."

"The sick-bay? Where is it?"

"I'll show you."

"Would you? Please! He's my husband."

Each action seemed to be performed with a terrible lumbering slowness as the man spoke to one of his mates, pulled on a shirt without doing up the buttons or tucking it into his jeans, and then began to waddle ahead of her along the deck. He even paused for a moment to squint at an egg-plant, glistening in the sunlight, which had presumably tumbled from one of the baskets they had been carrying from the boats.

In a claustrophobic little room, painted a vivid, oily green, Larry and Gwyneth were seated in wicker chairs before a square wicker table on which they had thrown all the paraphernalia with which they had set off to the shore. "What's happened? Where is he?"

"The doctor's in with him now." As Christine crossed to the door which was opposite her, Gwyneth added: "You mustn't go in. Mummy, you mustn't go in."

"Here, sit down," Larry said. "Sit down." He was in the act of lighting a cigarette, although as a rule he smoked his pipe.

"But I ought to . . ."

"You can't go in," Gwyneth repeated; with what to Christine seemed almost satisfaction. "The doctor said not."

Between them they began to tell Christine of how, as repeated efforts were made to get the engine started, the fumes had begun to nauseate the passengers and make them cough. For Adrian it had, of course, been worst, but when they nagged him to return to the ship, he had stubbornly refused. At last they set off, but he had continued to cough, growing paler and paler, until as they neared the shore, the haemorrhage had started. Fortunately the ship's doctor and a girl who was a trained nurse had both been there and had at once taken charge of him. But there had been a delay while they had argued whether to take him on to the hospital in the town or back to the ship.

"I told him it was madness to try to go ashore. I kept telling him."

"Oh, Mummy, what's the good of saying that now?" Gwyneth said harshly. There was a pallor about her eyes and her mouth, and her large hand trembled as she turned over a page of the *Illustrated London News* that rested across her knees; otherwise she appeared completely, even aggressively, composed.

There was a silence, in which Larry puffed out cigarette-smoke as he tweaked at the hair of his forearms and stared upwards at the ceiling. Gwyneth read, or appeared to read, and Christine creaked about in her wicker chair, glancing from one of them to the other until, noticing that Adrian's camera lay open on the table, she put out a hand and drew it towards her. At first, the stickiness did not seem to her odd, for, in that temperature, most things felt sticky: but, when she looked down to click the case shut, she gasped out in horror: round the rim of the lens blood had congealed into minute black beads that might have been ants.

"What is this?" she demanded.

Larry and Gwyneth both stared at her for a moment; then Gwyneth leant forward and snatched the camera from her. "He had been taking photographs when he—when it started," she said roughly. She clicked the camera shut: "I'll give it to the steward to clean."

Christine, like most women, was not usually squeamish about blood; but on this occasion she felt an impulse to retch which she could only control by getting up and walking up and down the little room with her hands clasped before her.

Gwyneth said, after watching her for a long time over her paper: "Oh, do sit down, Mummy. It's so disturbing. Sit down." But she was checked by a look from Larry.

Eventually the young doctor came in, mopping his face on a towel. The nurse who followed him, a plain dark girl in a simple cotton dress, with bare legs and arms on which the hair grew thickly, was at once recognized as a Eurasian by Christine

20

who, like all those who have spent years in the East, had developed an extraordinary, if pointless, insight about such matters. "He's asking for you," the doctor said; and when Gwyneth rose from her chair, made his statement clearer by adding: "For you, Mrs. Cornwell."

"For me?"

"You shouldn't let him talk. But go in to him. We've stopped the haemorrhage now." And because Christine still hesitated he repeated, almost angrily: "Go in to him. But no talking, mind!" He was a tough, ungainly young man and now, as he continued to rub his round, shiny, bright-red face on the towel, he looked as if he had just emerged from a rugger scrum.

Christine went in to Adrian. She crossed to the narrow bed, one of three, where he lay on his back, his eyes open and his jaw relaxed sideways, as though some blow had dislocated it, while he drew in air in one long, snorting breath after another and expelled it again on a kind of brief, hiccoughing sob.

"You mustn't talk." She drew a chair up beside him and took one of his hands, oddly cold and clammy, between both of hers. Slowly he began to turn his head, and it appeared to cost him so great an effort that she wanted to cry out: "Oh, don't, don't, don't!"

Then they were looking into each other's eyes; and as, unflinching, she held his gaze, she thought of how, more than twenty years ago, they had looked at each other like that after an accident in which he had been thrown from his horse on the first occasion when they had been out riding alone together. Then it was a question of no more than a broken collar bone and a couple of ribs; but as she had knelt on the dusty pathway beside him while the *sayce* was sent off to fetch help, and had held his hand in hers, as she was holding it now, there had been that same silent mingling of gaze and even his face, though so much younger, had looked oddly the same. They had been closer to each other at that moment than ever before or since: united by their sudden discovery, on the verge of the Indian jungle, that they were in love. Yet now another discovery, that of his imminent death, had brought them no less close; and though there was fear and despair and grief yet, as on that occasion twenty years ago, there was also an unbounded, almost triumphant relief that the secret which each had hidden from the other was now no more a secret. She heard a click

21

at the back of his throat and then slowly he began to give a lopsided smile.

III

Because she had been unable to sleep, Christine had gone out on to the verandah where her friend, Rosemary Maddox, in whose house Adrian had died, emerged sleepily to find her. "What are you doing here?" she asked. "Why aren't you in bed?"

"I couldn't sleep."

"You took the two tablets?"

"I took three. But I couldn't sleep." Christine, who was wearing nothing but slippers and a silk nightdress which rustled in the night breeze, was hunched on the edge of a wicker chair, her knees drawn up and her arms clasped about her, as though in some acute physical pain. The moonlight glittered on the diamond of her engagement ring. "How did you know I was here?"

"Oh, I seemed to guess it; I don't know how. I woke up because Geoffrey was snoring—listen!" From the room behind them they could hear the noise, rhythmical and oddly soothing, of Rosemary's husband refreshing himself for his coming day on the Canals. "You haven't been worrying, have you? Not again?" Rosemary, a tall, thin, childless woman, who spoke in a muffled, indistinct voice which, in the past, had always seemed to Christine to be only another symptom of a generally muffled and indistinct personality, had been Adrian's friend rather than his wife's. She was regarded as an intellectual, on the strength of a book of nineteenth-century memoirs translated from the German, and a couple of cookery books, and before Gwyneth had joined them, she was one of the few women with whom Adrian could bear to converse. Christine, whose intelligence, though wholly untrained, was far more logical and practical than her husband's, tended to regard Rosemary as an over-educated fool; but Adrian could not allow this—"She probably has far more brains than any other woman

22

in India; certainly more than you," he would add with a laugh. "And you really think a woman can be intelligent who rings up her Christian Science practitioner when one of her cats falls ill?" Christine had asked on one such occasion. "Oh, that! People stop being intelligent when it comes to religion. It's too much to expect from them."

Rosemary now drew her wrap close across her flat bosom with long fingers on which she never wore anything but her wedding ring, pushed her horn-rimmed glasses up to the top of her slightly beaked nose, and then, looking away from Christine at the moonlit expanse of the tennis-court, said: "Don't keep thinking about the future. It's by imagining all the terrible things that might happen in it that you make the things happen."

Christine remembered an occasion when Rosemary's husband Geoffrey had repeatedly grunted how intolerably hot the weather was, until Rosemary had reprimanded him, in her staccato yet gentle voice: "Darling, it's your saying how hot it is that makes it such a reality for the rest of us." Even Adrian, though feverish and in pain, had laughed when Christine went to his room and repeated the remark to him. Yes, though she felt she ought to regard Rosemary as a vaguely absurd and even exasperating figure, during these weeks when Adrian had been dying in her home, Christine had grudgingly come to find in her an extraordinary strength, calm and even nobility of character so that there were now often times when she would regret having held her up to ridicule to Adrian and to other women in their circle, and ask herself whether she had perhaps done so out of jealousy for her friendship with Adrian.

"I miss him so terribly," Christine said, rocking herself back and forth on the edge of her chair. "Oh, Rosemary, I feel I shall never get over that. And it's not as if I were old—there are so many years ahead."

For a long time Rosemary said nothing, sitting erect in her chair, her long legs extended before her, while the other woman continued to rock back and forth. Then she put up one hand to pat the curlers which made her head look absurdly small for her clumsy body, and said slowly and, for her, oddly distinctly:

"I shall miss him too, you know."

It was as if a frosted pane had smashed at a blow, and the things that had moved behind as no more than dark, amorphous shapes for Christine's imagination to guess at had, in that second, stood revealed. The creaking of the chair in which Christine had been rocking all at once ceased. She stared at Rosemary's profile and at last said: "You also loved him, didn't you?"

While she waited for an answer, there was a rustle and flurry in the struggling bushes which flanked the verandah: one of Rosemary's many cats. Then a jackal howled, a noise which, in spite of her many years in India, never ceased to fill Christine with desolation, and a few seconds later the mail-train could be heard thudding and clanking out into the vast Rajput desert. Rosemary still sat motionless, and the contrast between the two women—the one no longer pretty, but beautiful in her bereavement and desolation, and the other vaguely absurd, her large feet pushed into a man's bedroom slippers, the moonlight glinting on the metal of her curlers, her lower lip thrust out—had never been more extreme. Without either knowing it, it was precisely this contrast that had afforded the dead man so much pleasure.

At last Rosemary said faintly, on a sigh: "What does it matter now? I was very fond of him. I don't suppose I've cared so much for anyone in my life."

"Oh, Rosemary!" Christine put out a hand, but she felt inhibited from placing it on her friend's, and instead let it rest on the arm of her chair, where she began to pick at the wicker with a forefinger.

"These mosquitoes! To-morrow we shall be covered in bites. I'll get some of that stuff to burn." Rosemary shuffled back into the house and came back bearing a saucer which she balanced on top of the rickety wooden balustrade. Drawing some matches from the pocket of her wrap, she struck one, and at once an aromatic cloud rose up round them as the powder began to crackle with an electric blue flame.

Rosemary sat down again, and they began to speak in low voices about the dead man: the two families had shared houses together and had nursed each other through illnesses ever since, within two months of each other, Adrian and Geoffrey had got married, so that their store of shared memories was limitless. Even Adrian's faults of irritability, selfishness and

24

arrogance were now transmuted by their love. "Do you remember the time he was so cross with me?" Rosemary would say and she would forget how some rebuke had stung her and left her resentful for days.

Eventually Christine began to weep, her tears trickling down her girlishly smooth cheeks and falling on to her hands; and Rosemary, who had all her life shrunk from physical contacts and would each time have to brace herself for her husband's rough, unsubtle caresses, made clumsy attempts to console her. But she felt at her ease with words, never with actions; and so, after patting Christine's shoulder, she began to speak to her in jerky, muffled sentences, many of which were lost in the noise of secret rustlings from the bushes, the cries of wild animals, or the other woman's sobs.

She said what she believed, and as Christine listened to her, talking of the unreality of death and the ever-living presence of Adrian and of the need only for faith, she tried, in her anguish of spirit, to make that composure of belief her own. But she could not accept the unreality of death, for she had seen Adrian go from her unwillingly and in desperate agony, and to her literal mind that had been more real than anything else she had ever experienced in her life. She could not think of Adrian as a presence near to her, because within her, all through these days since his hurried burial, there had been an appalling emptiness which not even her memories of him could fill. As for faith, she had never had any and Adrian, an agnostic, had never encouraged any: she was too literal-minded and he too subtle. But now, in her grief, she wanted to tear from Rosemary some scrap of this consolation which the other woman enjoyed but which was denied to her.

"But, Rosemary, I can't understand, I can't understand!" she cried out at last. "Illness does exist; pain does exist; evil does exist; death does exist."

"Only in our minds, only in ourselves."

It was useless and both women felt it. They had been momentarily united by their love for the dead man, but his death had also separated them, for to each of them it was something different, as their loves had been different.

Now they began to speak of the future: of Christine's departure for England; of the sale of her furniture and Adrian's books; of money and the children. The last of these topics produced a dominant resentment which, all through the years that Rosemary had known Christine, had never ceased to surprise her. Christine was naturally so kind, unselfish, understanding and forgiving: but from time to time, out of some dark source within her, there would well up this bitter tide of vindictiveness, and not merely her personality, but her actual physical presence, would undergo a change. She would appear to crouch, as though to spring on the person against whom her momentary hostility was directed; her eyes, usually so large and serene under her smooth forehead, would appear small and baleful; her generous mouth would thin.

First she spoke about Gwyneth: "Sometimes I think that her father's death has meant nothing at all to her. She was supposed to be so devoted to him. But, do you know, I've never seen her cry—not once!"

"Oh, don't be so absurd, Christine. Tears are no measure of grief, are they?"

"It's not only tears. It's her whole manner—just as if nothing had happened."

"She's reserved; she takes after Adrian in that. Because she shows nothing, it doesn't mean that she feels nothing. You know that's the Cornwell way."

Christine did know, and it had always exasperated her. When Adrian met one of his sisters or brothers after an interval of years, they would say "Oh, hello" to each other and often omit even to shake hands. To Christine this seemed "unnatural"— this was the adjective she used; for her family was clannish, over-demonstrative, bound each to each by a curious nexus of love-hate relationship in which possessiveness and jealousy played at least as great a part as loyalty and love.

Later, it was Larry's turn: he was not, after all, Christine's own child and so, having expected less of him, she was less disappointed. Besides, in his clumsy way, he had been good for her during these days; and the long journeys back and forth from Rajputana to the North-west Frontier, where he was stationed, must, at the height of the hot weather, have been trying even to one of his health and physique. But it had become increasingly obvious that he was infatuated with the Eurasian girl who, by an evil chance, had been present on the boat when Adrian had had his haemorrhage, and had then stayed on to nurse him till his death; and there were often times when Christine asked herself if it were really a devotion to herself and his father, or a devotion to this girl, Louise, that made him endure those appallingly hot and tedious journeys. The girl was, of course, entirely unsuitable; and Christine now speculated what Adrian would have thought, if he had known. "He had such a horror of that kind of thing. And in the case of Louise it is so obvious, isn't it? It's not only a question of the *chi-chi* accent: it's the whole way she looks. Yes, poor Adrian would——" she was going to say "would rather have died", but she not unnaturally shied away from that phrase, and went on— "would have been utterly appalled at the thought of a son of his marrying such a girl."

"Does he intend to marry her?"

"Oh, I hope not. I do hope not! But he's obviously very keen on her, isn't he? Anyone can see that."

"Would it really matter so much if he *did* wish to marry her?"

"Rosemary!" Christine stared at her friend in horrified surprise. "Well, of course it would! In a regiment like his it would be utterly disastrous—unthinkable." She was not, in any other respect, a snobbish woman; but she had been brought up to have the same eye for pigmentation and "a touch of the tar-brush" as a connoisseur has for the pigment and brushwork of an Old Master and, since Adrian had been an old-fashioned imperialist, equally cynical about the motives of the British in India and about the benefits of the British raj but never questioning the British right to be there, she had never, during her married life, learned to modify this discrimination. It was not, with her, a question of reason: but of reflexes, habits, nerves. It never ceased to surprise her that Rosemary should have developed this racial tolerance, for their backgrounds had been almost the same: but Rosemary was "odd", as Christine and her women friends often reminded each other.

"I wonder how long this regiment will continue to exist," Rosemary said.

"What do you mean?"

"Well—if we get out. As I suppose we shall have to in the end. In five or ten or fifteen years."

But Christine had no patience with talk of a kind that had often elicited Adrian's most withering sarcasms. Indeed, only a few days before his death, Rosemary had rushed out of his

27

room, her sallow cheeks flaming after an argument on just such a theme.

"Anyway, I shan't be sorry to get out myself," Christine remarked. She had said this repeatedly, but there were times, when lying awake in the prison of her mosquito-net, she had cringed, as though from a physical blow, at the thought of the long voyage back to England and of attempting to make a life there for herself and her children on the pension which, apart from two hundred a year of her own money, was all she possessed. Rosemary had suggested that she should remain on in India: but she had seen the lives that other widows like herself eked out on the fringes of society, their fourteen servants diminished to two or three: the invitations to Government House becoming less and less frequent and then drying up altogether: without a position, often even without the money to afford to pay their subscriptions at the Club or their losses at bridge. Besides, there was Tim, of whom she must think; for, when she said that she must go back to England to make a home "for the children", it was for Tim that she meant. In the dark abyss where her bereavement had thrust her, this seemed to be the only light by which she would steer a course. "I never want to see India again," she added.

"And I sometimes think that I never want to see anything else."

"I seem no nearer to understanding the country or the people than when I first came here. And that incident of Amir Ali—that was what really drove the lesson home." She gave a little shudder, although the gritty wind that was blowing off the desert to rustle her nightdress and shake her greying curls was tepid, not cold. "He was with Adrian for more than thirty years. We had both been so good to him."

Amir Ali had been Adrian's bearer and it was he, sobbing wildly, who had rushed on to the verandah after dinner one evening, from the room in which he had been sitting beside his master while the nurse made a hurried meal, to announce that he was dead. Geoffrey had shouted at him to pull himself together, giving him a rough push as he thrust past him into the sick-room. The Indian had then thrown himself on to the floor of the verandah, clutching his head from which his turban had fallen off while he emitted a series of cries and groans that seemed to be more the expression of physical pain than grief.

28

Rosemary had afterwards told her husband that this, for her, had been the most horrible and heart-rending part of the whole death: certainly worse than Christine's tears, which had about them a *human* quality—Rosemary stressed that word, for it seemed to be the key—and were therefore somehow different. Often now, when she heard the distant howls of wild animals through the stifling night, she would remember, with a clenching of her large hands at her sides, that paroxysm of savage lamentation.

But, a few days later, it was discovered by Larry that certain small belongings of his father were missing: a pair of cuff-links, a broken fountain-pen, a comb, a half-finished bottle of Caron after-shave lotion; even a pack of cards. Amir Ali was the thief, as Rosemary soon discovered through her ayah. To Christine this act was the most bitter of betrayals: and it had both bewildered and exasperated her that whereas Gwyneth and Geoffrey had agreed with her in this, Larry and Rosemary had stubbornly refused to do so. "Oh, what does it matter?" had been Larry's cynically tolerant attitude: but whether he expected less than his mother of the Indians, or of the human race in general, he never, with characteristic inarticulateness, succeeded in making plain. Rosemary's reactions had been more complex and, since they were unintelligible to Christine, that much more annoying. She had maintained that Amir Ali had loved Adrian, and that there had been no element of hypocrisy in his noisy grief at his death. But there was a lack of connection in the Indian mind, and to love a man and yet to rob him after his death were not incompatibles. "I always think that the psychology of Indians can only be explained in terms of Elizabethan humour," she had declared: which was a remark that might have interested Adrian, but could only mystify his widow yet further. Amir Ali, in spite of a disagreeable scene during which he embraced Christine's knees and begged her to forgive him, was summarily sacked: and Geoffrey told him how lucky he was not to be handed over to the police.

"That, for me, was the end as far as India was concerned," Christine would say; and all her bitterness and rancour against this country to which she and her husband had given so much only for it to cheat them—Adrian had been going to a job in Delhi which carried a certain knighthood with it—was concen-

29

trated on this one symbolic betrayal. Amir Ali owed everything to them; and then he had done this thing. What they had owed to Amir Ali she did not, of course, calculate.

Once again, Rosemary tried to explain her attitude; but after a few minutes, she saw that Christine's hand had slipped sideways and forwards and that her eyes were shut. Then she tiptoed into the bedroom and brought out a rug which she placed gently over her friend's sleeping body. Again she went into the house, this time with the saucer from the balustrade, in order to renew the powder. Probably the mosquitoes would bite Christine anyway: but better a few bites than a whole night of insomnia. As she stretched herself out beside her snoring husband, whose bulk paradoxically seemed even more gross in sleep than when he was swilling beer, guzzling food or making clumsy love, she wondered whether she herself would be able to sleep at all. But that, of course, was holding the wrong thought, she hurriedly reminded herself. Of course she would sleep: and she turned on her side, closed her eyes, and began to draw in one deep breath after another in time with her husband's snores.

When Christine awoke, purple metallic smears had appeared above the desert. There was none of the sense, so usual on summer dawns in England, of the countryside expanding, refreshed: rather it seemed to huddle and cringe—the trees of the night now appearing as overgrown bushes, the drive curiously shrunk to what was almost a pathway, even the sky itself seeming to extend lower and lower—as though in preparation for a fresh onslaught from the sun. She was stiff, but, so far from being chilled, she felt her hair disagreeably sticky from where it had rested against the cushion and her hands, imprisoned by Rosemary under the rug, were damp as though from fever. What had woken her was the sound of the hooves of two horses being led around the house by the diminutive *sayce*. Sleepily she watched him, in the greyness of a dawn against which his own face was no more than a greyer smudge. He did not come near her but, chewing some betel-nut under a tree, stood and stared at the horizon, motionless except for the movement of his jaws under the pock-marked skin. She had slept without dreams for the first time since Adrian's death, and her sleep had been deep; and now she had woken without any of the anguish of loss or the

30

terrible sense of a day ahead which she must somehow endure. She yawned and stretched her arms above her head, holding them there for several seconds as she wondered at the pinkish glow which they caught from the brightening sky. Suddenly, from behind her, she heard footsteps and the noise of suppressed laughter. The *sayce* turned and came forward, spitting as he did so; and the crimson trajectory spattered the bottom step of the verandah. Rosemary was never severe enough with her servants; but it was not that, but the sight of the blood-like fluid issuing from his mouth, that made Christine draw in her breath sharply and turn her head aside.

"Good God! What are you doing here?"

"Good morning, Mrs. Cornwell."

It was Larry and the Eurasian girl Louise, who even at this hour, Christine noted with distaste, had heavily powdered and rouged her face and taken pains to cover her hands and bare arms with calamine lotion. They were both of them in riding clothes.

"Oh, I couldn't sleep," Christine said, "so I came and sat out here."

Larry at once assumed that she had not slept at all: which was what, unconsciously, Christine had intended. "My poor Mummy!" he exclaimed, putting an arm round her and kissing her on the cheek. He was unshaven, and probably unwashed, since a white crust could be detected along his bottom eyelids.

"Did you take your pills, Mrs. Cornwell?" Louise asked. Because she guessed that Christine did not like her and disapproved of Larry's interest in her, and therefore felt ill at ease, she often spoke with a stilted formality which Christine mistook for insolence.

"Yes, I took my pills." Christine answered without glancing at her. "Where are you both going?"

"Oh, for a ride," Larry answered.

"Yes, I had realized that. But where do you think you will go?"

"Oh, probably down by the railway lines, and then across the Canal. We want to practise some jumping. Louise is frightened of jumping, you know."

"Well, I suppose for someone who has only just taken up riding—and taken it up so late in life—it *is* a little frightening."

31

Louise was at least five years older than Larry: which was another, if lesser, reason for her being unsuitable.

Also, she was heartless: for Christine had never forgotten how, on the evening after Adrian's funeral, the two nurses had gone out to play a round of tennis. Christine had been lying down in her room, with the blinds all down, and Rosemary had been seated, silently doing accounts, when all at once the far-off thud of a ball on a racket could be heard. Christine had listened for a time, while she had had the impression that Rosemary, her head bowed over her work, had deliberately pretended not to listen, and then she had said: "Is that someone playing tennis?" "Sounds like it." "Who can it be? . . . Have a look, Rosemary." And Rosemary had got up reluctantly, raised one of the blinds, and then turned to tell her. Christine had exclaimed how unfeeling it was; Adrian had always been so good to them both, no nurse could ask for a more considerate or generous patient. To which Rosemary had muttered: "Well it's their work, isn't it? They must be used to people dying. *I* don't expect Geoffrey not to play tennis when one of his bridges collapses, after all. And probably they lose many more of their patients than he loses bridges."

But Christine still thought it callous; and she had subsequently told the story to many of her other friends, who had said: "Well, what can you expect?" or things to that effect. One did not expect much from a Eurasian girl; almost as little as from an Indian servant.

Christine now dozed again, for the three pills which she had rashly swallowed could not be resisted. But her sleep was light and troubled, and she kept waking, out of some nightmare of Adrian displeased, Adrian ill, Adrian lost in a vast, crowded railway-station, Adrian unfaithful to her, to slip off again, as though down some chute, into a pit of horrifying shapes and sounds.

Eventually she was fully awoken by the return of Louise and Larry. As she opened her eyes, fluttering the lids against the glare of the newly-risen sun, she saw them coming towards her with their hands joined and the identical, self-consciously idiotic smile on their faces. Even the *sayce*'s pock-marked little face seemed to be wrinkled into a furtive smile as he led off the horses. "Go and change, darling," she heard Larry say. "I must have a word with Mummy." But he still grasped Louise's hand, as though reluctant to allow her to leave him, while his other hand was plunged deep in the pocket of his breeches. "Run along!" And only then did he release her.

Still grinning, he lowered his perspiring bulk into the chair where Rosemary had sat that night and then, taking a corner of Christine's rug in both his hands, began to plait the tassels as he said: "Did you sleep that time?"

"Off and on. . . . Why on earth does that girl use so much make-up? Even Rosemary was remarking on it—those extraordinary orange blobs she puts on both cheeks."

The large hands, with the square, not too clean nails, went on with their task, of plaiting and unplaiting the tassels. Then, at last, he looked up: and it was as if he had heard nothing of what she had been saying. "Tell me, Mummy. What would you feel about having Louise as a daughter-in-law?"

"Louise?"

"Yes."

"Larry, are you mad?" Then she realized that he was in earnest. "I can't imagine anything that I'd like less," she said. "You can't mean it."

"Certainly I do." He laughed: "She's just agreed—I've asked her!"

"Well, of course she's agreed! Naturally! I don't imagine she'd say no. What a chance! A girl like that—it must be beyond her wildest dreams."

Either he deliberately ignored the tone in which she had spoken, or else, in his stupidity, he was unconscious of it. In either case she was exasperated to fury by the good-humoured calm with which he replied: "Oh, I don't think I'm really so much of a catch as all that. Do you? Probably you're prejudiced in my favour. After all I'm not rich and I'm not clever, and I don't suppose I shall ever be anyone of much importance."

"You have something to offer which most girls like Louise would give anything to have."

At first he looked puzzled, and then, slowly, he began to flush, the colour deepening under the tan of his unshaven cheeks and mounting to his forehead. "Louise is quite as good as I am," he said coldly, his fingers dropping the tassels.

"Well . . . not quite. Not in all respects."

Abruptly he jumped up. "Anyway—we're going to get

33

married." He began to flick his riding-crop against his booted leg, and suddenly gave his lopsided smile: "I'm afraid that's how it goes, Mummy. Sorry."

"Anyway, I'm glad that your father was spared hearing this news. It—it would have broken his heart."

Still he was smiling, to reveal the small, nicotine-stained teeth under the red moustache. "I don't expect that *really* it would." He glanced down at his watch: "I must go and change before breakfast." Stroking his chin, he added: "And shave—I'd forgotten that."

"But Larry—wait a moment. We must—we must talk about this. We must discuss it. Please." She got up and the rug slipped to the floor, so that, unseeing, as she stepped forward, she almost tripped over it.

"There *is* nothing to discuss. We're engaged. What more can one say? You're not pleased, I know, but there the thing is. I'm really quite decided. You mustn't expect to be able to make me change my mind." He stooped forward and kissed her on the cheek, saying: "What you need is some breakfast. Your hands are quite cold."

After he had left her, Christine's first impulse was to take the astonishing and disagreeable news to Rosemary: but when she hurried round the verandah and heard Geoffrey booming away about a bridge hand which he had played at the Club the previous evening, she hesitated and at last decided to wait until he had left for work. Geoffrey would of course be equally shocked at the idea of Larry marrying Louise: but since his prejudices were, as it were, unconscious parodies of those of his colleagues, he often succeeded in making what had previously seemed an entirely reasonable point of view utterly absurd. In the end it was to Gwyneth's bedroom that Christine went.

She was sitting up in bed, with a tray across her knees and a book, which Christine recognized as one of Adrian's diaries, held in one of her hands.

"Daddy wrote so well," she said, after they had said good morning to each other and pecked at each other's cheeks.

"Yes, he ought to have been a writer. But there were so many things he could have been," Christine said ingenuously. "He was such a wonderful actor too. In many ways Tim is so like him. . . . Darling, I'm awfully worried."

"Are you? Why?" Gwyneth asked, obviously not interested. "Would you like a cup of tea?" She gulped noisily at her own.

Christine shook her head: "Larry wants to marry Louise," she announced. "He proposed to her this morning—and she accepted."

Gwyneth did not stop swallowing the tea until the cup was finished: it was hot, and when she raised her face her nose was unbecomingly red and there were tears in her eyes. "I thought that was coming."

"But it's impossible—quite out of the question!"

"I don't see why. I don't find her either attractive or interesting, but that's his business. Isn't it?"

"That *chi-chi* accent!"

"It's certainly not attractive," Gwyneth admitted.

"Your father would have been appalled. That his eldest son—an Indian Army Officer—should—should . . . Oh, I'm only thankful it didn't happen before we lost him."

Gwyneth winced; but only because she disliked euphemisms like "lost him" for "died".

"Yes, I daresay he *would* have been upset. But I don't suppose that would have put Larry off. After all he disapproved of Larry wearing sandals and not shaving before breakfast each morning and of lots of other things. But Larry didn't take much notice."

In mounting exasperation, Christine continued her attempt to win the girl over to her own point of view, but, beyond admitting that the match would hardly be a source of pride or even convenience to a man in Larry's position, Gwyneth was not prepared to go. Eventually Christine rose:

"I had hoped that I could look to you in troubles of this kind. I thought that you were old enough to—to begin to take your father's place." Christine's lower lip began to tremble at this reference to Adrian, making Gwyneth simultaneously sink deeper into the pillows and tug the sheet up to her chin, as she used to do when scolded as a child. She knew that her mother thought her unfeeling and hard, but she was not really so, as Rosemary had divined: and the spectacle of Christine, with her small, girlish hands clasped before her, her eyes darkly ringed and her unusually crisp hair sticking in clammy wisps about her temples and cheeks, gave her a horrible sensation of combined pity, disgust and inadequacy. She knew that she ought to jump out of bed, put her arms round her mother and attempt to comfort her: but she could no more do that now than she had been able to mix her tears with Christine's at the moment of Adrian's death. Grief was something private which one did not share with others: and in this her father would have agreed with her.

"If you knew how alone I feel! Larry's no comfort and now he rushes into all this. I thought that you and I—well, you're too young, I suppose. You don't understand that if one's lived all one's life with someone else who's taken—taken every decision from one—being always there—been . . ." She became incoherent.

There was no doubt of the strain of self-pity and facile emotionalism, for they had always been present in Christine's character and were indeed family traits; but equally there was no doubt of the genuineness of her grief, her sense of abandonment, and her terror of a future in which Adrian did not exist. Gwyneth saw all this; but still she was incapable of running to her mother. All she feared was that the quivering lip would begin to tremble more and more violently until the face all at once contorted itself into that of a beaten child and the tears begin to stream. That, for her, was the worst thing of all.

"Well, I must go and dress," Christine at last said, to Gwyneth's relief. But after her mother had trailed forlornly out of the room, relief was followed by shame and a nagging sense of failure. Having gulped another scalding cup of tea, she once more applied herself to Adrian's diary. What she now read was his account of that ride when he had been thrown by his horse and had first realized that he and Christine were in love with each other. The black ink had faded to brown and the white paper to yellow: but because he had had real talent as a writer, the sensations of that day had not faded. Indeed they seemed to Gwyneth so much more real than the scene which had just passed: even though one of the chief events had been in both cases the same.

The cycles of grief are not unlike those of physical pain: and now, as she went on reading, sipping from time to time at a third cup of tea, one nerve and then another and another slowly began to throb within her. Isolated words slipped past her consciousness and then whole sentences were carried away, as though on some black, rushing stream. Faltering, she tried to go on reading: then she pushed the tray to one side, and, still clutching the note-book, turned over to bury her face in her arms. She began to cry as she always did, silently and alone, with sobs which, like some desperate kind of retching, left her whole body aching and torn.

IV

At last they had sold up all the belongings which they were not going to take back to England with them, and the time had come for Christine and Gwyneth to leave. For both women the sorting of possessions had been even more trying than the long interviews with lawyers, the answering of letters of condolence, or the auction sale itself, when things for which Christine declared that Adrian had paid "a small fortune" were knocked down for a handful of rupees.

Christine had been reluctant to part with anything, and Gwyneth had had to reiterate to her that, when they returned to England, they would be living in a small flat or a cottage. "Yes, I know, dear," Christine would then say. "But your father was so fond of that piece. Did I ever tell you how he came to buy it?" For there were few "pieces" that did not have a story.

Often Christine would obstinately insist on the value of some object which Gwyneth knew to be worthless, as in the case of a bronze copy of a Greco-Roman head.

"We'd better take that back to England," Christine had said. "No one here is likely to appreciate what it's worth. We can have it sold at Christies or Sothebys or somewhere like that."

"But Mummy, it's not really valuable. It's only a copy, you know."

"A copy—don't be absurd! It's an original, though I can't remember whether your father said it was Roman or Greek. A copy—what an idea! Your father bought it in Naples. I remember quite well."

"Honestly, darling—the original's in the Vatican Museum."

"Your father had a wonderful knowledge about such things.

37

I'm quite sure he could never have mistaken a copy for an original. He was a real connoisseur."

"But I'm sure he always *knew* that it was a copy."

"Well, of course, he would have known. But in this particular case I remember his telling me—I remember it quite clearly. . . ."

Such arguments were not rare; and the business of sorting became, in consequence, even more tedious and exasperating for Gwyneth and painful for Christine. Everything was clutched at by the older woman, because to everything some memory attached itself; and to prise away what was either useless or too bulky for transportation was a task that made Gwyneth feel that she was guilty of the most abominable cruelty.

At first Christine had secretly hoped that, before they left for England, Gwyneth would succeed in becoming engaged to one of the many young men that were invited to the house. As she would often say to Rosemary: "In England there are so few opportunities"—whereas in India, though she did not add this, there were so few women. But Gwyneth was obviously as little interested in these possible suitors now as on the ship, and they themselves were, equally obviously, more interested in her mother than her. They found Gwyneth odd and frightening, and did not feel at their ease with her. But with Christine it was impossible for them not to feel at their ease, for even at this oppressive time of grief her gaiety and charm would suddenly bubble up, against her will and almost without her knowing, as soon as some guests arrived. After some such evening of joking and laughing out on the verandah with half a dozen subalterns, Christine would feel a depression intensified by a cruel sense of guilt: she had forgotten Adrian, she had betrayed him. Then she would cast herself down on her bed in a passion of remorseful weeping.

Realizing, at last, that she would not succeed in marrying off Gwyneth before they left for England, Christine began to ask about her future plans; and she was astonished when the girl finally announced that she intended to study medicine.

"What an extraordinary idea! You're not serious, are you?"

"Perfectly serious. Why?"

"You know it may be difficult?"

"Difficult, how? I'm prepared to work hard."

"I didn't mean that."

"Then what do you mean?"

Christine hesitated: "Well, dear, you know that kind of thing costs money. We're not going to be very well off."

"I suppose you expect me to go straight into a job at three pounds a week."

"No—that wasn't my idea." Christine tried to be conciliatory, sensing the force of the girl's resentment. "But couldn't you take some sort of training that doesn't need quite so much time or money—a secretarial course, for instance? Or a diploma in domestic science, like the Halliday girl? She's got an excellent job for herself at a prep. school somewhere near Exeter."

"Things like that get one nowhere," Gwyneth said sombrely. "Except to preparatory schools."

"Oh, I don't know. Anyway, in the end, you'll get married. . . ."

"No, I shall not!"

"Of course you will, darling. Sooner or later you'll meet the right sort of man—and then what will be the point of all that time and money wasted on learning to be a doctor?"

"Oh, you don't understand!"

"Of course I understand, or try to understand. I know that I've not had your education—that you regard me as a fool—but after all I have had many more years of experience of life . . ."

"Mummy, please!" They were sorting and dusting books and Gwyneth now banged two together, sending out a cloud of dust which made her mother choke and cough. "Can't you see that I want a career—something that I can do for all my life? I'm not interested in getting married and having children and running a home."

"You say that now, dear. But every girl is interested in . . ."

"Every girl is not! Anyway, I'm not."

Christine sighed: "But where is the money to be found? It's going to be hard enough to keep Tim on at school. Even if they do give him a grant, as well as his scholarship, as Geoffrey hopes they might."

"Is it necessary for him to remain as a boarder?"

Christine was amazed: "Well, dear, of course he must. It would be terrible to have to take him away after he's done so well in his first year."

"He could go to Westminster or St. Paul's, couldn't he?"

"It's not quite the same." Christine herself would have been delighted to have Tim at home with her as a day-boy; but Adrian had always insisted on the superiority of boarding schools, and it was still too soon after his death for her to reject any of the opinions which he had always imposed on her with such ease. "One has to think of his future. And then, afterwards, there is the University—you know Daddy always hoped that he'd go to his old college. We'll have to save for that. Of course, he'll probably win a scholarship, but still— these things all cost money. I showed you the letter from Mr. Hiskett, didn't I? Such a nice letter." Mr. Hiskett was Tim's housemaster. "He seems to think Tim quite outstandingly brilliant."

"I wasn't considered exactly backward at school," Gwyneth said bitterly.

"I never said you were, dear."

"You're always talking about Tim's future career, but what about mine? Aren't I entitled to a career?"

Christine was bewildered; for in her mind women and careers had never been associated. "Well, we must see," she eventually sighed, turning over a copy of *The Portrait of Dorian Grey* given to her by Adrian as a birthday present before they were married. A silver-fish scuttled across one of the pages which the damp and heat between them had yellowed and blotched and then disappeared into the spine. "We shall have to see how things work out." She began to shake the book, but the silver-fish did not emerge. "That's all."

Whenever her mind was confronted with a problem that, in the past, she would have left to Adrian to decide, this was how she disposed of it. All her life she had been naturally optimistic, and experience had done nothing to alter her conviction that, in the end, "things work themselves out". When, therefore, Gwyneth attempted on other occasions to discuss the subject again, her mother merely said: "Let's leave that till we get to England and see how everything goes, shall we, darling?"; which infuriated Gwyneth, but seemed to Christine the ob-vious way of solving the dilemma.

The engagement of Larry and Louise had meantime been announced in the *Pioneer* and the *Statesman*, and Christine, realizing that this battle had been lost even before she had had the opportunity to fight it, set about making friends with the girl. Secretly, she was still chagrined and dismayed; and when her friends asked her about the match, she had to brace herself for the humiliation either of their ill-concealed astonishment and contempt, or, far worse, of their gushing sympathy and pity. With Larry she made the journey to the small town on the edge of the desert where Louise lived with her father, a widower who was a driver on the railway, and two younger brothers who were even darker than she. The brothers asked Christine to go to a dance at the Railway Institute, and although she was aware of Louise scowling at them when she thought she could not be noticed, she gladly accepted. Having once made up her mind to something, she had an extraordinary capacity for carrying it through without misgivings or hesitations; and she had now decided that she must accept Louise, her family and her background. So she danced in turn with the two brothers, and with the elderly station-master, whose sweat-stained blue suit was permeated with what seemed to be the smell of guavas; when Louise's father brought her a glass of what he called "port wine", she raised it and drank to the health of the engaged couple, although the sweet, warm, tacky liquid nauseated her.

When the train at last carried them away from all this, into the desert, Larry took both her hands in his. "You were marvellous," he said. "Thank you so much."

"But I enjoyed it," she replied: and this was the truth.

To Louise she gave a share of her jewellery, and when the girl protested, cried out: "Take it, my dear. And take this too!" she added, pulling out an opal brooch. "You're also an October birthday. What will I do with all this stuff in England?"

"But what about Gwyneth?"

"Oh, there's plenty still for her. And anyway she's not really interested in such things." Gwyneth never wore jewellery except her father's signet-ring on her little finger, and occasionally a Victorian cameo which he had given to her when they had left England.

There was no doubt that Louise's looks had improved since she had become engaged to Larry. Previously she had always had a brooding, sulky expression; when she had walked, she had slouched, and when she had stood still, she had looked ungainly and tense. She had suspected Christine's hostility to

41

her, and had been in no doubt of Geoffrey's: and in consequence when she was with either of them her defensiveness
had seemed to take the form of insolence. But now that she
was sure both of Larry's love and Christine's friendship, an
extraordinary change had happened. She would never be a
pretty woman, for her sallow features looked too much as if
they had been hurriedly formed from putty, and her hairy arms,
culminating in small, pudgy hands, dimpled at the knuckles,
were almost cylindrical; but she had all at once acquired a
vivacity which made even Geoffrey exclaim: "That girl's got
something!"

Louise had the air of being as surprised as all Larry's and
Christine's friends that he should have wished to marry her,
and there was an occasion, fraught with embarrassment, when,
venturing to put her secret doubts into words, she had asked
Christine and Rosemary whether they thought his career was
likely to be affected by the match, and what sort of welcome
they imagined that she herself would receive from the other
Army wives in Quetta. Both women were generous rather than
truthful in their assurances; and since she was hypersensitive
where her race was concerned, Louise guessed this. Often
during their love-making, having astonished Larry by the
passionate abandon of her caresses, she would all at once falter,
become grave, and beg him: "Larry, is this all wrong? Is this
a mistake? Are you sure it can work?" Then he would laugh
and say something like: "Don't be such a little goose!"; for it
was obvious that he was as unwilling to discuss the matter with
her as with his mother.

"He'll have a rough time," Geoffrey predicted.

"And she'll have a worse," Rosemary sighed.

"Oh, I expect things will sort themselves out," Christine
said.

"I certainly hope so." Rosemary, who had lost one child in
infancy and another in childbirth, and whose life had been a
series of undramatic disappointments, had less faith in the
ability of things to sort themselves out satisfactorily than either
her exasperatingly cheerful husband or her friend.

There was a wedding, quiet, but less quiet than Christine
had wished, at which Gwyneth caused resentment by refusing
to be a bridesmaid. It was assumed by Louise's family and
friends, who were as over-sensitive as Louise, that she wished

to show her disapproval of the marriage; whereas, in fact, as she had already explained to Louise, she merely felt too shy. A number of lengthy and embarrassing speeches were delivered by leading members of the Eurasian community, and Christine's old friends pulled wry faces and exchanged sardonic looks as they were invited to drink innumerable toasts in port wine or lemonade. It was all different from what Christine had imagined that Larry's wedding would be; but since Adrian's death, she had stoically come to face the fact that most things would now be different from what she had imagined. There were times when this realization that she had been cheated out of all that the future had promised—Adrian's new job and the knighthood that it carried; years passed happily and serenely between Simla and Delhi; and then the retirement to Florence, of which Adrian had always dreamed—would fill her with bitterness and despair; but there were other times when, with a pang of guilt, she would find herself thrilling at the idea of having to choose for herself a road that had ceased to be predictable, through a country wholly strange to her. She was a naturally adventurous woman whose adventurousness had always been subordinated to her husband's wishes: to be free now was as exciting as it was terrifying.

The day came for their departure; and Gwyneth envied her mother for the ease with which she said what was exactly fitting to all those friends and servants who had been with them during those last months. Gwyneth herself became surly and tongue-tied on such occasions, and she knew that many of the people who had helped them would, for that reason, say that she was ungrateful. Even when Rosemary, who was her godmother, attempted to kiss her good-bye, she squirmed and abruptly turned her head sideways so that the kiss landed somewhere on the firm line of her jaw. Yet she was probably fonder of Rosemary than she was of anyone else except her mother, Tim and Larry.

Even Christine's tears were beautifully managed. She would look into the countenances, one by one, of those who had come to say good-bye, and then slowly her eyes would fill, while the rest of her face still kept its grave composure. She had spared no labour to find new jobs for all her servants; and worst of all for Gwyneth had been the noisy lamentations of these middle-aged men and women as they begged their former

43

mistress not to leave them for ever. Of course, it meant nothing, Gwyneth told herself; they would forget soon enough. But there remained with her, as with her mother, long after they had completed their journey back to England, the terrible guilty sense of having abandoned a group of distraught children alone in a jungle.

At the station there had been a moment of comedy amidst the tears when the old ayah had rushed up to Christine shouting: "Memsahib forgot this! Memsahib forgot!" In one hand she held a bottle in which was the appendix that Christine had had removed more than five years previously. The Indian surgeon had presented her with this gift during her convalescence, and chiefly because she did not know how to dispose of it, she had pushed it into the back of the bathroom cupboard. No doubt the ayah had thought it some sacred relic.

While they were all laughing, Christine suddenly noticed a figure, standing apart from all the other servants, with his head bowed. It was Amir Ali. He had always been fanatical in his cleanliness and tidiness, imitating Adrian in this, and it was a terrible shock to see his clothes tattered and dirty, his face covered with white bristles in which the dust had lodged, and his turban askew. Although less than fifty, he had aged as Indians age, but in the past he had always been an upright and vigorous, if venerable, figure. Now he had shrunk and withered, the skin on his bare legs sagging in cracks and wrinkles like a toad's.

Christine went across to him; and all her bitterness and resentment at having been betrayed by him were swallowed up in pity. She remembered him as a young man with a hawk-like profile and over-full red lips who had obviously been jealous of the new memsahib when she had first married Adrian; and then she remembered him as the devoted servant of many years, and the best of all those who had helped in nursing the dying man. Once, when a disgruntled *chuprassi* had attempted to stab his master, Amir Ali had stepped between and he still bore on his forearm the jagged grey scar. Somewhere in the hills he had a wife and children and grandchildren; but he had given them all up to work for his English master.

"Amir Ali . . . good-bye."

He threw himself at her feet and there knocked his head on the ground, moaning "Forgive me . . . forgive me. . . ."

"Of course, I have forgiven you. Get up," she said in Hindustani. "Get up!" The tears had made deep runnels in the dust of his face and, as he bowed down before her, she was horrified by the way his shoulder-bones protruded through his clothes, and the back of his neck was criss-crossed by innumerable wrinkles that looked like black incisions on his brown skin. "You must write to me," she said. "Get a babu to write a letter for you. Will you do that? Will you?"

"Yes, yes," he cried.

"And thank you. . . . Thank you." She had never touched a male Indian servant in her life, but now she caught one of his trembling hands in both of hers.

Somewhere a whistle blew. Geoffrey called: "Come, my dear! Quick! Quick! Come!"

Doors slammed; more hurried kisses were exchanged; the servants huddled together, swayed and groaned, as the English called out: "Good luck! Good journey! Take care of yourselves! God bless!"

Christine sank back on to the cracked leather upholstery of the seat and turned her face, which was white and glistening with sweat, to look out at the town retreating jerkily behind them. She took a handkerchief from her bag and mopped at her forehead. "So that's over," she said.

Suddenly Gwyneth leant forward as though to be sick.

"Oh, don't, my dear, don't!" Christine cried; and she put out a hand.

The terrible dry sobs went on long after the town was no more than a grey blob under the immense sky.

V

"Yes, really the poor little chap took it remarkably well," Mr. Hiskett said. "Of course, it's to a woman that they want to turn at an hour like that, and fortunately he seems to have taken a liking for my housekeeper, Miss Downes. You must meet her. Yes, I must leave you alone to have a chat with her." Mr. Hiskett was a middle-aged bachelor; an

45

excellent scholar and sixth-form master who relished personal relationships with his boys only after they had passed through his hands to return to the school as visitors, and with their parents only if they were distinguished or rich. Otherwise boys or parents were alike passed on to his housekeeper.

He opened his study door and shouted: "Miss Downes! Miss Dow—nes!" on a long descending note.

"Yes, Mr. Hiskett." A thin woman in woollen stockings and shapeless tweeds, her straight grey hair cut in a fringe low on her forehead and in a line that just revealed the large waxen lobes of her ears, ambled wearily down the corridor, clutching a sheaf of papers in one hand. "Oh, I thought you wanted to see these," she said, vaguely waving the papers to and fro.

"No. I called you to meet Mrs.—er—Cornwell. She is the mother of—er—little Tim Cornwell."

"Oh, yes." The two women shook hands.

"I so much wanted to thank you for being so kind to Tim," Christine said. "As I was abroad myself and my only relatives were up in Scotland . . . I know what a difference it must have made to him at such a time."

"I expect you two would like to have a little talk together. Why don't you take Mrs.—er—Cornwell to your room, Miss Downes?" Mr. Hiskett now suggested quickly. "Er—Tim won't be out for another—for another twenty minutes."

Miss Downes's room was almost entirely filled by a desk covered with papers, out of which the spout of a brown teapot poked itself upwards. "You'll have a cup of tea, won't you?" She rummaged in a cupboard, causing innumerable receipt-books to cascade to the floor, and eventually produced a cup and saucer and poured out some tepid tea as brown as the pot in which it had been standing.

"An epidemic always keeps me so busy," she said.

"An epidemic?"

"Oh, only German measles. But parents get worried even about German measles, and letters have to go back and forth." She picked up a handful of papers and then let them drop. "I like Tim," she said.

"I'm so glad."

"Yes, he's one of the boys I like. He's what I call a little gentleman. I don't mean that he doesn't get himself into

46

scrapes like the rest of them. . . . Do you smoke? No? I'm afraid I'm a real chain-smoker. Such a bad example!"

Christine, wishing to ask Miss Downes how Tim had first reacted to the news of his father's death, had been doubtful in what way to begin. But now Miss Downes took two or three staccato puffs at the cigarette which she held in what appeared to be a miniature pair of lazy-tongs, and herself leant forward: "My heart bled for the poor child after Mr. Hiskett had broken the news to him. We had him spend the night over here in the private wing. After that, Mr. Hiskett thought it best for him to get back into the routine again—to keep him busy and keep his mind off it all." She spoke of how she led Tim up to the guest room and of his bravery: "I knew that he was just waiting for me to leave him so that he could have a really good cry. But while I was there, there wasn't a tear—not a single tear." She had given him a hot-water bottle because she had thought that would be "comforting"; but it had leaked during the night and she didn't suppose that the poor chap could have slept hardly a wink.

Christine pictured to herself the child's misery as he lay awake in that strange bedroom, with the bedclothes wet about him.

"It's funny how the shock seemed to come much later. He was as chirpy as a cricket after a day or two—and then, all at once, he had that trouble at night."

"What trouble?"

"Oh, didn't Mr. Hiskett tell you?"

"No. What trouble?"

"Well, I expect he didn't wish to add to all your worries. Another cup of tea? I'm as bad with the tea as with the cigarettes. Look at the colour of that—and the darker it is, the better it suits me! Oh, it's nothing serious; only to be expected in the circumstances. Of course, we asked the school doctor, Colonel Blackmore, to have a chat with Tim—and to give him a look-over. He said that he was as sound as a bell, no cause for worry about his general health. Just delayed shock, he said. He prescribed a sedative at bedtime and that seems to be doing the trick."

"But what—what has been the trouble?"

"I suppose it's what used to be called night-terrors when you and I were children. Every so often he wakes up screaming

47

his head off; and, of course, in a dormitory that causes a certain amount of fuss, as you can imagine! The poor little chap doesn't seem to know much about it afterwards; he doesn't even want to talk about it, I think. Other times he wakes up crying." She noticed the look of consternation that had appeared on Christine's face, and leaned forward, scattering cigarette-ash over the front of her grey woollen jersey: "Oh, you mustn't worry. He's *much* better already—much, *much* better." She began to dust off the ash with one of her swollen, blue hands: "He only does it about once every ten days now. His work, of course, is excellent; and what's so rare is that he's not just a swot—you know that he won the Junior Fives, don't you? Tomlins, who got into the Final with him—he's in Foote's House—is really a year his senior." Miss Downes knew far more about such sporting successes than Mr. Hiskett. "Yes, Tim's a real little all-rounder. Often the death of a father pulls them back a little. But in his case it seems to have had just the opposite effect. . . . Ah, there's the bell. He'll be out of school now. Shall I take you along?"

The first thing that Christine noticed as Tim began to come towards her at a leaping trot, some books under his arm, was how much he had grown. The blue serge suit, which she had bought for him at the Army and Navy stores only seven months before, was already too short for him in the trouser-legs and sleeves. He looked thinner, too, and his face seemed to have lost its babyish fullness and pinkness. He and some friends had just emerged from schools, and she had the sensation that he was coming towards her faster and faster as he shouted: "Mummy! Mummy!" With his one free arm he gripped her about the shoulders and she in turn stooped to kiss his upturned face. Momentarily he clung there to her, as he used to cling to her in terror when he was a small child; then, aware of Miss Downes beside them and of the other boys who were streaming out of class, he pushed her away.

"How are you, darling?"

"Oh, all right. . . . Are we going out to lunch together?"

"Tim, your voice has changed! It sounds so deep and gruff."

Christine knew, the moment she had spoken, that this was not what she ought to have said; and Miss Downes, instead of ignoring the remark, now laughed: "Yes, you weren't a treble in the choir for long, were you, Tim? Don't they grow up quickly!"

As Christine walked with Tim down towards the suspension bridge, she longed to put an arm round his shoulders, over which the blue serge had already rubbed shiny; to stoop and kiss that cheek, showing its first down; to brush back the lock of blond hair which fell in jagged prongs across his wide forehead. But she did not dare to do any of these things: she knew that she must not.

As soon, however, as they had left the school grounds, his hand, unsolicited, was slipped into hers.

"Where are you staying, Mummy?"

"At the Swan. Why?"

"Oh, the Swan's all right." Reflectively he added: "The Westgate is better. That's the best of all."

"Is it?"

"The Dragon's the worst. That's where most of the commercial travellers go. *Sometimes* parents go there. Not often."

"How have you been getting along, my darling?"

"All right. . . . Where are we going to lunch?"

"I thought we might as well go back to the Swan. What do you think?"

"Couldn't we go to the Westgate?"

"If you'd rather."

"Mummy, may I have some cider?"

"Is that allowed?"

"Of course—if one's with one's parents."

"You're happy here, aren't you?"

"Oh, yes. . . . Mummy, that's where old Josephine lives. His real name is Mr. Joseph, he's my form master. We call him Josephine and his wife Napoleon. She hen-pecks him."

"You want to stay here, don't you, Tim?"

He had been walking a little ahead of her, banging with a stick on the iron struts of the bridge. Now he stopped in his tracks, his mouth slightly open: "Well, of course I do, Mummy! Why?"

"I wanted to know. Don't look so upset, dear. If you want to stay, then, of course, you must stay."

As for most children, to leave school abruptly was associated in his mind with irremediable disgrace. Only in the middle of the last term a boy had been removed for mysterious reasons

49

and Mr. Hiskett, addressing the whole house, had spoken sternly of this unfortunate "having chosen to jeopardize his whole career". "I do not know," he had added, "what kind of school will choose to accept him now"—the implication being that, if such a school existed, it was one of a despicable lowness.

"But, Mummy, I couldn't leave now—I couldn't! What would I do? Where could I go?"

"Gwyneth thought that you might like to live with us, and go to Westminster or St. Paul's. They're very good schools, you know, dear. But I quite agree that there's nothing like boarding-school, that's what Daddy always said. And as you've settled in so well here, and seem to be doing so marvellously . . ."

"You know that I've gone up from eleventh to third place in the weekly order, don't you, Mummy?"

"But, darling, that's wonderful. I *am* so pleased. It's obvious that you take after Daddy and not after your poor brainless mother!" She squeezed his arm: "Now you mustn't go worrying about what I said. If you want to stay, you shall stay."
Christine had still to discuss with Mr. Hiskett the size of Tim's grant for the school: but in her own mind there was no doubt that, however small the sum and however large the sacrifices which she and Gwyneth might be forced to make, the boy must stay on.

During luncheon, Tim began to question her eagerly about the flat which she and Gwyneth had found in Earl's Court. "Please wait until I come home before you have my room painted!" he begged her, when she had told him that he would have a room to himself. "And can we have a piano?" he asked a moment later.

"We shall have to see, darling. We shall have to see how the money goes. First we must get all the essential things, mustn't we?"

"Oh, but we must have a piano! I can now play much better than when you left. I can play a Beethoven Sonatina and one of the Mendelssohn Songs Without Words."

Since he had been sent from India as a child of eight, he had never had a home of his own, spending his holidays with relations or friends of his mother or father, or at school, and this enthusiasm of his touched her unbearably.

"Is there a garden?" he next asked.

"No, I'm afraid not. You see, we're on the very top floors. It's what's called a maisonette.

"Then there's a lift!

"No, only a hundred and eleven stairs. Gwyneth has counted them. But that will worry your poor old mother far more than you both."

"It'll be wonderful to live in London. And we shall all be together," he added a moment later. Then, reflectively, he stared down into his tomato soup, his spoon poised in his hand, while Christine gazed across at him.

She wanted to add, "Except for Daddy," for that was the thought that had come unbidden at his last remark; but she knew that this reminder would be unnecessarily cruel.

After luncheon they played cards for a while in the lounge of the hotel. Tim always won, except on one occasion when she defeated him at a game of bézique. "Oh, that's a silly game," he then said crossly, stirring the cards in a heap with fingers that were covered with ink. "Let's go for a walk. We can have tea at Welland's afterwards."

He took her down to the Old Quarry where the river, making a vast loop, had created what was almost an island.

"They want to cut down these elms. They say that they're not safe," he explained to her. "Won't it be a pity? Look, there's a primula in flower! It's early for them. You should have seen the forsythia two months ago." She was astonished by the maturity of his interests; and even more so when he took her into the Priory and pointed out one of the brasses: "I did a rubbing of that. Mr. Sheldon showed me how. It's really quite easy. Now on Sundays Cooper and I often go out to the churches around." But a moment later he was telling her how, on one such expedition, he and Cooper had fought a battle with three "oiks"—this was apparently school slang for the boys of the town; and when they walked back for tea, he made her halt outside a shop with a number of model aeroplanes in the window, and admired them until she went in and bought one for him.

He ate a large tea, during which it pleased her to press on him cake after cake and ice-cream after ice-cream until, becoming boisterous, he started to do imitations of the Headmaster, Mr. Hiskett and "Josephine" which made the

51

people at the other tables turn round and smile: in his excitement he even knocked the milk-jug over. "Oh, Tim, it's such fun to be with you again!" Christine exclaimed. But only too soon the hour struck for her to take him back to the school in time for lock-ups and for her interview with Mr. Hiskett. "What sort of man is Mr. Hiskett?" she asked, as she peered into the mirror of her handbag and ran a comb through her greying curls: for she was simple enough to imagine that she might perhaps be able to charm him into increasing the size of the grant.

"Oh, he's clever. But Downie really runs the house. He's not interested in anything but his books and his gramophone records and his bugs."

"His what?"

"He runs the Entomological Society—you know, caterpillars, that kind of thing. That's his hobby."

"He's not married, is he?"

Tim laughed: "Some of the chaps say that he and Downie . . . I don't believe it. I don't believe he ever *looks* at a woman."

Christine lowered the comb.

A spring mist was coming off the river as they crossed the bridge. Christine coughed and shuddered involuntarily, for now the air was chill; then she slipped an arm about her son's shoulders. He would not mind, she thought, for no one could see them. "It's been lovely to see you again, darling—and to see you so well." Tim did not answer.

"I have some things—some things of Daddy's for you. His watch, and his fountain-pen and—and his camera." Suddenly the thought came to her of those beads of blood, huddled like ants, around the rim of the lens, and of Adrian's last photograph, of the ship taken from the boat, perfectly composed and focused even at that hour of illness.

"His camera!" Tim was excited. "Do you mean the Leica?"

"Yes, darling. We kept it for you."

"Oh, do send it to me, Mummy—as soon as you get home. Please, Mummy! Don't forget!"

"Christine hesitated, wondering what Mr. Hiskett would think if, after she had extracted the grant, she then sent her son a camera worth almost a hundred pounds. "I really meant you to have it when you were a little older," she said; for she shrank from telling him the real reason. "It's a very,

very expensive camera, you know, and someone here might steal it."

"Oh, but Mummy, I'd take such care of it!"

"Or you might go and break it," she added. "No, darling, really, I think I'd better keep it for you—for another year or so. Of course you can use it in the holidays," she added

"Oh, Mummy! I do think it's mean of you. After all it *is* my camera. Isn't it?"

Desperately she said: "Look, I'll tell you what. I'll give you another camera for use at school. I'll get you a Box Brownie."

"Oh, *not* a box camera!" he wailed.

"Well, a Kodak then."

"I don't see why I shouldn't have the Leica," he grumbled. "Lots of the boys have cameras as good as that." But she could see that her promise had appeased him, as he began to tell her about the Photographic Society and the exhibition which its members held every year in the school library.

Already the schools had begun to loom up at them through the mist, and she tightened her grip on his shoulders and drew him closer towards her as she said: "Tim, darling, there's still one thing I've not asked you about."

"Yes, Mummy." Almost as if he had guessed already, he took the opportunity offered by a piece of wire lying in their path to break himself away from her.

"Miss Downes—Miss Downes tells me that—that sometimes at night—that you don't always sleep very well."

He had picked up the wire, and was winding it round and round his wrist as he trotted ahead of her.

"Tim," she said: for he had given no indication of having heard her speak to him.

Silence.

"Is there anything worrying you, or upsetting you?" The wire was now drawn taut, so that she could see the flesh ridged between its coils. "Darling, did you hear what I said? Tim!"

"Of course there is nothing. Downie just fusses," she heard him mutter. Then loudly, almost viciously, between his bared teeth: "Nothing, nothing, nothing!"

"Take care, dear—you'll hurt yourself with that wire." She was relieved when he began to unwind it. "Because if there *is* anything on your mind, you must tell your old mother.

We mustn't have any secrets between us, must we? Must we, Tim?"

"Oh, we ought to hurry! Listen, there's the bell! It only rings for five minutes." As he trotted ahead of her while she struggled to keep up, he kept rubbing the weals left on his wrist by the wire, with the fingers of his other hand.

She had the tact to kiss him good-bye before they turned the corner which brought them into the quadrangle where both the schools and Mr. Hiskett's house stood. "Good-bye, darling," she said and her hand trembled. "Good-bye." His cheek was cold and damp, and his fingers were icy. "Only two and a half weeks until the holidays."

"You won't forget about the room, will you, Mummy?"

"What, dear?"

"Not to have it painted until I get back."

"All right. I'm seeing the decorator to-morrow."

"And the camera, Mummy."

"I won't forget. . . . Take care of yourself!"

"You, too, Mummy."

The bell, which had been clanging timidly out of the mist above them, all at once ceased. Tim bolted into the house; Christine walked slowly round to the private wing to find Mr. Hiskett.

VI

As Christine and Gwyneth began to trudge up the dark stair-well, each with a heavily loaded basket in either hand, a voice shrilled from below: "I suppose it was necessary to slam the door like that!"

Christine paused and seemed about to descend once more; until Gwyneth checked her: "Oh, leave it, Mummy! You know that she's dotty."

"I will not have her shout at me like that. As if that creature living with her didn't make noise enough! Do you remember that night when we heard him screaming for hours on end? No, dear, I don't see why we should put up with it."

But when she said this Christine had already resumed her climb.

"He was ill that night. That's different."

"Ill! Delirium tremens, you mean. And not surprising, considering how he drinks."

"We don't know that, Mummy. She says it's his nerves."

Panting heavily, the two women at last faced each other before the front door, whose shiny brownness, enclosing three ovals of green frosted glass to form a clover leaf, always suggested to Tim the wings of some insect: he had a horror of insects, even of ladybirds. Christine tried to fumble in her bag without putting down both her baskets, for which there was barely room on the top of the stairs. "Have you got your key?"

"No. Let's ring for Tim to open."

"Oh, don't do that, dear. He may be at work."

Gwyneth gave a sardonic smile: "More likely to be reading a detective story," she said. But by this time Christine had succeeded in balancing one of the baskets on the step below her, and had drawn out her key.

The maisonette into which the two women now entered occupied the top two floors of a tall, narrow house in a square between the Brompton and the Fulham Roads. Facing the front door was a steep flight of stairs which led up, carpeted in nigger-brown drugget for cheapness, to a bathroom and the two long attics in which Gwyneth and Tim slept. Downstairs there were a kitchen, Christine's bedroom, a sitting-room which was also used as a dining-room, and another room, called by the agent, "the slip of a room", where there was a table with the sewing-machine on it, the ironing board, and a camp bed for visitors. Gwyneth had soon ceased to take any interest in the furnishing or decoration of the flat. "You are an odd girl," Christine said to her on one occasion. "One would think you would be interested in how your home was going to look. One day you'll be setting up a house of your own." She did not guess Gwyneth's discouragement as they trailed up and down Tottenham Court Road, buying shaky limed-oak cupboards, dressing-tables and chairs; her disgust at so many shoddily cheap purchases turning into an apathy which would make her snap at her mother: "Oh, take which you prefer! It doesn't really matter," when asked for her opinion.

Only once she ventured: "Don't you think we'd do better if we went round the junk-shops?"

"But antiques are so terribly expensive!" Christine had then exclaimed.

"We needn't buy *antiques*. I meant just ordinary second-hand stuff."

"One's never sure how clean it is, is one? One hears stories of second-hand furniture being absolutely *infested*."

Christine was appalled by dirt, and whenever she made the climb up to the flat, she would feel the same disgust, as strong after six months as when they had moved in, at the layers of dust and grime that clung, like some sort of fungus, to the sash-windows; at the smell of stale garbage from the basement which Mrs. Campion and her lover inhabited; above all at the scurf of wrappings, twists of newspaper and cigarette-ends invariably lying, as though cast up by some nocturnal tide, each day in the entrance-hall and even on the stairs themselves.

It was other, more subtle, things that depressed Gwyneth: the wallpaper of the stair-well, for example, which flowered into enormous puce dahlias, the pixie-knocker of the couple below them (Christine thought this "sweet") or the pram, one of the rusty struts of its hood broken, which never moved from the landing of the second floor.

Tim, alone of the three, was capable both of ignoring this squalor below and around them, and of keeping his enthusiasm for the tasks of decoration and furnishing. His tastes were naturally immature. He had his attic room distempered an apple-green, then fashionable in tea-shops, and against this hung prints of Van Gogh, Peter Scott and Brangwyn, interspersed with photographs of fives teams and cricket teams in which he appeared. He had painted his book-case a darker green than the walls, and from the ceiling were suspended, by a nexus of wires, a number of model aeroplanes which were also his handiwork. Often Christine would take visitors up to this room, when Tim was out or at school, and say proudly: "Hasn't he made it nice?" When she was alone, and the next school holidays seemed depressingly far, she would find some excuse to go upstairs and would wander about, examining the photographs, unfolding and folding his clothes in the drawers, and even opening notebooks in which he had begun to scribble stories which rarely progressed beyond the first three or four paragraphs.

". . . Oh, it's muggy to-day!" Christine exclaimed, as she began to take out of the baskets the things they had bought. Along her upper lip there were small bubbles of sweat. "I wonder if Tim has got in." She went to the bottom of the stairs and began to call: "Tim, Tim, darling!"

Eventually Tim appeared from the bathroom, his blond hair dripping in prongs over his forehead, his neat, sinewy body naked except for a towel he had wrapped about the loins.

"Oh, there you are! How long have you been in?"

"About ten minutes. I've had a bath." He wandered into his own room and spoke to her from there: "I beat Jimmy Tomlins hollow."

"Did you, darling? Oh, good!" Christine had no idea whether he had been playing squash, fives or tennis.

"They have a super court. Richmond is lovely, you know, Mummy. Their house is by the river, the garden goes right down to it. They have a motor boat *and* a sailing dinghy."

"Who is Jimmy Tomlins, darling?"

"Oh, he's in Foote's—captain of the Colts' Rugger. His father is almost a millionaire, I should think. The old people are terribly common, even Jimmy's ragged about his accent." He came once more out on to the landing, doing up his shirt. "Talk about stupidity! Jimmy would have been sacked long ago if he weren't so good at games." He laughed. "He's a great boozer too!"

"A boozer!"

"Oh, he's always getting into trouble—breaking out of lock-ups, that sort of thing."

"I hope you never do anything like that."

"Well, if I do, I'm careful not to be caught." Once more he went back into his bedroom and this time returned with his trousers. "Mummy—there's something I want to ask you. You know that racket of mine, well, it's not awfully good."

"But, darling, we only bought it two months ago."

"Yes, I know. But it was a mistake to get one so cheap. If I'm going to be serious about tennis—and you know, I'm awfully keen about it now . . ." He broke off: "Oh, Mummy, you never sewed on this button!"

"I asked Gwyneth to do it. I expect she forgot."

57

"I didn't forget. I was too busy," Gwyneth shouted from the kitchen. "I'll do it this evening."

"That's not much good. I need the trousers now."

"Well, give them to me," Christine said. "It won't take a jiffy."

Tim came and sat beside her in his under-pants, his bare legs crossed, leaning over the dining-room table where she had placed the trousers and work-box. He patted her hand: "You look tired, darling," he said. "I wish you wouldn't overdo things."

"Mrs. Crutchfield didn't come again to-day. That son of hers has had some more ear trouble."

"Why on earth don't you get rid of her?"

"Oh, no, dear! I couldn't do that. She's such a nice woman."

"She smells."

This was true; but Christine exclaimed: "Tim, she doesn't!" out of some obscure loyalty which Mrs. Crutchfield certainly did not either appreciate or return. "It's unfortunate that she has all those young children who are always falling ill."

"That cotton is not quite the same colour, is it?"

"It's the nearest I've got. Oh, dear, do you think it will show? Surely it won't." Tim had just begun to be interested in his appearance, after years of childhood indifference and untidiness. "I wonder if perhaps Gwyneth . . ."

"It doesn't matter. It doesn't matter," he repeated, putting out a restraining arm as she began to get up. After a moment he said: "Jimmy suggested that I might like to go and spend a few days with them at Richmond."

"These holidays?" Less than ten days of the holidays now remained.

"H'm, h'm. . . . They're having a dance, you see, next Saturday." He began fiddling with the buttons in the open tin before him. "Would you mind?"

"For how many days do you want to go?"

"Oh, I don't know. Three or four, I suppose."

That left approximately six. She sighed: "Yes, all right, if you feel that you *really* want to be with them."

"Well, of course I do." He had not yet been driven in the Lagonda, sailed in the dinghy, or been to Hurlingham, of which Jimmy and his sister so often talked.

"Then you must go." There was a silence, while she put the

58

thread to her mouth and bit it. "That's done." As he took the trousers from her, she said: "Why don't you ever ask Jimmy round here? You could have him over for the day."

"It's so far for him," Tim mumbled, stooping to put on the flannels.

"It's equally far for you. And they have a car—haven't they?"

"Two."

"Well, then." He did not answer. "Or the Patterson boy. He's just round the corner in the Boltons, isn't he? I do want you to feel that your room is entirely your own. You can do what you like there."

"Yes, Mummy." He stooped over her, to kiss her cheek. "Thank you for doing this for me," he said. He squeezed her shoulder with one of those delicate, yet muscular hands which always reminded her of Adrian's. "Are we going to eat soon? I'm terribly hungry."

"Gwyneth is just getting things ready. I must go and help her. We've got some strawberries."

"Oh, we had strawberries for tea at the Tomlins." He saw the look of pleasure fading from her face and hurriedly added: "But it'll be lovely to have them again. I'll be upstairs. Will you give me a call?"

Christine went into the kitchen, a large, square, high-ceilinged room where the family usually ate their meals when by themselves, and found Gwyneth seated back to front at the table, stringing beans. She had on her face an expression of sulky abstraction usual to it when she was engaged on household chores.

"Darling, you're not leaving much of these beans for us to eat," Christine said, picking up a knife to join her.

"I can't help it if they're all string."

Christine, although in India the only cooking she had ever done was to make fudge on a spirit stove on the verandah with Amir Ali's assistance, had in the course of the few months she had been in the flat already turned herself into a cook with the same efficiency that she had taught herself to iron clothes, mend fuses and deal with her bank. Gwyneth, on the other hand, obviously hated an occupation for which she had no aptitude, and sometimes even gave the impression of intentionally exaggerating her clumsiness at it, as though to annoy her mother.

59

"What a snob Tim is becoming!" Gwyneth suddenly exclaimed, after they had worked together in silence for a time. But she said the words without expression, as though she intended them merely as a statement of fact, not as a criticism, though Christine bridled at once.

"Why should you think that?"

"Oh, it's natural enough. At a school like that, it must be difficult for him. Did he ever tell you about the overcoat?"

"The overcoat? No. What about it?"

"You remember that it used to be mine?"

"Yes, but it fitted him perfectly. And it was the regulation shade of blue."

"Unfortunately it buttoned on the wrong side. They ragged him about that." Having tipped the beans into a colander, Gwyneth went on inexorably as she held them under the tap: "It's no use asking him why he doesn't invite his friends back here. It's obvious."

"Take care, you're splashing yourself!" Christine cried out, making this trivial accident the pretext for voiding all her pent-up exasperation. Like her father, Gwyneth seemed to enjoy dragging out into the open all the disagreeable things which Christine preferred to push out of sight into some inaccessible lumber-room of the mind. "What do you mean— 'it's obvious'?"

"Oh, his grand friends might turn their noses up. They wouldn't. But he's afraid they might. It's such a very smart and expensive school, isn't it?"

"It was your father's school. And he always said there was no finer education. Anyway, they give so many closed scholarships to Oxford. That'll be useful, we must remember that."

"To Christ Church," Gwyneth said. "Where exactly the same thing will happen all over again."

"You're very hard on Tim"

"No, I'm not, I'm not!" And it was true that she was not; she cared for him more than anyone else in the world except for her mother. "I feel terribly sorry for him."

"I don't know why you should. He's doing remarkably well, and seems to be happy."

"When, a few seconds later, Christine went into the sitting-room, she was disturbed to find Tim already seated there with a book. "Oh, I'd no idea you were downstairs!" She wondered how much he had heard.

Slowly he looked up: it was impossible to tell, for he was becoming adept at concealing his emotions. "Those upstairs rooms get so hot," he said. "It's much cooler here. Can I give you a hand?"

At each meal he would say this, when the table was being laid and when it was being cleared; and Christine would always reply by telling him to go on with his book or with listening to the radio. "This is a woman's job," she would often add. But even when there were a man's jobs to be done, like carrying coal from the kitchen to the sitting-room fire or hanging the curtains, she would insist on doing them herself. "How you spoil him!" Gwyneth would exclaim, although she too spoiled him in her sullen, undemonstrative way. Christine was not unconscious of this spoiling, and from time to time she would force herself to be exacting and severe; but that mood would not last, for eventually her need to lavish her affection on someone would prove far too strong.

As they ate their meal, the two women said little, while Tim amused them with his chatter. He enjoyed teasing them both, and they enjoyed being teased, even though Gwyneth's face would become red and even more heavy than usual at his playful jibes, until eventually she would burst out: "Oh, don't be such an ass!" He liked to imitate their friends, and there was always a certain malicious truth in these impersonations, as when, for example this evening, he began to take off a coy exchange between Christine and the new, and excessively handsome, milkman.

"Isn't he wicked?" Christine cried out. "I'm sure I never giggled and squirmed like that. And he never called me 'lady'—he called me 'madam'."

"How's the job going?" Tim later asked his sister.

"Oh, not too badly."

Suddenly Tim said: "I do wish you could have become a doctor yourself."

Gwyneth carefully cut a potato in half, and then cut the halves in quarters: "Well, it was not to be."

"You'd have been awfully good."

"I don't expect so."

"Wouldn't she, Mummy?"

Christine replied, with downcast eyes: "Things would have been very different if Daddy had lived."

"I don't suppose he would have wanted me to be a doctor."

"I'm sure he would have been delighted! Why should you say that? What an extraordinary thing to say!"

There was a silence, until Tim tipped his chair backwards so that it rested against the wall, and his face, shadowed by an ugly cretonne curtain, became invisible to her. "If I left school—if I went as a day-boy—would it—would it make any difference?" Neither of the women answered, though both were deeply touched. "Because if it would, well, I'm quite willing. I could go to Westminster, couldn't I? Couldn't I?"

The offer, like his offers to help with laying or clearing the table or washing up the things, was certain to be refused; and really he knew this. But his sense of guilt, his pity for Gwyneth condemned to do a secretarial job which she detested, and his desire somehow to help her were none the less genuine. Only to change schools would have been too high a price: a price which, with the natural egotism of the young, he would never be prepared to pay.

"How nice of you to say that, darling!" Christine said. She had got up to clear away the plates, and now, balancing the stack with one hand against the edge of the table, she used her free hand to caress the back of his head and his shoulders. "But Gwyneth and I have discussed all this, and we both feel that, whatever happens, you must stay where you are. Anyway, it wouldn't make such a difference, if you left, that we should be able to pay for Gwyneth's medicine. Would it, Gwyneth?"

Gwyneth sadly shook her head and stared out of the window, her chin supported on one arm, the elbow of which rested across the table, while her body slouched forward. But as soon as her mother had gone into the kitchen she mumbled:

"Yes, thank you for the suggestion, Tim. It was sweet of you."

The words sounded grudging and even ill-tempered; but her brother was used to her inability to say things with the fluency which he, even at the age of sixteen, could so easily command. The contrast in their manners was extreme, as he now leant across smiling to take her forearm in his hand and said: "I feel you had rather a raw deal. And you've been so plucky about it. It's been much worse for you than for either Larry or myself. Hasn't it?"

"Oh, I don't know. . . ." She got up clumsily and called out: "Do you want any help, Mummy?"

Christine came in with the ice-cream that she had been emptying from the soggy cardboard carton and, seating herself, began with a knife and a tablespoon to divide it up. "It's so sad," she said, "Mrs. Crutchfield has broken another of these cut-glass dishes." The dishes, though of no great value, had been a wedding present from a District Inspector-General long since dead: and each such loss gave her what was almost a physical pang. "What a clumsy woman she is!"

"Why do you use the best things?" Tim asked.

"Well, what's the point in hoarding them?" But there were quantities of ungainly Victorian silver and plate which lay in the unopened crates in which they had been dispatched from India, upstairs in the attic. "Oh, Gwyneth, did I tell you that there was a photograph of Dr. Hope-Ashburn in the *Tatler* last week? I saw it at the hairdresser's."

"No, you didn't tell me. But he himself showed it to me."

"He looks terribly nice."

"Well, he isn't."

"Oh, darling! Hasn't he been treating you properly? I hope there hasn't been any nastiness. Why ever didn't you tell me?"

"He treats me all right," Gwyneth said laconically. She added: "He's an awful fraud, though."

"You mean, he's a—a quack?"

Gwyneth laughed at her mother's ingenuousness. "No, of course not. In fact he's fairly good at his job, I imagine. But I find his snobbery and his passion for making money both rather unpleasant."

"He must be rich," Tim said, "to live in that house in Park Crescent."

"He is—or rather, his wife is. But he'd like to be richer."

They continued to question Gwyneth, but since she wholly lacked her mother's delight in gossip and Tim's facility as a raconteur, she had little to tell them that they did not know already. Christine had seen from the photograph in the *Tatler* that Hope-Ashburn was "extremely handsome", without Gwyneth saying so; and the few meagre details which they were able to extract from her about the house in Park Crescent fell far short of their imaginings of its splendour. She omitted to inform them that in the course of the three weeks she had been working for the doctor a friendship had begun to grow up between herself and his wife: but Christine had already guessed this when, the day before, she had found a copy of a French novel on the sofa, with the name in it "Myra Hope-Ashburn", printed neat and small in green ink.

Christine was tirelessly inquisitive about her children's friendships, and there were times, since Adrian's death, when they even caused her the briefest of pangs of jealousy; so she now took the opportunity to ask:

"And do you ever see Mrs. Hope-Ashburn?"

"Sometimes"

"What is she like?"

"Oh, very nice."

"Has she any children?"

"No."

"What age is she?"

"Really I don't know!"

"Yes, I know I get on your nerves with my questions. I'm sorry, darling. But I do like to know about my children's lives. Is that wrong of one?"

Tim laughed: "You seemed to be wanting to know about Mrs. Hope-Ashburn's life. I certainly do," he added. He had walked past both the consulting-room in Harley Mansions and the house in Park Crescent, outside which the doctor's Daimler happened to be standing, and had thrilled to an opulence so remote from the Earl's Court Road. For him the highly burnished car had a beauty far greater than the Regency portico of the house itself, though that too excited him, as did the massive red-brick mansions, with their uniformed porters, their glittering brass plates, and the heavy curtains, wine-red and old-gold, that he could glimpse on either side of the windows of the ground floor where Gwyneth had told him that Hope-Ashburn worked.

Gwyneth herself was contemptuous, rather than admiring, of her employer's obvious delight in his new car, his collection of porcelain, and the rapid extension and improvement of his practice; and in this, though she did not yet know it, she resembled his wife.

"Now, dears, I know you both want to get along to the

cinema," Christine said, when the ice-cream and strawberries were finished. "Unless you'd like some cheese?" She pushed towards Tim a plate on which she had symmetrically arranged, in a star-pattern, five silver triangles of Swiss cheese, and added: "Or there's some honey, if you like."

Tim shook his head. "What about the washing-up?" he asked.

"I'm going to do that. And I don't want any help. Otherwise you'll make yourselves late."

As they were leaving Christine kissed both of them in turn: Gwyneth merely putting her face forward to receive her mother's lips, whereas Tim threw his arms about her and himself kissed her noisily on each of her cheeks, saying: "Now take care of yourself, darling. And be good, won't you?"

"As if I'm likely to have the chance of being anything else!" Christine exclaimed, delighted. "I may go to bed early. In which case I'll leave out the things for your cocoa, and Gwyneth can make it. I feel just a little weary."

When she had finished the washing-up, which she already did far more quickly and expertly, after little more than a year as a housewife, than Mrs. Crutchfield after a lifetime, Christine went and sat by the open window and began to darn Tim's socks. She felt tired, but she also felt restless. For a few minutes she divided her time between the work she was doing and looking down into the gardens below. Mrs. Campion's lover, Major Knott—"though I'm sure he has no right to call himself a Major," Christine would often say—was pushing the mower up and down, while Mrs. Campion herself, in a white cotton dress and white plimsolls, sat outstretched in a deck-chair, her dachshund in her lap. From time to time she would put her long face, which was growing indistinct in the light of evening, down to the dog's, or would scratch at her legs, which were covered, as Tim once put it, with bites where they were not covered with varicose veins. Soon, the Major, who was wearing a shrunken pair of khaki trousers, with boots beneath them, and a tartan shirt, gave up the mowing and went into the house, from which he returned carrying a glass and a bottle. Mrs. Campion said something to him, and he replied, pouring out from the bottle as he stood above her; then the dog began to yelp, a peculiar sound from where Christine was sitting, not unlike the squeak of an unoiled hinge, and Mrs. Campion got up, stooped once more to scratch her long thin legs, and trailed into the house, followed by the Major, and eventually the dachshund, who first, however, cocked a leg at the mower.

Christine had been fascinated by the whole dumb-show; for, although her inquisitiveness was at its strongest where her children were concerned, it was by no means confined to them. Screwing up her eyes, even though they were already smarting from staring down at her work, she now tried to make out what sort of person it was that was washing her hair at the back-room window opposite. There were many evenings that she passed in this kind of watching: but though, when she was alone, she was invariably drawn to the window if there was nothing else to be done, yet it always carried with it, like some drug, an aftermath of depression. Out there Mrs. Campion and her lover quarrelled; a girl washed her hair, a man, shadowy and vague, could be seen crossing and recrossing a room. Here, she herself was alone. Then when the consciousness of that solitude began to grow acute, she would look, as she looked now about the darkening room, at the possessions, here a Persian miniature, there a pair of Georgian candlesticks, which seemed to glow at her out of the dim trash among which they stood. She could remember how they had bought a picture together; even if she now forgot that she had wanted to buy another and Adrian had exclaimed: "Trust you to pick out the most sickly of them all!" She would recall an antique shop off the via Tornabuoni; a visit to Jaipur in search of carpets; or a sale in which, in order to get a single decanter, they had had to bid for a lot containing among other things thirty bolts and screws.

She put aside the darning and got up: on a table between the two Georgian candlesticks she had just seen the French novel which Gwyneth had been lent. It was Colette's *Chéri*, but that meant no more to Christine than the pages which she automatically flicked over, glancing at a sentence here and there. Gwyneth's place was marked with a bus ticket. Once more Christine turned back to the fly-leaf, and peered at that signature, the green ink of which now, in this fading light, appeared to be black. "Myra Hope-Ashburn." She tried to imagine what this woman would look like: young and prettily delicate, she decided, with anxieties about her health that kept her from having children; her hair black and smooth except

66

for some small curls over the forehead; large eyes on which she would put too much mascara. . . . It was Christine's habit to visualize unknown people, unknown houses, and even unknown situations in this way: and though such imaginings almost always proved to be wrong, at the time she was certain they were right.

She continued to stare at the name and with the curious foreknowledge that had so often operated in the case of Adrian in the past and, since his death, in the case of her children, she was sure that this woman, who, at the moment, was no more for her than some minute letters in green ink and a number of imaginary characteristics, would one day play a rôle of importance in their lives. When she at last put down the book, she took great care to leave it exactly as she found it, for Gwyneth and Tim both often complained of her inquisitiveness.

VII

Vaguely, through a half-sleep, Christine was aware that the children had returned. As they mounted the stairs she even called out, but neither of them heard her. The night had grown sultry, and turning over she threw off a blanket. It was still early, only eleven o'clock, but she had the sensation of having slept profoundly through a long space of hours.

After what seemed many hours more, she was roused by a scream and jumped from her bed: two more screams followed, and then there was silence. Five times before Tim had woken her like this, but that had been during the last holidays and since then, neither at school nor at home, had he had a nightmare. On the previous occasions she had always found him sitting up rigid in bed, staring before him; once, when she had approached, he had even raised a hand, as though to defend himself from a blow. "What is it, darling? What's the matter? It's only me. There's nothing to worry about." As he felt her arms around him he would put his head on her breast, and gradually horrible gulping sobs would burst from his mouth. She never knew how conscious he was, for he never answered any question she asked him and the next morning neither of them would refer to what had passed. The sobs would grow less and less frequent until, with a hiccough, they would come to an end, and almost at once she would be conscious of his deep breathing and of his body heavily relaxed against hers. Then she would lower him on to his pillow, draw the bedclothes over him, and, having kissed his forehead and smoothed back his hair, would tiptoe to her room. Usually she would find Gwyneth at the top of the stairs, and to her she would whisper: "Go back to bed, darling. Back to bed. Don't catch cold." Afterwards she would lie sleepless: for even though both the school doctor and the doctor who lived in the house next door had told her that there was no cause for worry, yet when she thought of Tim as he was during the day and set that cheerful, self-assured image beside that of the panic-stricken child she had just soothed to sleep, rocking him in her arms and murmuring softly to him, she would fear that something was hideously amiss of which she knew nothing.

Now, in her haste to go and comfort him, she slipped on the narrow stairs and, falling, twisted her ankle. For a moment the pain was intolerable. Doubled up on one knee, at the foot of the staircase, she closed her eyes and used both hands to grip the torn muscles in an effort not to scream. Eventually she managed to stumble over to the light-switch; then, leaning heavily against the wall on her right, she began to draw herself up, slow step by step. The agony was subsiding—soon she was oblivious of it, in her determination to reach him.

Thus absorbed, she did not see Gwyneth until she heard her from above: "All right, Mummy, I'll go. I'll go."

The words, so far from checking Christine, merely spurred her on. "It's all right," she gasped. "Go back to your room, Gwyneth!"

But the door had already shut.

When Christine at last hobbled into the room, Gwyneth was standing over the boy, their two opposed faces grey in the moonlight that streamed down from the attic-windows, shaking him by the shoulders as she reiterated in a voice that to Christine seemed cruelly harsh: "Tim, what's the matter?

What's the matter with you? What have you been dreaming? Tell me!"

Suddenly, instead of staring over her shoulder, he threw himself forward and clutched at her body. "Oh, Gwyneth, Gwyneth!" he wailed. "Gwyneth! I killed him!"

"Killed him? Killed whom? Whom, Tim? Whom?" she repeated.

"Daddy!"

"What do you mean?"

Suddenly the gulping sobs started, his hands still clutching at her as his shoulders rocked in the moonlight.

"It was a dream," Gwyneth said. "Only a dream."

"No, it wasn't, it wasn't. You don't understand."

"Of course it was a dream." She tried to loosen the fingers that were gripping her shoulder. Come, lie down, and then you'll tell me. Come, Tim."

Gradually she eased him on to the pillow, herself kneeling on the floor beside him, and his sobs began to quieten. "Tell me," she said. "What was your dream?"

"But it wasn't a dream!" he cried out in petulant exasperation. "Oh, Gwyneth, you remember how unhappy we were when we lived with the relations? Do you remember? You used often to say that you wished you were dead."

"Yes, I said it. But I never really meant it."

"Well, I did. And then—then I used to think how different it would all be if our parents were in England instead of India." He was staring up at the ceiling, the sheet pulled up to his chin in fists that were so tightly clenched that it seemed as if he feared that someone would rip it away. "And that's—that's how it started."

"How what started?"

He tossed his head from side to side on the pillow, as though in a fever. "I—I used to imagine that Mummy was in England. Other children's mothers came home every year. Don't you remember the Bennett children? But we—even when we went up to the hills—we—we—had to stay with other families. And I blamed Daddy for that, it was his fault. It was, wasn't it?" Gwyneth did not answer, but continued to kneel beside him, her hands under her armpits and her head bent forward to catch the disjointed, whispered phrases. "Then I began to think—oh, this is the dreadful part!"—his whole body writhed,

69

as Christine's had writhed when she had first twisted her ankle—"I began to think what it would be like if we had Mummy with us always—for ever. But that seemed impossible while—while *he* was alive. He'd never allow it, he'd always kept her from us. Hadn't he? Hadn't he, Gwyneth? He even used to hate it when she came to see us before they went out to dinner-parties and stayed far too long. You remember that, don't you?" Christine, now huddled over on a chair beside the door, remembered it too. "Oh, for God's sake!" Adrian would call out in exasperation. "Can't you say good night to them once and for all? We're late as it is. The dandy has been out there for the last twenty minutes. Christine! Come on!" It was as if he had been jealous of her love for the two children, just as she in turn had been jealous of his love for Gwyneth.

Tim suddenly put out a hand and clutched Gwyneth's forearm, raising his head from the pillow as those horrible gulping sobs started again. He struggled for a time against them and then, having at last controlled them, managed to continue in a voice that seemed oddly level and toneless in contrast: "The only thing was for him to die. To die. That's what I decided. I didn't *want* him to die, not—not at first. But sometimes, at night, when I was miserable, I would think of it happening." He went on, whispering almost dreamily: "It made me sad, of course, at the same time, it also made me glad. Can you understand that? Until, one night—it was after that time when old Auntie Jessy refused to allow us to go bathing with the cousins because she said we had broken the swing—I suddenly began to wish it. I began to wish it, Gwyneth, to wish he were dead. And then almost every night—before I went to sleep . . . almost every night . . ." He shut his eyes for many seconds and when he opened them again he was staring again at the ceiling: "So when it happened, it was as if I had made it happen. Do you think I did? Do you?"

"Of course not, darling—of course not." "Darling" was a word which Christine had never heard Gwyneth call Tim before. "One can't make such things happen. How can one?"

"But I loved him, I loved him!" he cried out in a renewed anguish. "Truly I did!"

"Of course you loved him."

70

"Then why do I have these dreams?"

"What dreams?"

"Dreams—dreams about him. Sometimes it's—it's he who wants—wants to kill me. . . . And sometimes. . . . Oh, Gwyneth, it's horrible!" Once again he threw himself upon her, burying his face on her shoulder.

After that she was able gradually to calm him; and Christine, watching and listening from the chair by the door, was astonished by the extraordinary tenderness that seemed to transfigure her. No longer did she appear sullen, unsympathetic and clumsy, as she knelt beside her brother, her hair falling about her shoulders, and spoke to him as Christine herself would have done. There was an unaccustomed grace about her movements as she began to arrange his disordered bed-clothes, and an unaccustomed softness about her face and voice as she leant over him to say: "Now don't worry. Go to sleep and don't worry."

It was this astonishing change, more than the throbbing of her ankle and the bewildering shock of what she had just heard, that prevented Christine from herself approaching the bedside.

Gwyneth at last prepared to leave him; and only then, as she made for the door, did she notice that her mother had been present. The two women looked at each other, Christine rising painfully from the chair while Gwyneth stood beside her, her hand on the door-knob; then, without their speaking to each other, the older woman followed the younger out on the landing.

"Did you hear that?" Gwyneth asked.

"Yes."

They did not know what to say to each other. Eventually Christine said, wringing her hands before her:

"Why did you never tell me that you both were so unhappy?"

"Oh, we weren't, we weren't. Not really so unhappy."

It was a lie: but Christine looked so pitiful, her cheeks blotched with tears and her lower lip trembling while she continued to twist her hands together, that an impulse of mercy prevented Gwyneth from telling her the truth. What that truth was, was simple enough: children accept unhappiness, without rebelling against it, as they accept authority;

and then soon they even forget that happiness ever existed.

"If I had known—if I had only known!" You never said anything in your letters. You always sounded content."

Gwyneth thought of all the thousands of children who never said anything in their letters; and she remained silent. But eventually she put her arm about her mother's shoulders and, in doing so, she felt, as she so often felt, that it was she who was the older woman, and Christine the girl. "Why are you limping?" she asked, as they began to descend the stairs. "What's the matter?"

"Oh, I twisted my ankle. I was running to Tim, you see, and I didn't put on the light. . . ."

"But it's swollen—it's swollen horribly! You poor thing!"

With relief the two women set themselves to the task of dealing with this physical hurt; for from that other hurt they both of·them cringed away. Gwyneth, kneeling on the floor of the kitchen, began to apply cold compresses while Christine, her hands clasped in her lap and her high cheek-bones still glistening with the tears she had shed, stared out into the sultry night. From time to time there was a flash from behind the darkened houses, but whether it was lightning or a late train along the cutting, Christine did not know.

Gwyneth, gazing up at that youthful, calm face under the grey hair, murmured, as she wrung out the cloth: "How brave you always are!"

It was what Adrian would tell her: and Christine smiled now, as she used to smile then, and put out her hand to the bowed head beside her.

VIII

Christine first spoke to Mrs. Hope-Ashburn on the telephone when she had to ring up to say that Gwyneth had a chill and would not be at work that day. The chill was a euphemism.

"Oh, dear! Poor thing. Well, tell her not to worry. I've nothing to do myself. Nothing to do to-day. So I can take over." The voice was staccato, deep and slightly hoarse, as though the speaker had a cold.

"I couldn't get him, he'd already left for the hospital," Christine then went and told poor Gwyneth, now crouched over a hot-water bottle on the sofa in the sitting-room. "But I arranged to speak to her. She sounded so—so different. Different, I mean, from what I had expected."

Gwyneth gave a small, wry smile: "Well, what did you expect?"

"Oh, she sounded so determined, and definite. I thought she'd be vague, fluttery—you know."

"Why on earth did you think that? She's an immensely capable woman. How do you suppose she does all her refugee and political work?"

"I didn't know she did." Christine sighed: "You tell me so little. Not like Tim. He's so interested in people." Gwyneth had picked up the novel that lay, face downwards, on the table beside her. "I don't believe that you're interested in people at all. Only in books. Mrs. Hope-Ashburn asked if you needed anything. She said she'd come round and see you, if you liked. She told me to ask you, and to give her a ring at lunch-time, if you said yes."

"But didn't you say that there was nothing serious wrong?" Gwyneth demanded fretfully.

"Well, of course, darling. Would you have liked me to tell her what was really the matter?"

"I expect she guessed."

Christine began first to pat the cushions and then to fidget with the beige rug that always seemed to get crumpled in front of the fireplace, while Gwyneth watched her balefully. "I suppose she does all this refugee work you were speaking about for the—for the Jews."

"Well, most refugees from Germany *are* Jews, aren't they?"

"Yes, I suppose they are." The tone in which Gwyneth had answered did not encourage Christine to go on with her probing. But having blown some dust from the chimney-piece, she once more succumbed to curiosity. "Is Mrs. Hope-Ashburn Jewish herself?"

"Yes."

"A practising Jew?"

73

"No. An Anglo-Catholic. If you're really interested, before she married she was a——" Gwyneth mentioned the name of one of the oldest Sephardic families in England, at which Christine exclaimed:

"Oh, but one of them used to be financial adviser to the Viceroy! He and Daddy got on extremely well together. You must tell Mrs. Hope-Ashburn, don't forget."

Gwyneth pursed her lips, and crouched yet lower over the hot-water bottle.

"Do you think he would be her uncle? He was never married, as far as I remember, and I suppose he would have been far too old to be her brother. Cousins perhaps. How old is she?"

"Who?" Gwyneth did not look up from her book.

"Mrs. Hope-Ashburn."

"Oh, about forty-five, I suppose! . . . Now, Mummy, do please let me get on with my book. I really don't want to chatter."

As she went into the kitchen, Christine said: "You never seem to think that I might perhaps feel lonely at times. That doesn't occur to you." But Gwyneth, peering down at her book, gave no sign of having heard.

Only four days later Christine had an unexpected opportunity of seeing Mrs. Hope-Ashburn for herself. Gwyneth had come home at midday instead of at half-past five to announce that she was driving down to Glyndebourne with the older woman: it appeared that a New York friend had not arrived from Paris, and that there was a ticket to spare. "Oh, how very nice of her to ask you!" Christine exclaimed.

"I expect that she only asked me because it was too late to ask anyone else."

"Why should you think that? I expect she likes you. And you know so much about music. Have you told her that you play?"

Christine could not understand her daughter's growing moroseness as they started unpacking the trunk in which the girl's evening dresses had lain unworn since their arrival from India. "Which do you want? The black lace, or the flowered chiffon? I never cared for lace, it makes you look so matronly. Do you remember how we quarrelled when we bought it at Harvey Nicholl's?"

But it was the lace that Gwyneth chose: only, when she put

it on, she found it was too small for her since her body, always big-boned and solid, had thickened even further during these recent months. "Oh, what am I to do? I can't go, that's all. There's nothing else for it." Gwyneth tended to plunge into this kind of fatalistic despair, when things went amiss.

"Don't be absurd. I can unpick that seam. It won't take me a moment. You go and have your bath, and let me get started."

"Can you? Can you really?"

"Now run along, darling."

"Oh, Mummy, be quick! Be quick! It's half-past two already."

It was true that Gwyneth was not going to a ball, but to an opera, and that she was going, not with a young man, but with a middle-aged woman; but this apart, the whole scene, with its bustle, suppressed excitement and now this last-minute intervention to stave off disaster, was one which, in the year before Gwyneth grew up to disappoint her, had so often been pictured by Christine in her fantasies of bringing out a beautiful and talented daughter in Delhi and Simla. Joyfully she set to work, while Tim, who had been helping her pack his tuck-box, sat in a chair and watched her.

"It's an awful dress," he said.

"No, it's not awful. But it's wrong for a girl." Christine, who was an excellent needle-woman, spoke with at least half a dozen pins in her mouth.

"Sometimes I think that Gwyneth *wants* to look plain."

Christine noticed, with dismay, that the hot bath made the girl's skin all blotchy: she hoped that when it was powdered over and she was wearing a fur wrap, it would not be noticed. "Let me just touch up your face. A little lipstick. Only just a little." But Gwyneth obstinately refused, grumbling a moment later, "Oh, don't fuss me so!" when her mother protested against the way in which she was thrusting her feet into her shoes without using a shoe-horn.

Tim came in: "I think she's here," he announced. "A green M.G. has just stopped outside. Aren't you ready yet?"

"Oh, God! . . . No, no, I'm not. Where's my comb?"

The bell pealed out.

"Now don't get worked up, dear," Christine soothed. "I'll go and ask her to wait a moment." Each time the bell rang, it was necessary to descend to open the front-door. "She might

75

like a cup of tea. It won't take a minute. Tim, put on the kettle. Quick, dear!"

"No, no!" Gwyneth shouted after her. "Don't ask her up. Don't!"

The bell rang again as Christine, whose ankle was still bound up with an elastic bandage, attempted to hurry down the stairs. But when she rounded the last bend, she saw that the front door had been opened and simultaneously heard that deep and vaguely rasping voice, saying: "Thank you so much."

"Delighted, madam."

It was Major Knott: Christine saw him first, in the tawny tropical suit which he wore during the summer, his Panama hat in one hand and his stick in the other, as he held the door ajar. Ignoring him, for they were not on speaking terms, Christine pushed past to greet the visitor.

"Oh, Mrs. Hope-Ashburn! Gwyneth is almost ready. Just a few seconds. Would you mind waiting? Here, or upstairs?"

As she spoke, she kept glancing at the other woman, noticing now the vast sapphire-and-diamond ring on the wedding-finger, now the extraordinary transparent pallor of the skin of her lean face, and now her teeth, which as her lips parted in a slow smile, were revealed as growing shorter and shorter as they neared the centre, so that they gave the effect of having been filed to make this crescent beneath which her pointed tongue could be glimpsed.

"Oh, it's not worth climbing upstairs." She glanced at Major Knott, who was disappearing into the basement, and gave him a brief nod. "It was short notice, I'm afraid." She wandered out on to the top of the outside steps, where Christine followed after her.

"Your car looks new," Christine remarked: for she could think of nothing else to say.

"Yes, this year's model. My husband always hogs the other. So I decided. Must have one of my own. I'm not sure I care for the colour though."

Mrs. Hope-Ashburn's bobbed hair was the same grey as Christine's but its texture was different, each curl seeming to have the spring and crispness of a wood-shaving. Her legs and arms both seemed unnaturally long for the slender boyish torso, the chest of which, with bonily protruding collar-bones, was almost completely flat. Her hands also seemed disproportionately large; and this largeness was exaggerated by the generous finger-nails, the bright red of which was in striking contrast to the pallor of her skin. Her face itself was a triangle except for the small rounded chin which seemed to have been added, as an afterthought, to the apex. Above her hooded green eyes the eyebrows, almost meeting in the centre, extended themselves in a straight line up to the temples. She was, there was no doubt, an ugly woman; but she also exerted the fascination of elegance, intellect and power.

"I like the colour," Christine said. She shook her head and mumbled, "No, thank you," as Myra Hope-Ashburn clicked open the flat gold cigarette-case she had fished, with those bony talon-like fingers, out of her bag. "It's awfully kind of you to give Gwyneth this treat. She's so fond of music, and used to play the piano so well—I think she even once thought of taking it up." Christine sighed: "Now of course she has so little time for practice. Yes, it'll be a real treat for her." Christine began to feel even more ill at ease as Myra Hope-Ashburn kept raising a cigarette-holder to her wide mouth, without once looking in her direction or making any answer. "I'm afraid life hasn't been much fun for her since my husband's death last year. She was so fond of him. It was a terrible shock to her—although she never shows it, of course; she's not that sort of a person." The other woman's impassivity and silence had the paradoxical effect not of checking, but accelerating, this flow of confidences, as Christine rushed on: "I wish I could do more for her, but I just don't know what. My boy's all right, my boy Tim. Perhaps Gwyneth has mentioned him to you? He's off to school to-morrow; he's very happy there. Very happy," she repeated, on a falling note. Then at last she fell silent: and in that silence she grew conscious of the heavily potent aroma of Mrs. Hope-Ashburn's Turkish cigarette; of the heat of the summer afternoon; and of a disagreeable throbbing from her bandaged ankle.

The other woman turned to her: "Is Gwyneth your only daughter?"

"Yes."

"She's intelligent," she said.

"Oh, yes, Mrs. Hope-Ashburn, she did very well at school."

"Pity she couldn't get to the university."

77

"She wanted to study medicine so much. But after my husband's death—well, on my little pension. . . . It was a great disappointment to her, a bitter disappointment. But she took it as bravely—as she takes everything. She never complains. She could have been a marvellous doctor, I'm absolutely certain. She has a real feeling for it." Once again Christine was conscious that nervousness was making her say too much.

At this point, Tim appeared behind them. Christine was glad of this intrusion. Putting her arm round his shoulders she said: "This is my son, Tim, Mrs. Hope-Ashburn. He goes back to school to-morrow. Don't you, darling? He's sixteen and a half."

Tim pulled himself free from his mother's embrace and held out his right hand, while with the left he pushed the hair from his forehead. He was a boy who could at once charm any grown-up with whom he came in contact, and who was gradually becoming conscious of this power. It was therefore a shock to him to realize that Mrs. Hope-Ashburn was completely uninterested in him—indeed, appeared to have hardly noticed him. Stubbornly desiring to turn this defeat to victory he at once asked:

"That's the latest M.G.—isn't it?"

"H'm, h'm." She tapped the cigarette-holder against that odd crescent of teeth.

"How fast can it go?"

"I've no idea—yet. Running in."

He walked down to the car, and wandered slowly round it. He did not intentionally show off his body, but each of his movements seemed to have a calculated easiness and grace just as Gwyneth's clumsiness seemed often to be calculated. As she watched him Christine felt an extraordinary pang which she used often to feel when he was a baby. What if she should lose him, she would then ask herself. What if anything should happen to him? He was too gifted and too beautiful; she loved him too much. Often, when he was lying in his cradle, the waxen pallor of sleep would seem to her that of death, and she would stoop in panic over him to try to catch his breath. Each infantile illness had seemed to her to be mortal.

"Are you going to have a picnic?" he asked, noticing the basket.

"That was the idea."

"We played the Overture to the *Marriage of Figaro* in the School Orchestra last year."

"Did you?" the deep voice rasped. Mrs. Hope-Ashburn's lids were so low over her eyes, as she stared out into the glare of the street, that they might almost have been closed.

"Tim is learning the clarinet. He only took it up a few months ago—he learned the piano before—but he's made tremendous progress. They've now formed a jazz-band at the school: Gwyneth's rather contemptuous of that!"

There was a clatter from the stair-well, and Gwyneth herself appeared, hurrying towards them with ungainly strides that drew her frock in tight rucks over her thighs. The blotches on her bare arms and neck were, Christine noticed with dismay, still visible in spite of a hurried and inexpert dabbing of powder. The powder was also far too heavy over her nose. "Oh, dear, I'm terribly sorry. I've kept you waiting hours. Please forgive me." Unused to high heels, she all but fell over as she hobbled down the stairs and was saved by Tim stretching out an arm.

"Take care, take care!" he said. "We don't want another sprained ankle."

On the morning after Christine's accident, when he had asked how she had hurt her foot, she had said vaguely: "Oh, I tripped on the stairs last night." He had made no comment, and put no other question; and that had been the only reference to the happenings of that night. But she had noticed his restlessness and lassitude, two things from which, unlike Gwyneth, he had never previously suffered; and these moods had continued until he had left for his visit to his friends in Richmond.

"Enjoy yourself, darling!" Christine cried out, as the engine started up. "Good-bye, Mrs. Hope-Ashburn. It was so nice to meet you at last, after hearing so much from my daughter. You and your husband have been so very good to her."

Mrs. Hope-Ashburn said something which, in the accelerating uproar of the car, Christine did not hear. Then they shot off, Gwyneth staring straight ahead of her to ignore Tim's waving arm, and there was no more trace left of them than the fumes of the exhaust mingling with the aroma of the cigarette that lay, half-smoked, at the bottom of the stairs.

"How fast she drives!" Christine exclaimed. "I do hope she'll be careful." The habit of worrying about the children when they were not with her was one that was growing, now that there was no longer Adrian about whom to worry.

"That's not fast," Tim said. "A car like that can go very much faster."

"It's an odd sort of car for a woman to drive. I don't know what sort of state their hair will be in by the time that they get there."

While they had been standing out on the steps, they had left the front door open behind them. Now, as they approached it, someone began to close it from the side, and only a spring from Tim prevented it from being shut in their faces. "Wait a moment!" he cried. Then he pushed and the person on the other side pushed; until at last he won, and the door burst open. Mrs. Campion was in the shadow of the hall, clutching her bony wrist as she shouted out in fury:

"What do you think you're doing? My arm! Do you want to break my arm?"

"I asked you not to close it. We hadn't got our key."

"Well, you ought to have had your key." Mrs. Campion tugged angrily at the floppy brim of the straw-hat which was tied with a black ribbon under her sagging dewlap so tightly that it looked as if she had two goitres. "You've no right to leave the front door open—particularly after my letter to the landlord, and his letter to you."

"We were only just outside, Mrs. Campion. I cannot imagine what harm could possibly come of it."

"It's not a question of harm. It's a question of principle." She stooped and scratched at one of her legs on which, winter and summer alike, she never wore stockings. Glancing down, Christine noticed that the bites had begun to fester; and at that moment she was so exasperated that the discovery gave her pleasure.

"While you're here, Mrs. Campion, I may as well mention about your dust-bin. If you don't put it out for collection each time, the smell seems to fill the whole house."

"Your nose must be uncommonly sensitive." There was a certain well-bred grandeur about Mrs. Campion, like that of a retired racehorse, as she tossed her head contemptuously from side to side and seemed to paw on the ground with one of her large plimsolled feet.

"It's unhealthy too. Come, Tim! Be sure to close the door

80

properly," she added, "otherwise we may annoy certain people who are fussy about such things—if not about other things."

Tim giggled uncontrollably all the way upstairs, following behind Christine who was flushed, still irate and yet tingling with the friction of the squabble.

"And remember the light!" Mrs. Campion suddenly boomed out from below. "On Saturday that daughter of yours left it burning till morning."

"Impertinence!" Christine exclaimed, as they entered the flat.

"One of her shoes was laced with string," Tim continued to giggle. He had developed an unfailing eye for such things, and when he felt shy or at a disadvantage, he had discovered that to remind himself of them invariably restored his confidence in himself.

"I suppose we should feel sorry for her," Christine said, who had often felt sorry for Mrs. Campion in the past, but was certainly in no mood to feel so at that moment. "To cut oneself off like that from one's family and friends—to sink to that condition . . ." The thought of Mrs. Campion sinking gave her the same pleasure as her glimpse of those festering bites. "After all she comes of an excellent family, and is a woman of education. Miss Bedworth was telling me the other day that her husband was a Naval Captain—a *real* Captain, not like Major Knott. Her children have never forgiven her for leaving him while he was dying, and going off with someone more than twenty years younger than herself. Well, she's suffering for it now, that's all I can say."

At those words they could hear from below a confused uproar of voices, culminating in a shrill cry: "Liar, liar, liar!" One door slammed, and then another. The voice became even more piercing, as it screamed: "Terry! Terry! Come back! I didn't mean it! I didn't mean it!" At these last words it wailed out like a siren and then wobbled into silence.

"You see," said Christine. "You see what I mean?"

"Did you enjoy it?" Tim asked. He was wearing only his pyjama trousers, because of the heat, and was seated at the kitchen table, eating a water-biscuit on which he had liberally piled butter and honey.

"Oh, yes," Gwyneth said flatly. She pulled off her mother's

81

fur wrap, kicked off her shoes, beneath which her stockings were soggy, and inserted a hand into the biscuit-tin.

"Tell us all about it," Christine urged.

Gwyneth began to nibble, flakes of her dry biscuit catching on the lace bodice of her dress or scattering to the floor. She had about her an extraordinary air, at once excited and secretive: her cheeks were flushed, and her eyes usually so sombre seemed to burn with the inward enjoyment of some mystery which she would not communicate. Tim did not notice this: but Christine, who had become abnormally sensitive to her children's moods ever since Adrian's death, guessed it at once. All her questions, however, about the opera, the performance and Mrs. Hope-Ashburn herself brought her scant satisfaction: Gwyneth continued to nibble at biscuits, wriggle her toes, and tilt her chair so far backwards that more than once she almost fell over, but she would tell her nothing at all.

It was only when Christine went in to say good night to her and was actually stooping over to kiss her on the forehead that she gazed up and announced: "By the way—I think I shall be able to study medicine after all." The words were spoken softly, almost inaudibly, in a deliberately casual tone: yet to Christine they seemed to carry with them a suppressed, half-mocking, half-malicious triumph.

"What do you mean?" she asked.

"Mrs. Hope-Ashburn has offered to lend me the money. I—I think I shall accept."

"*Lend* you the money?"

"Yes, lend it. It'll be difficult to pay it back, of course. It may take years."

"I don't suppose she really means you to pay it back."

"Why don't you think so?"

"Oh, I expect she just said that in order to make it easier for you to accept. Don't you agree? After all, a woman with all that money can't possibly——"

"I shall pay it back if it's the last thing I do!" Gwyneth broke in violently. "I—I wouldn't dream of accepting such an offer if that weren't understood. It's simply a business deal. That's all. There's nothing else to it."

"Well, anyway, I'm delighted, darling." Christine put her lips to her daughter's forehead, to which the blood was mounting, crimson from her cheeks. "Delighted," she repeated. Then in the unconscious desire not to allow Mrs. Hope-Ashburn to have all Gwyneth's gratitude, she went on: "Perhaps my little word may have had something to do with this news."

Gwyneth stared up at her from the pillow: "What do you mean?"

"Oh, I told her how much you had always wanted to study medicine. And what a bitter disappointment it had been to you that you couldn't go up to the university." She smiled brightly. "I said a lot of nice things about you."

"Oh, Mummy, you didn't!" Gwyneth was appalled.

"Well, why ever not? Surely I'm allowed to say nice things about my own girl if I want to? What's wrong with that?"

"But it must have seemed as if you were—you were begging."

"Don't be so silly! I'm sure Mrs. Hope-Ashburn never thought any such thing. And certainly nothing was further from my mind. The news has come as quite as much of a surprise to me as to you." The excitement that had burned so obviously, even if suppressed, in Gwyneth's eyes now seemed to be fading: and contrite at her realization of this, Christine stooped again and put her lips to her cheek. "I think she intended to make the offer long before I said anything to her at all. She obviously likes you, dear. She even said as much."

Gwyneth turned over, away from her mother, and drew her bedclothes up.

"Well, good night," she muttered.

"Good night," Christine answered. Then she added: "Good night—*Doctor* Cornwell."

IX

Although Rosemary had arrived two days before at the hotel where Christine and her children were spending their holidays that summer of Munich, this was the first opportunity the two women had had to talk alone together.

Tim and Gwyneth had gone out for a ride in the forest of Fontainebleau, and Geoffrey was playing ping-pong on the terrace below with the young German girl who had been supposed to go riding too. Geoffrey had once been chubbily handsome; now he was fat, with a body that had become increasingly pear-shaped, the shoulders narrowing and the hips broadening, through years and years of over-eating and drinking in sub-tropical climates. As she looked down from the balcony, Christine could see him, even more oddly shaped when fore-shortened by the height. He had on khaki shorts, grease-stained from tinkering with his car, and a pale-blue aertex shirt against which his breasts pushed pointed and small, like those of an adolescent girl. He flung himself from side to side, and sometimes even across the ping-pong table, with cries of "Got you!", "Hell and damnation!" and "Well played, sir, well played!" The last of these phrases was used to applaud good shots, whether by himself or his female opponent. Even at this distance, his round face could be seen to be glistening with sweat.

Opposite him, the German girl, Lise, who was obviously not exerting herself, played an accurate game. She was pretty and blonde, and the crisp white frocks which she always wore contrasted attractively with the brown of her skin. Her mouth was always slightly open, the lips soft and moist and her small teeth dazzling. Christine now noticed, for the first time, that she was double-jointed at the elbows: when she changed from backhand to forehand, it was as if the bone in her arm had suddenly snapped in two. Secretly, Christine was pleased that Lise had changed her mind and decided to play with Geoffrey instead of going riding with Gwyneth and Tim. Christine often said that Lise was a vulgar little thing; really, without knowing it, she was jealous of her.

"Geoffrey should be more careful," Rosemary said. She was working at the petit-point which, in recent years, had absorbed the spare energies that she used to expend on her painstaking translations of German historical works, only one of which ever got published. In her embroideries she followed the patterns of others, and when it was suggested to her that she should invent her own, she would give her melancholy smile and say: "Oh, no. I haven't a speck of original talent," as she used once to say

84

to Adrian when he urged her to write a book on her own account.

"Is his heart really bad?" Christine found it hard to reconcile Rosemary's obvious anxiety with her Christian Science principles.

"No, but he eats too much and drinks too much. He ought to get much thinner." She sighed: "It's a vicious circle. He always wants to eat and drink when he's feeling unhappy, and he's unhappy about missing his promotion. But he doesn't get promotion because it's begun to get around that he drinks. I don't imagine that we shall ever get to a large station now. Not that I care. But he does. If I can't be in London, Rome or Paris, I'd just as soon live on a small dust-heap as on a big one."

Geoffrey and the girl had changed sides, so that the two women now looked down on to Geoffrey's back, across which a damp oblong was gradually extending itself. It was obvious that he was flagging; often, instead of hurling himself at a ball that nicked the side of the table, he would let it go, contenting himself with a gasped: "Good shot, good shot!"

"She's an attractive girl," Rosemary said. "The type that Geoffrey likes." She spoke without any trace of bitterness. "Except that as a rule he prefers a fuller figure." She herself, in the three years since Christine had last seen her, had become even leaner and more angular as the result of dysentery. Geoffrey would mock her: "Faith may move mountains, but it certainly won't shift the amoeba out of your guts": a remark often produced in front of others, with the mistaken intention of amusing them at his wife's expense. "Tim and she seem to be good friends," Rosemary went on.

"Oh, yes, they're much of the same age. I think she really bores Tim, she's so empty-headed. But of course it's pleasant for him to have someone to take around." Christine yawned and stretched lazily, gazing at her outstretched hands. "These girls all seem to fall for him. I hope it won't make him vain."

"Well, he *is* very good-looking, isn't he?"

Christine had become used to having this said to her: but it still continued to give her a thrill of pleasure. "Yes, I suppose he is. Of course he's far too taken up with his work and all his other interests to pay much attention to his admirers. I don't think he's really aware of the effect he has on people." This

85

was not true and Rosemary, who thought Tim conceited, knew that it was not true.

Rosemary put a hand to her forehead to pull off the heavily horn-rimmed glasses about which Geoffrey would also tease her. "My eyes are beginning to ache," she said. "This work quickly tires them. It was meant to be a Christmas present for you—heaven knows on which Christmas it will be ready. Certainly not this one! . . . You must be very pleased about Tim's progress."

"Yes, I am. Mr. Hiskett seems to be convinced that he'll have no difficulty in getting a scholarship to Oxford. To Christ Church. That was Adrian's old college. If only this wretched war doesn't come!"

Rosemary said gravely: "Well, I'm afraid it will."

"Oh, Rosemary, you don't think so! Do you? Do you really? I was speaking to Kingsley Woolcott—you remember, he was in the Secretariat, and now he's an adviser at the Colonial Office. He says it's all a scare—that there's no need to worry."

"Kingsley always was a fool. I never knew how he managed to get as far as he did. He's far more stupid than poor old Geoffrey—and that's saying a lot."

Christine was always vaguely shocked when Rosemary spoke in this manner whether about Geoffrey or about men who had left India respected and with knighthoods: although this very detraction gave an even sharper poignancy to the unreserved praise which she would lavish on Adrian whenever they discussed him.

"I dread a war. I can't tell you how much I dread it," Christine said. Her only brother, whom she had adored, had been killed at the age of eighteen at Gallipoli; and she was haunted by the fear of Tim being killed too.

"Funnily enough, I don't really dread it. I suppose because Geoffrey is too old, and too short of breath, and I have no children to lose."

"I dream of it sometimes." Christine watched the ping-pong ball flashing back and forth in the sunlight, her eyes screwed up, as she said: "I think I would kill myself if anything happened to Tim."

"Why should anything happen? He's always had such luck. He's one of those charmed people who go through life unscathed."

It was true: as a child he had once fallen out of the window, three storeys high, of a Cromwell Road hotel, but when he was picked up, he had suffered nothing but shock, a broken rib, and a number of bruises. At games at school, his luck had become a legend: easy catches would be dropped for him, tennis balls which he played would graze the net, his stronger opponents would scratch from finals with influenza or measles. But such good fortune terrified Christine: "too good to last" was the phrase that repeatedly came to her mind.

"I used to think that about Adrian," Christine said sombrely. "Who would have thought he would die like that? Just—just when he had got that wonderful new job, and he seemed to be on the way to the very highest things."

"Is Gwyneth happy?"

"She's terribly keen about her work, and does seem to be doing well at it, *very* well. Little else seems to interest her." Many other things did, in fact, interest Gwyneth: politics, literature and music being the chief. But she was interested in none of the things in which Christine would have liked her to be interested: she still wore many of the clothes that had been bought for her, four years ago, on their departure for India; she still preferred to eat bread and jam or bread and cheese to a cooked meal, if someone were not there to cook it for her; and she was still neither engaged nor the possessor of a "boy friend". It was true that she now had a few male friends—elderly refugee professors, married doctors or musicians, and half a dozen young men, fellow-undergraduates, who were often described by Christine as "limp" or "odd" and were rarely liked by Tim who was, after all, as Christine sometimes said in indignant justification to Gwyneth,"at least a real man".

"I seem to see less and less of her," Christine went on. "I suppose that's bound to happen as children grow up." Although she often said this she found it hard to accept. "She has this great friend of hers, Myra—you must have heard her speak about her. We're expecting her and her husband any day now. He's been at a gynaecological conference in Rome, and they're driving back in their Daimler. He's Sir Noël Hope-Ashburn, you know—apparently he has a great reputation." Christine was jealous of Gwyneth's friendship with the Hope-Ashburns and yet she liked to boast about it: just as she liked to boast about Tim's friendship with Jimmy Tomlins and other boys at the school whose families were well known or rich. She sighed, and went on: "I've had to reconcile myself to the fact that Gwyneth's not interested in most of the things that interest other girls."

"Why should they interest her, when so much else does?"

"Oh, I'd like to have her settle down in a home of her own."

"She can do that anyway."

"Yes, but the lives of old maids are so dreary, aren't they? I know something about that: I mean about living on one's own, when the children are away. But I do have the children and that makes all the difference."

"And Gwyneth will have her work; and that will also make all the difference."

"Oh, there they are!"

As the two children walked up the gravel path, Tim now about a head above his sister, who had grown even more thick-set and clumsy with the years, Lise threw down her ping-pong bat and went smiling towards them, while Geoffrey lowered himself into a deck-chair, where he started mopping his face and neck with a crumpled, much-used handkerchief. Lise said something to the children, in a low voice, since they both bent their heads forward to hear her, and then she and Tim laughed together, while Gwyneth gave a vague embarrassed smile, looking away from them, sideways, at the garden. Christine guessed that some remark had been made about Geoffrey.

Soon Tim and Lise began to play ping-pong, Geoffrey ordered a drink, and Gwyneth, who was never at her ease with him, made her way up to the balcony where the two women were seated. She was wearing an aertex shirt, not unlike Geoffrey's, the top button of which was missing, crumpled jodhpurs, and a pair of brogue shoes far more heavy than Tim would ever have bought. Her nose was peeling in the sun, which had also bleached to a light yellow the hair drawn back on either side of her temples. She was fond of Rosemary, and she now took a cushion and placed it at the foot of her deck-chair, sitting on it cross-legged in a manner which Christine disliked. She gave the impression of a person inside whom there was a constant turmoil of suppressed energy, which would at any moment explode through its envelope of flesh and bone, just as her body appeared to be about to explode through the clothes which were far too small for it. Even on this holiday she had seldom relaxed. She, Tim and Lise would lie down on the roof of the hotel to sunbathe, but after a few minutes she would jump up and begin to wander about. Then, pulling on her clothes she would set off on one of her long solitary walks through the forest of Fontainebleau, from which she would return holding in one fist some limp specimens of plants which she would then show to Rosemary. As she read or wrote in her rapid, bold hand in a number of notebooks which she stacked all around her, she would smoke cigarette after cigarette, inhaling deeply and occasionally brushing the ash off her blouse.

Now, having chatted for a while to Rosemary about her petit-point, she got up and leant over the rail of the balcony to stare down at Lise and Tim below.

"You must get some new jodhpurs, dear," Christine said. "Those are almost threadbare."

Gwyneth did not reply, or even look round at this remark. But after a while she wandered back to query: "Did anyone telephone while we were out?"

"No. Were you expecting a telephone call?"

"Not really." Gwyneth fiddled with the leather strap of her watch, and then glanced down at its broad face, the glass of which was cracked.

"Have you no idea when the Hope-Ashburns are arriving?"

Gwyneth scowled and threw herself once more on to the cushion. "Oh, sometime this week. If one's motoring, how can one be sure?"

"It oughtn't to take them long in a car like that." Christine turned to Rosemary. "Poor Tim would so like us to have a car. He has this modern craze for speed."

"Yes, he was rather contemptuous of 'Mademoiselle Citroën'." This was the nickname which Geoffrey had given to their second-hand car, and Rosemary, when she used it, seemed to put it into invisible inverted commas, as though she was making fun, not so much of it, as of him.

Gwyneth again got up, and walked up and down the balcony, whistling one of the waltzes from the "Rosenkavalier" to which they had listened on the wireless the previous evening.

"Oh, don't whistle, dear! I do so dislike it."

"I think I'd better go to my room."

"Now don't be silly, Gwyneth. There's no need to take offence simply because I ask you not to whistle. It's so childish to be annoyed at such things. Gwyneth! Come back, dear!"

But, whistling aggressively, Gwyneth clattered down the iron stairs from the terrace to the garden.

"Oh, sometimes she's so difficult, Rosemary!" Christine exclaimed.

"She's obviously on edge." Rosemary held out her needle and a length of silk, saying: "Do thread that for me. Your eyes are so good."

"She works too hard—far too hard. Have you noticed how she simply cannot relax? That's tiredness, of course. Exhaustion, nervous exhaustion. I wish I understood her better."

"I think she's in a state about the Hope-Ashburns," Rosemary said slowly. "Are you sure——?" She broke off, taking the threaded needle, and said nothing more.

"Yes?"

"Well, are you quite sure that she and Hope-Ashburn—that she's not in love with him?"

"In love with him!"

"It's just a guess of mine. Because, of course, I've never met him, and never seen them together. But it did strike me, all this tension. She's obviously very anxious to see them and yet"—Rosemary smoothed the stitches she had just put in, rubbing them with her lean fingers—"and yet—she's in a state about their coming."

"Oh, I'm sure you're quite wrong! She's always been so critical of him. Says he is a snob and a go-getter and really not in the least intelligent. Well, not by *her* standards."

Rosemary shrugged her bony shoulders over which, even on this day of heat-wave, she had thrown a woollen cape.

The Hope-Ashburns arrived that same afternoon when all of them, except Gwyneth, were digesting an enormous luncheon on their beds. Gwyneth had been typing, and through her half-sleep in the room next door Christine had been conscious of the maddening click-click and the ting of the bell. How thoughtless it was! But the paradoxical effect of this noise ceasing was to wake her up completely. Outside her shuttered window she could hear voices, one of which, deeply rasping, was unmistakably that of Mrs. Hope-Ashburn. Christine lay for a while, staring up at the ceiling, while she tried to hear what was said; then, getting up, she began to wash and dress. Although she had often seen Lady Hope-Ashburn since that Glyndebourne visit, she had not yet met the doctor, and her eagerness to do so had been sharpened by Rosemary's suggestion.

Sir Noël turned out to be a man still excessively handsome, in spite of the creasing of fat below his jaws where his chin was retracted, a certain fleshiness of his lips, and the small purplish blood-vessels over the end of his Roman nose and his cheeks. He was wearing espadrilles, pale-blue linen trousers, and a white silk shirt, and his bare arms and face were sunburned to a curiously dead shade of chestnut. He was professionally jovial and yet, Christine suspected, bored, as he talked to Tim about his riding, the car and the latest cricketing scores from England, or described to the whole company the festivities which had been arranged for the congress he had left. "Of course, we tended to give most of the official junketing a miss, and go out with our own chums. We had a marvellous day at the villa of some Italian friends of ours in the Alban hills," he said, while on this last topic. "The food was superb. Wasn't it, darling?"

Myra, holding her coffee-cup to her wide lips with both of her hands, gave a brief nod and then smiled down at Gwyneth who was seated at her feet.

Geoffrey, who had been liverish and bleary after what he called his "shut-eye", now roused himself to ask Sir Noël if he had come across a chap, an absolutely first-class chap, a Eurasian, who had done some kind of research into some kind of tropical fever. He couldn't remember his name, off-hand, but they had often played a game of snooker together. Brilliant, he was.

Sir Noël patiently suggested names, and with an equal patience asked Christine how she was enjoying her holiday and congratulated Rosemary on her petit-point. From time to time he would look down at the gold signet-ring on his little finger, or twitch up his trouser-legs so that the line should not crease. His ears, which were over large for his head and entirely lobeless, sprouted the same coarse grey hair as pushed up between the lacing of silk cord that took the place of buttons at the opening of his sports shirt. "Well, you can't do better than that," he said to Tim when he had asked him what was his school, and what college he intended to enter. He himself, though he liked to forget this, had done considerably worse, and his marriage to his wealthy wife had been a part of his determination to make that worse better.

He did not stay for long, because he had to reach Paris that evening in order to attend a ball at the Embassy. "It's an awful bore," he yawned, cracking the joints of his fingers as he extended his joined hands in front of him. "But I don't want to offend them. They are such a nice couple." He went on to describe how he had first met the Ambassador and his wife on the yacht of some minor Balkan royalties—"he, of course, poor chap, was assassinated less than a year later. His wife is still one of my patients." When at last he got up to leave, everyone except Gwyneth, who knew otherwise, assumed that his wife would be going with him. Christine even said: "Well, good-bye, Lady Hope-Ashburn," and held out her hand. "It's been pleasant seeing you even for such a short time."

"Oh, Lady Hope-Ashburn isn't going," Gwyneth said. "She's spending the night here."

"If I can get a room."

"My wife hates social functions, and she's had so many in Rome that she's decided to rebel. I can't say that I blame her."

"Would you mind if I travel with you as far as the village?" Tim asked. "I have something to do there." He had nothing to do there at all.

"Delighted, old chap!"

"And may I come too?" Lise next stepped forward. Tim scowled.

As the car crunched away down the drive, Gwyneth turned and said: "Shall we go and see about the room, Myra?" It was the first time that she had used the Christian name in her mother's hearing.

Rosemary and Christine at once began to discuss the Hope-Ashburns, and continued to do so until it was time to change for dinner. Rosemary, as might have been expected, preferred Lady Hope-Ashburn, whereas Christine preferred Sir Noël. Geoffrey, who sat almost completely silent in a deck-chair, pulling at his pipe and tossing off glass after glass of Pernod, thought them both "a splendid couple".

92

From time to time he would strike his forehead with his fist and exclaim: "Damme, if I can get the name of the chap, he was brilliant."

When Christine arrived in the dining-room, Myra Hope-Ashburn was seated alone at a table for two. It was the best table in the room, in a quiet corner, overlooking the garden. It was obvious that she was a woman to whom the best table was usually given. Christine was embarrassed, not knowing whether to ask her to join their party or not. But Geoffrey, who entered at that moment behind her, boomed out: "All alone, Lady Hope-Ashburn! That won't do at all, at all. Won't you come over to our table?"

"Thank you so much. But you seem such a very big party already. It would mean adding another table. Wouldn't it?"

Obtusely, Geoffrey waved aside this objection: "No difficulty about that! I'll tell the waiter. He can do it in a jiffy."

"As a matter of fact I have some things I must discuss with Gwyneth. Afraid it would bore you all. It's better, I think, if we stay as we are. Thanks all the same." The staccato phrases, delivered in that rasping voice, left no doubt, even in Geoffrey's mind, that it would be useless to persist.

While Tim told them excitedly about the car and then went on to tease Lise, who giggled until tears appeared on her long blonde eyelashes, Gwyneth and Myra talked together in low voices, leaning across to each other while they sipped from glasses, not of the *vin du pays*, but of what Tim called "real wine, wine from a bottle". As soon as they had eaten, they left, without even glancing in the direction of the other table; and on the terrace, where coffee was usually served, no trace of them could be found. Even Gwyneth's novel, which she had thrown down on a wicker chair when she had gone to change for dinner, was no longer there.

"They seem to have a lot to say to each other," Tim said. Like his mother, but for other reasons, he felt obscurely jealous. It was he, not Gwyneth, who was usually lured away from the family group: indeed something of the kind had happened less than a week ago when an elderly American widow had swept him off to dinner and the opera in Paris. Gwyneth was the one who was ignored, or, at best, tolerated for the sake of her lively and handsome brother. This reversal was odd. "What do you suppose they're discussing?"

"Well, don't forget Gwyneth's obligations to Lady Hope-Ashburn."

"Oh, do you imagine that they're working out the interest on the loan?" Tim joked, with an edge of spitefulness as he searched through a pile of records. Already he was a graceful ballroom dancer, and he and Lise usually performed after dinner, pretending to be unaware of the older guests who sat and looked on. "That would be very Jewish."

"Lady Hope-Ashburn has been extremely generous," Christine checked him. She did not like to hear him mock in this way; and yet from the mockery she also derived a certain guilty pleasure. She had decided long ago that she did not trust Gwyneth's friend, and she had been annoyed and hurt by her unfriendliness now.

"I suppose we're not good enough for her," she said to Rosemary as the children began to dance. Geoffrey had already excused himself and lumbered towards two fattish, somnolent Greek girls who were, as he himself called them, his "second strings", when Lise was monopolized by Tim.

"Oh, I don't think that," Rosemary said quietly. She was at once far more astute and far less conventional than Christine, and in these three hours she had already realized what Christine had not even begun to guess in the course of three years. "After all, she doesn't know most of us, and it *is* rather alarming to be plunged into a large party when you're feeling tired and anti-social. She must have had far too much of that kind of thing already in Rome."

Later in the evening, Tim made the excuse of wanting to borrow Gwyneth's pack of cards in order to go upstairs to her room to find her. But he returned to announce that she was neither there nor in Lady Hope-Ashburn's room.

"Tim! You didn't go to Lady Hope-Ashburn's room, did you?" Christine was appalled.

'Yes. Why ever not? I thought that they might be jawing together up there. She's got the big double-room on the corner—the one with the bath. I'd never seen inside before, it's super."

"You'd no right to go in, if there was no one there."

"Well, the door was unlocked. She'd left a lot of jewellery out on the dressing-table. Come on, Lise!"

He swept the German girl off into a waltz before his mother

could scold him further. Christine turned to Rosemary: "I wonder where they've gone."

"For a walk, I suppose. It's a marvellous night. We ought to have done the same." Neither of the two women had, in fact, ever explored deeper into the forest than the two or three hundred yards to the stables from which the children hired horses. "What's the matter, Geoffrey? Aren't you feeling well?"

Geoffrey had begun to mop at his face and the palms of his hands, from time to time emitting a sigh that sounded almost like a stifled groan.

"It's this damned heat," he said.

"It's not all that hot. It's the cognac."

"Anyway, there's nothing wrong with me." He lumbered to his feet. "Do you think I can ask that one over there for a dance?" He pointed to one of the two English school-teachers who had arrived that morning, wearing ankle socks and heavy flat-heeled shoes, with rucksacks on their backs.

"Why not? But take care that she doesn't tread on your toes," Rosemary added tartly. "She might break one for you."

In silence Geoffrey and the girl began to circle, under a petrol-lamp suspended from a tree in a cloud of winged creatures. Her shyness and his clumsiness caused them repeatedly to stumble or bang into others, but Geoffrey, who was already hazy with drink, made light of such accidents, mumbling in the first case, "I beg your pardon, my dear," and in the second shouting out, "Watch out, old boy!" or even, "Bumped you again! Down to the bottom of the river!"—a reference to the days when he had stroked a crew to victory in the school summer races which, not unnaturally, was incomprehensible to most of the couples to whom it was made.

"He oughtn't to be dancing," Christine said, feeling sorry for the girl, who was obviously young and inexperienced.

Rosemary, misunderstanding her, agreed: "You're right. I don't care for his colour."

A moment later, Geoffrey tottered and spun round, with the girl in his arms, to knock over a wicker chair which an elderly Frenchman, seated near at hand, picked up with an expression of angry disdain. "I think we'd better stop," said the girl, freeing herself from him. Her face now the same colour as her salmon-pink ankle-socks, she clumped over to her older friend, who leant forward, a malicious smile revealing long, butter-coloured teeth, and said with a trace of a Yorkshire accent: "Well, you asked for it."

Geoffrey had meanwhile stumbled over to Christine and Rosemary, pushing his way between couples, his arms extended, as if he were negotiating a series of swing-doors. He slumped into a chair, and picked up his glass of cognac; but put it down again when Rosemary said: "Now, Geoffrey, please! Oughtn't you to go and lie down?"

"Lie down! Why the hell should I lie down? I'm perfectly all right. Perfectly all right." But even as he spoke, he was pressing one of his freckled hands to his breast-bone, while his breath came in abrupt whistles, from between clenched teeth.

Lise and Tim continued to dance on tirelessly, appearing and disappearing in the blue arc of light cast by the petrol-lamps. Lise, who had ambitions to go on the stage, had her eyes half-closed and her head tilted back in an altogether too self-conscious rapture: but there was no doubt that, when they were contrasted with Geoffrey and his embarrassed partner, there was both a poignancy and a charm in their grace, their grave abandon and their extreme youth. Suddenly Rosemary exclaimed:

"There they are! Isn't that them?"

"Who?" Christine asked.

"Gwyneth and Lady Hope-Ashburn."

Shadowily indistinct, two forms could be seen on the other side of the ring of concrete on which the dancers were moving, one leaning against a tree, while the other, and taller, smoked a cigarette, the heavy Turkish fumes of which all at once reached Christine's nostrils.

"Why don't they join us?"

As Christine said this the figure by the tree straightened itself, and came close to the other; then, together, they both wandered off into the darkness of the garden, so near, with arms linked, that they soon became indistinguishable.

Christine felt a renewed annoyance: "It's not very polite," she said. "Is it? It's as if they were deliberately avoiding us. . . . Come along, Tim! Time for bed."

"Oh, Mummy! It's only half-past ten."

He pleaded with her, as he always pleaded on such occasions; and, as always, succeeded in cajoling her into allowing him first one more dance and then another. "Lise's only four months older than me, she can go to bed whenever she likes. It's not fair."

"I can't be held responsible for the way that Lise is brought up."

"Anyway, I'm going to get Geoffrey off to bed—and he's much, much older than you," Rosemary said. "Up you get, Geoffrey! You've had enough for to-day."

Christine lay on her bed. She did not deliberately try to keep herself awake, but, without knowing it, she was waiting to hear the sound of Gwyneth's return to her room next door. She heard much else—the murmuring of French voices somewhere in the garden below, the running of water, gurgling and plopping through antiquated pipes, a far-off train, which reminded her of those terrible nights of insomnia after Adrian's death—but she dropped off to sleep before she heard Gwyneth.

When she next awoke—after what seemed many hours of sleep, although the clock, luminous on her bedside table, told her that it was still not yet midnight—they were both of them next door: their talk no more than a general confused murmur, flowing in and out like some erratic tide and casting up here a word, here a phrase, here even a sentence for her drowsy mind to grasp at.

It seemed as if they were arguing, perhaps even quarrelling. At one point she heard Gwyneth exclaim: "Oh, you don't understand!" to which Myra Hope-Ashburn snapped back: "No, it's you who don't understand. Who don't even try to understand."

Later Myra Hope-Ashburn again raised her voice: "Don't you see that Noël has nothing to do with this. Nothing at all!"

"But you can't just exclude him."

"That's exactly what I do want to do."

"Sh!" Gwyneth said.

When they next spoke their voices were so low that they were inaudible. A few seconds later, there were the sounds of feet going to the door, and of the door being opened and closed. Silence followed.

Christine was jarred awake for the second time by the noise of repeated knocking on Gwyneth's door, and a reiterated urgent: "Gwyneth! Gwyneth! Gwyneth!"

Christine jumped out of bed, and as she appeared in the

passage, blinking her eyes against the unaccustomed light, was in time to see Rosemary, in a night-dress and a sleeping-net, disappear into Gwyneth's room.

"What is it? Rosemary, Rosemary, what is it?"

The two women came face to face, as Rosemary reappeared in the doorway.

"It's Geoffrey. He—he seems to be in the most terrible pain. I thought that perhaps Gwyneth could do something for him. But she isn't there. Surely she must have got back."

"I'll try Lady Hope-Ashburn's room. You'd better go back to him. If she's not there, I'll see about a doctor. . . . Now, don't worry, don't worry!" Christine pressed Rosemary's hand. It was the only occasion she had ever seen her friend give way to panic, and the spectacle shocked and dismayed her, as children are shocked and dismayed when they realize, for the first time, that their parents are neither infallible nor invulnerable. She hurried down to the room, which she was able to locate because of Tim's description of it. There was a light under the door.

"Who is it?" Lady Hope-Ashburn answered to the knock.

"It's me—Mrs. Cornwell. Is Gwyneth there? Is she with you?"

Feet hastened to the door which was wrenched violently open: "Mummy, what on earth is all this? What do you think you're doing, coming at this hour of the night——?"

"I'm sorry, dear. It's Geoffrey. It's Geoffrey, dear—he's ill." In her fury, Gwyneth seemed to be incapable of grasping the words. "He's in pain and Rosemary thought that you—that perhaps you'd come and see him. I think we must ring up for a doctor, but at least until he comes . . ." She broke off. Behind Gwyneth, Myra Hope-Ashburn had appeared, in a black tussore-silk dressing-gown, with a crimson sash. Her pointed tongue could be seen under the crescent of her teeth from which her lips were drawn back in what looked like a grimace of disgust. "I'm sorry to disturb you, Lady Hope-Ashburn. But as Gwyneth is going to be a doctor, my friend thought . . . her husband . . . he seems to be in agony. . . ." There was no reason why, in a crisis of this kind, she should continue to excuse herself; and yet she felt obliged to do so.

Geoffrey was lying on his bed, in pyjama trousers but without his pyjama jacket, like some stranded whale. The pyjamas were in a pattern of grey stripes on lighter grey, and the hair that curled all over his body, the soles of his feet, and his face, which was screwed up in pain, were also grey: the only points of colour were his two nipples which stood out a bright pink.

He clutched at Gwyneth's hand: "Gwyneth . . . help me . . . I can't stand this . . . the pain. . . . It's not near the heart . . . my arm . . . and here, under the chin. . . ."

Gwyneth examined him and then consoled and soothed him until the doctor arrived, with a tenderness which recalled for Christine that occasion when Tim had had the last, and the most terrible, of his night-attacks. "What do you think it is?" he kept asking. "What do you think is the matter? It's indigestion, I suppose. It can do this to one, can't it?" He was pathetically eager for reassurance and they no less eagerly gave it to him.

The doctor arrived, a fussy, ill-tempered little man whose breath smelled sour from his interrupted sleep and the cup of coffee which he had drained before setting out. He told them afterwards, in the deserted lounge, that it was a characteristic attack of angina, and that Geoffrey must nurse himself with care.

Christine went back into the bedroom with Rosemary and noticed the copy of *Science and Health* that lay open on the table between the two beds. "Well, what did he say?" Geoffrey asked.

"He said what we've all been saying—that you must take things easy," Rosemary replied.

"Is it serious?"

"Serious enough for me to want you to go and see a specialist as soon as we get back to London. And, darling"—suddenly she sounded tearful, as she sat beside him and held his hand in hers—"do try and do what the doctor told you to do. That game of ping-pong, all that dancing—it wasn't wise, now, was it?"

"Yes, you're right. I must be careful, must be careful," he murmured, his speech sounding slurred, as though from the continued effects of his evening's drinking. "You're quite right, my dear. You know—you know, when I was dancing with that girl, suddenly—suddenly it all went black. I wasn't drunk, though I know that you all thought I was. I felt like hell—suddenly. Must have frightened her."

Christine kissed Rosemary on the forehead: "Good night, my dear." She was thinking of Adrian, for the look in Geoffrey's eyes was the same look that there had been in Adrian's after the haemorrhage on the boat. "Good night, Geoffrey."

"Good night." Suddenly he said, like a plaintive child: "I feel so cold."

Rosemary began to pull the bedclothes over him, while Christine went to the french windows in order to shut them. As she struggled with the latch, she heard Geoffrey say:

"Read to me a little, dear, if you're not too tired."

"Read to you?"

"Yes. Read from where you left off."

As Christine went out, Rosemary began to read from the copy of *Science and Health*. In her voice there seemed to be a terrible, suppressed sadness and despair. Geoffrey's eyes were shut, and his mouth was open; one of his hands was gripping his wife's.

X

As they boarded the boat, Christine met an old colleague of Adrian's, "Fozzy" Blackstone, and his wife, Eunice, who were returning to England on leave. They were a childless couple whose energies in India, when not expended in getting Fozzy promotion, were devoted to the rearing of plants which, in normal circumstances, would not survive the climate. Fozzy had been Adrian's deputy in his last job, and having been appointed temporarily, on Adrian's death, had succeeded in staying on. He was a man without either deadly enemies or close friends, mild, urbane, and cultivated; he stammered and he was short-sighted, peering from behind glasses with gold rims, which tended to slip lower and lower down a sheep-like nose which had the appearance of having been recently smeared with grease. He was always "poor old Fozzy" to his superiors; but his subordinates could feel for him neither the affection nor the contempt that that implied. His wife Eunice was plump and pink, and had once been a masseuse: from her former profession she seemed to have acquired a dogged, torpid strength in breaking down any opposition which Fozzy might meet. Both of them were fond of children, provided they were not their own, and when Gwyneth and Tim had been young enough to remain with their parents out in India, they had often been invited over to breakfast, at which they devoured sausages and mash and pancake-scones which Lady Blackstone, a Scotswoman, herself had prepared.

She now kissed Christine on both cheeks, although they had never been close friends, and exclaimed at the way in which Gwyneth and Tim had grown up—"I'd never have recognized them!" A moment later she was asking them if they remembered their breakfast parties, and telling some story of how Tim had quarrelled with some other boy. "And, my word, didn't you give him a licking!" she added with sadistic relish. "By the time Fozzy separated you both, his mother wouldn't have recognized him." When she found out that Gwyneth was studying medicine and that Tim intended to go up to Oxford, she exclaimed: "Oh, you brainy ones! You were always little highbrows. I remember how Timmy used to write the most marvellous little stories. Do you remember, Fozzy? You remember Timmy's stories, don't you?" Tim had not been called Timmy since he had been sent home from India to go to his preparatory school.

"Well, my dear, this is the most marvellous coincidence! We must have a long, long talk. Why did you never let us have a word from you?" Eunice Blackstone had apparently forgotten that it was she who had failed to answer a letter in which Christine had asked her to make enquiries about one of the old servants who was said to be dying in poverty. "We often wondered what had happened to you—though, of course, we were always getting word from here and there. That friend of yours—with the poor husband who never seems to be *quite himself*—we ran into her, when Fozzy was sent to represent H.M.G. at the opening of a police-college or something. A tiny little station on the edge of the Rajput desert. Rosemary something-or-other, that's her name, isn't it? Anyway you know who I mean. Well, of course, she gave us all your news."

At this point, Christine and the children, as second-class passengers, were told to go in a different direction from the Blackstones who were, of course, travelling first. "Oh, no, we must keep together!" Lady Blackstone exclaimed. "Fozzy, Fozzy dear!" She pushed her round, pink chin forward to indicate first the tickets which Tim held in his fist and then the officer who was responsible for checking them. Fozzy slowly drew out a wallet made from the skin of a crocodile shot by a young man to whom he gave consistently poor reports, and began to pay the excess.

Christine protested; but Lady Blackstone cried her down at once. "Let old Fozzy pay! He doesn't know what to do with his money. He hasn't any children, and he hasn't any vices. Come, let's go and sit down. This steward can find two chairs for us. I wonder if the children would like some lemonade or an ice-cream." But Tim and Gwyneth, of whom she was talking as if they were still at the age she had last known them, had already escaped out on deck.

"You knew, of course, that we took on Amir Ali?"

Christine knew, since she herself had written to suggest that they should do so. She nodded and said "Yes."

"What a servant! What a marvellous servant! And he's become so devoted to us. He treats Fozzy as if he were a great big baby—which, of course, he is. When I had sprue so badly last hot weather, I can't tell you how beautifully he nursed me. He's one in a thousand. Yes, of all the servants I've ever come across in India, he is definitely the best. No doubt of that. Don't you agree, Fozzy? And he really seems to adore us."

From this subject she moved on to that of the house in Delhi, which went with the job that Fozzy had inherited from Adrian: "Of course, in many ways it's madly inconvenient for us to run. It's such a barracks of a place, and our tastes, as you know, are really *simple*. Our little bungalow in Lucknow—do you remember?—was really our ideal. That was cosy." She laughed: "No one would call Mount Pleasant cosy, could they, Fozzy? Well, thank goodness we took all that furniture off your hands. It helps to fill those acres of spare bedrooms. It looks nice too. In the drawing-room we have those chairs—Queen Anne, are they? Are they, Fozzy?" Fozzy nodded. "Anyway they're very much admired."

Mention of the spare bedrooms and the dining-room carried

her on to the subject of guests: "Of course, Fozzy and I prefer a quiet home-life. But these last six months there's been hardly an evening we could enjoy alone together. We had the Parliamentary Mission—three of them, we put up, didn't we, Fozzy?—and after that the new C.-in-C., who was at Wellington with Fozzy, came to stay until his wife, who was ill, arrived out to join him. We shall be pleased to relax in our little place in Westerham, I can tell you! We're longing to see all the roses we put in during the last leave."

Next, she spoke about the Viceroy: "He's really such a dear, and utterly *simple* and *good*. That's what you feel about him: *good*. Well, Fozzy knows more about this than I do, but if it weren't that his saintliness had so much impressed Gandhi, things might be very much worse. Oh, yes, everyone thinks that. She and I have our gardening in common, of course, we're always rushing over to ask each other for cuttings. And like me, she's a great reader, always got her nose in her book."

At this point Christine rose and said: "I think I'll go up on the deck for a breath of air. It's so stuffy in here. . . ." She put a handkerchief to her mouth.

"Oh, you poor thing! Fozzy and I are so lucky, we never feel sea-sick."

Nor did Christine: but she merely nodded, and hurried from the saloon.

She was found, leaning over the rail, many minutes later, by Gwyneth and Tim.

"Hello, Mummy! How did you manage to tear yourself away?"

Almost simultaneously Tim exclaimed: "Mummy, what's the matter? You've been crying." Putting his arm round his mother in one of those shows of affection which always came so easily to him, he rested his cheek against hers. "What's the matter, darling?" he repeated.

"Nothing. Nothing's the matter."

"But your eyes are all red."

"It's this wind."

He laughed at her absurdity. "Don't be silly! There's hardly any wind at all. Tell me," he coaxed, giving her a little shake.

"Oh, obviously it's that terrible woman," Gwyneth put in. "Was she beastly to you? What did she say?"

"I'll give her a piece of my mind," Tim exclaimed.

"No, no, she didn't mean to upset me. They meant to be kind. But that smugness—that smugness of theirs! She went on and on about Amir Ali—the house—their life out in India. . . . And then I started thinking—if—if only your father had been . . ."

"But what's the good of thinking that?" Gwyneth demanded in mingled exasperation and pity.

"That house would have been ours. And your father was such a clever man, everyone said that, whereas—whereas Fozzy—he was just a laughing-stock—a laughing-stock, that's all."

"Oh, Mummy, why let yourself be obsessed by all these things that never happened? What's the point? Daddy died, and that fool got the job and a knighthood in his place, and here we all are. These are the facts—and we've got to accept them, whether we like it or not."

Christine seemed to cringe away from the brutality of this, drawing closer to Tim. "Yes, I know, darling. And I know that you're right. One can't live in the past. But sometimes, I feel so—so bitter. It all seems cruel and unjust, and one just can't understand it."

"After all, things could have been very much worse for us," Gwyneth reminded her. "Couldn't they?"

But Christine struck the rail before her with the open palm of her hand: "Damn them, damn them, damn them! I was feeling so happy after our holiday until they spoiled it all. Why did we have to meet them? Why did they have to spoil it?"

Meanwhile, in the saloon, Eunice was pouring out the tea which the steward had brought, gripping the handle of the tea-pot with her beefy masseuse's hands.

"Do you think she'll come back? Shall I pour out hers?"

"Better wait."

"It'll get far too strong. It's nearly black already." Having grumbled about a crack in one of the cups, until Fozzy irritably told the steward to fetch them another, Eunice bit into a finger of buttered toast and said: "What a nice little woman!"

"Yes, things can't have been too easy for her. Old Cornwell was always so extravagant—apparently he didn't leave much, apart from her pension."

"The girl is plain."

"Yes, poor thing. But somebody told me she'd inherited his

104

brains," Fozzy replied, with a grimace at the bitterness of the tea.

"The boy, of course, has all the good looks." She sighed: "He was such a sweet child, do you remember? I always said he was much the nicest child in Naini Tal." Now she was smiling in sentimental recollection while she continued to munch her toast: "I shall never forget when he turned up at that children's fancy-dress party we gave, dressed up as a Pathan. He looked bewitching, really bewitching! And did you notice those eyelashes? What a waste on a boy!"

Fozzy sipped and grimaced again. "She seems to have made a good job of bringing them up."

"Excellent," Eunice agreed. "But none the less, there's a certain sadness about the poor thing—didn't you feel that too? And, of course, she's terribly shabby. She used to be so fond of clothes, and always dressed marvellously. We had the same durzi, and the amount of money she spent! And then, every leave, she brought back what was really a trousseau from home. . . . Have some more sugar in that tea. Or shall I add some water?" She picked up a chocolate cake and inspected it from every angle, before cutting into it with a fork. She had always enjoyed food. "I expect she was pleased to hear all the gossip at first hand. She must feel out of touch. How lucky we met her!"

"Very lucky." Fozzy took off his glasses and began to wipe them on a silk handkerchief which he drew from his breast-pocket: "I was just thinking, dear."

"Yes, dear?"

"I know it's an awful bore. And I know that we did say that once we got down to Westerham, we were going to see no one at all. But I wonder if . . ."

"I know just what you're going to suggest!" Eunice cried out. "And I had the same idea too. You think we ought to invite her down for a visit. Don't you? That's it, isn't it?"

"Yes." Fozzy replaced the glasses gravely. "Once the children go back—she'll be on her own. . . . It may cheer her up."

They were a couple disposed to be kindly and generous if it did not cause them bother; and now, as they continued to munch cake after cake, they set about deciding what dates they would suggest and how they would best entertain Christine during her visit.

XI

Eunice Blackstone had described Christine as "shabby"; and with the years this shabbiness increased. Like Gwyneth, Christine had bought few clothes since her return from India, and those which she had already possessed had been dyed black when Adrian had died. "Oh, Mummy, you *can't* wear that!" Tim would often exclaim. "It's a disgrace." He would say this wholly unaware that the reason why Christine continued to wear the despised garment in question was because he himself had insisted on having a new winter overcoat, or had bought his pyjamas, not at the High Street, Kensington store at which Christine had an account, but in the Burlington Arcade. Tim was becoming a dandy like his father; and partly because she liked, in her own words, "to see him look nice", partly because she was becoming increasingly indulgent to him, and partly because any resemblance to Adrian she seized on with joy, Christine gave in to his extravagances instead of resisting them. After his first visit to Jimmy Tomlins, he had announced that he must have a dinner-jacket; and when Christine had demurred feebly, he had continued to sulk, until she gave in. "I felt so ashamed, turning up at their dance in my shabby old blue serge suit," he had explained. "It was miserable!"

"Well, if you *will* go and stay with the son of a millionaire," Gwyneth put in.

"I certainly shan't stay with anyone like that again."

"We'll have to see, darling. We'll have to see how things work out."

When Christine used this last phrase, it meant that she would deny something, usually to herself, but sometimes to Gwyneth, so that Tim could have what he wanted. On some occasions it even meant the selling-out of capital; and for Christine, as for so many people of her generation, this was an act almost as furtive, degrading and dangerous as theft. She would never tell the children about such sales, but lying awake at night, she would be prevented from sleeping by the guilty memory of them. To sell a ring, as she had once done in order to pay for Tim to join a winter-sports party in Austria, or to

106

sell a Coalport dinner-service, was, to her mind, far less reprehensible.

As she hurried along the Earl's Court Road from Gapps, where she would buy a pork pie for supper, to Jones, where she was having one of her hats remodelled, and so to the Post Office, Boots and Stewarts, she was indistinguishable, to the casual eye, from any of the other middle-aged, grey-haired women with whom she would stop to chat. But a close scrutiny would reveal that she was propelled by a more than usual energy; that, in spite of a growing stoop and the drabness of her clothes, she still looked extraordinarily youthful; and that her face, unlined under the softly waved grey hair, had gained, rather than lost, in charm.

There was still a childishness about her: eager, naïve, confiding, easily roused to enthusiasm or plunged into despair. Like a spoiled child, too, were her occasional moods of petulance, when, for example, a library book which had been promised to her was given to another subscriber, or the girl at the dairy inadvertently served someone who had entered after herself. At many of the shops at which she called, she would be asked how Tim had fared at Lords, or whether Gwyneth had yet qualified, by people who, in many cases, had never set eyes on either. The window-cleaner would spend more time in her flat than in all the rest of the house, because, when she had made him his cup of tea, she would talk to him about his ailing wife and his son in Canada, while she busied herself with the lunch. When she heard that an old woman, to whom she sometimes talked while waiting to be served at the grocers, had slipped and fractured her thigh, she called on her to offer to do her shopping; and when Tim grew out of, or discarded his clothes, she would pass them on to Mrs. Crutchfield who, instead of giving them to her son, would sell them, unknown to Christine, at a shop in the Fulham Road.

At eleven o'clock, in Stewarts, she habitually met a group of her friends. Many were, like herself, widows; and often they would be accompanied, unlike herself, by their daughters. Occasionally a husband would join them, or one of the elderly widowers or bachelors whose names the women would always prefix with the adjectives "poor" and "old". Christine, who had, as her friends chaffed, "a sweet tooth", would usually eat a chocolate éclair with her cup of coffee, and would laugh and blush simultaneously, like a child caught out in some petty misdemeanour or deception, when the widow of some Indian Army general shook her finger at her and said: "And then you wonder why you are putting on weight!"

Often these friends would suggest that "our young people" should "get together"; and that would always embarrass Christine. "Oh, no, Mummy!" Tim or Gwyneth would groan, when she passed on to them an invitation to a tennis party or one of the "Monopoly" parties which seemed to be so much in vogue among her friends' children and were so despised by hers.

"But, darling, it's rude to keep on refusing. She's such a nice woman, and this is the third time she's asked you."

When Tim and Gwyneth still refused, she would sigh: "Really, you are an odd couple! I just don't understand you."

"Oh, Mummy, do let us choose our own friends! . . . Would you like it if we forced you to go to parties given by parents of people whom we know?" Gwyneth would add with a certain logic; and at that Christine would lapse into a sulky silence from which Tim would have to coax her.

During these years, Christine was happy. There were, it was true, occasions like that of the meeting with the Blackstones, when there would rise in her the bitterness of a spoiled child who has been suddenly punished unjustly; and there were other occasions when, as she read in some novel a description of Florence, came across some forgotten letter or possession of Adrian's, or wandered alone, on summer evenings, through Kensington Gardens where they used to wander together during their first leave from India, she would feel a physical longing that was like some dizzying blow, struck upwards within her. Once, when Tim put on a record of Elisabeth Schumann singing "Du bist die Ruhe", she hurriedly put down her sewing and rushed into the kitchen where Tim, who had developed a sensibility to her mood that was almost morbid, soon came out to join her.

"What's the matter, darling? Something has upset you."

"Nothing, nothing." Savagely she clicked at the lighter for the gas-cooker, showering sparks downwards. "I thought I'd put on the kettle for a cup of tea, that was all."

Then, suddenly, she clutched him to her, in a despairing frenzy of tenderness. "That song—you wouldn't understand.

... It was one that Daddy and I ... in Geneva ... ah, it must be twenty years ago ..." Her mouth became shapeless; the lips began to tremble. She was unaware of the irony that when Adrian had taken her to the concert, as so often when he had forced her to listen to music, she had been bored and impatient to get out once more into the sunlit streets. Yet somehow the song to which she had not even been conscious of listening had managed to lodge itself in her mind, with all its associations of shared happiness and love.

"I understand, darling. I know what you mean."

"You always understand me so well—always."

"Come, dry your eyes! Here, use my handkerchief." He laughed: "Goodness, what a noisy blow!" She began to laugh with him, weakly and hysterically.

"Oh, Tim, if you knew how alone I sometimes feel!"

"Well, of course, I know."

"Thank God I have you and Gwyneth. But you'll grow up, and Gwyneth will want to lead her own life. And then I sometimes think—what will become of me?"

"You'll be able to enjoy yourself at last, without having to worry about us."

"But that's not what I want!" she cried out. "I have to be needed; I have to be of use to someone; I have to have something to do. I couldn't live like—like old Mrs. Bainbridge or Miss Nolan—playing bridge, reading books, and going to the cinema. I couldn't!"

"Well, you'll have me to look after for a long time yet."

"But when you get married?"

"Oh, I shan't get married for years and years and years. And, when I do, you can look after your grandchildren."

"Your wife may say something to that."

They spoke, as they usually spoke to each other when they discussed something serious, in tones of gentle banter. But now, suddenly grave, Tim said:

"Seriously—I do wish that you could marry again."

Shocked, she exclaimed: "Tim! How could you?"

"Well, why on earth not?" Once more he slipped back into the old jocular tone, as he said: "After all, you're an extremely eligible widow. And you get more and more beautiful as the years pass."

She liked him to flatter her in this way; and yet she still felt a resentment at what seemed to her the heartlessness of the suggestion. "No, dear. I'm afraid I don't feel that I shall ever want to marry again."

"But why not, why not?" he persisted.

"Tim, please! Please!" she cried out. "Don't! I don't want to hear about it!"

Nevertheless it was an idea that had sometimes obtruded itself into her consciousness, to be summarily and guiltily rejected. It was unthinkable; and yet—she would begin to relent—perhaps for the sake of the children, and especially for the sake of Tim. . . . A boy needed a father. Rarely, and then only for a guilty moment, did she admit to herself that she might wish to marry, not merely for the children, but for herself. Yet her moods of depression and bitterness, especially when Tim and Gwyneth were away, often had their origin, however obscure to her, in the exasperated sense that these last years of her early middle-age were wasted and lost. She was not yet old, and she was vain enough to know that she had not yet lost her beauty. But she was approaching nearer and nearer to that gulf across which Rosemary had already slipped, and the thought of it appalled her.

Often she would say of Adrian to Gwyneth or Tim: "I miss him as much as ever." What she meant was that she missed him still: for naturally, that first wild passion of grief and despair had burned itself out, as those terrible days beside the Rajput desert used at last to burn themselves out into a chilling dew. Now she rarely dreamed of him, as she used once to do, waking up to the slow realization that he was dead, and she alive and alone, and she had come to derive almost a pleasure from the melancholy which was induced by thinking about him; whereas, once, the mention of his name during a conversation had been like the inadvertent biting on a decayed tooth.

Sometimes she would find herself wondering what had become of her old suitor, Reggie Benson. They had met in Simla, when she was only seventeen and he twenty-three, and for three weeks of his sick-leave from the plains they carried on a flirtation which to him had been more serious than to her. He was haughty, courageous and narrow-minded, a subaltern in an Indian regiment who came of an old Roman Catholic family of which he was as proud as of his skill as a shot and a pig-sticker. When, before they had an opportunity

110

to meet again, Christine became engaged to Adrian, he wrote her a series of violently passionate or recriminatory letters which Adrian, when he was shown them, had held up to derision. But though she had joined in his laughter at the mis-spellings, the grammatical solecisms and the wild extravagances of expression, yet she had secretly been touched. Later she heard that he had married, lost an arm in the war, and eventually settled down in an English village with a rapidly growing family. They had never met again and, in the years between then and Adrian's death, she had given him hardly a thought. But there were times now when she caught herself, with a guilty start, thinking about him. Was he still alive? What was he doing? What had become of his wife? Once she mentioned him to Tim, when he happened to be looking at an old photograph-album and asked who he was; and with that extraordinary sensibility of his to all her hidden moods and feelings, he seemed at once to guess that this yellowing face was that of the first man she had loved. From then on, he would often tease her about Reggie, saying, when she confessed to him her fear of old age: "Well, perhaps we can get Mrs. Benson out of the way for you." As if he were being serious she would then point out that Reggie had probably forgotten her; that Mrs. Benson was no older than she; and that she certainly did not wish to take over Reggie's large family even were she willing to take over Reggie himself.

But as she thought of the years ahead, the idea of marrying again, so indignantly repudiated when the children suggested it to her, would again insinuate itself. Tim would eventually marry; and although she was convinced that that would make no difference to their love for each other, yet inevitably their lives would diverge. Gwyneth would not marry; but, always secretive, her insistence on being left to lead a life of her own had become an obsession. Whereas Tim, when he received a letter, would at once tell Christine from whom it had come, Gwyneth, if asked, would harden the line of her mouth and make some answer like: "Really, Mother! Of what possible interest can it be to you?" Already Christine was seeing less and less of both of them. Tim, being popular, had invitations to stay with numberless friends like Jimmy Tomlins; one summer holidays he was even taken abroad for two weeks. Gwyneth tended to remain on after the end of term at

Cambridge, working in the laboratories, and to go back before the term had started. Often she would go away to stay in the cottage which the Hope-Ashburns owned in Dedham.

Of Larry, although every fortnight an air-mail letter would arrive in his large, sprawling hand, Christine seldom thought. He moved from army station to army station, now at Quetta, now at Allahabad, now at Poona; he always said that he was well, and that the kids, of which he had two, were both doing fine. He had missed promotion, he was chronically short of money, and ever since the birth of the second child, Louise had rarely felt well: but this he did not say. Louise herself would write occasionally, enclosing photographs of the children which would make Christine exclaim: "Oh, dear, they are dark!" and giving news about them. Before Christine had left India, an affection had grown up between the two women, in spite of the prejudice of the one and the defensiveness of the other. But it was an affection which, having existed for so short a time, necessarily had only a few shared experiences on which it could feed itself; and slowly, as their memories of each other dimmed, that warmth dimmed also. Louise continued to write to Christine as "dearest Mother" and Christine would, in turn, call her "My own dearest Louise"; but the phrases, once living, had ossified into conventions.

When Rosemary and Geoffrey came to say good-bye to Christine before they returned to India, Christine gave them some toys for the children she had never seen. She was a generous woman, and she had spent far more than she could afford, as she tended to do, except on herself. Rosemary had seen Larry and Louise once in Bombay, and she had been depressed by the meeting: Larry, who was growing bald, seemed to be harassed, and that old vigour which had carried him back and forth across India when his father was dying, now appeared to be sustained only by an effort of will; Louise had plumpened, but she was tired and apathetic, and when she spoke to the children, her voice, always sing-song, grew even more so in querulous exasperation. One of the children had impetigo round his mouth, in unattractive scabs which made it appear as if flies had clustered there, while the other child screamed alternately with over-excited laughter or paroxysms of rage. But of all this Rosemary said little to Christine, for it seemed pointless to worry her.

Geoffrey left before his wife to go to buy some socks, and the two women at once began to discuss him. His heart was certainly bad, but not, apparently, as bad as all of them had feared. The climate, drink and exercise would all of them worsen it; but there was little likelihood of his being willing to give up any but the last of these three. Rosemary begged him to resign, but stubbornly he refused, asking her what kind of life she imagined he could make for himself, at his age and in his state of health, in an England from which he had been absent, apart from spells of leave, for the last twenty years. They would have a pension, but since he had never risen far, it would be even smaller than Christine's. Tacitly, he gave Rosemary to understand that he would prefer to die within five years at his post in India, than within ten years in some boarding-house in the Cromwell Road or Earl's Court Square.

As the time came for her to leave, Rosemary said: "It's been such a relief to see you. One can never judge from letters and I was afraid you were unhappy. But you seem to have coped with it all so well. People can say what they like about the British in India, but that kind of life seems to develop an extraordinary adaptability and toughness and resilience. When I think of your life out there, with at least fifteen servants, and of how Adrian wouldn't even allow you to do so much as sign a cheque or pay the monthly wages, it seems so astonishing."

"One had to do it—and so one learned to do it," Christine said simply.

"And you're not too miserable, are you? Are you?"

Christine frowned in thought; and, as the two vertical lines appeared down her smooth forehead, that face, so untouched by bereavement or the anxieties of these years, seemed to Rosemary no less amazing than the things of which she had spoken. "No—not for the present," Christine at last answered slowly.

"Why—what do you mean?"

"It's the future that terrifies me so. At the moment I have the children. Just as I told you at Fontainebleau." In a rush she began to pour out her fears.

Rosemary listened patiently, and said at the end: "Yes, I know exactly what you mean. I sometimes think the same things, too. If Geoffrey were to—if I were to lose him."

"But, don't you see, for you it would never be quite so bad.

113

You don't depend on *people* in the way that I do. You have so many things that interest you, which can't be taken from you."

"Yes," said Rosemary truthfully. "Yes, I suppose I have." She stared down at the frayed beige drugget which carpeted the stairs, trying to imagine to herself a life without Geoffrey. It seemed forbiddingly bleak; and yet she admitted to herself, with that peculiar honesty of hers, that it would also have its compensations. She would be able to attend concerts and theatres again, to look at pictures, and to spend her days in libraries.

"Sometimes, looking ahead, I wonder how I'm going to fill all the years in front of me," Christine said, on a note of subdued hopelessness.

Before the next summer was over, she was to have an answer, of a kind, to that question.

II
WAR

I

Gwyneth and Tim were arguing about politics, as the warning wailed out over baked and empty acres of concrete, brick and asphalt. While they shouted at each other, finding a release from tension in this savage bickering, the sweat glistened on their faces and darkened their clothes. "Keep away from the windows, children—please!" Christine implored them. But in spite of the heat, each seemed to be drawn from the shadows into the brilliant square of sunlight, as though into a spotlight.

The day before, Gwyneth had been arrested at Marble Arch for "obstructing the police in the performance of their duties". It had not been the first of such skirmishes, but in the past she had always been let off with a caution. When she stood outside High Street, Kensington, Station, selling copies of *Peace News* and the *Daily Worker*, her sturdy legs apart and her face impassively glowering, or when on a corner of the Earl's Court Road she harangued a crowd exhausted by the night's sleeplessness and the day's work, it was inevitable that, eventually, some embarrassed constable would be forced to ask her to move on, even to give her name. But doggedly she would persist, outside some other station or on some other corner, when the next afternoon of that torrid summer, noisy with sirens and bombs and far-off explosions from the docks and the city, began to freshen to evening. Tim accused her of enjoying this cheap martyrdom of jeers, insults and threats; and certainly when she returned home to supper, there was a curious remote exaltation in her silence and stillness as she sat facing the window, between her mother and brother, and then slowly began to eat.

Christine, who knew little about politics, but had thought Chamberlain a wonderful man at Munich and thought Churchill a wonderful man now, was perplexed and dismayed, and tended to blame Myra Hope-Ashburn, confessedly a Com-

117

munist, for leading Gwyneth astray. "Of course, you're entitled to your views, darling," she would say, "and I think it extremely plucky of you to do such unpopular things. But is it really necessary to *antagonize* people so—particularly, at a moment like this?" But Gwyneth, who was always willing to argue with Tim, rarely bothered to answer such remarks from her mother, merely shrugging her shoulders and allowing her lips to curl in a brief smile of contempt.

Tim, like his mother, was convinced that Myra Hope-Ashburn was to blame: "We never heard anything about these half-baked ideas until they became friends. Did we?" But this was not true, for even out in India, Gwyneth had been called a "crank" for championing Independence.

Yet Tim sensed that it was through Myra Hope-Ashburn that Gwyneth, in other respects so maddeningly invulnerable to all his jibes and arguments, could best be assailed; and on this particular occasion it was his mention of her, as they sat and listened to the distant thud-thud of bombs falling over the city, that had started their quarrel.

"Well, I hope your friend Myra will feel satisfied after this," he had remarked.

"What do you mean?"

He pointed out of the window: "It looks as if enormous fires had started."

"And why do you suppose that she would be satisfied by that?"

He grinned, and pushed his lips outwards. There was a silence, until another thud rattled the windows over which, all that morning, Christine had been laboriously sticking strips of net.

"You're so childish, Gwyneth said. "Can't you see that it's precisely because we want to stop all this crazy destruction that we take the stand we do?"

"It's an odd stand for *her* to take—let's face it."

"Odd? Why odd?"

"As a Jewess, I don't suppose she'd survive very long after the Jerries come over." He used the ugly word "Jerries" intentionally since he knew that she disliked it: normally, he would have said "the Germans".

"Then isn't that a proof of her sincerity?"

"What I can't understand is the way you allow yourselves to

be switched from one extreme to another, at the drop of a hat from Moscow. You were both so violently anti-Nazi, until last year. Weren't you?"

"Children! Children!" Christine pleaded. She had slept hardly at all the previous night, not because of fear, but because of the din, and she now had that curious sensation of dryness around the eyelashes and on the tongue which so often accompanies extremes of physical exhaustion. "What is the use of these arguments? They never get you anywhere."

"No, you're right," Tim said. "Some people are incapable of being persuaded of anything they don't want to believe."

"And some people will spend all their lives following others like sheep!"

"I'm not a sheep!" Tim shouted angrily. "It's people like you who are sheep—you and Myra Hope-Ashburn."

"Why do you go on and on about Myra Hope-Ashburn? Haven't I any other friends who think as I do?"

"I go on and on about her because she strikes me as the most silly and illogical of you all. If she's so keen about Communism, why does she employ all those servants and keep two cars? And if she's so anxious to stop the war, why does she leave it to stooges like yourself to get arrested, instead of going out herself to shout from a soap box? And, incidentally, why doesn't she stick in London? Or does she feel that she can view the whole war better from that cottage of hers in Wales?"

"She often is in London. You've no right to make insinuations like that! She works extremely hard and deserves her week-ends away from the bombing. Myra isn't a coward."

"So many of them are."

"What do you mean by 'them'?"

The childish and futile argument jarred Christine's nerves far more than the distant thud and rattle of bombs; she could never bear quarrels, especially quarrels between the children, unless she herself were participating. "Stop it, stop it!" she cried out, tearful with weariness and exasperation; but neither of them listened. "I can't bear this bickering. What is the point of it?"

Of course she agreed with Tim, but, as she often told him, it was useless to argue. What she did not understand was that at this moment, when he had finished a year at Oxford and was waiting to join the Air Force, he found a peculiar kind of

119

release, not unlike that which he found in intense physical exercise, in taunting his sister. It was true that he felt strongly about her views, and that to see her gesturing and shouting in the centre of a hostile crowd, as he walked home, would fill him with shame and rage; but it was not so much because of those views, as because of some explosive need inside him, that he was continually driven to quarrel with her. Already stored up within him was a frenzied craving for adventure, for violence, for chaos, for heroism. At Oxford he and his friends would perform absurd, reckless feats of daring: racing bicycles round the darkened quad late into the night; climbing into the colleges as though they were mountains; executing a series of savage practical jokes either against unpopular members of the High Table or against fellow undergraduates who seemed to them "dim" or "arty".

Oxford and the prospect of so soon going into the Air Force had between them put an extraordinary nervous edge and burnish on his personality, as on those of so many of his friends. Gwyneth, who had always loved him profoundly, now found herself shrinking away, repelled by a new arrogance, nihilism and insensibility; his teasing of Christine, once so gentle, now seemed to her cruel, and his heedlessness, when his mother sacrificed herself to him, appeared to her to have exaggerated itself into the most gross kind of selfishness. But she was alone in thinking this. Others, whether women or men, felt that the spell had never been so potent; he was generally adored and admired, and the indulgence which Christine had always showed was now also accorded to him by people like his scout, his harassed tutor or the dean of the college.

It was only when the all-clear sounded that the children's angry, recriminatory voices at last fell silent. Exhausted, as if after a wrestling-match, they sat back in two facing armchairs and deliberately stared away from each other. The brilliant square of sunlight had moved towards the fireplace, fading as it went. A breeze sprang up, causing the brass curtain-rings to jingle and the curtains themselves to rustle and flap. As the evening slowly darkened to night, the pinkish glow beyond the window darkened and intensified with it.

Suddenly Gwyneth put her hands to either side of her head, where the hair, already prematurely greying, was drawn back smoothly to a bun. She rocked from side to side, and then

120

pressed her right hand, clenched tightly, against her twitching mouth. Turning round in the chair, she brought her face against its back, making an ungainly twist in her green tweed skirt. There was a sob like a hiccough, and then another. Tim stared at her, his hands resting along the padded arms of the chair and one of his legs crossed high over the other. Christine came in and said:

"Well, that's over at last." She meant that the raid was over. "I wonder if we shall have a peaceful night's sleep. I've bought some ear-plugs. Perhaps they may help." She put a hand to the switch of the standard lamp beside the fireplace: "What about some supper?"

Gwyneth made a snuffling noise, as though she were blowing her nose into the back of the chair; Tim sat impassive.

"Gwyneth! What's the matter? You're not crying, are you? Gwyneth!" She went and placed an arm round the girl's shoulder, to lever her gently round. But Gwyneth cried out:

"Oh, leave me! Leave me alone! Don't touch me!"

"Now really—you mustn't be hysterical. I cannot understand why you children persist in having these absurd arguments. Why don't you agree to differ—and respect each other's opinions? At a time like this . . ." She sighed. "You used to be such good friends once. And now—now you sometimes behave as if you hated each other. Tim, make it up with her—say that you are sorry."

"But why should I be sorry?"

"Tim!" She frowned at him in rebuke, and then changed the frown to a look of silent entreaty. Reluctantly he rose, and crossed to his sister.

"I'm sorry—Gwyneth," he mumbled.

"Gwyneth . . . Gwyneth dear . . . Tim is speaking to you."

"Well, of course, if she doesn't want an apology . . ."

Again Christine's gaze implored him: but at that moment there was a ring at the door and he went out to answer it. Christine seated herself on the arm of the chair where Gwyneth was now huddled, motionless and silent; then put her lips down to the ear which was almost touched by one of the girl's upraised shoulders. "Now, come, darling," she coaxed in a whisper. "Don't be silly. Pull yourself together. Gwyneth!"

In the hall, they heard a voice which they recognized simultaneously as that of Major Knott. It was a curious voice,

121

at once over-military and over-refined, which when he was quarrelling with Mrs. Campion or complaining to her neighbours, would get out of his control and produce an occasional odd falsetto note. Even Tim, usually an excellent mimic, was defeated by it.

"If you'll wait a second, I'll just go and see," Tim was saying. "She may have gone out."

He came into the sitting-room, shut the door behind him, and pulled a face. "It's the Major," he said. "For you, Gwyneth."

Gwyneth jerked her body round and sat stiff and upright. "For me?" she queried in a flat voice. "Why does he want me?" Her face was red and mottled, but there were no tears on it; she looked as if she had just been roused from a deep sleep.

"Search me," Tim replied. "Are you in, or aren't you?"

"Well—all right . . . I wonder what he wants."

Major Knott entered, bending slightly forwards as though he had misjudged the height of the door, with the *Evening Standard* trailing open from one hand. He was said, by gossip, to be at least twenty years younger than Mrs. Campion, but there was an air about him of stiff, wiry decrepitude which he had no doubt observed among elderly retired soldiers and, whether consciously or unconsciously, set himself to imitate. He wore a grubby checked bow-tie, with a twisted knot that revealed the bone collar-stud holding together his high stiff collar. A triangle of linen handkerchief protruded from the pocket of his shiny, blue pin-stripe suit, as though it had been sewn there; his trousers, although they fell wide over his pointed black shoes, also had the appearance of being hitched far too high above his girlishly narrow waist, so that one imagined, though could not see, that their belt must be fastened somewhere under his arm-pits. The skin that lay taut over his prominent cheek-bones, before it subsided grey and puckered to the reddish tuft of a moustache above the small mouth, had the same rough texture, and the same tint as the lips which he was now drawing back from his uneven, nicotine-stained teeth in a simpering smile directed at Gwyneth. Yet, in spite of all these characteristics, he was not wholly absurd: under the thick eyebrows, the restless eyes were fine, and above them the forehead, jutting out, had a grandeur wholly out of keeping with the almost effeminate cast of the rest of his features and his puny body.

"Ah felt ah had to come and see you the moment that I read this. Ah wanted to bring you mah congratulations. Ah never realized that we were fellow-spirits."

"What—what do you mean?" Gwyneth said.

He held out the paper at arm's length. Then, screwing into his right eye a monocle which dangled by a cord from his button-hole, he glanced down the columns and eventually pointed. "Thar," he said.

It was an account, no more than half a dozen lines in length, of Gwyneth's appearance at Bow Street, of the magistrate's rebuke to her ("whatever your private views, which we respect in this country as they would not be respected in certain other countries of which you seem to regard yourself as the champion, people like you must be taught to realize that at a time like this, this kind of provocative behaviour cannot be tolerated") and of her fine of three pounds.

"Had you seen it?" Major Knott asked.

Gwyneth shook her head.

"What is it?" Christine took the paper. "Do sit down, Major Knott, won't you?" He tweaked his trousers at the knees and saying "Thank you, Madam," lowered himself on to the edge of an arm-chair.

Christine read: then, without saying anything, she folded the paper carefully and handed it back to the Major. She was horrified at the thought that many of her friends would probably read the account, and was bitterly ashamed; yet had anyone made an adverse comment, she would have defended Gwyneth with all the vehemence of which she was capable.

"Your daughter's an extremely plucky young woman," Major Knott said. He opened a battered cigarette-tin, and made a *tch-tch* noise, with his tongue on the roof of his mouth. "Ah knew ah'd forgotten something."

Tim glowered, slumped in a chair with his legs thrust out, while Christine got up and fetched a cigarette-box.

"Ah, thank you. One of the invaluable products of Messrs. Players. What could be nahcer?" When he smoked, Major Knott always put the cigarette to the exact centre of his lips, making what looked like a Boy Scout salute with his middle finger and index finger over his pointed chin.

He seemed to be wholly unaware of Tim's hostility, of Christine's stiff formality or of the embarrassment of Gwyneth, who was now standing by the window, looking out. "Of course, ah know that we don't agree in *all* respects, Miss Cornwell. But we *do* agree on the most important point and that's what now matters, isn't it? You're a member of the Peace Pledge Union, aren't you? But I was wondering if there was any chance of interesting you in a group we're forming here in Earl's Court. We call it 'Soldiers for Peace'—our ahdea is that it should be a *militant* organization fahting for peace. Yes, ah think that's the best way to put it. Fahters for peace. Now mahy stand is, of course, very different from yours; and ah daresay that most of our members would stand somewhere between us both, wouldn't they? But the important thing is that we are all unahted by one aim—" slowly he enunciated the words, one by one—"Stop—this—war."

Major Knott was a Fascist: he was an Irishman who had worked as a teacher of English in Munich between the two wars, and, like many such teachers who lived abroad for years, out of touch with their fellow-countrymen, he had exaggerated his pronunciation for the benefit of his students to the same absurd extremes as he had exaggerated his political opinions. Rarely had he come into contact with people who could correct either his vowel-sounds or his delusions about an England brought to decadence and catastrophe by a small group of what he called "Refujews"; and by the time he retired to England to settle with Mrs. Campion, the errors were too deeply ingrained for correction to be possible. He was a man curiously literal-minded for one of his race, and would fly into passions when, for example, he heard a choir of schoolchildren singing on the wireless:

> ". . . Till we have built Jerusalem
> In England's green and pleasant land":

on that occasion, as on many others, writing off a letter, the violence of the language of which would have prevented its publication even if its opinions had been saner. He was a Roman Catholic; a man capable at once of the most abominable cruelty and of the most unselfish tenderness towards the woman with whom, and on whom, he lived. Christine thought him mad.

He was talking now about the way in which the government were "persecuting" conscientious objectors. When he became excited, as he was at this moment, a yellow froth appeared in the puckers on either side of his mouth and he would nervously push his tongue outwards between agitated phrases, as a dog does when it is eating grass. From time to time he would wriggle a skinny arm and tweak his frayed cuffs so as to pull his sleeves lower. He spoke about a boy he knew—"You couldn't ask for a fahner specimen of an English, a *real* English, lad"—who had spent many weeks in solitary confinement. All those about him had been utterly corrupt and depraved: his fellow-prisoners, the warders, even the prison visitors and the chaplain. Each night he would be tormented by bugs, but, when he complained to the doctor, showing him the lumps, he was told that they were nervous in origin. "Nervous! Can you imagine it? Nervous! Ah ask you!" Major Knott gave a whinnying laugh, shaking his head from side to side as though he had water in one of his long pointed ears. The next night, he went on, the boy decided to collect the bugs, and having caught hundreds—"literally *hundreds*"—he laid them out on a saucer for the doctor to examine. When presented with this tribute, the doctor peered down at it and complained that, in the dim light of the cell, it was impossible for him to see. He would have to take the saucer out into the passage. When he returned, he said: "My poor boy! You're suffering from the most terrible delusions. There is nothing in that saucer at all. Look!" He held up the saucer, empty now, since he had shaken off all the bugs. "If you go on like this, you'll end up in a strait-jacket."

"Imagine!" Major Knott cried. "Imagine the dahabolical cunning of that! He was determined to drahve that poor creature out of his mahnd." At this Tim got up and walked from the room.

"Imagine!" Major Knott repeated, ignoring the exit. He leant forward to Christine: "Imagine, Mrs Cornwell! And yet we call ourselves a civilized people. . . . And that doctor, believe it or not, was a graduate from Edinburgh University, and ah believe very hahly regarded in his profession."

Christine said with a fatuous brightness: "Oh, from Edin-

125

burgh University, was he?" She looked at Gwyneth for help but, still standing at the window with one of her hands gripping the curtain which the dust and grime of that summer had turned from beige to grey, Gwyneth appeared to have not even listened. "This is the first time you've seen our flat, isn't it, Major Knott?" Christine went on.

"Yes, Madam, that's so. The first time, the very first time." Now he appeared to be brooding on something as, hands clasped, he stared sideways into the empty fire-place while, like a donkey trying to chew a thistle just out of its reach, he attempted to nibble at the small reddish-white moustache that covered his upper-lip in an untidy oblong.

"I hope it won't be the last time," Christine added politely.

"No, indeed, indeed! People lahke us ought to stick together."

"Well, I think we should all stick together, whatever our opinions. Of course, I ought to tell you, in all fairness, that my son and I—well, we take a rather different view of the war from my daughter."

But Major Knott, still standing at the grate and still attempting to bite on what appeared to be the bristles of a rather tired and stained tooth-brush, seemed not to have heard. He had begun to wonder, though Christine did not know this, if he would be offered anything to drink; and if he were not, whether Mrs. Campion would have any money for him to go round to the Redcliffe. To the public-house at the end of the road he could no longer go: since, less than a week ago, he had there struck and been struck by a drunken Irish labourer who unfortunately came from Belfast, was about to join the Guards, and resented being called "a stooge of the Jews". Major Knott now recalled the moment when, on the pavement outside, he had squirmed, covered his stomach with his hands, and had screamed out "You'll kill me, you'll kill me!" while he felt the heavy boots jarring his spine, women screamed and the brute himself grunted in rage and shouted obscenities. All those secret fantasies of his boyhood in a seminary in Ireland and later of his manhood and even middle-age, had suddenly been realized. There had been pain, of course; and shock and the disgrace of being insulted, when half-drunk, by someone who was completely drunk, in the black-out, on a pavement which was slithery with some nameless and invisible muck; and worst of all, his abject helplessness, when in those fantasies he had always been heroic in his martyrdom. But though the reality was like some horrible travesty of the dream, a work of art reduced, as it were, to the dimensions of a strip-cartoon, yet it also filled him with exaltation: so that as he went home stumbling and dizzy, he felt as if he were the triumphant victor of the encounter, rather than its cowardly and cringing victim.

"Ah wonder if ah maht trouble you for a glass of water?" he suddenly said.

"Of course. Would you like some orange in it?"

"Yes, some orange would be very nahce—if it won't be too much trouble. Very nahce indeed."

As Christine went into the kitchen, where she took the opportunity to turn down the oven in which their supper was cooking, Major Knott recalled with a shudder the coarse, not unsympathetic voices of the crowd who had dragged him to his feet. "A shame to pick on an old gentleman. . . . Well, what if he did say that? It's a free country, isn't it? Oh, I've seen him about often. They say he's not quite . . ." Until his wild eyes, shooting hither and thither in a vain attempt to see them by the light of a solitary, dimmed-out torch, caused that last voice to trail away into silence.

"There we are!" Christine said brightly. All at once, feeling sorry for him, she forgot her resentment at his noisy quarrels with Mrs. Campion, the smell of their dustbin, and their aggressive complaints.

He took the glass and gulped at it, his Adam's-apple jumping up and down like a ping-pong ball in his scrawny neck. "Thank you, Madam," he said, wiping his moustache on the handkerchief which was not, after all, sewn into his breast-pocket. He began to fold it carefully.

Tim opened the door and said: "Can I please have a word with you, Mummy?" retreating at once so that Christine had to follow him out into the hall.

"Yes?"

"When is he going to go?"

"I don't know, dear."

'Well. . . . At any rate I must be off."

"Off! Where to? You haven't had any supper."

"That can't be helped. I've got a date—Café Royal half-past eight."

127

"A date? You never told me, darling. You must eat something first."

"It's now five past eight."

"Well, I'll explain to Major Knott. . . . Everything is ready. The fish-pie will be over-cooked, if anything."

"No, dearest." He kissed her on the temple, and then on the cheek. "Too late now, I'm afraid. Besides"—he laughed—"you know fish-pie isn't exactly my favourite dish."

"Oh, dear!" she sighed. "Food is so difficult. I don't know what to do. You don't like rabbit, either."

"Never mind."

"I've got some eggs. Shall I make you an omelette?"

"There isn't time, darling. There isn't time. What I *would* like is some cash."

"Well, of course. How much do you need?" Christine picked up off the hall-table a black bag which, from use, was growing grey at the corners.

"Darling, that bag's terrible," he said.

"Yes, I know." There was no need for her to click open the purse, because the clasp had broken off, leaving a jagged spur. She had another bag, a present from Rosemary, but the shabbiness which had once been a disagreeable necessity had now become a habit and such things she usually pushed into drawers where they were hoarded and forgotten.

"And you really can't go on going about in those boats," he added, referring to her shoes. "You're not yet a grandmother—only a step-grandmother."

"Yes, darling, they *are* worn, I know. But I find them so comfortable on the hot pavements. They were good shoes once; I had them made for me in Italy."

"But that must have been at least six years ago!" She had pushed a folded pound note into his hand, furtively, as though she were tipping him, and having glanced down at it he asked: "You couldn't manage another of these, could you?"

"Oh, dear." She had taken ten pounds out of the bank the previous day and two pound notes and a handful of silver were all she now had left for the week-end ahead.

"A pound doesn't go far on an evening out," he said. "And I'm broke."

She handed him the other note, deciding that she would

have to try to borrow some money from Gwyneth: who, no doubt, would guess why she had to do so and would make some sour comment.

"Thank you, darling. You're an angel!" He kissed her on the cheek. "You pressed my tennis shorts, didn't you?"

"Yes, dear. They're hanging in the cupboard."

"Good. I shall need them to-morrow." He looked at his watch: "God, I ought to fly!"

"Who are you meeting?" She could not resist the question as he opened the door, although she knew that nowadays her curiosity exasperated him almost as much as Gwyneth.

"Oh, a friend," he said.

"Jimmy Tomlins?"

"No. A *female* friend, darling." He stressed the word mischievously.

She laughed, although his refusal to tell her was, as always, tantalizing: "Oh, you and your girl friends! Now be a good boy, won't you. Don't break her heart." But he was already clattering down the stairs, leaping them in twos and threes, as he shouted out good-bye.

Major Knott was standing at the window with Gwyneth when Christine went back. She excused herself for leaving him for so long, and he replied: "Oh, please, please! Ah've been glad for this chance to have a word with the younger generation. Ah was telling Miss Cornwell about a little brush which ah mahself had with the police less than a month ago. Oh, a nasty affair it was, though I did get the better of them." And he began a long and confused tale of how a policeman had called to complain about their black-out; of how eventually he had been taken to the police station; and of how he had vanquished a bullying oaf of a sergeant in the course of an argument of a Socratic subtlety and length. During this narration, which she had endured once already, Gwyneth walked out into the kitchen, from which she could be heard whistling and clattering dishes: so that Christine and the Major were now left alone together.

Christine did not ask him to sit down, and intentionally remained standing by the door herself. He drew closer to her; and, at this proximity, she became aware for the first time of an odd, peppery smell which in later years she was always to associate with the basement flat in which he and Mrs. Campion

129

lived. It was a smell neither agreeable nor disagreeable, and it did not suggest dirt, though that was its cause.

Eventually Christine interrupted: "I'm most terribly sorry, Major Knott, but we must have our supper. Do please forgive us."

"Oh, of course, of course!" But he still lingered, detaining her first in the doorway, then in the hall, and finally on the stairs, in the hope that perhaps she would ask him to join them. Finally, he told her that if they ever wished to shelter in the basement, he and Mrs. Campion would be delighted. To this Christine replied that as a general rule they went down to the shelter in the garden owned by the tenants on the ground-floor; but that it was none the less extremely kind of him to make the suggestion.

"Do you mean those terrible Bedworth women?"

"Yes, the two Misses Bedworth," Christine answered coldly.

"Couple of sex-starved spinster fuss-pots!"

One Miss Bedworth was a probation officer; the other taught music at a girls' school in East Sheen.

Christine made no reply to this last comment, beyond saying: "Well, good-bye, Major Knott," and shutting the door. As she went into the kitchen her annoyance with the Major also included Gwyneth: for it seemed to her a proof of the absurdity of Gwyneth's views that they should have brought about this reconciliation with someone so obviously crack-brained and perhaps even dangerous.

"Well, your friend has gone at last," she announced.

"Not *my* friend," Gwyneth answered.

"Well, I don't know who else's friend he could be. Quite mad, of course. . . . You didn't have much to say to him," she added a moment later, as she plunged a spoon into the dry centre of the fish-pie. "Did you?"

Gwyneth was silent.

"What a lot of odd people there seem to be in the world nowadays! Far, far more than when I was a girl. Or perhaps one just didn't come across them."

"What did Tim want?"

"Oh, to say good-bye."

"Money?" Gwyneth queried.

"Now, darling, it's natural for a boy of that age to wish to enjoy himself. Particularly"—Christine raised a piece of bread to her mouth, her expression suddenly mournful—"when one thinks of what lies ahead of him."

"That lies ahead of all of us."

"I hardly think that either of us is likely to fly in a bomber."

"No, but we spend a lot of time under bombers, don't we? And that's probably worse."

"I can't understand your hardness where poor Tim is concerned!" Christine burst out.

"Nor I your softness. . . . Anyway, don't let's start that old argument again. I wonder what sort of night we shall have."

"One day you may regret saying such things about him." But to this Gwyneth made no answer, continuing methodically to scrape butter over one piece of bread so that it would last for two others.

"I wonder who he's meeting," Christine said eventually.

"Didn't you ask him?" There was a silence. "Or didn't he tell you?"

"I suppose I am inquisitive. But is it a crime to be interested in the doings of my children?"

Every two or three days since the vacation had started the post had brought Tim a letter in a pale blue envelope, addressed in an italic script of a kind still rare at that period. Christine used to examine each of these envelopes, though all were the same, as though expecting that eventually one would yield up the secret of its authorship. The post-mark was that of Axton, a village near Oxford, and it seemed to her no less affected than the heavy, black script itself that *Esq.* should always be written out in full, *Esquire.* "Another letter for you from your lady-love," she would sometimes chaff Tim: but the only response he would make would be to give her a brief, seemingly absent-minded smile, as he slipped the envelope into his pocket.

That morning, however, when she was putting the tennis shorts in his cupboard and some socks and shirts in his drawers, Christine, who was alone in the house, began a hurried search. She knew that she was doing wrong, and she felt ashamed; and she also knew that at any moment he or Gwyneth might return. She tugged at one drawer of his desk to find it locked, and at another only to reveal a dusty disorder of used pen-knibs, indiarubbers, elastic bands, charred lumps

131

of sealing-wax, a rusty pen-knife, some patience cards and a fives ball. It was not until she put her hand into the pocket of his grey flannels, as she went to hang them up, that she found what she wanted. It was a note both brief and of a formality which was yet further exaggerated by the way in which the lines were carefully placed, wide apart and with margins that extended for at least two inches on either side of the stiff sheet of paper.

MY DEAR TIM (Christine read),

It will give Alec some pleasure and me very much more so if you can come and stay with us from Saturday to Monday as you promised. Alec has what he calls sciatica, and Nanny what she calls lumbago; but they seem to be suffering from the identical ailment, and the identical bad temper. The children are waiting for you to complete the tree-house for them. I, of course, am always waiting.

Love,

P.

At first Christine assumed this was the letter which had arrived that same morning; but a later glance at the date showed that it had been sent more than two weeks previously. The week-end to which it referred was therefore presumably that which Tim had said he was going to spend at the Tomlins. But the deceit of this was less of a shock to her than the discovery that this "P." must, obviously, be a married woman, and that the address embossed on the paper was "Axton Vicarage".

But Christine had extraordinary powers of recovery, and by the time she and the two children sat down to luncheon, she had persuaded herself that the first affair of every boy was always with a married woman; that, indeed, it was better if it were so since there was much less chance of his "doing something silly"; and that with such an address a divorce was, in any case, unlikely. The afternoon she spent in imagining to herself what "P." must be like: and as she darned Tim's socks, she decided that she must be called Pamela or Penelope; that she was married to an elderly widower whose children she looked after; and that Tim had met her and her husband at the house of a retired colleague of Adrian's, who now lived in

Oxford and interested himself in the Society for the Propagation of the Gospel.

Later that evening, while Gwyneth read a book and she herself finished the washing-up ("No, dear, really I prefer to do it alone, in my own time"—for she knew how Gwyneth detested this chore), she went on to picture to herself how Tim and "P." would be spending the evening. Were they really meeting at the Café Royal? Surely a small French restaurant in Compton Street or Dean Street was much more likely? But why had he lied to her? Why? It was so unnecessary and so wounding.

At this point she heard Gwyneth call: "The siren, darling! . . . Oh, don't stand by the window."

"I've only the plates left."

"Well, leave them. We'd better sit in the hall."

Gwyneth began to put up two deck-chairs in a space under the stairs, where a friend of Christine's, an air-raid warden, had optimistically told them they would be safer than anywhere else. Christine knitted and Gwyneth continued to read. But the bombs were falling near, and neither of them could concentrate. Eventually Christine said:

"Darling, I think it might be wiser if we went down to the shelter."

Gwyneth closed her book, taking care to mark the place with a used bus ticket. "As you like," she said.

"In any case, you know that those two hate to be on their own. It's really a kindness to join them. . . . Oh, I do hope Tim is all right!"

But although they knocked and rang repeatedly at the door of the ground-floor flat, neither Miss Bedworth appeared to answer: until, suddenly, Gwyneth remembered that one of them had said something to her about spending the day with relatives at Bromley.

At that moment the front door to the basement, which faced that of the Bedworths, creaked open and the Major's head poked out. "Come on in!" he cried. "Come on!"

"Thank you, Major Knott. But we have the key to the shelter. Thank you very much." Christine backed away; but the Major persisted:

"Oh, you'll be far more comfortable with us—and just as safe. Anyway, you've never seen our humble abode, have you,

133

Mrs. Cornwell? Come on!" At that Christine gave in. "Mind that top step!" He gripped Christine's arm and kept hold of it, going down the dark stairs crabwise before her. "This black-out!" he grumbled. "We had to paint over that bulb, as you can see." The uncarpeted stairs wound round, to fetch up in a large, low-ceilinged room which had once served as the kitchen of the whole house. There was a vast, sagging double bed, covered with what had obviously been a curtain, since at one end a row of brass rings could be glimpsed, and on this bed a dachshund was sleeping, its nose to its tail. Mrs. Campion, who was wearing a pale blue kimono and a pair of man's carpet slippers, trodden down at the heels, was seated in a deck-chair, reading a book through glasses that rested half-way down her large, fleshy nose. A kettle was puffing steam into the room from the gas-stove placed in a recess.

"Gladys, here are Mrs. Cornwell and her daughter. I've brought them down to shelter with us."

Mrs. Campion got to her feet, smiling in welcome as though there had never been any animosity between her and the Cornwell family. "Do sit down." She indicated the other deck-chair. "Perhaps you wouldn't mind sitting next to Fritzy, Miss Cornwell, would you?" As Gwyneth lowered herself on to the creaking bed, the dog opened one red-rimmed eye and gave a little snort and then a deep groan.

"Poor Fritzy, he does so hate the bombs," Mrs. Campion said. "But don't we all? . . . Make the tea, darling," she said to Major Knott. "And don't forget to warm the pot first."

There were two good pieces of furniture in the room: a Regency chest-of-drawers and a small, octagonal Dutch marquetry table on which were piled a dusty profusion of books, newspapers, periodicals and pamphlets. One felt that if one removed even one copy of *Action*, an elaborate system of stresses and counter stresses would at once be upset and the whole heap would crash and slither to the floor. Otherwise the furniture was of a kind used when camping: two folding tables, one of which had a wad of yellowing newspaper jammed between its struts; two deck-chairs; a packing-case covered with a piece of carpet.

The tea was black and bitter, and had obviously been made by pouring water once again on to the leaves of a previous brew. There was one Crown Derby cup, standing on a pink saucer, two pink cups and saucers, and a blue mug. Mrs. Campion removed the tea-cosy, which looked like a nigger-brown Balaclava-helmet, and said, in her deep ringing voice: "Milk and sugar, Mrs. Cornwell?"

Major Knott had begun to search for a cutting of *The Times* which he wished to show to Gwyneth, pulling out first a suit-case and then a hat-box from under the bed and rummaging among their contents. "Now come along, Terry!" Mrs. Campion exclaimed. "Your tea will get cold."

A bomb exploded, making Christine splash hot tea over her skirt and Fritzy sit up and whimper. Mrs. Campion took the dog on to her lap to comfort it, while Major Knott fetched a rag, that appeared to have been used for polishing shoes, for Christine to mop herself. Gwyneth stared at an early nineteenth-century water-colour which hung on the wall opposite, flanked by a photograph of Hitler, obviously cut from a newspaper, and another of Mosley with his signature across it.

"That used to be my old home," Mrs. Campion explained. "Do you know the Essex-Suffolk border? Both Constable and Gainsborough painted that wood on the right, just above the Stour. And that's me as a little girl," she went on, pointing to a sepia photograph, in a chipped gold frame, of a child seated on a cushion, with ringlets falling about her shoulders; it might, as recognizably, have been a photograph of Major Knott.

"I do hope Tim is not wandering about the streets," Christine sighed. In her anxiety for him, she had paid little attention to what either Mrs. Campion or the Major said: "He's so rash . . . listen! Do you think that's him? Have a look, Gwyneth."

Gwyneth went up the stairs grudgingly and then returned to report: "Nothing." She stared at Christine for a moment and then added: "Now, don't worry. What's the good of worrying? We left that note for him to say that we had gone to the shelter. And we'll certainly hear him if he knocks at the Bedworths', won't we?"

Major Knott had begun to fiddle with a radio set which lay, festooned in wire, on the floor beside the gas cooker. There was a series of whistles, snorts and coughs, and eventually a voice said: ". . . extensive damage to the City of London and the docks."

Mrs. Campion eyed Christine, who immediately stiffened,

135

her tea-cup gripped between both her hands. "Oh, turn it off, Terry," she said. "It's such a bore. And besides, it disturbs poor old Fritzy—doesn't it, darling?" She bent down and appeared to insert her long nose into one of the ears of the sleeping dog.

"But don't you want to know what's really going on?" He explained to Gwyneth: "We always listen at this time. There's not a word you can believe from the B.B.C. now—and as for the newspapers!"

"Terry, turn—it—off!" Mrs. Campion rapped out the command, stamping at the same time with one of her slippered feet on the worn linoleum, to emphasize each of the last three words. "Let's try to forget the war for a moment. We're all sick of it. . . . How about some more water in this pot?"

Christine noticed that the Major picked up not merely the tea-pot to carry into the recess, but also his own cup, which was still three-quarters full; and that Mrs. Campion, though she continued to talk about an occasion when Fritzy had almost died of food poisoning, was nevertheless watching each of his movements. First he poured the boiling water into the pot; next, Christine saw, he opened the door of a cupboard, in such a way that he was almost entirely concealed; then he put down the tea-pot and picked up his cup-and-saucer, saying as he did so in an unnaturally loud voice: "It's that younger Miss Bedworth. A'm sure she put out some poisoned bread. She really loathes poor Fritzy, ever since he chased her cat." From behind the cupboard door, Christine could hear a gurgle-gurgle. When he returned to sit beside her an unmistakable smell of whisky rose from the cup, which was now full to the brim.

"How about some reading aloud?" Mrs. Campion said. "Terry and I often read to each other during the raids. Terry, would you like to get *Emma*?"

Obediently he fetched the book from the top of a pile stacked against one wall.

"Who'll begin?" he asked. "Shall ah?"

"Yes, you begin," Mrs. Campion said.

In that extraordinary accent of his, he began the chapter about the picnic to Box Hill, breaking off from time to time to sip from his cup or, as a bomb fell particularly near to them, to make some admiring exclamation like: "They're having a field-day to-night!" or "There must be thousands and thousands of them over us this minute." Christine shut her eyes; the black-out had made the room horribly stuffy, and since she was, in any case, exhausted, she soon fell asleep. The Major went on reading. Nearer and nearer, and louder and louder the bombs crashed around them, until suddenly be broke off and shut the book: "Ah can't continue," he said. It was only then that Gwyneth noticed that the skin over his cheek-bones and his lips, which usually had the identical rubbed, crimson tint, had suddenly faded to the yellow, glistening and cracked, of Cheddar cheese which has been kept for too long; and that his hands, in which the book still rested, were trembling uncontrollably. "How can one read such stuff when all that is going on around one?" he demanded petulantly.

"All the more reason to read it," Mrs. Campion said. "To remind oneself of sanity, when the world's gone mad. Go on, Terry."

"No, that's enough." He lifted his tea-cup and drained it to the dregs, even at this moment cocking his little finger in a gesture of hideous refinement. Then he took the handkerchief from his breast-pocket and mopped first his lips and then his forehead and the reddish palms of his hands.

"Your mother's quite done in," Mrs. Campion said, looking across at Christine, who had fallen asleep.

"Yes, I'm afraid she's very tired. She can't sleep properly, you know. And then she has so much to do—now that Mrs. Crutchfield has gone off to munitions."

"Why doesn't she go to the country?"

"Oh, we tried to persuade her. But she wants to keep a home for us. You see, I shall be starting next month at St. George's, and once Tim is in the Air Force, he'll be wanting to spend his leaves in London, I expect."

Mrs. Campion took the book from the Major, who at once disappeared behind the kitchen door with his tea-cup in his hand. She began to read slowly, over-emphasizing certain words, as though she were reading to children; from time to time stumbling or even jumping a whole line so that she had to go back. With the hand that was not holding the book she never ceased to stroke the sleeping dog. Christine lay in the deck-chair with her face hidden in the crook of one arm and her knees drawn up. Suddenly Major Knott rose and tugged at a blanket from under the bedspread which once had been

137

a curtain, in order to cover her. She sighed and murmured, "Thank you," as he explained: "Ah know it seems hot. But there's no easier way of catching a chill than sleeping like that, without any cover." A few minutes later, however, Christine pushed the blanket away from her in her sleep, so that it slipped to the floor.

At half-past twelve, Tim came home; and it was extraordinary how Christine, who had slept undisturbed by the bombs, the reading and the sporadic conversation of the others, at once sat up. "Tim—isn't that Tim?" she asked, pushing her soft grey curls away from her flushed forehead with a hand that felt wooden and prickly from the pressure of her head against it. She got up, staggering a little, and made for the stairs. "Yes, it must be him. He's gone past the second landing, hasn't he? I'll go and tell him that we're here."

"Ask him to join us," Major Knott said. "We can put up another deck-chair, can't we, Gladys? Ah suggest that you and Mrs. Cornwell share the bed, as she's obviously tired."

When Christine reached the flat the light shone down the stairs from the open door of Tim's bedroom into the dark hall. She called out: "Darling! Are you back? Did you see our note?"

He had already taken off his jacket and shoes, and the knot of his tie was loosened. "What a heat!" he exclaimed.

"I hope you weren't silly. You didn't wander about the streets, did you?"

"No, we had dinner and then we went to the Spider Club—it's in a basement. Then I took her to her hotel in Knightsbridge, and came on here. She didn't want a very late night as she has such a lot to do to-morrow before going back to the country." He seemed slightly drunk, as he stood at the top of the stairs, his legs apart and his hands on his hips, and talked down to her in the shadows.

"Was it fun?"

"Oh, yes—great fun." He swayed slightly, and gave a dreamy smile, using the same upward gesture which he habitually used to push the curly blond hair away from his forehead. A bomb thudded and the window-panes rattled for several seconds afterwards, making Christine exclaim:

"Not under the skylight, darling! It really is madness. Do come down—please."

"I'm not afraid."

"It's not a question of being afraid. But it's so rash. Why risk your life needlessly?"

He put his head on one side, listening to the drone of planes: it was a sound which always gave Christine the same sensation of nausea as the buzz of a dentist's drill, and the same apprehension of the possibility of pain. "Thousands of them!" he exclaimed. But he did not speak admiringly, like Major Knott, but with a sudden wild hatred. "Well, we'll give it to them back—with interest! You wait till I'm out over Berlin—you wait."

She shrank from the venomous force of that threat and from the way in which his face, under the electric light, had all at once grown cruel and old and no longer handsome.

"Damn them!" he muttered.

"Come down, darling," she coaxed. "We've been with Mrs. Campion and the Major."

"What!"

"Yes, I know it seems odd. But really they've been so kind to us. And what's the point of keeping up these feuds—particularly at a time like this?"

"Oh, you're so soft!" he exclaimed. "When I think how that woman has treated you for all these years. . . . And he's nothing but a traitor—well, he is, isn't he? What else is he? No, I'm not coming down. Not on your life!"

"Then go to the shelter," she pleaded with him, mounting the stairs with the key outstretched towards him. "I'll join you there."

"Oh, it's so uncomfortable. No, I want a decent night's rest, on my own bed. If I'm hit, I'm hit. But if I'm hit, do you imagine that you'll be any safer down in that basement?"

"Don't talk like that, Tim." It reminded her of how Adrian would talk about dying. "It's wicked."

"You silly, superstitious darling." All at once his exultant hatred against the Germans and his resentment against Mrs. Campion and the Major faded from his face, as he put his arms about her. "Now you go on downstairs, and leave me to sleep, will you?"

"I'll stay with you."

"You'll do nothing of the kind. Come!" Gently he began to propel her down the stairs, and towards the front door. But when he opened it, he suddenly drew back, with an abrupt gasp.

"What is it?" she queried.

"Another of these bloody cockroaches." He let go of her and stamped out wildly: but the insect had already scuttled away into a crack in the wainscot. "That's the fault of those wretched people in the basement," he said. "The dirt down there breeds them, of course; and then they start coming up here. It wouldn't surprise me if we had rats soon."

"I'll get some powder to-morrow," she attempted to appease him.

"It's disgusting to think of these things crawling about the kitchen." His face had again assumed the same expression which it had when he had talked about the Germans.

"Oh, but I keep everything covered. You know that." She sometimes wondered if his horror of all insects had originated in some childhood fear of the scorpions, centipedes and huge silver-fish which were so plentiful in the old wooden house which they had occupied in the hills: often, when one pulled a sheet of lavatory-paper from its packet, something fat and wriggly would plop to the floor and scuttle away to safety.

"Now, off with you," he said. "Have a good night's sleep. Look at those rings round your eyes! Look at them! You're not going to remain a beauty for long. Go on—sleep, sleep!"

But it was crass of him to imagine that she could sleep while he was upstairs. She tried, but she could not. Major Knott snored, and the dog snored, and whimpered; and Mrs. Campion would from time to time sigh, grunt and turn over on the bed beside her. Only Gwyneth slept without noise or movement, outstretched on a deck-chair, with her legs crossed before her and her hands crossed on her stomach. Christine thought of Tim's remark about giving it back to the Germans—with interest; but she could feel none of the exultation at that prospect, only a chilling despair, as she thought first of his flying over a hostile city, with guns blazing at him and searchlights opening and shutting like vast gleaming scissors, and then of the people huddled as they were now huddled, sleepless or snoring or whimpering or grunting, as the bombs descended on them. It was necessary, she did not doubt that; and whereas the thought of Tim losing his life caused her an acute anguish, the thought of these faceless people being obliterated caused her no more than a burdensome depression. If only she could force herself to hate them, if only she could feel Tim's passionate convictions. But hatred was an emotion which she felt rarely, and then not for long; and though she could be roused to passion by some personal issue, general issues had always had for her a remoteness and vagueness.

It was a long raid: and as she was thinking this, she heard a terrible shrieking whistle and an explosion so loud that it was as if someone had suddenly brought both hands together over her ears. Everything rocked wildly, and, in the din of the glass tinkling all around them, the dog began to emit one prolonged yelp after another, like a person in desperate agony.

"Good God!" Major Knott leapt to his feet, thrusting his hands through the darkness before him as though to ward off some falling masonry or advancing foe. Mrs. Campion clutched at Christine on the bed, while Christine herself struggled to get to her feet. Gwyneth said calmly: "That must have been near."

But simultaneously Christine was crying: "Tim! Tim! Tim!" She had a picture of the attic bedroom, with vast squares of moonlight under its windows. "I must go and see."

Gwyneth said: "I'll go."

"Wait!" said Major Knott.

"Whatever it was, is over," Gwyneth said stolidly. She began to mount the stairs, and Christine hurried after her. The dog was still yelping, while Mrs. Campion attempted to soothe it: "Fritzy! Fritzy, boy! It's all over, Fritz, boy! All over!" she crooned. "All over, darling!"

"Quick, Gwyneth, quick! Oh, my God! I told him not to sleep there. I told him to come down."

Tim was sitting up in bed and, as they rushed in, he was laughing weakly, as though from tipsiness and hysteria. Glass lay in long icicles over the bedclothes, slipping to the floor and smashing there as he moved; their feet crunched on glass; even the looking-glass was smashed.

"Are you all right?" Christine demanded. "Darling, are you all right?"

"Of course I'm all right. It'll take more than that to kill me. Not even a scratch on my face."

His luck had still held good.

141

II

"**W**ould you mind if I switched on the news?" Miss Celia Bedworth asked, as she and Christine prepared the salads at the club where both of them now worked. Like many people in the war, Miss Bedworth had developed an extraordinary faculty both for finding news-bulletins at hours when they were not usually known to exist, and, even more remarkable, for listening to them.

Christine said nothing, and Miss Bedworth at once took her silence for assent. At the end, after she had sighed deeply with satisfaction and turned off the switch, Miss Bedworth exclaimed: "Twenty-two thousand tons over Berlin during the last three months! It's unbelievable, isn't it? . . . Oh, but how silly I am!" she touched Christine's arm with a dripping rubber glove. "Of course, to hear that sort of thing must be terribly worrying for you, Mrs. Cornwell. But you must be proud, too. It's they who are really winning the war for us. Did you hear John Strachey's talk last Saturday? Well, he said as much in so many words."

"Fortunately Tim has only three or four more missions before he's grounded," Christine said.

"And what a relief that'll be to you, won't it?"

Of course Christine was worried; and of course it would be a relief. But the paradoxical effect of Miss Bedworth's sympathy was to make her want to deny both these things. Once again she restrained herself, and said nothing, as she continued to slice tomatoes.

Miss Bedworth was a small, worried-looking woman, with a bony chest of which, since she had joined the staff of the Club, she had tended to exhibit a greater and greater expanse. Her sister was in the War Office doing what Miss Bedworth called "very hush-hush work", and since, as a consequence, she felt lonely, she was willing to work far longer hours at the Club than any of the other volunteers. With the American service-men for whom the Club catered she was girlish and arch; and it was she who virtually forced them to use the nickname "Beddy", although she never ceased to exclaim delightedly: "Really, what cheek!" when she was so addressed.

She was vain about her small, white hands so that when she worked she would always wear rubber gloves, wheedled out of an American surgeon who frequented the Club. She was also vain about her ears, which were pierced to receive the various ear-rings invariably said by her to have belonged to her grandmother. Into both hands and ears she was often to be seen rubbing cold-cream, when she had nothing else to occupy her.

"Did I tell you that I had another letter from my nephew? He always writes so cheerfully, poor boy. But one guesses how much he must suffer." She sighed: "Well it won't be long now. Major Oppenheim doesn't give them more than six months—at the outside."

Miss Bedworth had a nephew who had been reported first as missing and then as a prisoner-of-war. Gwyneth said unkindly that the change from the one status to another had been a blow to his aunt; and though this was untrue, and Miss Bedworth would certainly have preferred to have the boy living than dead, yet there was no doubt that she had derived a certain morbid pleasure from her supposed bereavement. The boy, as Gwyneth also pointed out, had never once been mentioned by either of the sisters until he joined the Air Force.

"I hope he doesn't try to escape," Miss Bedworth went on, "though I suppose it's wrong for me to say that—it's their duty after all, isn't it? But one hears of so many of them either losing their lives or making things far, far worse. And he was always such a reckless boy, such a reckless boy. Always up to mischief of some kind or another. Why, I remember once, when we went for a holiday to Dymchurch, and my brother and his wife were there, and, of course, Mike was with them . . ."

Miss Bedworth had an endless succession of anecdotes about Mike, few of which seemed credible even to those who had never set eyes on this stolid and freckled youth whose chief interests in life were pigeons and electrical engineering. Often she seemed to sense this, and a look of peevish frustration would appear on her face. She also sensed that her American listeners were either more credulous or more patient than her British, and it was to them, as they drank at the bar and ate their meals, that she poured out her more exuberant imaginings. Secretly, she was envious of Christine: not because she was more attractive, or more efficient, or more popular than herself, all of which was true; but for the odd reason that she had a stepson who might be killed in Burma and a son who might be killed over Germany. It was also for this reason that Miss Bedworth spoke of her father being killed in the battle of Mons, when in fact he had died in the influenza epidemic of 1919.

Miss Bedworth could rarely work and talk at one and the same time, as many American officers, waiting to be served a meal, had discovered; and now she relinquished the lettuces which she was supposed to be washing, and came and stood over Christine, with her rubber gloves dripping water on to the floor.

"Goodness me—chatter, chatter, chatter!" It was Mrs. Worth-Dillington, the manageress, who at last stopped the flow as decisively as if she had given a sharp twist to a tap. "Come along, ducky. It's twelve o'clock, and there are at least sixty men out there ravenous for their luncheon. Get cracking," she added, in the slang in which she was always up to date, "or those boys are going to be more than a little cross with their Beddy—and so shall I." Mrs. Worth-Dillington went through into the bar, where she exclaimed to another of her helpers: "Really, that Bedworth baggage is absolutely clueless. Poor Mrs. Cornwell—I wonder how she stands her." It was because no one else, least of all Mrs. Worth-Dillington herself, could stand poor Miss Bedworth that she and Christine were almost always detailed to work together.

After a few minutes of holding the lettuces under the tap, in so perfunctory a manner that at luncheon many American teeth were to close on grit or even worse, she again came over: "I think you've made a conquest," she said.

"A conquest?"

"Now don't look so astonished! As if you weren't always making them. You know that friend of Major Oppenheim's, Colonel Liebman, don't you?" Christine frowned down at the tomato she held in one hand, and then shook her head. "Well, of course you do! You and he were talking yesterday evening."

"Oh, that one," Christine said.

Colonel Liebman called himself "an advertising executive"; a heavily built man, with light blue eyes set a little aslant in a face whose tan he himself admitted to come not from the sun, but from an ultra-violet lamp.

144

"Yes, that one. Well, Major Oppenheim asked me last week if I'd like to go to the new Gingold show with him," Miss Bedworth explained: she had worked as hard to extract that invitation as for the silk stockings she was wearing.

"Oh, yes?"

"And he then said that Colonel Liebman had suggested that I should bring you along with me—so that we could make up a party. Isn't that a good plan?"

"I'm sure that Colonel Liebman would much rather you asked one of the girls. Why not Miss Parker?"

"But he particularly asked for you! That's the whole point."

"Did he?"

Christine said the words in a flat, slightly peevish voice, as she herself began to wash the lettuces which Miss Bedworth would obviously never finish. But secretly she was flattered, even though she knew that it was rash to believe anything that Beddy told one. Christine had liked Colonel Liebman who had talked about his two grown-up children, his work for a women's fashion magazine, and the kind of food to which he was accustomed and to which he compared, politely but unfavourably, that served at the Club. His voice was deep and penetrating, and he smelled strongly of soap.

"You will join us, won't you?"

"So much depends on Tim."

"You mean, in case he gets some leave."

"Yes."

"Well, if that happens, you can always cry off. Naturally they'd understand." She giggled: "I'd feel much safer if you came along too. Oppy has been so fresh these last days. I tell him that the sooner they give him a real job to do, the better. Something to occupy his mind."

Christine handed Miss Bedworth a tray, with an expressionless face. "You'd better take these through for the early ones," she said.

"Goodness! Half-past twelve already! How the time does fly!"

As Miss Bedworth went out, Mrs. Worth-Dillington entered. Mrs. Worth-Dillington pulled a face, as soon as the other woman could not see her, and exclaimed: "Always on the ball—trust our dear old Beddy! I shouldn't think that neck-line could go much lower—or those skirts come much higher."

Briskly she began to help Christine with competent hands that before the war had never worked at anything but gardening or horses. "There we are, dearie," she said, when Miss Bedworth returned. "If you held the tray the other way, you might find it easier to get through the door. Like this," she demonstrated. "That's the girl."

Miss Bedworth picked up a lettuce-leaf and began to crunch it. "They were listening to Haw-Haw again last night," she said. "Sybil was home and I can tell you we banged on the floor."

"Who?" Christine asked, although she knew already.

"Mrs. Campion and the boy friend. I can't see what's the point of this 18B if people like that are allowed around."

"I don't suppose they do any harm to anyone."

"How do we know that? . . . Do you remember how last November East Croydon stopped packet after packet? Well, that was a retired vicar. They caught him at it. Signalling from a skylight."

"Where on earth did you hear that tale?"

"Oh, it wasn't in the papers. That's not the sort of thing the Ministry of Information would let by. Is it? But, of course, Sybil, in a job like hers, gets to hear about that sort of thing. . . . I shouldn't have told you really, I suppose," she added without regret. "But that Campion woman and her Major—they make my blood boil. I'm surprised you can bear to exchange a word with them, let alone visit them in their hole. And how they have the face to talk to a woman in your position . . .! Sybil and I just cut them now. It's the only thing to do," she went on, but Christine, hurrying to prepare the salads, paid little attention to her. Miss Bedworth was not an unkind woman, but the war had given her a craving for sensation which her life had previously lacked and now she was insatiable. Stories of panics in shelters, stories of women and children maimed, stories of spies, stories of rapes, torturings and mass-executions: all were gobbled up by her as she was now gobbling a quarter of one of Christine's lettuces, her little white teeth working like a rabbit's. "When I think of you, with two sons fighting and you staying on here in London in order to help us here—and then I think of those two who are doing nothing at all, except to make things easier for Hitler—well, it turns my stomach." Before

146

the German invasion of Russia, she used to talk about Gwyneth in the same strain; but that was now forgotten, with the Finland Fête which she had helped the vicar to organize, and so many other things.

Unable to hold her head up against this venomous torrent any longer, Christine murmured: "Oh, I feel tired!" and picked up a tray to go into the dining-room. But Miss Bedworth followed her, talking as they went.

Mrs. Worth-Dillington, who was an observant woman, at once came between them. "Would you like to take over the bar, Mrs. Cornwell? You've done enough heavy work for to-day." She turned to Miss Bedworth: "You and I can finish the salads, dearie. And we'll have to get weaving. Come along!" Reluctantly, Miss Bedworth trailed back to the kitchen behind her boss.

At the bar Christine found Major Oppenheim, Colonel Liebman and a young American Air Force lieutenant who was attached to Tim's squadron.

"Hiyah!" Major Oppenheim called out.

The other two were more restrained in their greetings.

"What's yours?" Colonel Liebman asked.

"Nothing, thank you. Mrs Worth-Dillington prefers us not to drink when we're on duty."

"Tell that to Beddy," Major Oppenheim exclaimed. "That dame would get herself lit on cough syrup. Man, oh, man! Did you see her last night?"

Colonel Liebman leant forward across the bar: "Mrs. Cornwell, you're doing far too much," he said in a deep, considered voice. "Some of those girls only come here to have a good time." He indicated a group with his glass.

"Well, they're young," Christine said.

"Well, for Christ's sake, you're not *old*!" he protested. "Why shouldn't you enjoy yourself too?"

"I have two grown-up children, so I'm considered to have enjoyed myself enough already."

"I've got two grown-up children, too. But I certainly don't consider that I've enjoyed myself enough already."

"Say, did old Beddy speak to you about our all having a night out together?" Major Oppenheim asked.

"Yes. It was sweet of you to suggest it."

"Well, what about it? Are you on?"

"It's simply a question of my son getting a forty-eight hours. If he does, then of course . . . I always like to keep myself free on those occasions," she added in explanation.

The young lieutenant said: "Well, Tim's lucky, but I don't suppose he'll be as lucky as that. When did you say—next Saturday? Well, it's not likely he'd get two forty-eights so near together?"

"*Two* forty-eights?" Christine frowned at him, bewildered.

"This one, I mean, and then . . ." He broke off, for he sensed already that he had said something wrong.

"Well, I expect it'll be all right," Christine said slowly. "Yes, I expect it'll be all right."

It was not the first time that she had suspected Tim of concealing from her one of his leaves. It was natural that he should not want always to be at home; and that, even though she longed to see him, was something she must and could accept. But this new secrecy, like Gwyneth's secrecy in the past, rankled and hurt her. She found it impossible to accept it as part of the character of the boy she knew; and she decided angrily that it was "P." who was "behind" it.

That she did not yet know what the letter stood for was another symptom of the change.

III

A few days after Miss Bedworth's outburst about Mrs. Campion and the Major, Christine received a visit from a detective. He was, like the majority of detectives at that time, a man in late middle-age, balding, and with the beginnings of a paunch that strained the top buttons of his trousers and rucked the cloth, a shiny blue pin-stripe, in a number of tightly-drawn horizontal creases from pocket to pocket. One would expect to see his hands, which were faintly grey and luminous from the dust and grime of London, patting books in some dark corner of a shop in the Charing Cross Road or wearily scratching away at figures in a ledger. He had come to ask Christine if she knew anything about the political views of her neighbours in the basement—"Just a little private chat," as he put it, "strictly between ourselves."

"Well, what do you want to know?" Christine asked defensively. She had grown fond of Mrs. Campion during the last two years; and even for Major Knott had begun to feel a protective affection.

He explained that in the past they had received a number of complaints which they had felt they could ignore: people who had nothing else to do were always willing to poke their noses into other people's business, weren't they? And to those who could take no active part in the war, such interference gave a gratifying sense of participation. "Oh, you'd be surprised how many letters we get, Mrs. Cornwell, you'd be surprised." His eyes, beneath which the skin sagged in discoloured pouches, became ruminative and even melancholy, making Christine decide that, so far from being odious, as she had at first thought, he was sensible, well-intentioned and perhaps even likeable.

"Recently," he went on, "we've had a whole flood of letters about this couple. Most of them anonymous—that's how they usually come." There was nothing against the so-called Major on the records, except that he was a member of the British Union. But in times like these—well, it was necessary to check and counter-check. What did Christine feel about him? Could she help?

"He's harmless," Christine declared, "absolutely harmless. Of that I am certain. Dotty, perhaps, but harmless." She continued in this vein: at once warmly defending Mrs. Campion and the Major, and attacking the anonymous busybodies who had made the complaints.

"Well, thank you, Mrs. Cornwell," the detective said at the end. "I think that is all . . . except—do you happen to know when Miss"—he consulted a note-book which he drew from a bulging pocket—"Miss Celia Bedworth or Miss Sybil Bedworth is likely to be at home?" Christine told him. "And Major Knott himself?"

"Oh, I think he's usually to be found in the basement. If not, round the corner. At the pub."

"Doesn't he work?"

"No. He only has one lung—he's never very well."

"This woman he lives with—she always says that he's out. We've asked him to call round to see us, but somehow he never comes. He seems to be avoiding us." He gave a faint smile which broke the pouches under his eyes into a number of irregular, brown segments. "We only want to question him."

"I expect he's frightened," Christine said. "He's frightened of most things," she added.

They were standing in the hall and, at this moment, Tim came leaping down the stairs from his bedroom: "I seem to have lost my clothes-brush. May I take yours?"

"Yes, just a moment, darling. Or can you find it yourself?"

"Oh, I can find it." He went into Christine's room and then up the stairs again, brushing one sleeve of his uniform as he went.

"Your boy?" the detective queried.

"Yes."

"One of mine was in the Air Force, too. . . . We lost him," he added heavily. "Yes, shot down over the Channel. December 1942. He was our youngest."

"I'm sorry."

"Well, that's how it goes."

He closed his note-book, and caressed it between his hands as though it were some prized volume, while he gazed down and sighed. Then he gave a visible shake to himself: "Well, thank you," he said again. "I'm sorry to have troubled you."

Tim, when told about his visit, at once became furious:

"It's monstrous! I knew they'd get us into trouble, sooner or later. I warned you they would."

"But, darling, what trouble have they got us into?"

"Having a special-branch man round to question you like that," he continued to fume.

"Well, I wasn't the suspect," Christine said.

"How do you know? When they see that you're the bosom friend of people like that, well, they at once begin to wonder. Stands to reason. And you can bet they know all about Gwyneth."

"They can have nothing against her now. She's become as keen about winning the war as anyone else."

"Well, I don't like to have a man like that poking his nose into our affairs. Particularly in my position," he added.

150

"Oh, don't be so silly. Tim really! He called it a friendly chat, and that's what it was. He seemed sensible—and unlikely to listen to hysterical gossip. Gladys Campion's been a good friend to me," she added. "How could I let her down?"

Tim glanced at his wrist-watch, and then, fingering his D.S.O. with a gesture that had become habitual, he said: "I'm going to be late. I can't tell you what a hunt I had for that vest. Why don't you always put them in the same drawer?"

"I'm sorry. Did I make a mistake?" She put a hand on his shoulder and then timidly ran it up to his cheek and his forehead. As she touched him, she thought that he had never looked more handsome: his skin had an extraordinary transparency and bloom, and his blue eyes, under the level brows, were glowing as though the fatigue and strain of those innumerable missions over Germany had been no heavier than those of a cricket-match. So many of his friends had grown haggard, tense and either morosely silent or hysterically talkative. Jimmy Tomlins had developed an extraordinary "tic" which convulsed the whole of the left side of his face, as though in agony at some recurring attack of neuritis: he had been grounded. The young American lieutenant, when he had last come to the Club, had had to rest his arm on the bar, when he offered her a cigarette, in order to control its shaking. Another boy was in a mental hospital, where Christine had found him crying endlessly to himself with the sheet clutched to his chin.

"Will you be late?" she now asked. She had been hoping that this evening, at least, he would stay at home with her. "I'm not going to the Club, and Gwyneth should be back from the hospital later in the evening."

"Can't say. It all depends," he answered.

"Who—who is it this time?" she ventured with an effort of playfulness.

"What do you mean? . . . Oh, just a girl. You wouldn't know her, darling."

"But I might like to know her. Don't you ever think that?"

"What's the point? One meets these girls, one takes them out to a dance or a theatre and then—then it's all over."

"Don't you ever have a—a special girl?"

He shook his head and smiled. "Much better not."

But she did not believe him: the letters, addressed in that

italic script, still came for him regularly, and she had begun to dread that an affair which had already lasted for eighteen months, might last, like the war, for ever.

One after the other, Miss Bedworth and Mrs. Campion came up to see her. Miss Bedworth was the first:

"Oh, thank goodness I've found you! Let me get my breath." She panted, with one of her small white hands, the nails of which were carefully cut to diamonds, pressed to her bony chest, and then sank on to the sofa, where she crossed her legs, to reveal not merely her knees but a considerable expanse of thigh. "Has he been up here too?" she queried.

"Who?"

"That detective." Christine nodded. "He has! Well! About time too! These complaints must have been going on for years and years—I remember that, when the war had only just started, old Colonel Vanson—you remember him, don't you?—said that they ought to be locked up. What's the good of all these posters about careless talk and not spreading alarm and despondency, when Fifth-Columnists like that are allowed to go around saying what they please?" Then, suddenly realizing that Christine, so far from being a sympathetic listener, was eyeing her coldly, even with distaste, she touched her ear-rings, pulling them downwards so that the pierced lobes were disagreeably stretched, looked absently out of the window, and fell silent.

"What did you tell him?" Christine prompted.

"Oh, of course I had to say what I thought."

"Which was?"

"Well, I had to mention about the radio, didn't I? And that time Sybil met that man coming out of their flat—that foreigner, with the blond hair. You remember, I told you?"

Christine did not remember; but no doubt it had been one of Beddy's innumerable fantasies transformed into truth for her, if for no one else, by endless repetition.

"It was you who wrote the letters, I suppose?"

"What letters?" The bony chest began to crimson, and she was now not so much gently pulling, as plucking at the ear-rings.

"Well, some of them at any rate."

"I don't know what you mean, I'm sure."

"The anonymous letters. Or did you put your name to yours?"

"Really, Christine, I don't know how you could think such things of me—or of poor Sybil." All at once Miss Bedworth ceased to be indignant, and instead began to whine. "Of course when I was interrogated—well, one must always tell the police the truth, mustn't one? Or what one *thinks* is the truth. Which is all I did. I don't know why you should fly at me like that. I'm sure I've never had any wish to harm others at all. I'd have thought you'd have known me better." She clicked open her bag and took out, first a handkerchief, into which she blew her nose until it grew as red as her chest and flaming cheeks, and then a packet of Chesterfield cigarettes. "Damn!" she exclaimed, when three successive matches blew out.

There was an obscure pathos about her which always prevented Christine from being angry with her for long: the same pathos which made the Americans allow her to extract from them the cigarettes, at one of which she was now jerkily puffing, the silk stockings and the countless tins of spam or boneless chicken. Christine said quietly:

"What about a cup of tea?"

"No, dear—no thank you." She was determined to be hurt. "It's sweet of you, but—no thank you. I mustn't waste your time." Only when she reached the hall did she relent: "Oh, by the way, I suppose you haven't heard from either of the boys, have you?" she ventured.

"I had a telephone call from Colonel Liebman this morning. He wanted me to go out dancing with him tonight. But, as Tim was home, I had to refuse."

"It's odd." Miss Bedworth spoke in a sad, tinny little voice, as she began to ease back the cuticles of one hand. "Oppy hasn't been into the Club for more than a week, and I haven't had a squeak from him. If you—if Warren Liebman rings up—or if you should see him . . .." She broke off, and again the skin of her bony chest began to redden as though rubbed vigorously by an invisible towel.

"I'll ask what's happened."

"Would you, dear? Oh, thank you. Because you know . . ." there was something ghastly about her jocularity—"I'm more than a little sweet about that boy. Yes, I am, I truly am."

Within less than five minutes, Mrs. Campion was at the door, in a dressing-gown, with her scant grey hair in curlers, so that bare patches of her scalp were visible.

"May I have a word with you?"

"Of course. Do come in."

She peered over the balustrade into the shadowy well beneath them, one hand, crooked with arthritis, curved round it like the yellowing claw of some bird of prey. Then she straightened herself: "I wanted to make sure." Her slippers padded into the sitting-room where she turned round.

"Has he been up here?" she asked.

"Who?"

"That man from Scotland Yard."

Christine nodded.

"Did you tell him anything?"

"Of course not." Mrs. Campion continued to eye her balefully, her head raised and her battered nose twitching as though to catch some scent which might betray Christine. "Really, Gladys—you trust me, don't you? Do you imagine that I'd *want* to get you and the Major into difficulties?"

"One never knows, these days." She stared down at her enormous feet, and then took a step forward: "No, of course not. Of course I don't. But I'm frantically worried. Suppose they lock him up, suppose they separate us. He says they've been following him."

"I'm sure he's imagined that."

Mrs. Campion shook her head: "The other night, when we came home, there was a car standing outside. There were two people in it, I saw them. A black car."

"What night was that?"

Mrs. Campion thought. "Tuesday," she said.

"Well, there you are—you see! Jimmy Tomlins drove Tim down that night. It was almost certainly them, having a last chat."

Mrs. Campion shrugged her shoulders: "People have been writing about us. He told me that."

"Nobody pays any attention to anonymous letters."

"Do you think that they think he's a spy?"

"Of course not, my dear! Really, you mustn't get yourself into this state."

154

"He's terrified. Absolutely terrified. He was hiding when the man came."

"Well, that's silly," Christine said. "It would be much better if he let himself be questioned. He ought to be perfectly frank and open. After all, he's got nothing to hide. Has he?"

"They have ways of getting at people."

Christine suddenly realized that not merely the Major, but Mrs. Campion, was terrified. It was as if all those delusions of plot and counter-plot, persecution and torture had been passed, like some infectious disease, from one to the other. In the past Mrs. Campion had sobered and steadied Major Knott, coaxing him or teasing him out of his wilder fantasies: she was the only part of the real world which he seemed capable of seeing and accepting as it truly was, undistorted by his growing paranoia. But that was obviously a rôle she could now no longer play.

"Oh, nonsense!" Christine said. "They wouldn't hurt a hair of his head. The worst that could happen would be for you both to be interned. And there's no great hardship in that from all accounts."

"That's what they say. But can one believe it?"

"Of course."

"You know as well as I do that, these days, none of us has any idea of what is really happening. Have we?"

"Anyway, I'm sure that the Major ought to let himself be questioned."

"He talks of going into hiding."

"What?" Christine all but added: "He must be quite mad." Instead she went on: "You must do everything you can to persuade him not to do anything so foolish. That would certainly arouse suspicion."

"Oh, what are we to do, what are we to do?" Mrs. Campion hugged herself, her bony arms, the skin of which was brown and wrinkled like an elderly plucked chicken's, crossed over her bosom, her hands gripping her shoulders. She rocked from side to side, in fear and despair, while her lower lip stretched itself and her chin began to wobble. "It's all so difficult, so difficult!"

Christine comforted her and reasoned with her; but the results were as unsatisfactory as when, in the past, she had seen Mrs. Campion herself attempting to comfort or reason with

155

Major Knott. It was as if a blind had descended; and any light which she attempted to cast into the darkness of Mrs. Campion's consciousness now would only reach it as a faint glow through that obstruction. One could never be certain; one could never know who might be watching one; certainly Miss Bedworth and her sister must be in the pay of the police. . . . To all this Christine would make no answer but a "don't be so silly!"; and the time had passed for reassurances of that kind to be of any use.

Soon after Mrs. Campion had gone, peering over the banisters, as she tiptoed down the stairs and hissing up at Christine about the light, "No, off! Turn it off! I can manage like this!", there was the sound of Gwyneth's key in the door and then her heavy tread in the hall.

Christine went out: "Hello darling. How early you are! I thought you and Myra were going to meet for tea together."

"We did meet." Christine glanced down at her watch, which showed ten past five, and Gwyneth added: "Not for long."

"So you decided not to go to the theatre after all?" Gwyneth did not answer. "Much the wisest thing. You need a good rest. You look tired, darling. Come and sit down, and let me make you another cup of tea."

"Yes, I'm coming, I'm coming." Gwyneth pulled herself away from the arm which her mother had put around her shoulder. "Do just let me get myself sorted out." She opened her brief-case which was, as usual, crammed with medical equipment, the remains of her sandwich luncheon, and two or three books. It had been an exhausting and ghastly day, with the victims of a V1 explosion, mostly children from a Council school, being bundled into the overcrowded casualty wards, either unconscious or screaming with pain and shock. She wanted to have a bath and change into other clothes, for in no other way did it seem possible to escape from the smell of charred flesh which, she had the illusion, must be still clinging to her person.

"Was it a beastly day?" Christine queried.

"They're all beastly days now." Gwyneth never spoke to anyone about the details of her work, not even to Myra. She found, strangely, that those endless hours passed in hurrying

156

from one mangled or burnt body to another acquired, in retrospect, all the guilty horror of some shameful dream which one shrinks from recounting. But unlike most such dreams, these refused to be forgotten.

"Poor darling. You're working too hard. Even someone with your stamina can't stand up to this."

"Oh, it's surprising what one can stand up to." Gwyneth was working under a surgeon already in his seventies, and his hours were usually longer and even more arduous than hers. "Yes, we can take it," she added sardonically. "Blood, sweat, tears, and all." She still liked to jibe at Christine's admiration for the man whom she herself usually dismissed as a "clown".

"Tim gone out?"

"Yes. He was sorry to have missed you."

"Nonsense. I don't suppose he gave me a thought, until you reminded him."

"Darling, he did! He said, of his own accord . . ."

"Where has he gone?"

"Oh, one of his girls, I suppose."

"*One* of them? There is only one—isn't there?"

Christine did not deny it. "Does he ever—does he ever talk to you about her?" she asked.

"Is it likely?"

Christine had already confessed to Gwyneth about the letter she had read: "He left it on the kitchen-table and I began to read it without thinking, imagining it was for me," had been her excuse which, needless to say, Gwyneth had not believed.

"I'm afraid it's serious. It's gone on so long."

Gwyneth began to go up the stairs and Christine followed after, although she knew that Gwyneth disliked being trailed in this fashion. When they entered the bedroom, Gwyneth sank on her bed, her body twisted so that her feet touched the floor and her head touched the pillow. She felt too exhausted to stand up, let alone to begin to take off her clothes.

"What are you doing?" Christine, kneeling on the floor at her feet, had begun to loosen the laces of the heavy brogue shoes. "No, Mummy, no!"

"You'll feel much better if you get these shoes off. Then you can put your legs up and have a good rest."

"Please!" Gwyneth sat up and pulled her foot away.

"Why do you never want me to do anything for you?"

157

Gwyneth looked down at her mother, who still knelt before her, and replied: "Because, unlike Tim, I don't want to have you as my slave. Please get up. You've worked quite as hard as I have, and feel just as tired. Please!" She began herself to wrench off her shoes.

"How was Myra?" Christine asked, still from the floor, where she now sat, like a young girl, her hands in her lap and her legs crossed beneath her.

"All right."

Gwyneth and she had quarrelled, as they so often quarrelled nowadays. Gwyneth supposed that the fault was her own: exhaustion would make her irritable and morose, and Myra, instead of realizing this, would at once begin to ask her: "What is the matter? What have I done? Why are you in this mood?" For those long, eager conversations, during which they talked about the farm Myra had bought, Gwyneth's job, politics, books or music, they now had little zest. "More tea?" Myra would ask. "Thanks." "Busy?" "Pretty busy." Like two tired tennis players, they were content to do no more than lob the ball back and forward, back and forward.

"Is she going to drive you down at the week-end?" Christine asked.

"I'm not going."

"Not going?"

"No."

On this occasion, as Gwyneth had munched a scone and stared out into Curzon Street, Myra had all at once exclaimed: "It's obvious I bore you." She picked with the nail of her index-finger at the raw place she had already made on the side of her thumb. "Well, I don't blame you." "Oh, don't be silly, Myra!" "We have nothing to say to each other now, have we? Nothing at all." "If you could be a little less self-centred, and try to understand. . . ." "Understand what?" But Gwyneth could not begin to tell her about those charred and mutilated bodies, about those eight horrible hours during which she had only sat down for ten minutes in order to try to eat a spam-sandwich which her stomach had at once rejected, or of her present feeling that her clothes, her hair and even her skin were somehow defiled and contaminated. When Myra now touched her bare arm, she at once pulled it away: for she could not bear to see that contact between her own seemingly

158

soiled flesh and the country-fresh cleanliness of the other woman.

"But you need that week-end," Christine protested. "You know that you need it. It's too bad if you have to do another week-end of duty. That's three in a row."

"No, I shall be off at the week-end." Gwyneth had now raised her feet on to the bed, and was staring up at the ceiling. She always looked forward to the days she could snatch for a visit to the farm which Myra had been running ever since Sir Noël had left for Italy, with the rank of Brigadier in the R.A.M.C., more than a year before. As she helped Myra with feeding the pigs, milking, or cleaning out the hen houses, she would have the sense both of revival and of purification. "At last I feel clean again!" she would exclaim; and Myra, looking at her soiled hands and mud-stained gum-boots, would hear the remark with astonishment. Returning to London afterwards was like wading back through a tunnel, the clammy walls of which closed round her, nearer and nearer, until she felt that she would suffocate.

"It's not convenient for Myra," Gwyneth said, still staring up at the ceiling.

"Well, whether it's convenient or not, I think she *ought* to have you. It's the least she can do." Christine rose to her feet and stared down at Gwyneth, clasping before her hands which had once been smooth and white, but were now roughened and seamed to ugliness by her work at the Club. "Have you quarrelled?" she asked.

"Oh, Mummy, do stop—do stop! These endless inquisitions!" Gwyneth put a hand over her face, and Christine noticed how violently it was trembling: "Can't you leave me alone? Leave me alone!"

"But darling, what have I said? What *have* I said?"

"Can't you understand that she might want—that there might be times . . . Oh, what's the good?"

"I'm sorry, dear. Gwyneth, I'm sorry." She sat beside her on the bed: but when she attempted to take her hand, Gwyneth snatched it away. "Dearest, what's the matter?"

"Everything is the matter. It's all horrible. Can't you see that? Can't you see how it is?"

"Well, of course, I know things aren't any too cheerful at the moment. . . . But there's this wonderful news from Italy,

159

and at any moment now they say that there's going to be a break-through and . . ."

"Oh, you and your silly, silly optimism!" Gwyneth had begun to laugh, and Christine laughed with her, until she realized that this was not real laughter, but hysteria. "Everything is always going to be all right, isn't it? And we're all happy, aren't we? And as soon as we win the war, dear Mr. Churchill's going to . . ." She broke off and, turning over, buried her face in the pillow.

"But, darling, things are not really so bad. After all, we still have each other—haven't we? And the war is nearly over. And we've had lots of good times. Lots and lots. Darling, you mustn't let yourself be got down by your work—or Myra's behaviour—or anything else. There's still so much we can enjoy, and there's going to be so much more. Everyone says that . . ."

Suddenly Gwyneth sat up in the bed, swinging her feet to the floor and gripping her mother's shoulders so firmly that Christine almost cried out in mingled pain and fear. She brought her face close, and suddenly asked: "Have you ever seen a child of eleven with the top of his head blown off? Have you? Have you? Have you? At each reiteration she shook her mother violently.

"Gwyneth!" Christine squirmed away, and half-stumbled, half-ran to the door. "What's the matter with you? What's come over you?"

Gwyneth threw herself once more on the pillows, digging her fingers into them and letting out stifled moan on moan.

"Darling, please! Please! . . . Look, I'm going to go and run you a hot bath. And you're going to go to bed, and I'm going to bring you up your supper. The fishmonger gave me some plaice, and I'm going to poach it for you. That's how you like it, isn't it? Now come along, darling." She patted Gwyneth's shaking shoulders and then ran her fingers over her hair. "Tim may be back soon, and we must be cheery for him. Come! Come, Gwyneth!"

She could not understand this terrible fury of despair, and, as she went into the bathroom and turned on the taps, she began to say to herself, "Over-tired, that's what it is," and later, "It's that wretched Myra woman." Like so many people during these years, she herself found life more intense, more enjoyable and more attractive than ever before: but, like most of these people, she would have been shocked if anyone told her so.

"Darling!" she called. "It's beautifully hot. And I'm going to give you that cake of Blue Grass soap which Colonel Liebman brought. Come along, darling! There's a good girl."

IV

Christine, who could remember a time when Adrian used to say to her when she was moving a chair or a bridge table: "Don't lift that, darling! You'll only go and strain yourself", was walking home with the shopping. Somewhere she had lost a glove, and her left hand, into the palm of which her string-bag was cutting, was blue and stiff with cold. Through the years of war she had become shabbier and shabbier: her stockings were now usually woollen or lisle above shoes which had rubbed into grey patches at each heel and cracked into grey wrinkles over each instep; no longer did she even bother to have her hats remodelled, as once, at Jones in the Earl's Court Road, or her suits turned and dyed; the only jewellery she wore, day after day, was a pearl necklace which had been Adrian's engagement present. Tim still used to exclaim that she must do something about her clothes: but now that she had the two excuses of coupons and the lack of time, in addition to the old excuse of shortage of money, she could ignore him with an easy conscience.

Her energy, at any other time, would have been thought remarkable: but she was only one of innumerable other middle-aged women who ran a household single-handed, did an exhausting daily job, and yet entertained on a scale unimaginable before the war. There were few nights when someone—a friend of Tim's on leave, an American from the Club, or one of her own friends up in town from the country—was not occupying the little room which had once been used only as a storing place for the ironing board, the sewing-machine, Tim's tennis-rackets and cricket-bats, and innumerable dusty papers and boxes. If Tim or Gwyneth was away, there might also be a second, or even a third guest. Often, in the evenings, there would be impromptu parties composed usually of people younger than herself: for Gwyneth's and Tim's friends, having been brought first by them, would continue to drop in, even if the children were not there. The Americans, who tended to be sentimental, would write to Christine when they were sent abroad and say that they had regarded the flat as a second home and her as a second mother. Some of them even called her "Mother", to the disgust and derision of Tim.

Christine was an affectionate woman, and she willingly gave her affection to these home-sick boys, who brought her unasked the presents which poor "Beddy" had to extract from them with so much labour. They found her sympathetic, gay and uncensorious; and even her inquisitiveness, which so maddened Tim and Gwyneth, they merely took for a sign of friendship—as indeed it was. Many of them would later be killed, and when she heard the news she would weep for them with a grief not profound, but nevertheless genuine. That recurrent nightmare of being cast out, unwanted and useless which, as the children grew up, obsessed her increasingly, had slowly begun to fade. "What would we do without you?" a young pilot once said to her as, late at night, she put up a camp-bed in the sitting-room and then went into the kitchen to prepare some supper for him. What she, in turn, would do without him was a question which, fortunately, she did not ask herself.

"How are you, Mrs. Bryce?" she now stopped to say to a portly woman with a fox-fur slung about her nigger-brown overcoat as though it were a sash. "Is the knee better?"

Mrs. Bryce, who found that nowadays it was difficult to come across people who had either the time or the patience to listen to all the details of the ailments with which she was afflicted, at once launched herself into a saga of swollen veins, elastic bandages and radiant-heat therapy. Christine listened sympathetically, as she usually listened on such occasions. "Ah, but you're so lucky!" Mrs. Bryce at last concluded. "You never seem to have a day's illness. You must be as strong as a horse. Why, to carry even one of those baskets would be quite impossible for me. The doctor won't even let me lift an ordinary breakfast-tray—in spite of this new belt I have to wear." She made a kind of gouging movement with one thumb at her waist. "I'm not altogether happy about it. I should so like to have a word with your daughter about it, when she's not too busy. Just to set my mind at rest."

Christine knew that Gwyneth would refuse such a discussion, except on a professional basis; and because this made her feel guilty she parted with her week's cheese ration to Mrs. Bryce before she said good-bye.

Outside the house she noticed, as she approached, that a black car was parked: and she remembered how Mrs. Campion had spoken, less than a week ago, about such a car, and how she herself had laughed at the idea and explained it was Jimmy Tomlins's. She quickened her pace. She liked Jimmy and he might even have brought Tim with him, although Tim had said he would not be due for another leave for at least ten days. But when she got nearer she realized that this black car, a Wolseley, was not the black car which Jimmy had been given on his twenty-first birthday; and that the driver was neither Jimmy himself nor one of his friends, but a man in policeman's uniform. The front door was open.

She mounted the stairs and, as she did so, she heard Mrs. Campion reiterate in a loud voice: "But he's not in, I tell you he's not in. He's not in!"

"Then please allow us to go into the flat." It was the voice, patient yet stubborn, of the detective who had come to call less than a week before. "Please, Mrs. Campion."

"Take your hands off me! Don't touch me! Don't you dare to touch me!"

"Mrs. Campion—will you please let us pass?"

Coming from the street, full of wintry sunlight, into the hall, Christine had an impression of three dark figures, their backs turned towards her, of a white smudge of a face and of another oblong smudge which was Mrs. Campion's bare arm, barring the doorway.

"Christine!" she called out. "Tell them he's not here. Tell them he's gone away. They won't believe me. Tell them, Christine."

But as she said this one of the men ducked under her arm, and could be heard clattering down the wooden stairs into the basement. Mrs. Campion's arm dropped as she cried out: "Stop! Come back!" and another of the men followed. The detective said doggedly: "We only want to question him. That's all. We only want to question him."

Simultaneously there was a sound of scuffling from below, and an inarticulate bellow, either of rage or of pain. Christine put down her two baskets and her string bag, and attempted herself to push between the detective and Mrs. Campion in order to go down to see what was happening. "What are they doing to him? Oh, what are they doing to him?" Mrs. Campion gripped her arm. "Oh, Christine, what are they doing?"

At that moment the Major shot up the stairs and through the door in nothing but a pair of greying pyjamas, with his pursuers thudding behind him. Panic-stricken, he glanced in turn at Mrs. Campion, at Christine, and at the detective; then, with a curious choking whimper, he dashed for the next flight, while another tenant, who had been looking down, leaning over the banister, rushed into her flat and slammed the door behind her. With extraordinary agility for someone of his age the detective leapt the stairs in twos and threes until, at the first turn, he succeeded in catching one of the Major's pyjama sleeves. The Major pulled, there was the sound of tearing cloth. Again the detective grabbed, and this time he caught the Major's elbow. The Major struck out: a feeble blow, such as a woman might give, which glanced off the other man's cheek. But it was enough to make him lose his temper. "So you would, would you? That's enough of that! Do you hear? That's enough of that!" He began to twist the Major's arm, while Mrs. Campion, in an attempt to go and pull him off, stumbled on the bottom stair and eventually scrambled to her feet without one of her slippers. Major Knott writhed and groaned; then, with a scream of mingled rage and agony, somehow managed to butt the other man with his head. Both of them swayed; clung to each other, as though for support; and then came crashing down, rolling over each other, until they hit the marble floor at Christine's and Mrs. Campion's feet.

Mrs. Campion put her hands to her ears, as though to shut out some noise to which she could not bear to listen, and then let out three short screams, one after the other. Dazed, the detective rolled over, and tottered first to his knees and then to his feet. He gazed down; blood was beginning to trickle out from one of his nostrils on to his moustache, and he was panting heavily.

Christine stopped and eased the Major's body over. "You've killed him," she said.

But at that moment she did not really believe it.

V

Tim, who had so often teased his mother about Reggie Benson, now began to tease her about Colonel Liebman.

She had met Reggie, who was filling a temporary and unimportant post in the War Office, at the Blackstones' cottage in Westerham, and the disappointment had been bitter. Eunice Blackstone had smiled and said: "We have a surprise for you. Reggie Benson is coming to tea." "Reggie!" "Yes, had you forgotten that he was a neighbour of ours?" "But he used to live——" "Oh, that was years ago—before his wife died."

Reggie looked immensely tall and thin, in spite of a stoop which gave him the appearance of perpetually scanning the lawn on which they were seated, in order to pick out a weed. His right sleeve, where his arm was missing, was carefully pinned up; the other hand, as he coped with his tea, was wonderfully agile. He talked to the dog, but little to anyone else, and when he was not talking had the habit of nervously clearing his throat two or three times in succession. He was living with one of his unmarried daughters, who also ran a smallholding, while he went up to London each day in order to work. He seemed dry, lethargic and passionless: until someone began to speak about the war, when, like a sudden squall which spends itself almost as soon as it is aroused, the topic galvanized him into a few minutes of eloquent ferocity. Such a man, one felt, would be capable of administering a gas chamber; and Christine recoiled.

He seemed to be far less interested in Christine than in some rose-cuttings which the Blackstones had promised him; but when they both tactfully went off on this errand, he turned to her and asked:

"Why did you never answer the letter I sent to you when your husband died?"

"I never got it," she said in astonishment.

"But you must have done."

"Truly I didn't."

He put out his long hand and once again patted the dog, while Christine wondered first whether he was lying and then whether he thought that she herself was lying.

"And here we are now."

"Here we are."

There was a silence, until their hostess returned to say in an over-bright voice: "The last time the four of us sat at tea together it was in Simla. And I shudder to think how long ago that was."

Christine, when she returned home that evening, told the children about the meeting: and though she joked about it, yet they both sensed her disappointment and sadness. "He used to be so handsome, so wonderfully handsome. And now he's stiff and rickety, with a long red nose, and eyes that keep on watering." She sighed: "I suppose he thought that I had altered in the same way." But she did not really suppose it, for she had never lost her vanity and often, looking in the glass, used to congratulate herself on her unwrinkled skin and changeless features.

Tim came up behind where she was sitting, and put his hands on her shoulders: "You'd do much better to forget him and concentrate on the Colonel. You don't want to marry a retired Indian Army captain with a small pension, one arm and a red nose—especially as he has all those daughters. Do you?"

"Oh, really, Tim!" she giggled. "Isn't he awful?"

"Whereas Colonel Liebman—what could be better? He has only two children and both of them are married. You'd be mistress of his duplex, his Studebaker, and that washing-machine which will take—how many plates did he say? Really I can't remember."

"You mustn't make fun of him. He's such a kind man."

"There you are—you see! You're sentimental about him. I knew that you were."

"Don't be silly, darling. In the first place I wouldn't want to go to America and leave my two children. And in the second place, I'm sure that he's not in the least bit interested. We're good friends, that's all."

But, secretly, during this period when she so often accompanied him to theatres or dances and he came to the flat, she had found herself wondering how their friendship might end. She suspected that he was physically attracted by her; and, for the first time since Adrian's death, she was conscious of herself being physically attracted by a man. He had large, brown hands, which Tim had jokingly supposed he must also hold under his ultra-violet lamp, and she would catch herself looking at them, deriving pleasure from the gold watch-strap against the darker skin, the golden hairs which grew in tufts beneath each knuckle, and the broad, carefully tended nails. He danced easily and gracefully, and beneath his uniform his thighs and legs were as hard and muscular as those of a young man. Only his close-cropped, stiff grey hair and the skin of his face, which was beginning to sag and grow flabby under its tan, betrayed his real age. Like so many Americans, he had a passionate and dedicated reverence for youth; and one of the reasons why he so enjoyed being invited to the flat was that he there met, not his, but Tim's contemporaries. Tim he adored; and the overt mockery with which Tim so often repaid him could only intensify that adoration. Tim flew, whereas he was too old to do so; Tim could race up the stairs to the flat without any of the panting to which he himself would succumb at the top; Tim did not need to do exercises every morning to prevent his stomach and pectoral muscles from sagging, or to lie under a lamp in order to tone up his skin.

Liebman did not speak a great deal when he was in the company of Tim and his friends. He would lie outstretched in a chair, his legs wide open and his trousers rucked up, so that two or three inches of his bare shins would be visible, while he sucked at one of the midget cigars which he offered, usually unsuccessfully, to the other men. "That's right," he put in occasionally in his deep, attractive drawl, or, "You've said it, fellah!" He was always the first to chuckle at one of their jokes, and always the last to leave.

Alone with Christine, on the other hand, he became voluble; and she had to confess that she was even more bored by his

167

conversation than by his silences. He was wholly without any powers of selection and could not, for example, give an opinion of a play without first recounting to her every detail of his journey to the theatre. Never was there any variation of pace or of volume; and when she interjected a remark in the hope of forcing him to a short cut, he would merely listen politely and then go on: "Well, as I was saying . . ." He seemed to fear to be alone with her, usually preferring parties of four, to which he would invite a friend and she would invite Beddy or one of the other women at the Club: and this she would alternately interpret as being a favourable and an unfavourable omen.

With the shyness of an undergraduate, he would from time to time pay her a compliment, squeeze her hand, or ease his knee against hers while they were dining or in a taxi. But what was odd was that, in spite of that apparent shyness, he would usually make such demonstrations of affection, not when they were alone, but when others were present. At first, when he said good night, he would only shake her hand, in spite of Major Oppenheim's attempts to kiss "Beddy" and her excited squeals of response; but later he got into the habit of putting his lips, which were moist and wonderfully soft, to her cheek for a brief moment, murmuring as he did so something like: "Well, good night, sweetie. It's been loads of fun."

She used sometimes to talk to him about her own anxieties for the children; but, although he listened attentively, with exclamations like "Well, for heaven's sake!" or "Oh, you poor little thing!" he never had any other comments to make or advice to offer, except on one occasion when he said: "Well, I think you have been a wonderful mother to those children. Truly, Christine, I do. Wonderful." But he was a little drunk then, as he often became at the end of an evening.

Eventually he was transferred from London to an aerodrome in East Anglia, but he still came up to see her and his friends, staying usually at the Club, but sometimes at a hotel or even at the flat, if one of the children were there. Then he announced that he was expecting to be sent abroad, and, since he was also about to have a birthday, Christine decided to give a party for him. It was a week-end when she expected Tim home, but when Gwyneth would be away staying with Myra: Gwyneth was usually uncomfortable both with her mother's friends and with the Americans, and in turn spread a feeling of discomfort among them.

There were bottles of Algerian wine and beer which Christine had bought; and bottles of whisky and gin which were presents from her guests. Christine had made a chocolate cake, which tasted like sweetened cotton-wool, out of an American packet-mix, which was also a present. They played party games, acted charades, and eventually rolled back the carpet in order to dance. Everyone, except Christine, had already drunk too much; and everyone, except her, was in a mood of wild hilarity. She felt depressed: Tim had telephoned to say that he could not get away, although she suspected that he would get away to "P.", and Warren Liebman was leaving and she might never see him again. But she forced herself to dance as energetically, to dress herself as absurdly, and to talk and laugh as loudly as any of her guests. Eventually, at midnight, she went into the kitchen to fry some eggs, which Myra had sent her, and some tinned bacon. She was alone and it annoyed her that none of her guests, not even "Beddy", had followed her to help. But then suddenly, as she was heating the pan, Warren lurched in through the door.

"Let me give you a hand," he said thickly.

"Oh, it's quite unnecessary."

"Please, Christine, please."

"Well, if you insist—perhaps you could get us down some plates from the rack? . . . Oh, Warren!"

He had dropped the second of the plates and it now lay in pieces.

"Doesn't matter," he said. "Don't worry. I'll give you another. What is it—is it valuable?" He peered at the largest of the pieces of utility china, swaying as he did so.

"Of course not. You don't have to replace it. Especially after all those presents you've brought."

He had arrived with his car loaded with presents, not merely for her, but for Tim and Gwyneth, "Beddy", and even Mrs. Campion, whom he had never met, but whose story Christine had told him. He was, as people never ceased to say, kind, wonderfully kind.

Carefully now he took down the plates one by one, and then, when he had stacked them all on the kitchen table with the concentration of someone building a house of cards, he came over to the stove and put an arm round her waist. "Lovely party," he said.

"It has been fun, hasn't it?"

"And a lovely, lovely hostess." He put those moist soft lips to her cheek, and then, as though emboldened by her lack of opposition, to one temple and eventually her mouth. "I shall miss you," he said, in a voice which was husky from either emotion or drink.

"And I you."

"We've had some good times together. Haven't we?"

"Very good."

"You've been a real pal. You know, I didn't care much for England until I met you. Honest I didn't."

He kissed her again on the lips, swaying a little as he held her in his arms, and this time she responded with ardour. "Oh, Warren, shall I ever see you again? Shall I ever see you again?"

"Well, of course you will, sweetie."

"But won't you forget me?"

"Forget you! Say, are you kidding?" The smell of whisky, heavy on his breath, mingled with that of soap. "Is it likely?"

"This bacon will get burnt. And what will the others think?"

When she went back into the sitting-room, carrying a tray, her gaiety was no longer forced and artificial. Her face and neck were flushed, as though she had just woken up, and there was an extraordinary, almost feverish, brilliance about her eyes as she gazed round the disordered room where couples sat on the floor on cushions, their arms about each other, or little groups, usually male, conversed secretively in corners.

"Take care, Warren," she warned, as he followed behind her, with a tray of coffee-cups. "Don't drop them."

"Say, I'm not all that high!"

"Christine is the only Englishwoman who knows how to make a decent cup of coffee," Major Oppenheim declared tactlessly, since "Beddy" never tired of reiterating: "Of course Oppy says that ours is the only English home where you can get a decent coffee."

Christine refused the cup which Warren offered to her, and instead took a glass of whisky, her first of the evening, which she rapidly drained. After two more she was joining in a square dance, and after three she had to sit down, on the sofa beside Warren Liebman, who at once put an arm round her waist. "You look lovely," he drawled. "Like a million dollars. I want to whisper something to you." He leant over and put his lips to her ear: "I love you," he said; and gave her a kiss.

At last the guests began to leave: some were singing, some swayed arm in arm, one slipped and went down the first flight of stairs as though his overcoat were a toboggan. "Lovely party, Christine"; "Christine, that was marvellous"; "What about a good-night kiss from Mother?" . . . Then the laughter and the noise of cars faded below the windows, and she and he were alone.

Christine began to pick up cups and glasses from the floor and the tables, and to place them on a tray. Although she was tipsy, she was sober enough to be disgusted by the cigarette-ash and burnt-out matches that either littered the carpet or floated on the dregs of wine, whisky or coffee; by the rings, like dents in the occasional tables and on top of the book-cases, where glasses had stood; by the stale smell of smoke, drink and human bodies perspiring in a mass.

Warren was staring at her, as he undid his tunic and loosened his tie, his head lolling back on the sofa, from which the cushions had been thrown on to the floor. "Stop that," he said. "Come and sit down." Christine flung up one window, and then another, making him exclaim: "Christ! Can't we do without that blizzard."

Her head was throbbing, her eyes smarting from the cigarette-smoke, and her back and legs aching. She went and sat beside him. "You'll never get into a hotel if you leave it much later."

"Who says I'm going to get into a hotel? Can't I spend the night here?" He threw her over and began to kiss her until, as though terrified by the force with which she gripped his muscular shoulders and put her lips to his, he jerked her sideways so that her head was on his shoulder. "Well, what about it?" he asked.

"Why not?"

"That's my girl." He pulled off his tunic, and then began to loosen the laces of his shoes, cursing under his breath when he had to pick at a knot caused by his own fumbling.

"Warren," she said. All at once, feeling completely sober, she was overcome by a sense of desolation and bleakness, as though the ice-laden wind which she had let loose in the frowsty, sealed flat had also been let loose within her. She caressed his hand, and then put it to her lips. "Warren—you know, this is the first time . . . the first time since . . ." But he had dragged her over to his own inert body, and the rest of what she wished to say was stifled by his tongue. As a lover he was completely inadequate. "Drunk too much—that's the trouble. . . . Drunk too much," he mumbled. But desperately he went on draining glass after glass of whisky, picking the bottle up from the floor, where he had placed it under the bed, and splashing it into the tumbler so that it went over his shaking hand and over the bedclothes. Everything seemed to smell of whisky to Christine: Warren himself, the bed, even the air she breathed. Then all at once, exhausted, he began to sob on her shoulder in mingled frustration and shame, clinging drunkenly to her and still reiterating: "That liquor . . . that goddam liquor . . .", and later: "Next time, I'll show you. . . . You wait . . . another time. . . ." Eventually he fell asleep.

She put her lips to his forehead, which was as moist with sweat as his cheeks were with tears and his hands with the whisky he had splashed on to them. She caressed his shoulders, the two muscular squares which divided his chest, and then the flesh which, in spite of all his exercising, was just beginning to subside into a paunch below his narrow waist. "Warren," she whispered. "Warren, I love you." But he began to snore, and a few minutes later, unable any longer to hold up the weight of his body against hers, she eased him down on to the pillows. The wind blowing through the open windows of the sitting-room and on into the hall, was making the door rattle and shake. She began to tremble in spite of having him so near her, and soon her teeth were chattering.

Much later, when she had managed to doze off, she was aware of his rising from the bed with a groan and fumbling on a chair for his underclothes. He went out, and up the stairs to the bathroom. Her American friends never ceased to tease her about the plumbing of the flat, and now, as she lay listening, she heard first the plug being pulled and then the sound of water being run into the bath and of his splashing about in it. After that she heard him creak down the stairs again and go into the sitting-room. She waited: but when he did not return to her, she got up and found him curled up on the sofa, with his body covered up inadequately with his greatcoat, a coat of Gwyneth's, which had been hanging in the hall, and a number of cushions. She fetched two blankets and put them over him too.

After that she did not sleep: she felt exhausted, her whole body aching as though she had been physically beaten; she felt icily cold, and she was filled with a terrible remorse and nausea. Yet at the same time she could not stop thinking about that extraordinarily youthful body; and of all that promise which, pathetically, he had been unable to fulfil.

At dawn she heard him again go upstairs and again the bath was run: "Well! Good morning," he said brightly, when she went out in her dressing-gown, to meet him as he descended. "I didn't mean you to get up at this hour. But I've got to be back at the station by nine." She touched his arm, intending to draw him to her; but with the briefest of pecks on her forehead, he went into the kitchen: "I wonder if those socks are dry. I washed them out last night and put them near the stove."

She got him some breakfast, and sat down opposite him with a cup of coffee, as he gobbled his eggs and bacon. She wanted to talk to him about the night before; to tell him that it didn't matter and that there would always be other times; to joke with him about going to sleep on the sofa under all those cushions, when he could have had the spare room: to assure him that her affection for him had not changed. But as he munched the crisp bacon and swilled from the cup of coffee which she kept on replenishing for him, talking as he did so about the journey ahead of him, a look in his eyes, at once furtive, guilty and frightened, kept her from saying any of these things.

"Well, I guess it's good-bye, sweetie."

"Good-bye, Warren. Let me hear from you."

"Sure, sure. As soon as I get there, you'll hear. And thanks—thanks a lot."

"Thank you, my dear."

"Well, so long!"

She put her arms over his shoulders, so that he had to kiss her: at first perfunctorily on the cheek, and then, no less perfunctorily, on the lips she put to his.

"All the best!" he shouted out, all at once sounding cheerful as he clattered down the stairs. "And thanks—thanks again!"

173

She went back into the sitting-room and began to tidy up the sofa where he had slept; lodged down one side she found a ball of kleenex tissue. On the floor there stood a whisky bottle with less than two fingers of whisky in it. She put her lips to the mouth and tipped the bottle backwards. She felt that she needed it.

VI

Myra's land-girl was ill, and to their astonishment Mrs. Campion had undertaken the milking during the week-end which she was spending with Christine at the farm.

"But *can* you milk?" Myra asked.

"Well, of course I can. I imagine that it must be like riding a bicycle—once one has learned, one has learned. I spent my childhood in the country," she added, as she tugged at a pair of Myra's gum-boots, obviously too small for her. "The only question is—how on earth can I get these on?"

In the end Myra found another pair of boots that had belonged to a man she had employed for a few weeks before his call-up, and in these Mrs. Campion at last strode off, a pail in either hand and a tattered raincoat flapping around her. Over her head she had tied a red square of Christine's pirate-wise, so that even her eyebrows were hidden. Since the Major's death, she had become increasingly eccentric and unamiable, and now Christine was the only person whom she would ever admit to her flat or whose flat she would enter. That Christine had been able to persuade her to come away for this week-end had astonished them all; especially Myra, who had only given the invitation in the expectation that it would be refused.

Behind Mrs. Campion the dachshund, Fritzy, waddled along.

"Fritzy!" called Myra, and again "Fritzy! Come here!" Then she shouted out: "Oh, Mrs. Campion, please don't take the dog into the cow-house." But Mrs. Campion either did not, or would not, hear. "Oh, blast the woman! I've told her to keep that bloody little dog of hers out of the cow-house, time and time again. He *will* worry the cat and the kittens."

She began to hurry away in the direction in which Mrs. Campion had gone, and Christine and Gwyneth followed. "Hell!" From the cow-house they could hear the excited yapping of Fritzy, and Mrs. Campion shouting: "Fritzy! Naughty boy! Naughty boy! Leave pussy alone! Fritzy do you hear me? That's enough, Fritzy."

Myra snatched at the broom which was resting against the cow-house, and rushed in; after which the yapping turned into a series of squeals, followed by a cry from Mrs. Campion "Stop! Stop that at once! Stop that, you wicked woman!" and Fritzy bolted out, his tail between his legs. Christine and Gwyneth arrived a moment later: in one hand Mrs. Campion was holding the two pails, which clanked together at every movement, while with the other hand she was struggling to wrest the broom from Myra's grasp. "You're a thoroughly wicked and cruel woman!" she was saying in fury, as the two of them swayed back and forth. "To hit a poor, defenceless creature like that. . . . How would you like it if I . . .?" The cat, its back arched, was staring at them from a disused manger, in which its kittens were curled. "I've got a good mind to . . ." At that the broom snapped between both their hands.

"Gladys! Gladys!" Christine went between them. "Don't be so silly. Myra only wanted to stop Fritzy from killing the kittens. That's natural enough, isn't it?"

"Well, she can do her own milking now!" Mrs. Campion dropped the pails one after the other on to the concrete floor. "If Fritzy's not wanted, then I'm not wanted either. It's better for everyone concerned if we take ourselves off—far better."

She pulled the square from her head, and tossed it over one of the partitions between the stalls. "The N.S.P.C.A. would have something to say to behaviour like that. Beating a poor little dog, that never harmed anyone, with a broom . . ." She strode off, shouting over her shoulder, and Christine pursued her.

Myra began to laugh: "The woman must be mad. Absolutely mad. If she really imagines that I'd let that horrid little lap-dog of hers devour Suzy's kittens, and not say a word! The only bore is that I shall have to do the milking myself—unless I can

175

persuade Fuller to lend me one of his girls for the job. I'd better telephone.''

Christine pursued Mrs. Campion up to her bedroom, where she was flinging her few belongings into a canvas bag. "What do you want?" she demanded, when Christine walked in, after having knocked and received no answer.

"Come along, Gladys. There's no need to take this so seriously. It was natural enough for her to . . ."

"Natural! If you think it's natural to lay about a poor little creature who . . ." Fritzy was crouched under the bed, with only the tip of his nose appearing. "Look at him! Just look at him! He's terrified." She raised the bedspread: "Look how he's trembling.''

"He did attack the cat," Christine reminded her.

"He only barked at her, he never did anything else. There was no need for her to behave in that hysterical way, picking up a broom . . ." Savagely, Mrs. Campion pushed her night-dress into the bag and then thrust her slippers on top of it. "For the sake of that daughter of yours, you'll stomach anything. I won't!''

Christine continued to reason with her; but she would only cry out: "No, no! It's no good! Unless she's prepared to apologize, I shall go! Yes, I shall go! It's no good, don't try to prevent me! Simply because you're willing to smarm up to her in order to get invited down here, don't imagine that I'll do the same. No. No. Christine! No!" until Christine at last decided to go downstairs to find Myra.

Myra was seated at the telephone, one of her trousered legs resting high over the other, while, with the index-finger of her right hand, she rattled irritably at the cradle of the telephone. During these years on the land, her hair had turned as grey as Christine's own, and though the rest of her body was as gaunt as it had been, her stomach had begun to bulge and her hips to thicken. Gwyneth stood beside her. "Hell!" Myra ex-claimed. "What's the matter with this telephone? I can't get a sound out of it." She slammed the receiver down, and then kicked out at the edge of the carpet where it had got rucked. "It's extraordinary, Gwyneth, how carpets tend to curl up wherever you've walked.''

Christine said: "Myra, she's determined to leave. I've just been up to her room, and she's almost done her packing.''

176

"Well, good riddance!"

"I think . . ." Christine faltered—embarrassed—"I think she could be persuaded to stay."

"I daresay she could."

"She's really sorry for making that scene. But you know how eccentric she's grown, ever since his death. I think if you—if you went up to her, she'd appreciate it most enormously."

"*I* go up to *her!*" Myra jumped to her feet, pulling her jersey down over her little paunch. "Well, I must say the woman's got a cheek. Why should I go up to her? Why?"

"I suppose it's a question of face," Christine said feebly.

"I could slap her face, good and proper, for her." Myra threw herself down once more beside the telephone, and again began to rattle the cradle, repeating "Hello, hello! Operator!" in mounting irritation. "Oh, damn!"

"You are hard, Myra," Gwyneth said slowly. "You're one of the hardest people I know."

"Not at all. But I have no patience with silliness and mush. No one could say that I was unkind or . . ."

"I'm not saying that. But your sympathies are—well, limited. Let's face it."

"Yes, they are limited, if you mean that I have no sympathy for a crack-brained and disagreeable old woman who seems to have completely forgotten that it was I who not merely invited her down here but who even paid for the ticket which brought her. No, I have no sympathy with that sort of thing; I've no time for it. When I think of all the deserving people who would show a little gratitude for what one tried to do for them . . ."

"Must kindness always be repaid with gratitude?"

"Oh, I agree that it very rarely is." Again Myra rattled at the telephone, and then turned to exclaim: "Oh, really, Gwyneth! When there's a perfectly good scraper and a mat outside the door, is it necessary for you to come into the house with most of the cow-shed sticking to your soles?"

Christine stared in turn at Myra and Gwyneth: all that day they had been bickering in this fashion. Each of them found, in the other, certain failings at which to pick as though they were sores, and it seemed as if they exaggerated precisely these failings in themselves in a stubborn desire to annoy. Myra, Gwyneth declared, was callous, ruthless and cold in her efficiency; Gwyneth, according to Myra, was sloppy, graceless

177

and clumsy. Both of these accusations contained an element of truth. But Myra seemed to grow even harder when Gwyneth told her she was hard; and Gwyneth, when Myra pointed out she could touch nothing without its breaking, almost at once dropped a cup or knocked over a table-lamp by lurching into it. Christine sensed that for each of them to cause annoyance to, and to be annoyed by, the other, had become a destructive need; and by this she was both puzzled and frightened, as she had long been puzzled and frightened by their whole relationship.

"You seem to forget how much the poor old thing has suffered," Gwyneth pursued. "Much more than any of us in this wretched war."

"Could you possibly be quiet for one moment while I put through this call? Those poor cows can hardly be feeling comfortable."

At this moment Mrs. Campion could be heard thud-thudding down the wooden stairs, with Fritzy's paws scratching behind her. When he saw Myra, Fritzy at once scuttled into the sitting-room and from there leapt on to a window-seat and escaped into the garden. Without saying a word, Mrs. Campion marched past the three women and went to the front door; but she was so loaded with her canvas bag, two brown-paper parcels, a knitting-bag and a brief-case that had once belonged to the Major, that she could not get out until she had freed a hand.

"You're not going, are you?" Gwyneth said. "Please, Mrs. Campion! Do stay!"

"Would you let me pass, please?"

"But, Mrs. Campion . . ."

"Let me pass." One of the brown-paper parcels fell to the floor, as she attempted to tuck it under her arm; and when she stooped to pick it up, the other fell too. "Let me pass, Gwyneth!" she cried.

"Now, really, Gladys . . ." Christine interposed, putting an arm round her shoulders.

Mrs. Campion wrenched herself away, and the satchel joined the two parcels. "Open the door!" she commanded.

"Well, I'll come to the station with you," Christine said, realizing that, without the apology which Myra refused to give, the old woman would never be dissuaded. She opened the door. "But just wait while I put on my coat and hat."

"I don't want anyone to come to the station with me. I'm perfectly happy as I am. In fact I'd rather be on my own—much rather." Mrs. Campion stooped and, having hitched up the various fallen packages, then straightened herself and marched out into the wintry dusk. "Gladys, wait!" Christine called. "Wait for me!" Then, as she saw Mrs. Campion stride away down the drive, she raced to her room, pulled on her coat and hurried in pursuit.

At first in the mist she could not see the old woman at all; but then she heard her calling: "Fritzy! Fritzy, love! Where are you? Where have you got to?" A note of panic entered her voice, as if it were she who were lost, and not the dog. "Fritzy! Fritzy! Come here! Good boy!" she wailed.

Christine came on her at the same moment as Fritzy whisked out of one of the straggly laurels that flanked the drive, his snout covered with earth and his wagging tail scattering drops of water to left and right as he trotted up to his mistress. Mrs. Campion at once began to scold him: "Wicked Fritzy! Naughty Fritzy! Does Fritzy want smackies?"

"Do give me some of these things to carry," Christine said.

"I can manage perfectly well, thank you. Please go back to the others."

"Don't be silly, Gladys."

Christine attempted to take the canvas bag and one of the parcels, but Mrs. Campion pulled away, backing into the laurel-bush from which Fritzy had emerged. For a while the two women tugged, much as Myra and Mrs. Campion had tugged at the broom; but on this occasion Mrs. Campion at last relented: "Well, if you insist," she grunted.

They walked on in silence, while the mist, clammy and chill, closed in around them. After a while Mrs. Campion said in a deep and mournful voice:

"I knew that it was a mistake to come. I never liked that woman. It was a mistake all along for Gwyneth to get involved with her."

"She's been very good to Gwyneth."

"Oh, she likes to buy people with that money of hers! As she bought her husband. And as she wanted to buy me."

"That's not just, Gladys. She's an extremely kind woman. I used once to feel about her as you do now, but I've come to see that she can be a very good friend. No, Gladys, that's not just. Not just at all."

Mrs. Campion snorted: and although Christine knew that it was not just, yet it had given her a furtive pleasure to hear her friend say such things about Myra.

"Yes, it was a mistake to come," Mrs. Campion went on, striding ahead so rapidly that both Christine and Fritzy, who was plump and no longer young, had difficulty in keeping up with her. "I learned that lesson long ago from life—it's best not to rely on anyone. But this time I forgot it. To my cost." She was wearing a raincoat which had belonged to the Major, a beret which she herself had crocheted out of some wool left over from some socks she had knitted for Tim, and over her long, pointed shoes a pair of rubber boots which squelched with each swinging pace. "It's best to be alone. No, I mean it, Christine. Another woman—a woman like you—would be miserable at never seeing her children. You would, wouldn't you? But I'm not. I'm glad! I don't want to be under any obligation to anybody. I don't want anyone to rely on me." She sang out this declaration with a kind of savage joy, setting her long face, with the hooked red nose, sideways and upwards to the wind that blew icily towards them. "It's better to stand on one's own feet, in one's own place."

"That's not a very kind thing to say to an old friend," Christine remonstrated.

"Oh, you!" Mrs. Campion exclaimed.

"And what about Fritzy?"

"Fritzy, thank the Lord, is not a human being. He doesn't talk."

"But you talk to him," Christine reminded her with a laugh. "And you once said that he understood everything."

Mrs. Campion shifted one of the parcels from her right to her left hand. "If those children of mine came back on their bended knees to ask for my forgiveness, I'd—I'd shut the door in their faces."

Christine had never heard about the children from Mrs. Campion herself: but there had been gossip. "Beddy" said that there were two of them, a son who was now a naval captain and a daughter who had married and was mistress of what she called "a lovely home somewhere in Wales"; they had quarrelled with their mother when she had left their dying father

180

in order to live with a man at least twenty years her junior, and since then they had neither forgiven, nor been forgiven by her. So much for "Beddy's" story; but Christine knew that, when she did not positively lie, Beddy exaggerated, and it was wise to discount most of what she told one.

"You know, I don't even know how many children you have. You've never spoken to me about them."

"Is there any reason why I should?"

"None whatever. Except that it would interest me to know."

"You and that awful Miss Bedworth ought to have been novelists—or private detectives. You have such an extraordinary interest in what is no concern of yours."

Christine laughed, for she was no longer hurt or annoyed by such remarks. "But I *do* feel that you're a concern of mine."

"Anyway, the children have long since ceased to concern me, so why should they concern you? I last saw them twelve years ago," she added.

"And don't you ever correspond?"

"Never."

"Are they doing well for themselves?"

"Very—by all accounts. They were always ambitious." She was obviously unwilling to divulge anything further.

At the station Mrs. Campion had an altercation with a youthful porter who objected first to Fritzy sitting beside her on a leather settee in the first-class waiting-room, and then, when she told him to mind his own business, to their being in the first-class waiting-room at all. But she refused to budge either the dog or herself.

"Well, I'll see you to-morrow afternoon," Christine said, as Mrs. Campion climbed into a non-smoking compartment and reminded the only occupant that he ought not to be smoking. At the same time she settled Fritzy in a corner seat. "Please tell Major Van Wyze, will you?" One of the Americans from the Club had been lent the flat for the two days that Christine was away.

"I cannot understand your allowing that young man—whom you hardly know—to use your flat as a . . ." But the train whistled and jolted at this moment, and the last word became, perhaps fortunately, inaudible.

Christine began to walk back briskly. All the week she had an irrational feeling of optimism and buoyancy such as many

181

people experienced during that last winter of the war against Germany, and nothing—the silence of Colonel Leibman after his departure from the country, the quarrels of Myra and Gwyneth, and now this scene with Mrs. Campion—was able to destroy it. For so long the war had seemed to be endless; and now the end was in sight. What would follow that end she no more considered than Adrian had considered what would follow his operation; it was enough to survive. That survival never ceased to astonish her, when she thought back, as she did now, crossing the fields in a short-cut to the house, and remembered the bombings, the fears of starvation, the threat of invasion, and always that struggle to "Keep a home for the children" whatever else might happen. She had expended capital as recklessly as she had expended energy; but both the home and she had come through. Climbing over a stile, she began to sing to herself *"Du bist die Ruh"*: shockingly out of tune, since, unlike Gwyneth and Tim, she had no ear for music.

As she crunched up the drive, still singing, a voice called to her through the mist: "Mummy, Mummy! Is that you?"

"Yes, darling, what is it?"

She heard Gwyneth running towards her, and she sensed even then that something was wrong: no doubt the bickering had flared up into a real quarrel, and now she would have to try to reconcile them as she had tried, and failed, to reconcile Mrs. Campion and Myra.

Gwyneth's hand, chilly and damp, closed on hers under the dripping laurels. "Bad news," she panted. "Major Van Wyze has been trying to telephone us all afternoon. He's only just got through."

"Tim! Tell me, tell me!"

"He's all right, but he's—he's badly wounded. Shot down over the North Sea, but thank God they picked him up. No, he's all right—all right!" She gripped her mother's shoulder. "He's in hospital in Harwich. Myra will drive you there. I've just been throwing your things into your case, while she's getting out the car. He's all right!" she repeated so vehemently that it sounded as if she were angry. "But we must get started at once!"

VII

The giant grey grub was slung by straps over the bed, with a violet face upturned to the shaded light which its lidless eyes could not see through a thick mass of gauze. Consciousness flickered in and out of the swaddled head, bringing a renewal of agonies that were then alleviated with the prick of a needle and a further sleep crowded with nightmares of diving headlong into a pit of flame with fingerless hands and eyelids sewn together. Sometimes the grub would be aware of people about it; and sometimes it would even scream out when hands tugged at its mask or whipped away the violet deposit from the charred skin beneath.

Christine sat beside the grub, and sometimes Gwyneth sat with her. When the grub moaned or attempted to wriggle in its harness, she would say: "Darling, keep still! Keep still! It's me! It's Mummy!" But the grub either did not hear or did not understand her. Then she would cry out: "Oh, nurse, nurse! Please come and help him!" There were some nurses, middle-aged, grey-haired women, usually with Irish accents, who touched the grub and moved it about as though it were something inanimate like a mattress, often talking at the same time about the latest "break-through"—it was a time of break-throughs—or of the possible fate of "Him". But there were other nurses, young girls who turned out to have been students at the Royal Academy of Dramatic Art or the London School of Economics, daughters of clergymen, barristers, or stock-brokers, who could hardly bear to look at the grub and would handle it with their eyes averted, as though they were engaged on some shameful task.

Since the grub did not seem to hear her, Christine longed to touch it in order to comfort it in its terror and pain. But she could not put her lips to the grub's face, for she would only have put them to that thick wad of gauze; and it was impossible to touch the grub's hands, since each was compressed between what appeared to be two squash-rackets. She thought the grub would die: but when she said this to the glum doctor, who turned out to have once been an assistant of Sir Noël Hope-Ashburn, he said tetchily: "No, no, we shall pull him through." Then he added: "First we must let that burnt skin heal. Afterwards we can start the beauty treatment."

This was a period of insensibility for the grub, like that when it had been hooked wriggling out of the North Sea, too frozen for its nerves to send their futile messages of agony to its brain. But the agony had followed, as it now followed again when the prick of the needle became less and less frequent, the sounds around it more and more insistent, and it began to be able to make out that voice which so often repeated: "Darling, Mummy's with you. Mummy's here. It's going to be all right."

On the second day, when the mask had been scraped off and the glum doctor was picking with an instrument like a silver tooth-pick at what had once been the grub's nose, Christine, who had been asked to sit out in the corridor, suddenly heard a series of reiterated but muffled screams, all on one note, like those with which she used to be woken that summer before the war. The sounds at first seemed as inarticulate as the yelping of an animal in a trap, until she made out what the grub was trying to say:

"Pat! Pat! Pat!"

Gwyneth, who was also in the corridor, said: "He's calling for her. Of course we ought to have told her." She gripped her mother's shoulder, for she thought that Christine too was going to cry out in the same unbearable agony which her brother was suffering.

VIII

The omelet, which had obviously been made of dried egg, was brought by a stiff-backed waitress with rickety legs that looked like creosoted poles in their black stockings. "I've brought you a little surprise," she said, indicating a curl of bacon beside the omelet with the grimy murderer's thumb of the hand on which the plate was balanced. "I'm sorry I haven't one for your daughter too."

"We'll share it," Christine said. "Thank you so much."

"What news of the boy? . . . Oo, you've been real gluttons

184

for the marmalade, haven't you? We'll have to replenish that."
She picked up the marmalade jar and hugged it to her bony
chest with one hand, while with the other she pushed the
mustard pot across the table to Christine. "Is he better?" she
asked.

"Oh, yes, much better."

"A lot of pain, I expect. Poor dear."

"That's passing."

"That friend of my brother's—you remember I told you
about his accident, didn't I?—well, of course, those were
sulphuric-acid burns. He said that the worst came after the
first week; the healing, I expect. Oh, he had a terrible
time—sometimes he'd scream for a whole hour on end. You
don't want this toast, do you? I'll bring you some fresh." She
giggled maliciously: "We'll give it to old Mr. Redface Rawson,
shall we? That'll teach him not to shout for his food." If one
looked under her small, tight, straw-curls, one had the feeling
that one would find white cotton stitches, as on a doll, to hold
them in place: her cap, worn at a jaunty angle, also seemed
to have been stitched to her scalp—when she bent stiffly over,
to pick up the spoons, knives and forks that were always
scattering from the plates that she carried, it never budged an
inch.

She went away, and Christine attempted to force mouthful
after mouthful of the omelet down her throat; but it was as if
she were swallowing sand. The waitress was soon back.

"Of course it's marvellous what they do, isn't it? This man
Mc-something—you know who I mean. He's a real artist, they
say. I was reading something about it somewhere. Of course
they never look the *same*, but in some cases I dare say that they
even look better!" She giggled, as though she had made a joke.
"Well, that friend of Harry's. His wife told me 'of course I'd
recognize him anywhere, anyhow, but a lot of his old pals
don't'. Mind you, not that he looks *bad* any longer. You
wouldn't even know that anything had happened to him—
except that the skin looks a bit stretched like, and it's rather
an odd colour. But they say that'll pass. . . . Oo, just take a
look at our Mr. Redface," she bent over the table to hiss at
them. "You wouldn't believe the dirt in his room. I've often
told Miss Pritchard that I wouldn't be surprised if that room
of his was *infested*. Have you noticed the bites on the back of

185

his neck? They're bites—no pimples ever looked like that."
Mr. Rawson's arrival had been merciful; and now, as he began
banging with his fork on the side of his empty cup, in order
to attract the waitress's attention, she reluctantly left Christine
and Gwyneth, hissing: "At your service, my lord!" as she
teetered across the room.

Christine looked at her watch: "Her train must be late."

"Are any trains ever on time now?"

"Thank goodness he's being moved from here to-morrow.
I don't feel I can stand this hotel or that hospital a moment
longer."

"Oh, they try to be kind."

"Yes, they try. But what's the good of kindness if it has to
be so clumsy? I prefer Miss Hawsley"—this was the disagreeable, sharp-tongued sister in charge of Tim—"to any of
those girls who keep saying how sad it all is and go around
with tears in their eyes, and yet can't touch him without making
him want to scream. I expect that he prefers Miss Hawsley
too—even though she bullies and bosses him."

"There's your fresh toast, dear," the waitress said, executing
a little pirouette and depositing a plate before them. Gwyneth
took a piece, and found that it had been toasted on only one
side.

"That's what I mean," Christine said. "So kind and so
useless."

Miss Pritchard, the manageress, was weaving her way between the tables, nodding to right and left as though she were
performing an exercise for reducing her double-chin, which
swayed and wobbled with her as she walked. "For you, Mrs.
Cornwell, dear," she called out. "Your visitor has arrived."

Christine rose: "I'd better see her alone," she said to
Gwyneth. "At first. Then I'll bring her in for some breakfast."

"In the lounge, dear," Miss Pritchard said. "Her room isn't
ready yet. I'm just sending the girl up with the sheets. I
suppose you warned her to bring her own towels? . . . Ah, well,
never mind! We'll give her one of our Mr. Rawson's, shall
we?"

All the chairs in the lounge had been piled either on top of
each other or on top of the tables, and the threadbare carpet
had been rolled back to reveal a smaller and shinier rectangle
of nigger-brown linoleum which covered the floor from wall to

186

wall. A girl sat on a cane chair by the doorway, clasping with both hands a large black patent-leather bag which rested on her knees. She wore a tartan skirt and beige cashmere jumper and her coat and beret were thrown over an upright chair beside her. She looked up at Christine, who addressed her:

"Mrs. Nowell—I'm Tim's mother. It was good of you to come so quickly."

Christine put out a hand; but the girl said vaguely, "I'm sorry," and smiled, without putting out her own. "Is there some mistake?" She had an American or Canadian accent.

At that moment Christine was aware that someone had got up from a chair in an embrasure by the window, and was limping towards her across the linoleum.

"This must be the lady that I . . . I'm so sorry."

Patricia Nowell was extremely thin, with arms through the transparent skin of which the blue veins seemed to shine. She had a small crooked mouth, and a nose that was also slightly crooked, under a forehead that bulged out of proportion to the rest of her delicate features. She dressed badly, but expensively, and used no make-up except powder. When she put her long hand into Christine's it felt as cold, sharp and brittle as a razor-shell picked off the sea-shore in winter, but the smile on the crooked mouth was affectionate and warm.

She was a woman who appeared to be very little younger than Christine herself.

"I'm so bad at hospitals," she said. "Women are not usually squeamish, are they? It's usually men. Are you squeamish?" she turned nervously to Gwyneth in the taxi. "No, of course you're not, because you're a doctor." She tended to ask questions to which she would at once herself provide the answers. "Even the *smell* of hospitals upsets me. My friends often wonder how I managed to have three children—and I wonder myself." She kept licking her pale lips, and staring out of the window of the motor at the wind-blown, rain-drenched streets, while her hands twitched her fur coat tighter and tighter across her chest.

All around her, in her lap, on the floor, on the tip-up seat before her, there were innumerable parcels which were presents for Tim. She had brought him butter and eggs which, in her own words, she had "wangled" out of a farmer who lived next door; her own and her husband's chocolate-ration for the month; some books from Heywood Hill, with whom she had a standing order; a bottle of expensive eau-de-Cologne; and a large box with a Fortnum and Mason's label. . . . In turn she would either clutch at or touch each of these packages, as though they were possessed of magic properties of some kind, extending long skinny hands on which the nails were bitten savagely to the quick.

She talked, as she had been talking ever since they had met, as though she were trying to remember scraps of some amusing conversation in which she had been interrupted many years before, making frequent literary allusions which Gwyneth grasped, but which were wholly lost on Christine. But for the fur coat and for the large diamond-and-sapphire brooch pinned on her jersey, she might have been the dean of a woman's college at a provincial university. As the taxi drew up under the portico of the hospital, she fumbled in her crocodile-leather bag and took out a pill which she only managed to swallow after repeated efforts, jerking her head backwards on her spindly neck like a hen drinking water.

"Well, this is certainly a novel experience," she said, as, white-faced, her hands still making that gesture of drawing her fur coat tighter and tighter about her, she followed the other two women down the corridor. Behind her came the taxi-driver carrying her parcels. "I've so often had scenes in hospitals in my books, but all my children were born at home and it's years since I entered one." She gave a brief, nervous giggle, peering at the same time through a door which had swung open to admit a ward-maid carrying a tray. She began to lick her lips, and flickered her blonde eyelashes as though she were walking into a gale.

Neither Christine nor Gwyneth was at that moment listening to what she said and the significance of the phrase about her books was therefore lost on them. To enter the little room where Tim lay alone was for each of them like diving headlong into a frozen pool, and they were bracing themselves for the plunge and sudden shock. They tiptoed in and Pat Nowell tiptoed in behind them screwing up her eyes in an attempt to see in that gloom of curtained windows and shaded light. The nurse whispered: "He's asleep for the moment. But he ought to wake up soon." Neither Christine nor Gwyneth could ever tell whether he was awake or not. They sat down on two straight-backed chairs, leaving the armchair for Pat Nowell, who bared her teeth first at the nurse and then at them, and at last perched herself on the edge, arranging her parcels about her. "Shall I take those?" the nurse asked.

"Yes, would you, please?"

There was a silence in which nothing could be heard but the patter of the rain on the balcony outside and Pat's deep breathing. Every now and again she would put a hand to her mouth and tear at one of the already-bitten nails in self-absorbed ferocity. She was shivering, although the room was, if anything, over-heated, and she still repeated that pathetic gesture of tugging at the lapels of her fur coat, crossing them over her chest. From time to time her large, pale blue eyes would move over to the bandaged, amorphous shape, slung above the bed, and would then move away, while she swallowed hard.

Suddenly there was a cry, like a small child's, followed by a scream: "No, no! Take them away! Take them away!" Christine jumped up and leant over Tim: "What is it? What is it, darling? It's only a dream. We're here—Pat's here, too."

"No, no, no." He choked through the hole that was left for his lipless mouth and the nostrils that looked as if they had been eaten away by some loathsome disease. "No, no, no! Save me! Save me! Mummy, Mummy! Save me! The cockroaches! The cockroaches! Take them off my face!" His hands, suspended from the ceiling by straps, made pathetic scrabbling gestures.

Christine leant over to him, reiterating: "It's a dream, a dream! Of course your face itches, darling. That means it's begun to heal. That's all it means. Darling, it's a dream. A dream, darling!" Gwyneth stood beside her.

Suddenly both women were aware of a wind blowing through the room, sleet-laden and icy, and of a light that hurt their eyes after the gloom in which they had been sitting. The door on to the balcony swung back and forth, with a rattle and a bang.

Gwyneth said: "Go to her."

"No, you go."

Pat Nowell was bowed over in one corner, her head resting on her hands, which were in turn gripping the rusty balustrade, while her whole body shook in a useless, endless retching.

Gwyneth put an arm round her, and gripped her ferociously. "Stop it!" she said. "Stop it! You're all right. Stop it!"

"Oh, I . . . I can't . . . can't . . . I . . . can't. . . ." Her hair, soft and scant, was drenched with the rain which had also darkened the shoulders of her dress and was mingling with the tears that ran off her chin and the tip of her nose.

IX

Myra was an efficient, but uncomfortable, hospital visitor. When, on this occasion, she had volunteered to comb Tim's hair while Gwyneth was out of the room arranging some flowers brought from the farm, her sharp, aggressive tugs had made him want to cry out in protest, such was his present state of feebleness and over-wrought nerves. Yet he knew that, unlike Pat, she would be certain not to make the parting on the wrong side or leave a number of tangles and tufts.

"My God, Gwyneth! Couldn't you have done better than that. . . . Well, the vase is wrong in the first place. Mouth far too big. But why on earth did you cut the stems so short? Here, let me try." She plucked at the roses, two and three at a time, with irritable movements of her thin, muscular arms, and then, no less quickly, began to push them back. Gwyneth subsided into a chair, having first taken up the book which was lying face downward on it.

"*La Chartreuse de Parme.*" She was obviously surprised.

"Pat is reading it to me. I'm trying to improve my French. Or, rather, she's trying to improve it."

"That's better. You really can't stick flowers in a vase as though they were surgical instruments." Myra placed the vase on the table beside the bed. "Gwyneth, do you think Tim's man is any good?"

"They say that he is."

"I must ask Noël when I next write. He seems so young. And so vague. I suppose that he knows what he's doing."

Gwyneth said nothing: she knew that Myra's interference always annoyed Tim.

"Somebody really must have a word with him about that girl who came in to give Tim his injection. I've never seen anything so scruffy. I suppose they just have to use whatever labour they can get these days. But I should have thought that in a case like this, in which good nursing is so important. . . . Why don't you say something yourself? Coming from you—as a doctor . . ."

At first, Gwyneth pretended not to hear—this had become her most usual defence against Myra's proddings and pushings—but the other woman pursued: "Gwyneth, do put down that book, and listen to what I'm saying. Gwyneth! *Gwyneth!*"

Soon the two women were bickering, while Tim lay on his back and stared up at the ceiling. He wanted to shout at them, "If you're going to start all that again, get out! Get out of here!" but he felt too weak to do so. Fortunately Pat soon appeared.

She came over and sat down on the bed beside him.

"Well, did you eat something?" he asked.

"Scrambled egg on toast, and a cup of coffee."

"That's not enough!"

"Quite enough. Oh, and I bought some peaches, here they are, they were meant for you, but I ate one myself." She peered into the bag, and then exclaimed: "Oh, he's given me at least two that are all bruised. Look!"

Her dismay was so comic that they all began to laugh, while Tim shifted himself uncomfortably on his pillow and eventually put a bandaged arm round her shoulders.

Pat held out the bag to Myra, "Have one?"

"One of the bruised ones?" Myra carefully selected a peach, and then went over to a cupboard in one corner to rummage for a knife and plate: no one had told her that this was where cutlery and crockery were kept. "H'm! Delicious!" she said, as the juice ran down her chin.

"Don't use your handkerchief!" Gwyneth cried out. "The juice stains terribly!"

But Myra continued to mop at her chin with her talon-like fingers.

"Shall I peel you one?" Pat asked Tim.

191

Tim nodded. But when the peach was ready, he said fretfully: "Oh, I don't feel like it now. You eat it."

Pat began to coax him as if he were one of her children: "Now, come along, darling! Don't be silly! Look, it's perfect. It's just right. You know that you love peaches. I got them especially for you."

"I don't want it. I don't want it!" He sounded as if he were about to burst into tears.

"All right, my pet. Then you needn't have it. Gwyneth will eat it. Come on, Gwyneth!"

"You tell me not to get the juice on my handkerchief and you let it dribble all down your blouse," Myra cried out in triumph as soon as Gwyneth bit into one of the pieces. "You see!"

Tim wished that they would go: all of them, even Pat. Yet less than two hours ago, he had been fretting because it was already ten o'clock and no one had come to visit him; and when Pat had at last arrived, breathless and apologetic because she had overslept, he had half scolded, half whined: "You know how beastly it is for me to lie here for hour after hour, with nothing to do. If I could read it would be different. You know, you know—and yet you're always, always late."

"Yes, I'm sorry, dearest. I'm sorry, I'm sorry."

He had behaved like a spoiled child; and she like a foolish, over-indulgent mother. But he could not help himself. "Oh, Pat, Pat, Pat!" He had sighed and clumsily drawn her head down on to his chest with his two bandaged hands.

Fortunately, Myra and Gwyneth soon got up to leave: Gwyneth had to be in London by six o'clock that evening and Myra was to drive her. Myra, who liked Pat far more than she liked Tim, invited them both to come and stay at the farm "as soon as he's through all this nonsense".

"Oh, I meant to tell you, I've just finished *A Bird's Cry*. Awfully good. I've asked Bumpus to order me all the others."

Pat looked sulky, as she usually did when someone mentioned her novels, bit at the nail of her forefinger, and mumbled something inaudible.

"Thank God, that's the end of them," Tim said when they had left. Pat was looking down at him oddly, her mouth slightly open and her chin stuck out. "What's the matter?"

192

"Are you *bleeding*?" she asked.

"Bleeding?"

"The bandage round your mouth. . . . It looks as if . . ."

"Oh, that! It's something new they're trying. It must be soaking through."

"Oh, for a moment . . . for a moment, I thought . . ." she gave a sigh of nervous relief. "It frightened me," she said. She returned to the bed and once more perched herself beside him. "Don't you like Gwyneth then?"

"Like her? Oh, I'm very fond of her."

"You don't *seem* to like her."

"We're different; we go our different ways."

"Yes, I see." She frowned: "She's very fond of you. That's obvious."

"We've always been good friends."

"I wonder if you don't sometimes . . . I mean, if you could *show* her a little that you *are* good friends. You don't show these things, you know."

"Don't I?"

"You don't even show that you care very much about me."

"But I do."

"Yes. I think you do." She said the words with a strange assurance. "I know you do. But still. . . . It's the same with your mother. You're always so impatient, or ironic or snubbing when you talk to her."

"Am I?"

"Do you mind my telling you this?"

"Of course not. Why should I?" She felt that he was laughing at her; but she went on:

"She's such a wonderful person. And sometimes it upsets me, it upsets me horribly, when I see you treat her . . . I feel that she may think that *I'm* to blame."

"You?"

"For coming between you. Most mothers hate their son's wives. And I'm not even a wife, I'm something far worse. And I'm not even the conventional mistress, am I? Thirty-seven years old, three children. . . . And yet, you know, I feel that she *doesn't* hate me: that's the odd thing. She doesn't. Whereas Myra—well, she hates *her* really, doesn't she? Deep down. Doesn't she? . . . Tim, are you asleep?"

"No, dearest. Just bored."

193

"Tell me about Myra."

"Oh, I can't be bothered!"

"I suppose your mother *knows*—about them, I mean."

"In the way that mothers know: yes, I suppose she does. If you ever said it to her, in so many words, of course she'd be horrified." He gave a laugh which sounded vaguely sinister as it emerged from the hole in the bandages around his mouth. "But provided it's not put into words—well, she can accept it. The funny thing is that I'm sure that I knew about it long before she did. I remember, it was the summer we spent at Fontainebleau—I was only fifteen or sixteen. . . . Poor Mummy! I used to joke about it with a girl called Lena or Lisa or something like that. But Mummy hadn't a clue, not a clue in the world. Later, oh, years later, when she was angry with Myra about something, she once asked me if I didn't think there was 'something unhealthy' about their friendship." Again the soft, sinister laugh bubbled up out of the hole. "But otherwise she's never said a word. . . . Poor thing, poor thing!"

"But Myra likes her, doesn't she?"

"H'm h'm. Who doesn't? And she tries hard to like Myra back—for the sake of Gwyneth. Most of the disagreeable things she forces herself to do are for the sake of one or the other of us."

"You're so hard about her."

"It's a defence. It's only a defence. You're hard about Alec and the children: for exactly the same reason. Guilt. They've no right to make one feel so guilty. They've no right to suffer, and suffer again, and come back for more each time one kicks them!" Suddenly he had ceased to speak in a drawling, bored voice; she noticed that he was trembling.

"Darling, darling!" she calmed him, listening to the thudding of his heart, as her head lay on his breast.

At that moment Christine came in.

"Well, how's my boy?" she asked. She pulled open the zip-fastener of a brown canvas bag, after she had kissed him and greeted Pat, and took out some silk pyjamas. "They're not very well ironed; I had to do them on the table in my bedroom. But at least they're better than if you had allowed them to wash them here."

"I should have said that that was a matter of doubt." He

saw her look of dismay, and at once added: "No, darling, they're perfect! I'm only teasing."

"A man was selling peaches just outside the entrance, and so I bought you some. The first I've seen this summer."

"Pat bought me some, too."

"Oh, dear!"

"But I'm sure yours are not bruised like hers." He peered into the bag. "Clever Mummy."

"One has to be careful with these men who sell in the street. They always cheat one, if one gives them half a chance."

"I'm not good at shopping," Pat said crossly. "I always get cheated."

Christine was secretly pleased that her peaches were so much better; and Pat knew this. It was such things that would always prevent the two women from becoming the friends which they both wished to be.

"I saw Gwyneth and Myra just for a moment. As they were leaving. They were quarrelling again."

"Still quarrelling?"

"It seems so silly of them. Bicker, bicker, bicker."

"Since they enjoy it."

Christine looked at Pat; as she often looked at her when the two women were alone together with Tim: bewildered, pained, appealing.

"Now I want to sleep. I want to sleep, please. Pat—Mummy. . . . But would one of you draw the blind, before you go?"

Both women crossed to the blind, but in the end it was Christine who lowered it. Both lingered near the bed, saying things like: "Got all you want? Shall I ring for some more orangeade? What about your pillows?" Then they went out.

They sat in the garden behind the hospital: conversation came with inexplicable spurts and hesitations, as it always came when they found themselves alone.

"He seems much better to-day."

"Oh, but it all seems so endless."

"Dr. Ashworth thinks that they can move him to the other place next week."

"How he suffers!"

"Now, dear, you mustn't lose heart. It's very important that we should all . . ."

195

"Yes, I know, I know!"

Pat spoke so peevishly that a long silence followed. Then she slipped her arm through Christine's; she began to tell her of her plans. She was going to leave her husband; she had asked him for a divorce; but whether Tim wished to marry her—well, that was another question. She smiled as she made this last statement, but she was obviously near to tears.

Christine found herself saying: "Oh, he will, dear, he will. I'm sure that he will. Don't worry about that. I'm sure that he will."

X

Tim used to talk about "my beautician" and also about "my tailor". "I've ordered a new face," he used sometimes to explain, "and, my God, what a lot of fittings!" Once, when he saw someone staring at him at a party and then looking hurriedly away, he asked: "Well, do you like my patchwork quilt?" At that time the skin of his face consisted of a number of rectangles of different sizes, greenish-white for the most part, but an inflamed purple where their edges joined. There had been, at first, a period when he had had to be coaxed, and finally ordered, to go into the small market-town outside which stood the hospital where he was being treated; but after that there followed a period when he seemed to take a vindictive pleasure in forcing the gaze of the squeamish and watching them recoil. He would comment on the curious fact that quite as many people seemed to be attracted by his disfigurement as were repelled by it, and after one visit to London he had returned with a story, at once sardonic and revolting, of a naval padre who had pursued him, cosseted him and gushed over him, as though he were a young girl with a nose-bleed.

Pat had, by now, left her husband and her children, and had taken a furnished cottage near the hospital, and there Christine and Gwyneth also spent much of their time. "What does he see in her?" Christine would often ask her daughter, and Gwyneth would answer:

"Oh, a lot."

"A lot! What do you mean?"

"She has so much charm. And she's so intelligent. And she has that air of helplessness and hopelessness which so much attracts men."

"I wish I could look helpless and hopeless," Christine said, with a trace of the bitterness and self-pity to which, from time to time, she would give way since Tim had been shot down. "It must be convenient." She continued to weed the lettuces at which she and Gwyneth had been working all that afternoon, until she looked up and said: "But she's not attractive, is she?"

"I used to think not. But there's something about her."

It was obvious, even to Christine, that Pat and Tim were living together: neither of them made any attempt to conceal their relationship, and Tim would wander in and out of Pat's room in his pyjamas or say things like, "Pat and I were discussing that in bed last night", in front of his mother. Christine was shocked, not for the obvious moral reason, but because it disgusted her to think of someone so young lying in the arms of a woman who, in her own phrase, was nearly "old enough to be his mother". She would find herself examining Pat's soft grey hair, the faint lines about her mouth and on her neck, and her hands, which were far less youthful than her own; and then unwillingly she would begin to picture to herself Tim stroking that hair, kissing that mouth, caressing that neck, holding those hands. It was horrible.

Curiously, she never thought with the same disgust of Pat being obliged to put her face against that face which looked as if it had been made up inexpertly by an amateur male-impersonator: the features all reduced in size and sharpened to an edge, the lips two thin razor-slashes, the eyebrows stuck on askew so that it seemed as if a shake of the head would make them tumble off. Christine knew that Tim had been burnt terribly and that anyone who was squeamish could not bear to look at his face for long; but it was not a thing she herself felt, as she felt Pat's approaching middle-age.

"Do you find you can read her books?"

"The early ones. I liked *A Bird's Cry*."

"But they're good, aren't they?"

"Well, I suppose she's one of the six most highly regarded women novelists in England."

Gwyneth always became both uncomfortable and impatient when her mother wished to discuss books or politics or music, about which she really knew nothing. She could have given her reasons for not liking Patricia Nowell's novels, and had often done so to both Tim and Myra: "They're dead, that's the trouble with them. She's been to the best schools, of course—Virginia Woolf, Katherine Mansfield, Ivy Compton-Burnett, even Henry James—but that's not enough. Is it?" But if she said that now, Christine would frown, two vertical lines appearing down her smooth forehead, and would say: "Dead, dear? Yes, I think I see what you mean. And *A Bird's Cry* did remind me just the slightest of 'Mrs. Whatever-it-is'—you know, that one by Virginia Woolf which you lent me last year and I never managed to finish. Do you think she cribbed it?"

"Of course she cooks well," Christine went on, still trying to analyse Pat's attraction for Tim.

"Marvellously."

"And you wouldn't expect her to be able to do that beautiful jewel-work, would you? One wouldn't think she'd have the patience."

"I find three children more surprising. That would require even greater patience, I imagine."

"It's sad," Christine said.

"What's sad?"

"To think of that family without her. Oh, I know the old grandmother is looking after them, but still. ... Do you suppose that she and Tim will ever get married?"

"Will she get a divorce? She was so sure that dear Alec was going to oblige. But dear Alec seems to have been unexpectedly obstinate."

Pat limped down the gravel path from the house towards them. She was wearing a simple blue-and-white cotton dress and sandals showing surprisingly pretty feet beneath bare legs which, like her arms, had a curious blue-veined sheen. "I hope my terrine is going to be a success. I've just finished," she said. She came and stood over them, her hands crossed before her, while she tore at a thumb-nail. "Guy and Eva have just telephoned. They wanted to come for the week-end, but I managed to put them off." She always spoke of her friends by their Christian names, and it was only later, when they arrived, that Christine slowly learnt that one was an Oxford don, another the editor of a literary magazine, and a third a famous actress. "We shall have to have tea almost at once, if Tim is expected back in hospital by five o'clock." Tim was going for another of his "fittings": in this case to have the two horizontal razor-sharp lines of his lips broadened and curved into what he had begged the doctor, half jokingly and half seriously, to make a cupid's bow. Every three or four weeks he had to undergo some such adjustment.

"Poor Tim," Christine said. "I've lost count of how many of these operations he's had."

"Twenty-three," Pat said quickly. She put out a hand and broke off the dry head of a lupin. "Yes, twenty-three."

Gwyneth and Christine straightened themselves, and Christine looked down at her fingers. "I'd better wash these. Hadn't I?" She began to walk ahead up the path to the house, while Gwyneth and Pat followed behind her.

"How is the book going?"

"Oh, the book!"

"Aren't you writing?"

"I've put it away." Pat spoke in fretful dejection. "At the moment it's no good. I can't get on with it. The trouble is—well, I'm afraid it will die on me." She shrugged her shoulders and simultaneously flapped her arm at a wasp which was circling, closer and closer round them. "Oh, get away! Get away, wasp!"

"That's probably only a momentary thing. I expect it'll come back."

Pat sucked at her index-finger, the cuticle of which had now begun to bleed. "Since he—since all this happened, I haven't written a word—not a word that really *tells*. I scribble away and then I have to tear it up; and that goes on day after day, day after day. It happened at such a bad stage—just after the first ten thousand words. That's the crucial time for me, like the first month of a baby. And now I feel I've lost it, lost it for good. I don't feel I shall ever be able to get into it again."

"Why don't you start something else?"

"I thought of that. Of course I did that full page review for the Literary Supplement, and the broadcast talk. But things like that don't really count, do they? The terrible thing is that unless I'm writing I'm never really happy. There's a feeling of guilt which seems to sour everything—as though one were trying to enjoy oneself on stolen money!" They entered the sitting-room, through the french windows, and found Tim kneeling on the hearth before the ugly little fireplace, the electric kettle raised above the tea-pot. With a horribly forced jollity he cried out:

"Oh, you've arrived too soon. Now you've caught me making tea without first seeing that the tea-pot is warm! . . . That cake looks marvellous, darling—positively pre-war. Or should one say post-war now?" Such remarks he used once to make to Christine in order to please her, and she remembered this, the corners of her mouth sagging as she placed herself in an armchair and stretched out her legs, which had begun to ache after her hour in the garden.

Tim hated going back into the hospital; but he never said so, attempting to mask his depression with this desperate jocularity.

"I've been making a sketch for old Maddox—a ground-plan as it were. He's damn well got to follow it. These eyebrows might have been put on by a drunken child of five." On such occasions he could never stop talking about his disfigurement. "But have you noticed how my colour is improving? I prefer pink to green—don't you?"

Pat cut the cake deliberately into slices, but Tim shook his head: "Not after that stupendous lunch. One day you must explain to me how you get those vast sirloins from the butcher. I hope you're not doing anything you oughtn't to do."

When he went upstairs before leaving for the hospital, Pat turned to Gwyneth and said in a low voice:

"Gwyneth . . . I—I wonder if you'd do something for me."

"Well, of course. What is it?"

Pat crumbled the chocolate cake on the plate resting on her knee and then kneaded it with her fingers. "Drive Tim to the hospital for me. Will you?"

Both Christine and Gwyneth were staring at her, and she went on hurriedly:

"I've had a racking head to-day. I don't feel like driving— don't feel I'd be at all safe. Will you—will you take him for

200

me? I know I've always done it in the past. But I feel—I feel I must lie down. Will you, Gwyneth?"

"Of course," Gwyneth said stolidly and quietly, as though the request had not in the least surprised her. She gulped at her cup of tea, three or four times noisily, and then asked: "Shall I take my own car or yours?"

"Whichever you like." Tim came down the stairs, in his uniform, with a bag in his hand. "Darling, I've just been telling Gwyneth that I've got a vile head—one of my migraines—and she's offered to drive you. Is that all right?"

He paused for a moment on the last step, and the eyelids, which had been so recently grafted on that they moved with the unexpectedness and clumsiness of those of a doll, seemed to click audibly upwards. Then he gave his lopsided smile, which was now almost a grimace, as the already taut skin was stretched even further over his cheek-bones: "Of course," he said. "Anyway, I know how you hate hospitals. And Gwyneth has had a crush on them ever since she was a toddler. . . . Shall we go?" He turned to his sister.

In the doorway, he embraced first Christine and then Pat, who, as he was climbing into the farther seat of the car, suddenly rushed round to him: "Are you sure you don't mind? Are you sure, darling?" The way she licked her lips and flickered her eyelids reminded Christine, who was watching from the porch, of that time when they had walked together down the corridor of the hospital.

"Of course I don't mind." He put out one of his scarred skeleton hands, the joints of which he could still not properly articulate, and placed it over hers. "Cheerio," he said.

"Good luck! Good luck, darling!"

"Good luck!" Christine echoed.

The two women went back into the sitting-room in silence, where Pat crossed over to the writing-desk, a hideous piece of modern Jacobean furniture, and drew a pad towards her. For a while she alternately sucked the end of the fountain-pen and tapped it against her teeth, staring out into the garden. Christine asked:

"Shall I give you some more tea?"

"No, thank you."

"Whether Tim warmed the pot or not, it's excellent, isn't it? Where did you buy it?"

201

Pat did not answer.

"They say that one can get Earl Grey again—had you heard that? . . . Pat!" She went across to the desk and put her hands on the other woman's shoulders: it was the first time that she had ever touched her voluntarily. "Now don't worry. It's nothing. It's no worse than having a tooth out. That's what Dr. Maddox said. We can drive over and see him before lunch to-morrow, and I'll bet you that he'll be as chirpy as a cricket. This new pentothal—something—it's not like that horrible ether. Now come, Pat!"

The other woman's bony shoulders were jagging up and down as she bit on the knuckles of her clenched fist. There was a look of terror in her face. Suddenly she swung round:

"Christine, you've got to tell him—you or Gwyneth. I—I can't. I simply can't."

"Tell him? Tell him what?"

Pat got up, her body hunched and her head drawn down before her shoulders, so that from behind she looked like an old woman. "I can't face it any longer," she said. "There seems to be no end to it. Twenty-three times. I can't, I can't!" Again she bit on her knuckles, swaying her body from side to side as though in some physical agony.

"Come, you must lie down," Christine said. "I'll give you two of those American cachets that Major Oppenheim brought me. They're marvellous. Come, my dear!" She tried to put an arm round Pat, but at once she pulled free.

"You're tough, you're brave," she cried out. "I'm not. I'm weak and I'm—I'm a coward. I can't look at him any more. I can't touch him any more. I can't bear to have those hands of his touch me. I've done my best, truly I have. I have, haven't I? I left Alec for him—the children—everything. But the terrible thing is that I—I no longer love him." She threw herself on the sofa and covered her face with one of her skinny arms. "I used to think in the old days that it wasn't his looks that had attracted me. I used to tell him so. Yes, I did. But now I know—now I know that that was all that ever made me love him . . . his—his looks, and—and his physique—and—and—his youth. . . . All the things that Alec hadn't got—had lost, if he'd ever had them. . . ." She got to her feet again and confronted Christine: "You despise me, don't you? Don't you? But I can't love him, as you love him. I can't, I can't! You don't notice his skin, do you? Like, like rubber. Do you? Do you? He's unchanged for you. He's as he always was. When I saw him kiss you just now, I realized that. You didn't have to brace yourself. It was a pleasure for you, wasn't it? Wasn't it?"

"He's my son," Christine said quickly. "Any mother would . . . I should have thought any woman who . . ." But it would have been too cruel to go on.

Pat clutched her hand. "You'll tell him for me, won't you? Won't you? I'll—I'll write a letter, I can do these things in writing, I'm only good in writing. But you must tell him first. You will? Promise that you will."

"Of course," Christine said. Suddenly all her resentment against Pat, her jealousy of her, and the discomfort which she had always experienced in any physical nearness to her, blazed up and then blazed out. "Of course I'll do that. Of course." She had often thought and even said that Pat was nearly old enough to be Tim's mother; but now, as she put an arm about her shaking shoulders, she felt that she was young enough to be her own daughter. How could such a woman have borne three children? And how would she ever bring them up? She was fortunate to have her clergyman husband— and "Nanny" and "Grandmama", of whom she was always talking.

"I'll leave to-night," Pat was saying. "Tell him that he can have the house until the lease runs out. Tell him I'll write to him. Yes, we must write to each other. I shall try to explain it all. I can say things in writing which I can't—I could never say to his face. He writes such marvellous letters. Doesn't he? Don't you think so?" Tim's letters to Christine had never covered more than a sheet of writing paper and even to so indulgent a critic they had always seemed pathetically inadequate. But now she merely nodded her head: "Yes," she said. "Yes, he writes well, doesn't he? At school, he always won the essay prizes."

Suddenly Pat turned and cried out with something of the same absorbed ferocity with which she bit her nails: "But don't despise me! Don't despise me! And don't let him despise me! Please, Christine, please!"

XI

Tim drew the pad towards him and wrote on it: "Pat?" Christine explained: "Oh, she has a chill, poor dear. Nothing serious. She's spending the day in bed."

Tim shrugged his shoulders and then, putting a hand up to his mouth to finger his dressings with the same absent-minded gesture with which he used to finger his D.S.O., he stared out of the window to where two horribly scarred children, a boy and a girl, were quarrelling together with shrill cries of "You did!", "I didn't!", "You did, you beast!" When he again took up the pad, it was not to write anything further about Pat, but to scribble: "Silly bastards. Do that all day."

Christine was waiting for the time when he would be able to talk again. Each day she told him that Pat was still in bed with her chill, and each day he would shrug his shoulders at the news and write no comment. But, on the fifth day of such visits, the bandage had gone and in its place were two strips of sticking-plaster, stained orange as though from too much smoking, by the dressing beneath. When he talked, it was as if a village-idiot was babbling, and even Christine had difficulty in understanding him.

She kissed him on the forehead when she came in, put down the books she had brought, and then seated herself on a chair facing the chaise-longue on which he was stretched out.

"Well?" he prompted her, as if he had already guessed what she had to say to him.

"Darling . . . I—I don't know how to—break this to you. . . . Some bad news . . . I—I kept it until we could have a real talk about it. That's why I didn't tell you before."

"Pat?"

"What, dear?" The blurred sound could have been one of ten words; but it was silly of her not to recognize it at once. "Yes, dear. Pat. I—I'm afraid she's gone. She went that—that day you came back here." Christine opened the bag which, for so many years now, Tim had told her she must throw away. "I have a letter from her."

There was a silence; and then suddenly be began to laugh.

"Yes, I thought there would be a letter. A letter is so much in character."

"You mustn't be too cross with her. I know that—that she's behaved shockingly, and yet if you could have seen the poor thing as I saw her, on that last afternoon. . . . She tried, she really did try. Don't blame her too much!"

"Blame her! Why should I blame her?" Christine was leaning forward on the edge of the chair, like a child, in order to catch the words that fell from between the two swollen, discoloured strips of sticking plaster. "I don't suppose it could have been very nice to have to live with—with this." Once again he fingered the dressing. "It wasn't exactly what she'd bargained for—was it?"

Suddenly he had begun to speak with a bitter ferocity and self-disgust. Christine cried out: "But, darling, it's only something temporary. That's all. In six months' time Dr. Maddox says that you'll look just like anyone else.'

Again he laughed, the sound coming in strange, hiccoughing spurts from between the blubber-lips. "But I don't want to look like anyone else. I want to look like myself."

He had never spoken like this before, to her or to anyone else. "You've always been so brave," she pleaded with the unspoken corollary "so be brave now". "So brave," she repeated.

"And Pat was brave too—in her own fashion."

Christine did not know whether he was being ironical or not; but she answered, as if no irony were intended: "Yes, she was wonderful during those first weeks. That's why I—I can't understand her behaviour now. . . ."

He replied: "Oh, I expect she could take so much—and then could take no more."

Christine shook her head, her eyes filling with tears. "I know that to a man—how a woman looks. . . . But women don't feel like that, truly they don't. That's not what's important to them. When your father was ill, it never made any difference—it made me love him more, that was the only thing. . . ."

He closed over her hand the skeleton-fingers, the mere touch of which would make Pat want to shudder. "But, darling, you're different, you're different."

"Different! How am I different? Of course I'm not different.

205

There are millions of women who would agree with what I say. Honestly, Tim . . ."

"Then Pat is different." There was a silence. "Have it as you wish it. But I don't blame her! . . . Good God, supposing I was married to a woman who had—well—say—had to have a breast removed, or something like that. . . . Well, could I go on loving her? Could I go on making love to her? Could I? Could I? I just don't know."

Christine was horrified: she stared at him, her mouth slightly open, while with one hand she brushed the tears off her cheeks. Suddenly he jumped to his feet, and began rummaging in a drawer, pulling out letters: "Look at all these! The marriage of true minds! That's what it was—read them, go on, read them!" He tossed some of the pale-blue envelopes into her lap. "And really, all the time, she was just finding other, grander, words for what any stray bitch on heat wants. That's all." He went to the window, standing with his back to her; and all at once she realized he was crying.

"Tim . . . darling! Don't! Don't!"

"Don't touch me . . . please don't touch me. . . ." But as he said this he clutched her in his arms, putting his bandaged face down to hers and swaying with her in grief. Suddenly he cried out, in an agony of self-pity: "I wish I were dead! I wish I were dead!"

"Tim . . . Tim! You were so brave—you've been so brave all along. And now you're nearly at the end. The worst of it is over. It's over, darling. It's finished! You can forget about it."

"Over—finished! Look at me, Mummy—look at me! What do I look like? What will I ever look like?" Outside in the garden, the two children were playing with a ball, one shouting: "Harder, silly! Harder!"

"But you look quite all right—quite all right. And anyway you have so much else. You're clever, and you're capable, and you're young—and you have this marvellous war record. So don't despair, dearest. Everyone says how wonderful you've been—Dr. Maddox said that to me when we had a little chat yesterday. Even that nurse you so much dislike said it." She took him to the chair, as she talked, and made him sit down, herself lifting his legs up on to the support and arranging the cushion.

"Poor Mummy," he said, beginning to caress her hand. The

sticking-plaster stretched painfully as he attempted to smile: "You're always so optimistic, aren't you? Always so cheerful. Always so sure that everything's for the best."

"Now you're making fun of your silly old mother."

"I'm not, darling, I'm not!" He put her hand to his burning cheek. "What would I have done without you—then, or now, or at any time?"

She began to caress his hair, standing beside him as they both looked out of the window at the two children. One shouted: "You did that on purpose!" "No, I did not!" "Yes, you did!" "I shan't play!"

Christine had thought that the worst was over; but suddenly Tim flung himself off the chair and rushed to the window which he threw up with a single irate gesture. "If you can't stop that row, you had bloody well better go and play somewhere else! Go on! Beat it! Beat it! Beat it!" he yelled. Then he threw himself face downwards on his bed, in a paroxysm of weeping.

III
AFTER

I

"**B**eddy" was humming "Bless them all" as she made up before the looking-glass that hung above the wash-basin in the ladies'-room of the Club. She broke off to say: "Wasn't the King's speech lovely? I made Oppy listen to it. I think it almost persuaded him that the War of Independence had been a mistake." She patted at her cheeks, leaning forward and peering into the glass with a look of vague apprehension, her haunches stuck out, like a school-boy awaiting the first stroke of a cane.

In Christine's ears still buzzed the hesitant rhetoric of the peroration: '. . . If you carry on in the years to come as you have done so splendidly in the war, you and your children can look forward to the future, not with fear, but with high hopes, of a surer happiness for all. . . .'

"Like a father to us all," "Beddy" was saying. "That's how Oppy himself expressed it. But you can tell the strain has told, oh it's told on him all right. Sybil saw him last week, you know, as near as you are to me." The powder had settled thick along the edge of the wash-basin, like a layer of pink dust. "She said he looked *old*—really old now."

The swing-door banged open to admit Mrs. Worth-Dillington, who said: " 'Beddy', you bad girl! You've been at that flour-bin again," as she went into one of the two lavatories. "Beddy" pulled a face at the looking-glass.

"So it's over at last," she said. She pushed her lips in and out, and then pressed a tissue to them. "I often wondered if I'd live to see the end."

The plug clanked, and Mrs. Worth-Dillington hurried out. "Surely you're not all that old, duckie, are you?" she asked genially.

"Old bitch," "Beddy" exclaimed, as soon as she had gone. "At least I shan't have to be bossed around by her for much longer. That's my Fifth Freedom—Freedom from Bossing."

She giggled and hitched at her shoulder-straps. "Do you like my dress?" she asked.

"Very nice," Christine answered.

"That saucy son of yours asked me if I'd made it out of the netting we stuck on windows. I gave him the rough edge of my tongue, I can tell you—in no uncertain terms. Still"—she sighed—"he dances divinely."

Christine had been waiting to wash her hands, still sticky from the grasp of a plump Czechoslovakian major with whom she had been dancing. Now, as "Beddy" went out and she let the warm water swish into the basin, she leant against its edge in a fatigue which bewildered and annoyed her. It was true that she had worked hard, preparing for the dance; and "Beddy" had been even more garrulous and tiresome than usual. But the day had been no worse than many other days, and at least it had been free from anxieties about Tim or Gwyneth. Yet, at this moment, when outside the door they were all dancing "Knees Up, Mother Brown" she felt she wanted nothing more than to throw herself on to a bed and close her eyes, not for hours, but for days or even weeks.

"You don't look very happy," Gwyneth said when Christine joined her in a corner, where she was seated talking to a red-faced Dame of the British Empire who was a friend of Mrs. Worth-Dillington.

"I feel rather weary."

"There's nothing more exhausting than the hilarity of others," the Dame barked out. She was wearing a charcoal-grey uniform with quantities of silver braid, unrecognizable to the two other women.

Colonel Liebman came over and gave a little bow: "Would you like to dance?" He looked exactly the same as eighteen months before, except that on the back of one of his tanned hands he had a puckered, white scar from a superficial wound inflicted by a sharp-shooter off a roof in Paris.

Christine rose, because she feared that her refusal might make him think that she bore him some grudge. It was an old-fashioned waltz, and "Beddy" was already whirling round in the arms of Major Oppenheim, screaming out shrilly: "Faster! Faster! Faster! I can still see their faces!"

"Well, how has the world been treating you?" he asked, as

decorously as if they were no more than acquaintances. Earlier in the evening he had merely greeted her with a "Why, hullo there, Christine!" wrung her hand, and then hurried off to the bar, where she had seen him gulp down two glasses of Scotch, neat, one after the other.

"It's a relief it's all over. I can hardly believe it," she answered tritely.

"That's just how I felt—I still can't take it in. And in ten days' time I'll be back in Pelham. Well, well, well!"

"So soon," she said.

"Soon! Boy, I can hardly wait. Those ten days seem a lifetime." He began to talk about all the things he was going to do and see as soon as his ship docked, and then broke off to ask: "Say, what about Tim? How's he making out?"

"Haven't you seen him?"

"Nope. Is he here? I saw Gwyneth," he said. "Hear she's doing well. But where's the boy?"

"Just behind you."

Tim was seated on a sofa against the wall, one hand holding a glass of champagne while with the other he caressed the plump bare arm of a girl who was a corporal in the F.A.N.Ys.

Colonel Liebman manœuvred Christine round, and peered. "Where? Where do you mean?" he asked.

"On the sofa. With Maureen Phillibrand."

For a moment he stopped dancing, then: "Christ!" he exclaimed. "But his . . ." he broke off: and when she looked up at him, she saw that his tanned face had gone a lemon-yellow.

"He was shot down—badly burned," she said.

"Christ!" he repeated. He continued executing the movements of the dance, muttering as he did so: "Poor kid! My God, the poor kid!" Mercifully the record soon ended, and "Beddy" could be heard clapping her hands and screeching:

"Encore! Encore! Encore!"

Christine began to walk back to the corner where Gwyneth and the Dame were seated, but Colonel Liebman touched her arm and gently eased her sideways: "Let's go and have a word with him," he said.

"Now?" Christine hesitated.

"Sure—why not?"

"Oh, all right."

Tim was laughing uproariously, and the girl Maureen, who had become tipsy on two glasses of champagne, was throwing her head back and laughing with him, their two bodies, colliding and then bouncing away from each other though their arms still were joined.

"Oh, Mrs. Cornwell, you really shouldn't allow your son to tell such stories in mixed company!" she greeted Christine.

"Well, since you understand them . . ." Tim protested to her. Again they both rocked from side to side. "I had no idea that Roedean provided such a liberal education."

"Darling, you remember Colonel Liebman, don't you?"

"Hello, Tim. How are things?"

Tim did not get up to shake hands, but merely answered: "Oh, hello, Warren. You know our Maureen, don't you?"

"Sure, sure. Nice to see you, Maureen."

"Colonel Liebman knows Daddy."

"Daddy" was an Air Vice-Marshal who had been the managing-director of a Midlands catering-firm, and most of Maureen's conversation was prefaced by "Daddy says" or "Daddy thinks" or "Of course, Daddy". She was only just nineteen. Now as Christine and Warren sat down, she at once embarked on a confused story about the liberation of Paris, which appeared to be told solely in order to indicate that "Daddy" was on Christian-name terms with General de Gaulle and that Warren had been on "Daddy's" staff. In her tipsiness she could not decide whether "Daddy" had had luncheon or dinner with the General after his entry into Paris.

"Darling," Tim suddenly interrupted her, "you're becoming just a wee bit of a bore. Don't mind my saying so."

"Well, really!" Maureen snatched her hand from his, so violently that the champagne in the glass which he held in his other hand splashed on to his trousers.

"Now, now, don't get me wrong. We love having you with us. And we're all sure that 'Daddy' is frightfully clever and important and all that. But as a topic of conversation—well . . ." He pulled her back on to the sofa as she attempted to get up, and said:

"Now the person I'd like to hear about is Mummy."

"Let me go! You'll tear my dress! Tim, let me go!"

She struggled free, and hurried off through the door of the

214

ladies'-room, while Tim threw back his head and again laughed uproariously. Warren gazed down into his glass of whisky and gave a small smile.

"Tim, that was unkind," Christine said.

"Nonsense! She loves being teased. I do that all the time to her—and she always comes back to me for more."

"Darling, you forget how young she is."

Tim ignored this: "Well, Warren—tell us something about yourself. I see that they've given you a lot of medals." He pointed at the two rows of ribbons on the American's tunic.

"Oh, good conduct and that kind of crap. No heroics, I'm afraid."

"Well, that surprises me; that surprises me, Warren. I should have thought you were a very, very heroic person. Wouldn't you, Mummy?" Christine said nothing. She could not bear to hear Tim baiting people in this way, but never knew how to stop him; if she showed her disapproval or pain, it only seemed to spur him to fresh cruelties.

Warren, unaware of Tim's irony, smiled deprecatingly: "No, I guess I'm a very ordinary guy. Not like you. You're the hero, from all accounts." His voice suddenly becoming husky, as though with tenderness, he stared, brows furrowed, into the ravaged face of the boy before him and said: "Gee, Tim, I'm sorry about all you've been through. Christine was saying."

"Well, ektually, old boy"—Tim put on the caricature of a young war-time pilot with a "handle-bar" moustache—"ekt-ually all that was nothing at all. Bashed up the old face a bit, of course."

Obtusely Warren pursued: "When I get back home one of the first things I'm going to do is to tell them about the people like you. Yes, that's going to be one of my first jobs. The Battle of Britain, the Spitfire boys."

"Well, ekt-ually, you know, old boy, I was still at Oxford during the Battle of Britain. And it wasn't Spitfires, it was bombers. Not that I could care less." The imitation continued; and now, through the fumes of whisky that were mounting to his head, Warren was vaguely aware that Tim was making fun of him; that he found him ridiculous and boring; that perhaps he did not even like him. These thoughts were like a series of blows beneath the heart, leaving him breathless and dizzy.

215

"I know that some of you that did the real fighting must despise the guys like me. Christ, I wish I'd been fifteen years younger!"

"Be grateful you weren't."

But ignoring this, his pale-blue eyes fixed with a kind of yearning mournfulness on the scarred face of the boy, he went on: "We won't forget, Tim. Don't imagine that. We won't forget what you and all those like you did to save the civilized world——"

Suddenly Tim leapt to his feet: "Really, this is too much! Excuse me, Mummy. It's more than I can take." He began to weave his way across the room, while Warren lumbered upwards: "Say did I—did I put my foot in it? Did I say anything that I oughtn't to have said? Well, I didn't——"

It's nothing, nothing. Please sit down, Warren. He's highly strung and nervous. That's natural, isn't it, after all he's suffered?" Suddenly she felt more exasperated with Warren than with Tim.

"Well, I must tell him—I think I must go and explain . . ." He began to wander off while Christine called: "No, Warren, no! Come back! Warren!"

But stumbling, swaying and knocking into couples who were dancing, his glass of whisky clutched in one hand, Warren disappeared.

Apparently he did not find Tim, who returned a few minutes later to where Christine was sitting:

"Let's get out of here," he said roughly.

"But, darling, we can't. I can't. I'm supposed to be one of the hostesses."

"Doesn't matter. Nobody will notice. Come on!" He made a gesture with both of his hands to make her get up. "Come on, darling!" Leaning forward, he now got hold of both her wrists and began to pull.

"Tim, please! Let me get up on my own." She struggled to her feet, once again experiencing that terrible weariness, as though after some lengthy illness. "Where were you thinking of going? Home?"

"Home!" he exclaimed in incredulity. "At this hour—on this night? Don't be silly, sweetie. No, we're making up a party to go to the Beauchamp."

"Oh, the Beauchamp. Well, why don't you young people go

216

on your own, and I'll slip back to the flat? Wouldn't that be the best thing?"

"Certainly not."

"I'm tired, darling. Really I'd much rather go to bed than——"

But he would not listen to her, propelling her towards the cloakroom with one hand while with the other he waved good-bye to those of his friends who were still dancing or sitting around the room.

"You're not cold, are you?" he said to Christine, as he took her hand in the back of Gwyneth's car. She had begun to shiver, as she drew her shabby black-velvet wrap, a relic of the days in India, closer and closer to her shoulders.

"No, dear, no." But the shivering continued.

Gwyneth looked over her shoulder: "I hope you haven't got a chill."

"No, dear, just tiredness, that's all."

She could not understand why she felt this weariness and depression, like some physical weight crushing her downwards, and in an attempt to shake them off she pointed to the sports-car in front: "Jimmy must be pretty far gone. Look how they're swinging about the road. They'll have an accident, if they're not careful. Tim, do you think they're safe?"

But Tim, who had now turned his back to his mother, in order to fondle Maureen, who was seated on the other side, appeared not to hear her.

The Beauchamp was crowded; but Jimmy and Tim were known there, and the head-waiter, a Cypriot who looked like a harassed Greek Minister during a Government crisis, was both sentimental about their uniforms and mindful of the generous tips they had lavished on him in the past. "For you, gentlemen, there is always a table," he said, casting his eyes about in anguish looking for somewhere to squeeze them in.

"Good old Christo," Jimmy Tomlins said, putting his arm round his shoulder and hugging him to him.

"I wonder if we shall see Daddy here," Maureen said. "He thought he might come on after his dinner."

"Oh, God forbid," Tim said audibly.

The room seemed to Christine unbearably noisy, hot and crowded, and, though she was not as a rule conscious of her appearance, to-night she felt uneasily aware that her black-lace

217

evening dress, and her black wrap, her single string of pearls and her evening shoes all compared unfavourably with the clothes and jewellery of the women seated around her. She sipped some champagne, and then, resting her arm on the table and her chin on her palm, she stared at the swing doors through which the sweating waiters kept shooting in and out. Her eyes felt as if minute particles of grit were lodged beneath the lids.

Beside them was an empty table, far larger than their own, on which was a card "Reserved": and now a party of people, headed by Sir Noël Hope-Ashburn, strolled towards it, laughing and talking among themselves. Myra was the last, with a young, awkward-looking girl in an unbecoming ice-blue evening dress and silver slippers, whom Christine recognized as the land-girl who had just arrived on the farm when she and Gwyneth had last been there on a visit. She had freckles scattered over her prominent cheek-bones and her plump arms, and her uplifted breasts, which were large, were squeezed so close to each other by the constriction of the dress that a deep chasm was visible between them. When she walked she gave the impression that she was not used to wearing shoes.

Sir Noël, on seeing the other party, was immediately affable, patting Tim on the back, bowing to the rest of the company and making a point of asking about the rheumatism from which Christine had been suffering when they had last met. Myra was chilly: she gave the curtest of "Good evenings", as though to a group of strangers who had been fellow-guests at a party she had not enjoyed, and then turned away to see about arranging the seating at the table. "Sir Arthur here, I think. . . . And would you like to go over there, Lady Mablethorpe? . . . Many of the names were familiar to Christine from the newspapers; these were evidently what Myra herself called "Noël's smarty friends". Meanwhile the girl, whose name was Betty, stood shifting her weight from one sturdy leg to the other, behind the others. To her Myra eventually said: "Come along, Betty—over here," as though to one of the cows it was the girl's business to milk.

Christine had noticed that Gwyneth had shifted in her chair when the party had entered, so that she was seated in such a way that she presented her right shoulder and back to the table.

When Sir Noël had said "Good evening, Gwyneth. How are things?" she had merely replied "Good evening" without turning round. Previously she had been unusually exhilarated as she talked to Jimmy Tomlins about cars, a subject which had come to fascinate her; but now she had fallen silent, scowling down at her hands, which were clasped in her lap, while she drew in her lower lip.

Maureen hissed across the table to Tim to ask if one of the women was not a leading actress. Tim nodded, and Maureen then asked: "And the man on her left—surely I've seen him somewhere?" He was, as Jimmy Tomlins then whispered, a Governor of the Bank of England.

"Really, I find Myra's communism more and more absurd!" Tim exclaimed loudly. He laughed: "It's one of the things which even Gwyneth, who can explain everything else, has never succeeded in explaining to me."

"Sh, Tim! She'll hear you," Christine reproved him.

"But who is the girl with all the freckles?"

"Oh, she helps on the farm. Her name is Betty Something. Her father is one of Myra's neighbours. Isn't that so, Gwyneth?"

Gwyneth shook her head irritably: "What?" she said. "What? Oh, Betty—Betty Whitworth. Yes, you remember Mr. Whitworth, don't you? He's got the garage on the corner of the road."

"Oh, you mean the man that used to help Myra out with coupons."

Unintentionally Christine used the phrase "help out", which Myra herself used when talking about her illegal purchases.

"Yes," Gwyneth said. "That man."

'I think she's rather fetching," Tim mused. "Yes, I like little Betty. I imagine she'd be lots of fun, don't you?" he turned to Jimmy.

"Oh, come, old boy! Come, come! With legs like that?"

If they had drunk less, they would not have been talking so loudly; Christine was afraid that the others could hear them. "Sh," she said again. "Do be careful. Tim!"

"Oh, you have no eye for hidden possibilities, none whatever."

Maureen, who had been looking as sullen as Gwyneth during this conversation, now began to stare across the room at a young French officer, her lips parted and one eyebrow cocked. She felt both humiliated and infuriated by Tim's comments on the other girl.

Jimmy Tomlins asked Christine and Gwyneth in turn to dance, but both of them refused: he did not ask Maureen, because he assumed that Tim would do so. The other two couples in the party were already on the floor.

"You know," said Tim, "I think I shall ask her to dance." He looked meditatively at the land-girl, his eyes half closed, as he raised his cigarette to his lips.

"No, darling," Christine said.

"No, Tim," Gwyneth added with even more emphasis.

"Why on earth not? She looks terribly bored and out of things. I suppose she *can* dance."

"I think they would think it rude," Christine said.

"Well, why on earth should they think that? After all, they're friends, aren't they? And this is Victory Night." He got up: "Here goes."

They watched him as he went across to the other table, and addressed himself, not to the girl, but to Myra. They could not hear what he said, but they heard the reply delivered in her rasping, staccato voice. "Well, ask her and see." He turned to the girl, who put a hand up to the straight blonde hair which fell to her shoulders, as though she wished to conceal her eyes. Then she took the hand away, and said almost inaudibly to Myra: "Shall I?"

"That's for you to decide, my dear."

The girl shook her head. "I'm sorry," she said huskily, the freckles standing out now as the blood mounted under them. "I think perhaps—not. I'm sorry," she repeated.

"I wonder if she can dance," Maureen whispered maliciously. She turned, her champagne-glass in one hand, and made a little face at the French officer, who had now begun to return her gaze.

"Well," said Tim, returning. "That was a sad defeat. How about it, Maureen?"

"Thanks, no. I'm not a second best."

"Oh, come off it. Come off it!" He tried to pull her to her feet, and though she kept saying: "Leave me alone! I don't want to dance! I don't want to!" slowly she yielded. He was aware in the scuffle that Betty kept glancing up at him with a gaze that was at once contrite, appealing and frightened.

A moment later Jimmy Tomlins slipped away, hoping that they would think he had gone to the lavatory, when, in fact, in his present state of nerves, he could no longer stand the proximity of so many people. He would like to have climbed into his car and shot off into the night, alone, with the wind cool on his burning face; but instead he smoked a cigarette while he talked to the doorman.

Christine and Gwyneth were alone.

"One gets so used to seeing Myra in trousers that one forgets how smart she can look," Christine said.

Gwyneth did not answer.

"Tim shouldn't have done that," she went on, talking because it seemed to be the only way to combat her exhaustion and depression. "Sometimes a devil gets into him—of course he only did it to annoy Maureen, that was all."

"And to annoy Myra."

"Myra? Why?"

"He's never liked her, has he?"

But that was an answer to a different question from that which Christine had wished to put. "Fancy bringing that girl along in their party. She must feel so out of place. I suppose Myra thought she was being kind. But it does seem to me a mistaken sort of kindness. Don't you agree?"

"Must we go on discussing Myra? It's not a subject which I find as interesting as either you or Tim do."

Christine suddenly sensed with an inward jolt that Gwyneth was, at that moment, battling against an even profounder desolation than herself. They were both of them stoical: but whereas Christine would clutch at any sympathy with the greed of a child, Gwyneth would push it away from her. "Dearest, you're tired," Christine said; for she could think of nothing else. "Shall we go home? I'm tired too."

"Yes, let's go home."

They waited for the others to return to the table and then, in spite of their protests, said good night and left.

Neither of them spoke a word during the drive home. "There's Mrs. Campion," Christine exclaimed, as they drew up at the kerb. "Isn't it?" She got out of the motor, and at the same moment Fritzy waddled towards her from the basement next door where he had been scavenging in the bins.

221

"Fritzy! Fritzy! Fritzy love! Where are you?" the tall, stooping shadow at the end of the street began to call.

"Gladys! Why are you out so late? You know that I said I'd take poor Fritzy for his last walk," Christine began to scold her. "It's so silly when you're not feeling well."

"Oh, I'm quite all right," Mrs. Campion said roughly, as she approached them. "I'd no idea when you'd be back. You mightn't have been back until to-morrow morning."

"Well, as I'd promised you . . ."

Mrs. Campion gave a deep, humourless chuckle; she obviously did not lay much store by promises. "He always knows the time. And if one's late, he begins to fret."

"How are you feeling now?" Gwyneth asked.

"Oh, perfectly all right."

The three women began to climb the stairs; and it was obvious to the other two women that Mrs. Campion was in pain, as she limped along beside them.

"Can I make you a hot drink?" Christine suggested.

"No. You know I detest milk at night."

"An aspirin then."

"But I tell you, there's nothing wrong with me—nothing wrong with me! I'm all right! . . . Really, you are stupid sometimes, Christine!"

They said good night, and heard Mrs. Campion limping down the stairs, with Fritzy behind her. Christine put her arm through Gwyneth's as they began to mount slowly.

"Oh, I do feel tired!"

"Me too."

"And depressed—I can't think why."

If Gwyneth had said something then, instead of remaining silent, Christine would have tried to explain to her what she had been feeling all that day. All through the war, they had lived under the constant threat of death, and yet it was only to-day that she had felt that death was near to her. All through those years she had worked without any respite, and yet it was only to-day that she felt that she could work no longer. She had been happy during those years, and now she had this feeling of irrational despair and sorrow. She wished to tell someone about all this, but she could not tell Gwyneth: it had always been hard to confide in her, and now it had become virtually impossible.

Gwyneth stooped down as they entered the darkened flat and picked up an envelope from the mat. "A telegram," she said.

Often, in her dreams, Christine had seen such telegrams, waiting for her on the mat, when she came back home, and they always announced the death of Tim or Larry. But this merely said:

GEOFFREY DIED YESTERDAY WRITING
ROSEMARY.

II

The war was two years over.

Christine sat at her limed-oak desk, the edges of the drawers of which now protruded crookedly, and frowned at a letter. As she looked at it, she massaged her right hand with her left, squeezing the swollen joints as though the rheumatism in them were some poisonous liquid. Then she heard a key in the door, and the sound of Gwyneth blowing her nose loudly.

"Is that you, darling?"

"Yes."

"It was madness to go out in this rain with that cold of yours."

Gwyneth's nose was red, and her eyes, above which the eyelashes jutted thickly, were glistening with tears, forced into them by her trumpeting into the large, white, linen handkerchief still held in her fist. But it was obvious that she was, none the less, in a state of elation. "I've got it," she announced.

"Got it? Got what, darling?"

"The cottage in Highgate Village." Christine stared at her, still kneading her aching hand, as Gwyneth went on: "I had some tough bargaining, I can tell you. In particular over that dilapidation clause. But the place has possibilities—definite possibilities."

Christine said slowly: "I look forward to seeing it." She had said this, off and on, for the past ten days, but Gwyneth had never suggested that she should show the cottage to her. Once again Christine frowned down at the letter, like a child forced to read a lesson too hard for her. "This is from the agents," she said.

"Oh, yes." Gwyneth opened the battered portfolio which she had continued to carry about with her even after her move into a surgery of her own near Highgate Archway, and pulled out a pad, normally used for prescriptions, on which she began to do calculations with the stub of a pencil. She appeared not to have heard what her mother had said. But Christine pursued with a kind of dogged mournfulness: "They've put the rent up again. Really I don't know how to go on. If we'd only been paying ten pounds less a year ago to begin with, they couldn't do a thing. It makes my blood boil to think of those two Bedworth women paying not a penny more, while I have to fork out almost double. It's a scandal. The Government should do something about it."

"You're one of the class about which the Government is likely to do precious little," Gwyneth answered brutally, continuing with her sums.

"Old 'Beddy' "—the nickname was now spoken, not with affection, but with rancour—"must be earning three times my little pension. Goodness, how smug she has become!" Christine pushed irritably at one of the warped drawers, but it refused to go in any further. "They've just had their sitting-room done up. I feel ashamed of asking anyone to come in here now." She gazed round the room at the patched covers; the sofa on which so many guests had slept that its seat rose up in two symmetrical tumuli; the sunshine-yellow walls that had turned a dingy grey; the carpet with an ink-stain ineffectively covered by an occasional table which came to pieces if one attempted to move it. . . . "It was so nice once. And now——" Her voice became husky, as she swallowed on the last words, shrugging her shoulders.

"Why don't you give it up?" Gwyneth suggested.

"Give it up! And where am I supposed to go?"

"You could find something smaller."

"At a much larger rent. No thank you, dear."

"Or you could get yourself a furnished room."

224

"That sounds a most attractive suggestion."

"After all, what *is* the point of slaving away to keep up this flat, which is really far too big for you?"

"I kept it up for you both. That was my only reason."

"All right!" Gwyneth exclaimed in exasperation: the sight of her mother's doleful yet accusing face gave her a terrible sensation of pity and guilt, combined with the irrational impulse to inflict some further cruelty. "All right, that reason has passed. Hasn't it?"

"*Tim* still seems to want to stay here," Christine answered bitterly.

"But how often do you see him? Once in two months. Is it really worth while to go to all this expense and trouble for the sake of two days in every two months? Is it?"

Christine shoved again at the drawer: "Yes, it is," she answered shortly.

"You know you can't afford it," Gwyneth reminded her. "On your pension—and what capital you have left—you simply can't afford it."

"Well, I don't regret the capital. I suppose it was used in a good cause. I've never needed anything for myself . . ."

"Yes, I know you saved and stinted and denied yourself for us! But we never asked you to do so. Did we? We never wanted the sacrifice."

"I made it willingly."

"Then don't throw it in our faces now!"

Christine rose, trembling, the letter held in both her hands. "What a way to speak to me!" she cried.

"Oh, Mummy, Mummy, we've said all this so often before. Haven't we? And what is the good? I know that you think us ungrateful. But we have to lead our own lives—that's natural, isn't it?"

"Yes," Christine said stonily, "it's natural enough, I suppose. But it's hard for the parents." Suddenly she brought her swollen hands together in tearful appeal.

"I'm not possessive—I'm not! But I—can't understand—it seems to me so odd . . ." She broke off, because she feared she would burst into tears. "Well, don't let's talk about it. As you say, it's no use."

But when Christine said "Don't let's talk about it" it usually meant that, in some oblique way, she would again refer to the

225

subject; and a moment later, as she picked up some socks of Tim's to darn, she asked with a forced casualness:

"How big is the cottage?"

"Oh, four rooms, that's all."

"*Four* rooms?"

"Yes."

"I suppose a sitting-room and a dining-room—and then two bedrooms?"

"One of the bedrooms I shall use as a study."

There was a short silence; then Christine went on:

"I suppose that you'll have to have a daily woman."

"I suppose so. I certainly can't run the house myself."

"Will she cook for you? Is that what you had in mind?"

"Oh, really, I don't know."

"I'd have loved to be your housekeeper. But I know that wouldn't work. Would it?" Gwyneth did not answer. "You wouldn't want your old mother around, fussing and interfering." Still Gwyneth was silent. "It's fixed then, is it?" Christine said.

"Is what fixed?"

"The cottage."

"H'm, h'm." Gwyneth made an uncommunicative sound at the back of her swollen nose, beginning once again to rummage in her brief-case.

"Then it's no use my mentioning my plan to you."

"Your plan? What plan?"

Christine sat down again; she began:

"Well, I can quite understand, darling, that at your age and in your position you should want some privacy for yourself. You have your own friends and your own interests, and it would be silly of me to wish to share them. So I thought—I thought of giving you a sitting-room of your own. I don't mind moving into the little room, I don't mind at all. And if that room of mine were then done up, and we bought some new curtains—oh, I meant to tell you, I saw some very pretty stuff in Story's window when I was shopping to-day—well, I do really think we could make something of it." All that afternoon, which she had spent alone, she had been elaborating this scheme; and now, as she told it, forgetting that Gwyneth had already made her decision, she became excited and eager: "You could have the gate-legged table in there—you've always liked that—and the Cotman water-colour, and the two Persian rugs—though I know they're a little threadbare. And we could buy you a decent sofa, and two armchairs. . . ."

Gwyneth wanted to cry out: "Oh, stop, stop, stop!" for at such moments she felt she was being guilty of the most abominable cruelty to a small child. Was it all a mistake? Had she the right to abandon her mother? Ought she not perhaps to give up her life to her, as she had seen so many girls give up their lives to their parents, uncomplainingly, as a duty. But she was at once tougher, more ambitious and more ruthless than they. Some instinct of self-preservation warned her that she must stand alone—however deep the wound to her own conscience or to the feelings of her mother. But the pathos of this appeal, as of so many of Christine's appeals, was something intolerable. Gwyneth got up:

"Well, I'm afraid I'm now committed." She tried to be affectionate and tender, but neither the appropriate words nor the appropriate gestures would come. Clumsily she said: "It was nice of you to think of it," and equally clumsily she patted her mother's bowed shoulders. It was rarely that she touched her, and even more rarely that she kissed her, or allowed herself to be kissed. Christine was therefore grateful even for this gesture of contrition.

"Tim coming?" Gwyneth asked, edging towards the door.

"Yes, I think so. I hope so." Tim never let her know for certain whether he would be coming for a week-end or not. "I had a post-card from Bangor, and he was not sure how long his tour would take him. You'll be in, won't you?"

"No, I'm afraid not. I have a meeting."

Gwyneth was often out at "meetings"; but whether they were social, medical or political Christine never knew. Occasionally she would say, as now: "A meeting? What kind of meeting, dear? Couldn't you put it off?"

But Gwyneth replied: "No, I'm afraid not. I must be there."

"I hope poor Tim won't be hurt."

"Hurt! Why should he be hurt?"

Christine hesitated and then said: "You used to be so close to each other once."

Gwyneth sighed. "But, darling, things can't go on being as they've always been in the past." She mastered her exasperation, and began to explain patiently: "We're fond of each

227

other, of course we're fond of each other. But, well, we have different interests, different points of view, different friends. You can't expect us to feel exactly the same about each other as we felt when we were children."

But Christine persisted with a stubborn obtuseness: "You know that when you both were left with the relatives he regarded you as a mother."

"But things have changed! They've changed!"

Gwyneth picked up her brief-case and went up to her bedroom: she knew that if she stayed any longer with her mother they would have one of their useless, aimless, bitterly acrimonious quarrels which would culminate in Christine bursting into tears and Gwyneth rushing out of the house, slamming the door behind her. Moodily she sat down on her bed, her plump legs apart, and rested her chin on her arm which, in turn, she supported on a hefty knee. Although she was still only in her early thirties, her figure was matronly, and her hair, wisps of which always escaped from the bun into which it was drawn, was rapidly turning the same grey as the coats-and-skirts which she invariably wore to work, as though they were a uniform. The melancholy which would suddenly darken her face when she was a girl had become set, but in a less impassioned and more sullen mould. Yet she was kind and humane and, in the women's hospital where she worked, was adored by her staff and patients. Often, after she and Christine had quarrelled, and remorse would rise up in her, choking her, like some bitter vomit, she would say to herself: "But why am I like that to her?" And she would remember some old woman, who had cursed at her when she was trying to relieve her agony, or a young probationer who had been guilty of a carelessness that might have resulted in death: to them she had been merciful. She knew that her skill as a doctor lay, not in brilliant intuitions, but in her perseverance, her patience and her humanity: yet it was precisely these qualities that deserted her when she had to cope with her mother. She continued to stare out of the attic window, sitting, her hands clasped and her head thrust slightly forward, in exactly the same posture in which she sat by a difficult case: and on her face was the same expression of watchful, brooding tenderness, which gave to it a kind of monumental handsomeness. How could she help Christine? What was she to do for her? The cottage had been an extravagance which, while she felt herself under the obligation to repay her debt to Myra, she could barely afford. No, she ought not to have taken it; but there were reasons for doing so, apart from her wish to get away from Christine's clinging and cosseting and prying. There were reasons.

Meanwhile, Christine was making her way down the stairs to the basement flat, to visit Mrs. Campion. She had so often declared, "But I must feel that I'm wanted. I must feel that I'm of some use in life"; and yet she was unaware of the extent to which this need drove her to the other woman. Often she would exclaim what a nuisance it was to have to do this or that for Mrs. Campion; and she would add that it was not as if the old woman ever showed any gratitude or even pleasure at seeing her. But when the children told her that she was tired, that she had always done more than enough, and that surely Mrs. Campion's children should also take some of the responsibility from her, Christine would protest: "Oh, but the poor old thing has no one else in the world. I don't know how she would survive if I didn't go down to see her."

She knocked now and waited, as she heard the old woman moving about in the room below and then shuffling up the stairs, while Fritzy let out a series of sharp, plaintive yappings. Christine had often asked Mrs. Campion to give her a key to the door, but stubbornly she had refused, for to do so would have been to give up some fraction of that independence and privacy which were now her only possessions.

"Who is it?" she asked.

"It's me."

"What is the good of saying 'It's me'? How am I to know what that means?" Mrs. Campion grumbled breathlessly, one gaunt hand pressed to her side while with the other she held the door open for Christine to enter.

"Did I wake you up? Were you lying down?"

"At this hour! You know that I never lie down during the day." Mrs. Campion always kept up this pretence, in spite of the evidence of the nightdress she was wearing and the unmade bed in which was lying, face downwards, a large, old-fashioned volume of *Tom Jones*. Fritzy sat on the pillow, as breathless as his mistress; but whereas she had grown thinner and thinner, he had grown so fat that he could hardly move himself even to greet Christine, to whom he was devoted.

"How are you feeling?" Christine asked, although she knew that this question always annoyed Mrs. Campion.

"Perfectly all right," Mrs. Campion said, subsiding into a chair. Her face was haggard, an orange colour against which her lips showed deep purple, with grooves running like scars down either cheek and diagonally from her ears to her protuberant collar-bones.

"I've brought you some cold meat. We're going out this evening," Christine lied, "and I'm afraid it may not keep till to-morrow."

"What's the matter with the refrigerator?"

"I'm going to de-frost it."

"Well, put the meat down over there." Mrs. Campion pointed to an upturned packing case on which there already stood a cup without a saucer, half full of cold tea, a skein of wool, and some old football-stockings of Tim's rolled up into a wad, which Mrs. Campion wore in bed. "Fritzy can have it for his supper."

"Oh, but it was meant for you," Christine said, dismayed. "It was the best part of a joint of lamb."

"You know that I don't care much for meat. . . . Oh, stop fussing with that bed! You only disturb poor Fritzy."

"Shall I take him out for you?"

"No, he's got to go to the vet. I shall take him myself." Mrs. Campion rose slowly from her chair and pushed back a curtain behind which clothes hung from pegs or lay in disordered heaps on the floor.

"But you oughtn't to go out—really, Gladys. It's raining."

"Mind your own business! And give me those shoes." Christine handed her the canvas shoes. "I don't see why I should be cooped up in here all day long. You seem to want to make an invalid out of me." She was talking with the same fretfulness that Adrian would show whenever Christine attempted to dissuade him from something rash during his last illness; and there was the same lurking terror in her enormous, red-rimmed eyes.

"Of course I don't. But it's so stupid, when you're not feeling grand . . ."

"Who said I was not feeling grand? Now take care of those

230

cups!" she cried out. Christine had nearly dropped one while she began on the washing-up. "Take care! I can't afford to have you smash everything I possess. The Rockingham plate was only a luxury; but my teacup I need." Four months ago Christine had broken a plate which had already been riveted, and since then Mrs. Campion had never ceased to remind her of this accident. "You're so heavy-handed," she went on, as she began to lace up an old-fashioned corset, the pink satin of which had grown frayed and dingy with use. She paused, her bony hands clutching the two strings, and for a moment a look of intense pain passed over her face; her lips seemed to recede, showing her teeth, while her eyes moved helplessly about the room as though looking for some person who was not there to come to her aid. Then she drew a deep sigh, seated herself on the edge of the bed, and saying, "Now patience, Fritzy, patience," began to pull on her stockings.

Christine had repeatedly begged her either to go to the hospital where Gwyneth worked or to see Gwyneth privately; but this suggestion threw the old woman into such a temper that she no longer dared to make it. Instead she said: "Look, Gladys, do let me take Fritzy to the vet for you. I can telephone Rosemary and say that I'll be late."

"He'll be injected only if I hold him. He wouldn't let the vet touch him otherwise. Would you, Fritzy? Would you?" Once again she made the old gesture of inserting her long, battered nose into Fritzy's ear, as she leant across the bed in her tattered petticoat, drawing up her blue-veined knees.

"Haven't you finished that yet?" she demanded, turning.

"Almost."

"Well, when you've finished, get out the pram."

Under the stairs in a cupboard which contained an old uniform-case, a rubber "bone" with which Fritzy had long since ceased to play, a broken electric stove and some umbrellas, the coverings of which hung in dusty shreds, there was also a folding perambulator which Mrs. Campion had bought from a second-hand shop in the Fulham Road. It was a malevolent object which Christine detested from the way in which it closed on her fingers, inexplicably collapsed and let out a series of shrill screams which put her nerves on edge. The cupboard smelled, and the pram, too, had begun to smell; after touching it, Christine always wanted to scrub her hands.

Now, as she began to carry it up the stairs, it snapped on the hem of her dress, leaving two grey ridges. Mrs. Campion followed, panting noisily, with Fritzy in her arms, even though Christine had called out to her that she could carry the dog.

The belt of Mrs. Campion's raincoat had no buckle, and she knotted it together, after she had deposited Fritzy in his carriage, and then pulled a hat, which looked like a felt flower-pot, down over her eyes.

"I'd better wheel it for you," Christine said.

"No, no, no!" Mrs. Campion protested, thrusting Fritzy along the hall with a series of laborious forward movements which looked as if she were pushing a toboggan through deep, crumbly snow. "But help me now—no, the other end, the other end," she cried, as they came to the steps. The two women stooped, and between them, the icy wind whistling round their legs, carried the dog down into the street, while he whimpered at every jolt. "You ought to have the poor fellow put away," Tim had declared brutally, when he had last seen him; to which Mrs. Campion had retorted: "How would you like it if you were put away simply because you were old and suffered from rheumatism? Your mother has rheumatism," she added maliciously.

"I'll walk with you," Christine said, drawing her coat about her.

"Certainly not."

Christine was appalled by the fury of the wind, which threw stinging drops of rain on to her upturned cheeks and flapped at Mrs. Campion's raincoat as though it were a sail. "Then let me treat you to a taxi."

"Really, for someone who is virtually broke, your extravagance is astonishing. I suppose you now plan to go all the way to Portman Square in a taxi?"

Christine denied it: except when she was with Tim, she never entered taxis, even at times when her rheumatism made it almost impossible for her to walk.

"Well, good-bye," Mrs. Campion called, again making those odd forward movements of her tall, emaciated body into the rain and wind.

"Good-bye, my dear. I'll look in as soon as I get back."

Mrs. Campion made no reply; perhaps did not hear.

Christine walked to the next corner, and then looked round.

Mrs. Campion had stopped and was bending over the pram in order to cover Fritzy with a strip of tartan blanket. There were no other pedestrians and no cars in the street, which was already growing dark. The wind blew a violent gust, and the shadow-like figure seemed to totter before it again stooped to the task of pushing the perambulator forwards. Christine hesitated; she wanted to run after Mrs. Campion, to call out, to force her back into the house. But she did none of these things, for she knew they would be useless.

As she walked on, her first thought was: how lucky I am! Then another thought followed: if that should happen to me!

Rosemary had long ago told her never to come to the house without first telephoning. From a call-box round the corner, Christine asked: "Is it all right?"

"Yes. He's gone to Manchester on business, and she's at a bridge party. Only the old lady is here, and she very much wants to see you."

After Rosemary's return to England she had been forced, by lack of money, to look for a job. All her friends had supposed that she would teach, find some literary work, or undertake translations; but instead she had preferred to go as housekeeper to a rich, childless couple, who lived in Portman Square, in a house covered throughout with different shades of striped or starred wall-paper. Mr. English ran a chain of women's clothes shops, which went by the name of "Eithne McDonald". Since his wife was called Magda, and they had obviously originated from East London, not Scotland, this had puzzled Rosemary and the Cornwells, till one day Mr. English himself had explained: "I bought them out, you see. That's what I did. I bought them out."

"I can't think of any job less suited to you," Tim had told her. "What on earth made you take it? And what on earth made them take you?" he added.

Rosemary answered the second of these questions first.

"Well, I'm a lady," she said. "Apparently. And that's what they wanted. When I went to the agency, they took one look at me, and said, 'We've just the job for you.' And funnily enough, it suits me. I'm clever at taking down telephone messages, and nobody can live the best part of thirty years in India without knowing something about entertaining. I live in my little cubby-hole, and if I want anyone to talk to, there's always the old lady."

On the top floor, Mrs. English kept her partially bedridden mother as though she were a mad relation in some Gothic novel. Rosemary often suspected that the older lady did not go down the stairs, not because she could not, but because she dared not, for fear of annoying her daughter.

"But you ought to be using your brain," Gwyneth protested.

"There's little of that left. And what I have I can exercise on my subscription to the Times Book Club and my weekly copy of the *New Statesman*."

When Rosemary now opened the door, Christine hissed at her conspiratorially: "Out? You're sure?"

"Yes, I only hope she doesn't come home sooner than she said. She tends to, you know, if she begins to lose money." A maid crossed at the back of the long hall, and gave them an inquisitive, vaguely impertinent look as she went through a door into the basement. "That's the new German girl. I bet she sneaks on me."

"Oh, Rosemary, this is just like being at school!" Christine laughed delightedly.

They made their way upstairs, past the drawing-room and study on the first floor, the bedrooms, dressing-room and guest room on the second, the two guest rooms on the third, and so to the landing where Rosemary lived. The German girl slept on the landing below, and the cook above, on the same floor as Mrs. English's mother.

Rosemary turned up the grudging flame of the gas.

"I'm not supposed to burn that except when I'm in the room. The old lady has a paraffin stove. She says it 'turns her stomach'."

The room looked as if it had been planned either for a large dog or dwarf, and Rosemary's height only exaggerated this impression. There was a narrow divan bed, a narrow chest-of-drawers, like an enlarged match-box stood on one end, an upright cane-bottomed chair and a small armchair covered in a pattern of orange zig-zags, like forked lightning playing on a bright green ground.

It always surprised Christine that after at least six months in this room Rosemary should still give the impression of merely camping in it. There were none of the photographs in silver frames which Christine remembered from the house in India; no pictures; not even the bottles of medicine or toilet preparations which normally accumulate where a person has lived for any length of time. But for the wireless this might be a room in any small London hotel and Rosemary a visitor up from the country for a few days of shopping.

"Why don't you have some of your own things around you?" Christine asked, surveying the room. "Wouldn't it make it a little less depressing?"

Rosemary smiled: "But who said that I found it depressing?"

"Well, *I* do."

"What would you like me to have here? That skin of the man-eating tiger, which Geoffrey shot near Naini Tal? Or some of those mounted tusks?"

"You have other things," Christine reminded her.

Rosemary sat down on the bed. "You know, it's odd—I don't seem to have any interest in possessions now. I gave an awful lot away before I left India."

Christine, who had clung to her possessions and had cried out, with what was almost physical agony, when Gwyneth had attempted to prise the more unsuitable from her grasp, could not understand this lack of interest. After all, Rosemary had always had such nice things—as Christine would remind her. But the other woman's feeling that she could not be bothered with possessions seemed to Christine to be only a part—the least alarming part—of a general feeling that she could not be bothered with anything at all. Rosemary was glad to see her old friend, of course; but Christine often wondered how much she would mind if she never saw her again. She was glad to hear about Tim and Gwyneth, and their many mutual friends; but did she wish to hear about them any more urgently than about the family whose serial story she mocked at, but always followed, on the wireless? Sometimes Christine wondered if, since Geoffrey's death, Rosemary had lost the capacity for feeling.

The two women talked.

"Gwyneth is sure that the poor old thing has cancer. But I can't get her to go for an examination." They were discussing Mrs. Campion. "Didn't you think she looked terribly ill when you saw her last?"

Christine said such things before she remembered that it was unlikely that Rosemary would agree with her.

"Oh, I don't know," Rosemary said. "She seemed pretty cheerful to me. After all, one can't expect a woman in her seventies to show no sign of wear and tear. Can one?"

Tim often said that Rosemary's growing remoteness was the natural upshot of her stubborn refusal ever to come to terms with reality. She tried, by an effort of will, to see reality in a different, less painful, guise and when she could no longer do so, she shrank away from it, into a world of her own imagining.

"How terrible old age is!" Christine exclaimed, in the middle of their conversation. "I dread it so much."

Rosemary said nothing.

"When I look at Mrs. Campion," Christine went on, "and think that one day, perhaps, I shall also be reduced to that condition!" She gave a little shudder.

"But you never will," Rosemary protested.

"Why not? It might quite easily happen."

"Because you're not Mrs. Campion—that's why. She hates the world and life, and expects to find them vile. And so, for her, they are. Whereas you . . ."

But there were now times when Christine herself found the world and life vile—though to Rosemary she would never dare to say it. Often she would complain: "People have changed, now that the war is over"; or "Gwyneth has changed"; or even "Tim has changed". She did not guess that this change might be one, not in the world around her, but in her own self.

Soon she had begun to tell Rosemary about the cottage which Gwyneth had taken: for, like a thorn implanted in the recesses of her mind, she was all the time painfully conscious of this news. "Don't you think it extraordinary of her?" she appealed at the end. "After all, she must know how I have to scrape to keep the flat going. And though she's offered to make me an allowance of five pounds a month, that'll hardly make up for what I shall lose on her room. She sighed. "Well, I suppose I shall have to get a P.G."

"Would that be so terrible?"

"Tim would hate it so."

"Then he ought to help you, so that it's not necessary."

Christine was secretly aggrieved that, in spite of his new job with Maureen's father, at an excellent starting salary, Tim had still made no offer to help her with the expenses of the flat; but now she at once defended him, as she always did when Rosemary made any criticism of him, however oblique:

"The poor boy has hardly enough to live on himself. His digs in Birmingham are wickedly expensive."

If Rosemary had known where he lived, she might have pointed out that a two-roomed service flat in a modern block in the centre of the city could hardly be described as "digs"; but as she and Christine were equally ignorant of the nature of his accommodation, she merely shrugged her shoulders. "Well, I should have thought he'd have something to spare. After all, you only keep on the flat for him, don't you?"

This was not the whole truth, even though Christine herself imagined it was so. The flat had, during the war, been the centre of the lives, not merely of the children and their friends, but of a number of people, mostly foreigners, who now rarely wrote to Christine except to send her a postcard or a Christmas card. Since their going it had acquired the peculiar silence and melancholy of a dismantled power-house. The power-house would not work again; better for her to abandon it. But she had not accepted that fact. Somehow, some time, the dynamos would once more start to whirr and spark; the workers would come back; energy would begin to pulse, as it used to pulse, outwards in all directions. It was only necessary that she should hang on, hang on.

Also, she had reached that age at which all change is terrible. When Adrian had died, although she had been terrified and appalled at the prospect of having to start a new life, yet she had also been thrilled. But now the thought of packing up and beginning yet another life, probably alone, in some small flat, in the house of others like Rosemary, or in one of the drab boarding-houses where so many of her old friends now stooped over their gas-rings in order to prepare her a cup of tea, filled her with apprehension. Often she dreamed of standing outside her front door, her possessions all around her, with a sheet of paper in her hand on which an address was written so badly that it was impossible for her to decipher it. . . .

"Would you like to go and see the old girl?" Rosemary asked. "She's always asking after you. You made a great impression on her."

It was not unusual for Christine to be told that she had made a great impression on people such as Mrs. Swinson. Such old wrecks at once realized that here was someone who was interested in them; did not despise them or find them tedious or repellent; and would be kind and generous to them not, like their relatives, from a sense of duty or guilt, but because she happened to like them. Old Mrs. Swinson could discuss, as she was doing now, what she called "her water-works" without the fear that Christine would cry out: "Oh, Mother, please! Must we have these revolting details?" as her daughter would do; and when it was necessary for her to have the pan there would not be on Christine's face any of that look of patient, absent-minded stoicism which invariably appeared on Rosemary's.

"No one would believe you were only eight years younger than myself!" the old lady exclaimed, when Christine virtually lifted her up in bed.

Christine shrank at the thought of that brief interval which separated her from the decomposing huddle of flesh, wrapped about with shawls, that her hands were now touching. Eight years—so little! And who would come to hear her talk about her "water-works" or help her to perform these necessary, if now repellent, functions? She supposed that she would be in a hospital ward, and that some efficient, brusquely anonymous nurse would heave her around as though she were a package of meat.

Mrs. Swinson now began to talk about her daughter, in a plaintive sing-song Cockney voice: she felt she had a grievance, and yet she did not wish to be disloyal, so that every complaint was at once followed by the kind of excuse which Mrs. English would, no doubt, herself have provided. ". . . I used to know his mother and father so well," she related, for example, of a business-man who had been to dinner the previous evening, accompanied by his wife. "I remember him as a boy—that was when we were neighbours in the New Kent Road. I thought she'd ask me down, or at least bring them up to see me. Not a bit of it! I dare say they thought I was dead. . . . Well, I suppose she didn't want me to get tired, like. The doctor said I mustn't get tired. That's very important in my chronic condition, not to get tired. And maybe she also thought that I wouldn't be wanting them to see me like this, bed-ridden. I was always so active in those days, I'd never sit still."

Later, she began to complain that Mr. English had not been to visit her for nearly a week; but in this case, too, she at once began to excuse him: "Well, of course, he did have that cold, I do know that. And I expect he thought he was being considerate, knowing how easily I catch a cold—even sitting in a draught brings one on. And then, of course, Mr. English is such a very busy man. You know he began from almost nothing, don't you? And now he's given us this lovely home, and he and Mrs. English go abroad at least once a year, sometimes twice. . . ."

She suddenly clawed open a box of *marrons glacés* and handed them to Christine: "They brought these back from somewhere in France. They brought them back for me especially. Wasn't that nice of them? But I can't eat them, not now I can't. They bring on my heartburn something terrible. The doctor says it's some kind of acid—and when the acid and all that richness meet—well, it's sheer murder." She shook the box at Christine, who had declined: "Now, please, Mrs. Cornwell! No compliments, please, among friends!"

When Christine got up to go, the old woman clutched at her hand, turning her wedding-ring round and round between her fingers as she coaxed her: "Stay a little, Mrs. Cornwell, do stay a little! It's early yet. At any rate stay till the rain stops!" She poked her little beaked nose up at Rosemary: "You tell her to stay. You persuade her."

But Christine insisted, for she feared that Tim might arrive home before she returned.

Rosemary accompanied her down the street, even though Christine had urged her not to venture out in the rain. "Oh, but I love it! I'll see you on to your bus, and then I'll take a short stroll through the park."

"Shall I come with you?"

"Oh, no. You must get back to Tim. You mustn't be late."

It was obvious that Rosemary did not wish to be accompanied.

As the bus lurched off, Christine shouting good-bye to Rosemary over her shoulder, the conductor bawled out: "Hold tight, Grandma! Hold very tight!" It was absurd to be angry;

but she glared at him in rage as he punched her ticket. Grandma. . . . And then she thought gloomily of those eight years which separated her from "old" Mrs. Swinson and who could guess from what humiliations and horrors.

Tim was already home.

"Oh, darling, I'd no idea you'd be here so early," she cried out in dismay. "Why didn't you get yourself some tea? I'm really most frightfully sorry."

She insisted on making him some tea now, although he did not want it and, when it was brought, only took two or three sips. All the time she questioned him about his doings, while he mumbled his answers—"Yes." "No." "Not bad." "H'm, h'm." "Oh, all right"—turning over the pages of a woman's magazine which he had found on the sofa. "Isn't that ridiculous?" he asked at one point, holding up an illustration. "How would you like to see your old mother wearing a coat like that?" she laughed in response.

"I wouldn't allow it."

At last he put down the magazine, and gave her a beam, as though he were greeting her now for the first time: "Well?" he asked. "How is it going?"

She began to tell him first about poor old Mrs. Campion and then about Rosemary and Mrs. Swinson.

"I don't know why you visit those old hags when you always come back so depressed. Can't you make some other friends? When did you last see the Everards?"

"Oh, darling, you know I don't really like them. He's become so pompous since he joined the Colonial Office. And really she and I have nothing in common."

"Well, what have you in common with this—this old Mrs. Swinson, or whatever she's called? Or with Mrs. Campion and Rosemary for the matter of that? No, darling, I think you ought to get out of this rut. Before it's too late. I've been thinking about it a lot"—he had, in fact, barely thought about her at all in the three weeks since he had last seen her—"and I really do feel that the time has come when you ought to try to break out and away from this odd little set of yours."

"But how could I break away from Rosemary, after all she's done for me?" She was puzzled, committing the mistake of taking seriously what had been merely the idea of a moment. "And Mrs. Campion—how could I abandon her now?" She watched him as he drew a cigarette out of the gold case which he had talked her into giving him for his twenty-first birthday, but to these last two questions he offered no answer.

Puffing smoke-rings up at the ceiling, he drew his legs on to the sofa: "Guess who I saw, while I was driving from Cardiff to Swansea."

"That's easy—Myra."

"No, wrong! Betty," he announced.

"Betty?" She could not think to whom he was referring.

"Myra's land-girl. Don't you remember that evening at the Beauchamp when she refused to dance with me?"

"Oh, yes—yes, I remember now."

"Well, I took her into Swansea—and there was no reluctance about dancing this time, I can tell you! It was a complete coincidence," he went on, drawing at his cigarette. "Of course, I knew that I'd go near Myra's place, but I didn't much care to see her. And then it just so happened that I ran out of petrol—and who should come out to serve me but Betty, in some of the dirtiest overalls on which I've ever set eyes! She's not bad looking, you know—her figure is marvellous." He smiled in pleasurable recollection: "We had quite a time."

Tim seemed to take a pleasure in telling Christine of encounters of this kind, of which there were many; even though it should have been obvious to him that they shocked and dismayed her.

"Are you going to see her again?" she asked feebly.

He laughed: "Oh, God, no! I hope not. But Swansea is a horribly dull place on a Sunday, if you're alone."

She hated this callousness; and all the excuses which she made for him, whether in her own mind or in answer to Gwyneth's criticisms—"He's so young, and after all he's been through it's natural for him to want to enjoy himself"—would never entirely banish her uneasiness.

"Darling, I hope you weren't too naughty," she said.

"No naughtier than she."

Usually, at this point in such conversations, she began to talk to him about the need to "settle down", at which he would laugh at her until she fell silent. But now she merely began to put the tea-things on to a tray and carry them into the kitchen, for it had at last come home to her that nothing she said to

241

him would ever make the smallest difference to any of his actions.

"The rent has gone up again," she announced, when she returned. "They now want two-eighty."

Tim whistled: "The bastards!"

"Really, I don't know what I am to do. Gwyneth thinks I ought to give the place up." She perched herself on an arm of the sofa, from which she looked down on him as he lay outstretched, his head on two cushions.

"Well, why not?" he drawled. "Isn't that the most sensible thing?"

It was like being struck across the face with a cane; Christine even put a hand to her cheek and slowly began to massage it, as she stared at him in mingled pain, shock and astonishment.

"It's not for myself that I've kept the flat on," she replied to him slowly, the colour beginning to mount under her skin which her fingers were still stroking. "It—it was . . ." She stopped.

"Well, for heaven's sake, don't keep it on for us."

"That's what Gwyneth said. She's—taken that cottage."

"The one in Highgate Village?" Christine nodded. "Good for her!"

"It's you I'm still thinking about. I want you to have somewhere which you can regard as your home—where you can keep your books, the clothes you don't need, and where—where there's always a bed for you. . . ."

"Well, it's certainly been wonderful having this *pied-à-terre*. But if it means that you have to pinch and scrape and struggle to get along, it simply isn't worth it."

"Yes, it is worth it," she said. "For me it is."

He either ignored, or did not notice, the suppressed force of these words. "Nice of you to say so. But after all I'm likely to be less and less here; and if, as seems likely, I have a place of my own, well, then, of course——"

"Have a place of your own? Do you mean you want to . . ."

"Well, now, I'm taking our hurdles in the wrong order!" he exclaimed with a laugh. "The fact is, darling, that I've at last decided to follow your advice."

"My advice?"

"To settle down. Maureen and I have decided to get married." This was something which Maureen herself had

242

decided more than two years before, as Christine well knew. "It's not a bad idea, is it? What do you think?"

Christine paused only for a second, but he noticed that pause and it exasperated him.

"Darling, I'm delighted! Really delighted! You know how much I like her. And, after all, you can't go on being a gay bachelor for ever, can you?" She continued to say what she thought she ought to say, instead of what she felt, while he, without in any way responding to this forced enthusiasm, remained outstretched on his back, staring up at the light. At last, in a bored, slightly mocking voice he began:

"She's a good sort, and she seems to like me. We suit each other. We thought of getting married in the spring. 'Daddy'—as I suppose I shall now have to learn to call him—is going to give us a house somewhere outside Birmingham. We've seen one, as a matter of fact; beautiful William-and-Mary. It's more than he thinks he's going to pay, but we've both set our hearts on it. Then we shall probably also look around for a small central flat in London." He went on speaking of their plans, unaware of her growing misery, desolation and jealousy.

Of these emotions she was ashamed; but later she told herself that probably most mothers showed them, when their sons announced their engagements. Yet it was odd and disturbing that what was so obviously "a good match" in the case of Tim should upset her far more than what was equally obviously a disastrous one in the case of poor Larry. None of her former friends would now make those pitying or malicious comments with which they had greeted the news of Larry's engagement to Louise; for the snobbery of those Anglo-Indians was confined to colour and money, never to class, and on both these scores Maureen was unassailable.

"I'm sure she'll make you a wonderful wife."

"Probably a better wife than I shall make her a husband!" he retorted, laughing.

"I do like her so much."

"That's what I keep on telling her. She seems to have got some idea into her head that you dislike her or disapprove of her—God knows why."

"Did she say that?"

"Well, you have got that cutting way of putting things at

243

times. Which someone who didn't know you well might misunderstand. But I keep repeating to her that it doesn't *mean* anything at all, that it's just your manner."

"I'm sorry she should have thought ..." Christine began. Then she got off the arm of the sofa and said with a forced brightness: "Anyway, darling, I hope that you are going to be very, very happy indeed. You deserve to be."

"Bless you, old thing."

He patted her on the back as she stooped over to kiss him: genuinely he was fond of her, and Maureen's hostility to her caused him to worry.

"I must slip downstairs for a moment to see if Mrs. Campion is all right. I promised that I would."

"Now no skivvying for her! Just look in—and come back. I want to see *something* of you myself," he said, opening another magazine.

"But, darling, I must get her some supper."

"No, no. That's exactly what you must not do."

"Someone must do it."

"Then she should hire a woman."

"Oh, Tim! You know she can't afford it."

"Then what about those children of hers? I really don't see why she should live on your kindness and charity when both of them are so well-to-do."

"You know that she's quarrelled with them."

"Well, she ought to make up the quarrel."

"I'm afraid it's gone too far for that."

"Not if she didn't suffer from that insane pride of hers. . . . I thought that, once your children were grown up and the war was finished, you'd relax a little. Instead of which you wear yourself out on these quite unnecessary duties. Now don't be long—remember. I see little enough of you, as it is."

When Christine rang the bell to the basement flat, the wait seemed even longer than usual and Mrs. Campion's ascent of the stairs even more laborious and slow. When the door at last opened it revealed the older woman in her nightdress, with a candlestick in one hand.

"What's the matter?" Christine asked, peering at the gaunt profile the shadow of which, monstrously exaggerated, flapped on the wall behind it. "Isn't the light working?"

"Fused," Mrs. Campion said, almost inaudibly, between

clenched teeth; and Christine knew at once that she was in the most terrible agony.

"Well, why didn't you call us? Tim or I could mend it. Get back to bed."

Mrs. Campion took two steps backwards down the stairs and then, with a sudden abrupt gasp, put a hand over her mouth.

"Gladys," Christine said, terrified yet trying to be calm. "What's the matter? Are you in pain? What is it? What is it?"

But as she spoke, Mrs. Campion slowly sank on to the stairs, bowing her head over on to her knees while the candle, tilted dangerously, dribbled wax into the darkness below her. Christine heard the scrabbling of Fritzy's paws and then his whining as he edged under the skirt of his mistress's nightdress.

"Gladys!" she cried. She stooped and put an arm about the other woman, and as she touched the frayed cotton of the nightdress found it damp with sweat. "Come!" she coaxed. "Let me help you down to bed."

Suddenly Mrs. Campion gripped her savagely, emitting a horrible, retching groan. "Oh, oh, oh!" she gasped. "I—can't—stand—it. . . . Oh!"

Christine consoled her like a child; and when the worst had passed, took the candlestick from her, placed it on the topmost step, and then half dragged, half carried her down the stairs.

Mrs. Campion lay on the bed, staring with her mouth open at the ceiling, where shadows leapt hither and thither, like crinkly black flames. Fritzy was crouched beside her, his nose to her breast. "It'll pass," she said. "It's going. It'll pass soon." Suddenly she began to weep, her lips contorted and the large tears spilling sideways from her eyes which, each beneath its jutting ridge of bone, continued to search the ceiling as though for some invisible mark.

"Gladys, you must let Gwyneth look at you. I insist! You must!"

"Yes, dear . . . yes, I will . . . yes. . . ." She had never before called Christine "dear", and her normal rasping voice seemed curiously soft and tender. "Yes, I will." Suddenly she clutched at Christine's hand, and cried out: "But it's coming back! It's coming back!"

When Christine at last returned to the flat, Tim greeted her: "Well, really! You've been gone at least an hour."

"Tim, she's very ill," Christine said. "I shall have to go and sleep there. I'm sorry, darling, but—but I simply can't leave her."

She had done him the injustice of supposing that he would be exasperated by this news: instead of which he at once threw aside his magazine and leapt to his feet. There was no doubt from her expression that she was seriously alarmed.

"I'll come with you," he said.

"Will you, darling? That's very sweet of you. Bring some fuse wire—the lights have all gone."

It was with an extraordinary tenderness that he squatted by the old woman's bed and took one of her wrinkled hands between both of his own. "Now what's all this about?" he asked. "Eh? What is it?"

"Tim . . ." she murmured. "Tim. . . ." She gave a little smile. "Look, Fritzy recognizes you. He's wagging his tail."

They sat with her, while she alternately dozed and mumbled disjointed phrases to them; until, in the hall above, they heard a firm tread. "Gwyneth," Christine announced.

There was no doubt that Mrs. Campion was dying: upstairs Gwyneth murmured the terrible word "inoperable" as she prepared a syringe in order to give her an injection. "But how long will it be . . ." Gwyneth shook her head, obviously stricken. "We must get her into a hospital as soon as we can."

"She couldn't stand a public ward."

"Well, what else is there for her?"

"Perhaps I could help. . . ."

"Mummy—how can you? When you know that you've barely enough——"

"I wouldn't mind a public ward myself. I think I would prefer it. But for her . . ."

"We'll have to tell her children. After all, it's up to them," Tim said decisively.

"Oh, no, Tim, no!"

"Of course we must. Don't you agree, Gwyneth?"

Gwyneth nodded: "Yes, I think we should. After all, it's only fair to them."

"But she'd never forgive us. You know how she feels about them."

"Do you want her to go into the next world bearing that same terrible hatred towards them?" Tim asked. "Isn't it better for them to be reconciled before it's too late?"

"And think of their feelings of guilt, if they learn that she has died in poverty, in a public ward, unforgiving to the end," Gwyneth murmured, as she watched the syringe gently bouncing up and down in the boiling water. "No, I think we ought to tell them."

"I'm sure we're doing wrong," Christine still protested, as Tim telephoned to Directory, in an attempt to find out the Captain's number: and neither of the children could shift her from that conviction.

Late that evening, when she went down to the basement flat for the last time with a string bag containing her night-things, she found Mrs. Campion more aggressively herself.

"What is all this?" she demanded. "What have you got in there?"

"I'm going to spend the night with you," Christine replied.

"And where do you suppose you're going to sleep?"

"Oh, I shall manage in the armchair."

"You're such a restless sleeper," Mrs. Campion objected. "I remember from the air raids. You'll only disturb me."

"Gladys, I'm not a restless sleeper at all! That's the first time anyone has told me that. . . . But, before I undress, I'm going to make some cocoa for you, and Gwyneth has given me these two pills for you to take."

"I really don't know why the girl should use me as her guinea-pig." Mrs. Campion pronounced the word "girl" as "gal". "One would imagine that by now she'd know how to give an injection. It was like having a knitting-needle stuck into one."

While she prepared the cocoa at the gas stove, Christine gathered her courage to tell Mrs. Campion both that Gwyneth had arranged for her to go into a private ward at the hospital where she worked and that her son, the Naval Captain, had told Tim on the telephone that he would be arriving early the following morning. At last, having carried the steaming mug over to the bed, she managed to break this news; and, as she had expected, Mrs. Campion was furious. She did not intend

247

to go into a hospital, she shouted, the muscles of her scrawny neck standing out like cords; still less did she intend to see either her son or daughter. "How dare you interfere in my private affairs? How dare you? First you have the impertinence to push yourself, unasked, into this flat for the night and then you calmly admit to all this too. It's monstrous! Absolutely monstrous! I suppose it's because you have nothing else to do that you've become such a busybody. Well, I won't stand for it, do you hear? I won't stand for it!" A froth appeared at the corners of her mouth which had already broken down into a number of deep, inflamed cracks. "No, I won't see him! And I certainly won't be moved! And as for your spending the night, well, it's quite impossible!"

"Gladys, Gladys, Gladys," Christine chided her softly, while Fritzy snuffled and made a noise like a kitten mewing in distress. "You'll only exhaust yourself. Why go on like this? We only want to help you. That's all. Please, Gladys." She began to force the older woman back on to the bed, and, after a moment of resistance, Mrs. Campion subsided, throwing a skinny arm over her face as her body was suddenly racked by long, shuddering tearless sobs, one after the other. "Oh, Gladys, why do you resent everything one tries to do to help you?" Christine implored, herself near to tears. She tried to ease the arm away, but Mrs. Campion only squirmed round, drawing her knees up simultaneously, so that she was now huddled in a tense, ungainly coil, her face to the wall.

Fritzy was waddling up and down the stairs, scratching at the door from time to time or at Christine's shoes. "All right, Fritzy, all right," she said. "I must take him out, Gladys. Can I have the key?"

Mrs. Campion at once turned round, snatched the key off the table beside her bed, and then thrust it under her pillows. "No," she said. "Ring."

"But you can't get out of bed again. Don't be silly."

"Ring."

In the end Christine left the door ajar, even though Mrs. Campion shouted after her: "Shut the door! Shut the door, I tell you!" Fritzy trotted to the very edge of the pavement and there, as though with the purpose of displaying the same obstinacy as his mistress, squatted himself and began to strain with bulging eyes and protruding tongue. A woman passing by, exclaimed "Disgusting!" while Christine scolded, "Not there, Fritz, not there! Bad dog! Naughty dog!"

Delighted with his exploit, Fritzy then made a laborious attempt to whisk up the steps on three legs while the fourth, crippled with rheumatism, trailed, as though broken, behind him. Christine followed.

No sooner had he entered the basement flat, some two yards ahead of her, than the door shut with a defiant slam, so suddenly and unexpectedly that at first Christine assumed that a gust of wind had blown it. But when she rang and rang, and no one came in spite of Fritzy's yapping, the truth began to dawn on her.

"Gladys!" she called. "Gladys—don't be silly! Please, Gladys!"

She must have pleaded for at least five minutes until at last a voice came from within: "Go away! I don't want to see you again! Go away! Go on! Stop making that din!" Then there was silence.

When Christine at last gave up her useless ringing and knocking at the door and made her way upstairs to tell Gwyneth and Tim of these events, they both advised her to wait until the morning. "By then, she may feel different," Tim said. "It's useless hammering away now—you know how stubborn she is. Leave her to stew in her own juice."

But Christine remained anxious and distressed, and most of that night she lay awake, either thinking of Mrs. Campion in particular or brooding in general on the horrors of illness and old age.

The morning brought the Captain, a grey-haired man in a tweed suit too loose for his stooping, emaciated figure, and brogue shoes polished to a dazzling burnish. All of them went down and alternately knocked, rang and shouted. It was odd, as Christine pointed out, that Fritzy made no sound.

Suddenly the Captain's moustache twitched, and his red face began to whiten. "Do you smell anything?" he asked.

It was the question which they had all feared to put. Immediately he began to throw himself against the door while, simultaneously, Tim ran out into the garden from which, a few seconds later, they heard the sound of broken glass. "Take care!" Christine wailed. The stench of gas was now overpowering.

249

Like some vast, frozen bird, Mrs. Campion lay over Fritzy, clutching him to her bosom, as though to warm him to the end against the imminent ice-age. She must have fed him soon before their death; there was an enamel plate beside the bed, with the remains of some porridge in it, surrounded by curdled milk.

III

"It really is maddening to have to miss 'Façade'," Gwyneth's friend, Laura, exclaimed, slamming the car door. "I thought the whole point of coming was to see Margaret in it." Gwyneth remained silent, staring moodily at the back of the bus in front of them while her large hands, the palms of which looked as if they had been rubbed with sandpaper, beat a rhythmic tattoo on the wheel. "Well, wasn't it?" Laura pursued.

She was herself a dancer, with a narrow face and torso, and delicate wrists which threw into contrast the masculine sturdiness of her legs and thighs. She fingered the glossy black bun into which her hair was drawn, and repeated:

"Well?"

"Yes, my dear. That was the point. But as the programme was changed, and 'Façade' came last instead of first, I can hardly be held responsible. Can I? Can I? Well, can I?"

"Why did you tell your mother to come to-day of all days?" Laura at last broke her silence to demand. "We planned to come to this matinée weeks and weeks ago."

"Because she's visiting friends in Hampstead for lunch, and it seemed to be convenient to pick her up on our way home."

"Oh, we're picking her up, are we?"

"Yes."

"Well, then, good God, surely she could have stayed on with them until the show had ended?"

"Yes," Gwyneth agreed impassively.

"So?"

250

"So what?"

"Then I can't understand what we're doing in this car at the moment."

"I forgot."

"Forgot? Forgot? What do you mean?"

"I said we'd wait for her at Whitestone Pond at half-past four. I forgot about the show. And by the time I remembered, she'd already left home."

"You could have telephoned these friends of hers."

"If I'd known their name."

"But aren't they *old* friends of hers?"

"Probably."

"Then, surely . . ."

"Well, really, Laura, I can't remember where all my mother's old friends live. It might be one of a dozen couples."

There was a silence, until Laura demanded: "Why do you keep that wind-screen wiper going, when it's no longer raining?" She stared at Gwyneth's profile until, at last realizing that she would make no move to switch off the wiper, did so herself with an irritable gesture. "What has happened to that marvellous memory of yours?"

"My memory was never marvellous."

"Well, that efficiency of yours. I'm surprised you don't leave swabs inside all those wretched women you cut up."

"Oh, I have a sister to remember the swabs for me."

"You've taken the wrong turning!"

"No, I haven't."

"Yes, you have. If you cut down Downshire Hill——"

"Really, Laura, I know Hampstead far better than you."

They continued to bicker until they reached the Pond, where they found Christine seated on a bench talking to an old man in a cloth cap and crumpled blue-serge suit, a knobbly stick with a rubber ferrule extended between his knees.

"Who's your boy friend, Mrs. Cornwell?" Laura asked, her ill humour gone. As in the case of the performance of "Façade", she disliked not getting what she wanted; but she liked Christine. "Well, now, don't be so coy!"

"Oh, we got into conversation." Christine was always "getting into conversation" with strangers, who confided to her the most extraordinary secrets about their married lives, their health or their careers. Laura, who was inhibited by an

251

over-consciousness of class, never wearied of hearing of such encounters; and Christine, realizing this, at once ran on: "Such a sad story. It seems his only daughter fell in love with a German prisoner-of-war, and now it turns out that he already has a wife and family of three or four children in Düsseldorf— or Hamburg, was it?" So she continued, until they drew up at the cottage.

"Shall I get the tea?" she then volunteered at once.

"Oh, no, you sit down and take it easy, Mrs. Cornwell. That's my job," Laura told her.

"Yes, do sit down, Mummy." There was a note of irritation in Gwyneth's voice. She herself had already flopped into a chair, with one leg thrown over the arm, the calf muscles protuberant as a cross-country runner's.

Christine sighed, and placed herself on the sofa, pulling out two hat-pins and removing one of what Tim called her "pancakes", as she did so. Jabbing the pins back into the hat, she remarked:

"I didn't expect to see Laura."

"No?"

"Wasn't she supposed to be going on tour?"

"She is going on tour. Next week."

"You'll feel lonely without her." Gwyneth got up to put another lump of coal on the fire without answering. "Will she be away for long?"

"Ten weeks, or thereabouts."

"She must be thrilled. I've always longed to go to the States. Now I suppose it'll never be. Unless I win one of those football pools which Tim gets so cross with me about," she added. "He says it's a waste of money—throwing money away. But did I tell you about the man at Gapp's—the one at the bacon counter—well, they say he's now bought himself a . . ."

"Yes, you did tell me."

"Perhaps I might have the same luck!"

Gwyneth did not look as if she believed it.

"Then you'll have the cottage to yourself." Christine reverted to the theme from which she had been distracted. "It'll seem odd, I expect. Of course the place *is* small, really, but one does have such an odd sense of space. Doesn't one? That's what Rosemary said to me last Sunday. . . . You know that she's started her new job, don't you?"

Gwyneth nodded moodily.

"Four pounds a week—all found! I'm glad she left those terrible Englishes. Though I feel sorry for the old lady. Apparently she broke down completely when Rosemary said good-bye to her. But four pounds a week, think of that! I've a good mind to get a job myself."

"Don't be silly," Gwyneth said roughly. "With that rheumatic knee of yours how do you imagine you'd get on?"

"Oh, but it doesn't prevent my being active."

"You could barely hobble last week."

"What I *do* find trying is all those stairs at number twenty-one." Christine sighed. "Ah well! Beggars can't be choosers. I suppose I should be grateful that I have a roof over my head." Christine eyed Gwyneth sideways, and saw that her face was reddening either with exasperation or embarrassment. She knew that it was madness to go on with this prodding, and yet she continued to do so, out of an overflowing bitterness of heart: "Did I tell you that Tim and Maureen have asked me for next week-end?"

"No. How nice of them!"

"*Very* nice." Again Christine sighed. "But I don't know if I shall go."

"Why on earth not?"

"Well, I think that really they regard me as rather a nuisance. And—oh, I don't know—I feel uncomfortable when I'm with them. Not with Tim, of course, but all those smart friends of theirs—and Maureen's relations. . . ."

"Don't be silly."

"I'm not being silly. After all, it's natural that after a time children should begin to find their parents a bore. Even though that's hard for the parents themselves. But one has to face it. My one wish is not to be a burden to you both, that's what I said to Rosemary only yesterday. I don't want you to feel that simply because the room will be empty now that Laura is going——"

Suddenly Gwyneth shouted: "Oh, do stop it! Do stop it! I can't bear all these digs—all this hinting!"

"Well, what have I said? What have I said?" Christine demanded in feigned surprise. "Have I said anything? Surely we can have a calm discussion without your flying off the handle. . . ."

"I know that you think that Tim and I treat you badly. And I know that you feel you ought to have Laura's room. Well, say it, say it! Why don't you say it outright?"

"Really, darling, it's not a thing I expect. Not a thing I expect at all. I've always said—well, I was saying only the other day to poor old 'Beddy', when she asked why I didn't settle myself either with you or with Tim—I told her, at once, that even if you both wanted it, I'd never *dream* of such a thing. It wouldn't be fair to you. Of course, you must have your own lives . . ."

"Oh, Mummy, Mummy, Mummy!" Suddenly Gwyneth swung her leg off the chair, and jumped to her feet. Pulling down her grey cardigan, which was rumpled above her slightly protuberant stomach, she said: "One comes home exhausted after a hard day's work—hoping for some quiet—and then one gets . . ."

But fortunately at that moment Laura came in, bearing the tray. She looked back and forth, from one of the women to the other, and then placed the tea-things on a table, sat down beside them, and began to pour out.

"No, thank you, no," Christine said in a small, aggrieved voice when Laura broke the silence to offer her a piece of cake.

"Oh, but you must! I insist. I made it myself. It's the first cake I've ever made in my life, can you believe that? You must forgive the hole in the centre. Please, Mrs. Cornwell." She was making a special effort to be agreeable to Christine: for it was part of the peculiar relationship between herself and Gwyneth that each of them would always side with a third party in any dispute or quarrel.

Gwyneth now leant over to cut herself a piece of the cake, since Laura had omitted to offer her one; at which Laura exclaimed: "What an enormous chunk! No wonder you keep putting on weight." She gave a little laugh. "I wish I knew the secret of *your* figure, Mrs. Cornwell. In the distance at the Whitestone Pond, you looked like a young girl."

"It's nice of you to say that. But I'm afraid you only want to pay me a compliment," Christine replied, though she none the less believed it.

Gwyneth picked up a book and began to read, swilling tea and eating her piece of cake in voracious gulps as she turned the pages.

"Very social, I must say," Laura commented after a while.

Christine peered at the dust-jacket of the book, and then exclaimed: "Oh, it's Pat's new novel! I didn't know it was out. They've promised to let me have it first at Boots. I told the girl that she was a friend of ours. What's it about?"

"Tim."

"Tim!"

"Couldn't you have guessed that from the title?" The book was called *The Face*.

"You mean it's—it's about him and her?"

"Well, that was obviously her starting-point."

Christine was horrified, and her horror grew when she learned that the central theme of the book was Tim's mutilation. "Oh, no—no!" she exclaimed, as though repudiating some shameful suggestion. "No, she couldn't have done that. She couldn't."

"It's surprising what writers can do," Gwyneth said sardonically.

"But to make capital out of—out of all his sufferings . . ."

"They were her sufferings too."

"Not to the same extent! All that silly squeamishness, and then letting him down like that, at the time when he needed her most! No, that's something I can never bring myself to forgive her. And now—now this—this beastly book of hers. . . ."

"She's been far kinder to him than to herself in the book."

"Well, I should think so too. Let's face it—she could hardly have behaved worse. . . . I'm surprised that she's not afraid of being dragged into court," Christine went on. "That would teach her a lesson."

"Oh, don't be silly!"

"Yes, I agree with you, Mrs. Cornwell," Laura put in. "I think it's a shocking thing to have done. If I were your son I'd sue her—I'd sue her at once!"

Gwyneth eyed Laura contemptuously over the top of the book. "Well, you're such an exhibitionist," she said with a bitter smile.

"What do you mean?"

"You'd love all the publicity of a court-case. Wouldn't you? It would be even more exciting than being on the stage of Covent Garden."

"I don't know why you say that. Really, Gwyneth, sometimes

255

I think you take a pleasure in deliberately hurting people's feelings."

Gwyneth laughed: "Well, of course I do!"

"And I don't regard it as a joke." Laura got up and began collecting and stacking the tea-things noisily, her usually serene face distorted with annoyance. Christine looked in turn at her and Gwyneth: the scene, in some extraordinary way, was conforming to a pattern—one long since established by Gwyneth and Myra between them. "How they enjoy a scene!" Tim used to exclaim of those other quarrels; and though she could not understand why, Christine sensed that the two women derived the same kind of perverse pleasure from this one.

"Can I help you, Laura?" Christine asked.

"No, thank you, Mrs. Cornwell. No, thank you."

Christine and Gwyneth were again alone together; and now there was a long silence.

"Well, I hope you're satisfied," Gwyneth said at last.

"Satisfied?"

"Whenever you come here, you seem to manage to make Laura quarrel with me."

"What do you mean? How is it my fault? What do I do? If you and she get on each other's nerves I can hardly be held responsible. What an idea!"

Gwyneth snapped the book shut, tossed it across to the table where the tea-things had been, and got to her feet. Once again the cardigan was rucked up, to show a bulge of pink satin over her midriff, but on this occasion she did not pull it down. "You seem to have a genius for creating an atmosphere of tension," she muttered as she strode out of the room.

Christine said: "Well, really!" half aloud to herself; got up to examine an invitation to a scientific lecture which rested on the chimney-piece; then peered at the hand-writing on an envelope beside it, but restrained herself, with difficulty, from taking out the letter; and eventually sat down once more to examine Pat's book. "I wonder what she's made of me," was her thought.

From the kitchen she could hear Laura and Gwyneth quarrelling, at first in low, urgent voices, the actual phrases of which were inaudible to her, and then in a torrent of mutual accusations.

256

"You've no right to say that, no right at all! Have I ever accepted a penny from you, have I?"

"Oh, don't be so childish. I didn't mean that you were a parasite in that sense. I meant that you simply live off the emotions of others."

"Well, it would be difficult to live off *your* emotions," Laura shouted back, her tones now strident and slightly Cockney. "I don't believe you have any. I don't believe you feel anything at all. When I see how you treat that wretched mother of yours, who obviously adores you . . ."

"Leave her out of this!"

Suddenly, in the middle of this uproar, a slap could be heard. Then there was silence, followed, a moment later, by the noise of someone sobbing. But who had slapped whom? It was obviously Laura who was in tears, but from her experience of similar quarrels between Gwyneth and Myra, Christine knew that that did not necessarily mean that it was Gwyneth who had been the assailant. Once more the low, inaudible voices could be heard: no longer in mutual accusation, but in mutual apology. Christine, lingering by the door as she strained to catch what they said, muttered to herself: "How absurd! Really, how hysterical!" She found, as she often told Rosemary and Tim, something "unhealthy" and "morbid" about these scenes.

At that moment the bell rang.

Gwyneth called out: "Mummy! Oh, Mummy! Do see who it is."

Christine went to the front door, and let in a small, pale, blond young man and a middle-aged woman of almost twice his size. She remembered having met them once before, at a meeting of a Ballet Club to which Gwyneth had taken her, but they did not recognize her. The young man had some gramophone records under one arm, while from the other dangled an unfurled umbrella. He walked in ahead of the woman and at once began to take off his duffle-coat, peering at the same time at his chin in the looking-glass.

Gwyneth appeared, her face flushed and shiny: "Oh, hello, Frank! Hello, Lettice! You know my mother, don't you?"

Each gave Christine a nod and a quick, nervous smile; neither of them looked at her.

"I've brought round the Khachaturian records," the young

257

man fluted. "We want your advice. Lettice doesn't think the music will do."

The woman, who had a homely, slightly disagreeable face, turned as she hung up a black raincoat that looked as if it had been dipped in tar, and said sharply: "That's not what I said at all. You always get the wrong end of the stick, Frank. Always."

They continued to argue in this fashion, until Laura herself appeared, her long face coated in powder and her eyes glistening, no longer with tears, but with the mascara she had just applied.

"Now, Laura, let's have your opinion!" the woman demanded.

"Well, let me hear the music first," Laura said, taking the records from the young man. As she began to place them on the turntable, Gwyneth asked, in a voice which, to Christine's astonishment, was heavy with a kind of yearning tenderness in spite of their recent quarrel:

"Are you sure the needle doesn't need a change?"

"Well, you'd better judge." Gwyneth crossed over as Laura smiled helplessly at the others. "I'm terrible at mechanical things. That's Gwyneth's speciality."

They listened, first to the records which the young man had brought, discussing them as they did so, and then to innumerable other records which either Laura or Gwyneth would tweak from the shelves where they stood neatly arranged and catalogued. "Awful!" the young man would say, putting his little hands to his shell-like ears. "Take it off, take it off!" and the record would be removed. "I like that. Yes, that I like. That's nice," the woman would then pronounce, as though she were a middle-class housewife trying on hats. "It could do with some trimming. Properly trimmed, that would be a good choice, I think."

No one asked Christine for her opinion; no one looked at her, or addressed her. They were even unaware that, huddled as they were around the fire, eagerly arguing with each other, she was left to sit in a draught. She felt alone, exasperated, and bitterly sorry for herself. What a sissy the young man was! She would like to hear Tim's comments on him. And the woman, how untidy, with that egg-stain on the front, and all that hair which looked as if it had been cut off at different lengths by a pair of garden-shears! These were, no doubt, intellectuals. Intellectuals. She savoured the word contemptuously on her tongue as the old man to whom she had talked on the Whitestone Pond had savoured the phlegm brought up from his creaky lungs, before he leant forward to spit it out at his feet. Ever since Adrian's death it was among such people that Gwyneth had found her friends, and all of them were alike: affected, selfish, neurotic, grubby, conceited. Christine had forgotten the exceptions to this rule—the young violinist, a refugee from Poland, who had been so good to her; the journalist, a paying-guest for a few weeks, who had then gone out to edit a paper in Nigeria; the B.B.C. features-writer who had invited her to the studios—as she now crouched in her chair, scowling in turn at the backs of the four people whose bodies prevented any of the warmth of the fire from reaching her.

Suddenly she got up; but, though she pushed her chair back noisily, they were all so absorbed in their discussion that none of them looked round. In the hall, she pulled on her shabby black overcoat, with hands that were trembling and clumsy with rage, wrenched her umbrella out of the stand, and then re-opened the door into the sitting-room to say:

"Gwyneth, dear, may I have a word with you?"

Gwyneth looked up, and with reddening face joined her in the hall. "What is this?" she demanded.

"I think I shall go home now."

"Go home! Why?"

"Well, dear, my knee has begun to ache and I don't want to be late. And, anyway, I have some letters to write." Christine's "letters", so often an excuse if she wished to refuse an invitation or avoid some irksome duty, had become a family joke; even though it was true that since the end of the war she had been driven by the lack of anything else to occupy her into carrying on a growing correspondence with people, similarly idle, whom she would have regarded merely as acquaintances and therefore as not worth even a line during the busy and crowded years in India or during the war.

"But we were expecting you to supper," Gwyneth said indignantly.

"Yes, dear, I know. And it was very sweet of you—of you and Laura—to invite me." Gazing down at the ugly, battered,

red-leather knob of her umbrella, which looked like a red-hot poker withering between her black gloved hands, she went on in the same voice of quiet, reasonable, melancholy restraint: "But I really do feel very tired. I think I shall get back to my own little gas fire, and settle down for the evening. Now that you have this unexpected visit from your own friends, I'm sure you won't miss me." She opened the front door, and a gust of wind spattered her shoes and the bottom of her dress. "Oh, dear, it's raining," she exclaimed. "Well, good-bye, darling. Say good-bye to the others for me. I don't want to break in on their discussion. They seem to be so very absorbed!"

"Oh, do stay to supper," Gwyneth said impatiently. "Then I can drive you home afterwards."

"No, dear, I wouldn't dream of it. I wouldn't dream of dragging you out in this weather. The walk down to the bus will do me good. The doctor says that exercise can do no harm whatever to my sort of rheumatism. . . . Well, good-bye."

As she leant forward to kiss Gwyneth, her eyelashes were blinking rapidly and her upper lip trembling.

Gwyneth knew that Christine expected her to insist on her staying, but for once, perversely, she did not do so. Instead she said harshly: "Well, you must do as you think best. I'll telephone to-morrow."

Christine turned and made her way down the steps with what Gwyneth was sure was an exaggerated limp. Another bid for sympathy, she thought in exasperation; and what was even more exasperating was that the bid would succeed. As she peered out at the bowed figure, hobbling along towards the garden gate, where she had to struggle simultaneously with the latch and her umbrella, she was stricken by remorse. Laura had said that from behind, at the Whitestone Pond, Christine had looked like a young girl; but now she looked like an ancient old woman.

"Oh, Mummy, please, please!" Gwyneth ran out into the rain and put an arm under Christine's, propelling her back towards the house. "Please don't go! Or, if you must go, do let me drive you back."

Christine pulled stubbornly in the opposite direction. "No, darling, let me go, let me go, let me go. Don't bother about me, please. Gwyneth, let me go. You'll only get soaked." But at that she began to yield: and after a few seconds Gwyneth had succeeded in coaxing her into the house, and was helping her off with her coat and shaking out her umbrella.

"Why don't you spend the night?" she asked. "I can have the camp-bed and you can have mine."

"Oh, it's far too much trouble. I don't want to put you to any trouble."

"Don't be silly! It's no trouble at all. You will stay, won't you?"

"Well—all right, dear. If you insist." Christine's hand went out first to the umbrella which Gwyneth still held, and fiddled with the tassel; then timidly, as though she were a child touching some forbidden object in a museum, she raised it to Gwyneth's cheeks. "You're very sweet to me," she said. "Both of you. I'm lucky to have such nice children. Very, very lucky."

The words were without any intention of irony; but to Gwyneth they carried the smart of a rebuke.

"Now let me see what I can do about the supper," Christine went on. "There's no reason why I shouldn't get on with it, while you all are discussing your music."

Laura complained even if Gwyneth went into the kitchen to get herself a cup of tea. But Gwyneth had not the strength to deny her mother now: even though this weakness of the moment would certainly result in at least an hour of bickering later. "Well, I think almost everything is ready," she mumbled in lame excuse, following Christine into the kitchen and fiddling with a tin-opener. "Laura was planning an omelet. An omelet, cheese and fruit."

But Christine was not listening: "Shall I make that potato-and-bacon dish which you and Tim used so much to like?" she demanded eagerly. "Shall I?" She pulled at the door of the refrigerator: "You have some bacon, I see."

"Yes," said Gwyneth weakly. "Yes, why don't you do that?"

"Now you leave me to myself. You go back to the others!" Christine began to rummage for a pie-dish in a cupboard. "And don't tell Laura what I'm doing, mind! Not a word to Laura! I want this to be a surprise. Don't tell Laura! Let's see what she says."

261

Christine's visits to Tim and Maureen passed no more happily. They now had three indoor servants, one of them a German girl who was alternately bullied and snubbed and patronized by Maureen; a child said to be delicate; and a Nanny who, by virtue of having once worked for some distant cousins, was frequently described by Maureen to her friends as having "been with the family for as long as I can remember". Nanny had a disagreeable old-fashioned face, sepia-coloured with darker brown blotches, as though in a Victorian photograph, and her favourite phrase when she wished either to humble her mistress or to exasperate Christine was: "Well, yes, of course, Madam, if that's how you like it . . ." Christine often felt that, but for Nanny, she and the child, Jeremy, might become friends; but somehow Nanny, with her admonitions that the poor mite must not be over-excited or her reminders that one of his grandmother's minor indulgences would be paid for that night as like as not, seemed always to come between them, just as Laura and Maureen now seemed always to come between her and her own children.

Maureen herself was kind; but in that jolly, brisk way that usually signifies that the kindness is willed, not spontaneous. The first time that Christine stayed at the house, Maureen told her: "Now I want you to regard this room as your own. It's Granny's room, and you can have it whenever you want it." But when Christine left on the Monday morning, she heard orders being given to the German girl for Granny's room to be "done" first thing, as some other guests would be arriving before luncheon. Maureen ran her house efficiently, worked in the W.V.S., and entertained the "county". She was getting plump, because she was greedy, but it was an attractive plumpness except when she appeared in breeches to ride.

During her week-end visits Christine saw little of Tim. Sometimes he would take her out in his Jaguar, and on such occasions she was too frightened by the speed and recklessness of his driving to be able to talk to him coherently. Even at other times, however, he succeeded, like Gwyneth, in giving her the impression that nothing she said could possibly be of interest to him. "I suppose he finds me dull and stupid," she would think; but then why did he chatter away in so lively a fashion to the old wife of the parson, who was far duller, far more stupid, and deaf into the bargain? Sometimes Christine would exclaim: "Tim, I don't believe you're listening to a word that I'm saying to you!" And unashamedly he would reply: "Now how did you guess that?"

He had become increasingly cynical; liable to moods of alternate moroseness and gaiety; restless; cruel in his teasing of his wife, his mother, Nanny, and above all the child; feverish in the pursuit of women, and usually successful; intelligently Philistine, contemptuously social. Christine often confessed, either to Gwyneth or to Rosemary, that she was worried about him; something was wrong—though what it was that was wrong she could not define. Certainly he was not happy; and Gwyneth said that that was natural enough after all he had suffered. But the war was four years over; people had got sufficiently used to his new face to feel that it had always belonged to him; and after all he had made a good marriage, his job was an excellent one, and he seemed to be generally liked.

From time to time, whether through some careless remark of Gwyneth's, the visit of a friend or her own observation, Christine would become aware of one of his flirtations, usually with a married woman. On one occasion, when Gwyneth and Laura were going to Italy for a holiday, he had even borrowed the cottage from them in order to use it to meet the young wife of an elderly pianist. Christine had been horrified. "Oh, I suppose I shouldn't have mentioned it," Gwyneth then remarked. "One tends to forget how conventional you are. But, surely, in the old days in India, there was enough of all that? Or was Kipling wrong?"

"Yes, dear—but . . ." Christine hesitated; and did not go on. There was a certain decorum in those far-off times; it was unlikely that a man would borrow his sister's house in order to entertain a mistress. But it was hard to explain this to Gwyneth, and Christine was afraid that, if she attempted to do so, she would only be laughed at.

This particular week-end had been a failure from the start. It was Jeremy's birthday on Saturday, and Christine, having gone into an Oxford Street store with the intention of spending ten shillings on a present, came out with a toy train that had cost her three times that sum. "It's for my grandson, you know," she explained to the bored young man wearing the striped tie of a minor public school who had strolled over to serve her. As the young man fiddled with his cuffs, wondering if it was noticeable that they were frayed, she went on to tell him how Jeremy had this absolute mania for railway trains in spite of being only three. "Why," she continued in a sudden rush of confidence, "the only reason that he eats his cornflakes is because there are trains on the packet!" The young man thawed and slowly softened; his cuffs ceased to worry him: and Christine, mistaking this patience for a genuine interest in her affairs, at once began to talk at length about her family.

"Well, I bet he'll be pleased with that," the young man said, as he bowed and beamed good-bye to her.

"Oh, I hope so. I do hope so."

"You'd think they had nothing to do but gas all day," he commented to another young man, as Christine moved away. "Silly old trout!" But he said it without any rancour.

The train, however, pleased only Jeremy. When Tim pulled it across the floor of the nursery, first the string broke and then, more serious, one of the wheels came off. Jeremy screamed with excited laughter at both of these accidents, but Tim said something about expecting as much of toys made in Czechoslovakia and Maureen added: "It's a disgrace, a shop with that reputation selling such shoddy stuff."

Nanny then took a handkerchief from her belt, licked it surreptitiously, and ran it along the side of the engine. "Oh!" she cried. "Good gracious! She held the handkerchief out, smeared with what looked like a pale-pink lipstick. "Well, look at that. One lick of that and his tummy will be in an even finer condition than now. Look at it, Madam!" Nanny had already persuaded Maureen to cancel Jeremy's birthday party, because his tummy had been upset that morning; and when Christine had pointed out that this was probably due to excitement, she had fingered one of the dark-brown blotches on her face, squinted down her nose at a plate of porridge which she had liberally scattered with salt ("That's how we from the North of the Border like it") and had retorted: "Well, that was what I meant, madam. Other children mean excitement for him;

264

and excitement always leads to a bilious attack. Or worse," she added ominously.

Tim was even more restless and preoccupied than usual. He would play with Jeremy or chat to the women for a moment; then he would go off and weed the herbaceous border; then, half an hour later Christine would hear the Jaguar roaring away with him to some unknown destination. He had drunk a lot before luncheon, though not enough to go to his head, and then spent half the meal teasing them all in turn and the other half in complete silence.

"Do you ever hear from Pat?" he suddenly asked Christine when they found themselves alone with their empty coffee cups between them.

"What, dear?" Christine was astonished; for this was the first time he had mentioned Pat to her since that day in the hospital when she had had to tell him of her departure. "Oh, no, dear, no. And I can't say that I'm sorry. . . . Why?"

"This book of hers—I've been reading it."

Christine had also read it; but she had hoped that Tim, who now rarely read anything except the *Autocar*, the *Tatler* and the *Financial Times*, would fail to come across it.

"Yes, I've read it too."

"What do you think of it?"

Once again she was astonished: for Gwyneth and Tim now rarely asked her for an opinion on anything at all, let alone a book.

"Well, I suppose it's very clever," she said guardedly. "Gwyneth says that everyone thinks that it's her best for many years. But——" she looked across at him and nervously cleared her throat—"she shouldn't have done it, Tim. It wasn't right."

Unexpectedly, he exploded into a laughter that had something of the dry, persistent, struggling quality of a choking-fit, the stretched skin of his face darkening as he gripped the arms of his chair. "Well, really, you are priceless! You do say the most marvellous things, darling. And why wasn't it right? Why shouldn't she have done it? Hm?"

She looked both confused and hurt by this boisterous mirth. But stubbornly she repeated, "It wasn't right, Tim," shaking her head, her hands locked before her.

"My God, what a devilish understanding! All the little things that I thought she had never noticed—the feelings I tried to hide. . . . She had seen them all, all! It's terrifying, you know, to pick up a book and find out that someone has understood you better than you've understood yourself."

"It was a cruel thing to do. How would she like it if one of us wrote a book about her, and told how she——"

"But she's told it all herself!" he cried out in exasperation at her obstinate loyalty to him. "Oh, she's a writer in a thousand." He went to the window, and looked out at the beautiful formal garden, his hands deep in the pockets of his trousers, jingling his money. "And a woman in a thousand," he added. "I don't suppose I shall ever meet anyone like that again."

"And I hope not too!" Christine wanted to reply. But she remained silent as she gazed at the back of his head where the blond hair curled, slightly over-long, into small tendrils.

She had never been able to understand his love for Pat in the past; and now she could not understand his admiration for her. "Well, I suppose she's very clever"—that grudging phrase, which she had so often used about her, hardly seemed to explain the force of her attraction.

Tim drifted back to where his mother was sitting, placing his suede shoes gently on the thick pile of the carpet as though he were afraid to disturb someone who was asleep. He sat down opposite her, and stared intently at her face, and she stared back at him. Upstairs they could hear Jeremy screaming in the nursery: it was a usual occurrence. No doubt Nanny had told him either that he must rest longer or that he had rested enough.

Tim yawned, stretching his arms above him and then extending his fingers, which were still thin and claw-like after their burning, as he thrust his legs out.

"It's odd, you know," he mused. "We saw each other for occasional week-ends—an evening here and there—and then that short time when she took the house. . . . And yet she managed to know all about me. She knows me as no one has ever known me," he added, unaware that this remark might cause her pain. "And here I've lived with Maureen for nearly four years—day after day, day after day—and what does she know about me? Nothing at all!" He laughed: "We might still be strangers."

"But, Tim, she tries hard to . . ."

266

"Oh, she knows that I like two lumps of sugar in my coffee, and one in my tea; that I hate to see her wear brown; that I never eat celery or sweet-breads. . . . But of the things that matter, the things that count . . ." Again he laughed; then, seeing the look of consternation on her face, he went on: "Don't think I'm complaining. To have been understood, completely understood, once in one's life—well, that's quite a lot. I've been lucky, damned lucky. Think of the poor wretches who fail to achieve even that. Oh, one mustn't expect too much. One mustn't expect that kind of thing to happen twice in a lifetime."

"Tim!"

"Yes? What?"

"Oh, darling, you mustn't be so bitter, so cynical."

"But I'm not being bitter, not at all. You're the one who must beware against being bitter. I'm very satisfied. I've had all that any man can reasonably expect in life."

He frowned up at the ceiling as the child's screaming continued. Then he leant forward and took her locked hands:

"Truly, Mummy. What more can one expect? I have a wife who runs my home well, and a brat—not a bad brat, except when he screams—and a house which is one of the show-pieces of the Midlands. . . . And then there's that book to remind me of all the other things I've had—the other, less tangible things. . . ."

She did not know whether he was talking in mockery or not. But she mumbled: "Well, if you're satisfied, darling . . . if you're content. That's what matters."

"Oh, satisfied—content! Well, that's another thing, isn't it?" Suddenly he jumped to his feet. "God, that child! What is the point of employing an expensive Nanny if she can't even guarantee one quiet after luncheon?" He strode towards the door, and Christine, seeing what he intended to do, cried out from behind him:

"Oh, leave him, Tim, leave him! He'll calm down in a second."

Then she waited for those terrible screams which were so unlike the screams of rage that had gone before them. Adrian and she had never beaten the children, and she remembered how once, when they were staying with friends, they had

267

walked up and down, up and down, the garden in agitation, their arms linked together, while their host chastised his six-year-old son. Christine put her hands to her ears, and then, nauseated, opened the french windows on to the garden and was about to step out. But the noise stopped.

Tim was flushed and panting when he returned to the room. "That'll teach him a lesson," he said. He smiled, looking down at his hands which he extended, palms open, before him. "My own hands are stinging."

Christine felt momentarily repelled and disgusted: she knew that he had enjoyed thrashing the child, as he had enjoyed dropping bombs over Germany. But she was sentimental enough to shrink in horror from these facts: these were not pleasures that were generally acknowledged.

"You seem unhappy," he suddenly remarked.

"Now—now, you mean?" she asked, startled. "No, of course I'm not. I've loved this week-end. It was just Jeremy—you know, I don't think you ought really to treat him so severely. . . . After all, the child *is* delicate. Isn't he?"

"Doesn't do him any harm—quite the contrary. Probably if you and Daddy had slapped us more often we'd be better and more dutiful children now. The child is spoiled and coddled enough as it is by Nanny and Maureen—not to mention you."

"Yes," she agreed slowly. "But—but . . ."

"But what?"

Surprised by her own boldness, she confessed to him: "You enjoyed doing it, Tim. That was what was wrong. You did, didn't you?"

"Well—so what?"

"Why—why do you suddenly want to be cruel to people, darling? Why? I don't understand. You were never like that when you were young. You weren't one of those cruel children."

"Oh, shut up!" he said, with such profound weariness that the rudeness of the phrase seemed somehow to be dissipated. Then he sat bolt upright in the chair: "Enough about myself. Let's talk about you. What about this flatlet you're going to take? You've told me nothing about it."

She had told him nothing about it because he had asked her nothing about it. Now, excited by his interest, she began to describe it to him. It was in a basement, but there was light,

268

oh, a lot of light; it was not at all like poor old Mrs. Campion's flat, not at all. The bath tub was in the kitchen, but she liked the idea of being able to watch the toast while taking her morning bath. And, after all, Haverstock Hill was a nice neighbourhood, wasn't it? A little too Jewy, perhaps, but there were nice houses with nice gardens. What she particularly wanted was to have a few of her own things around her.

Tim expressed his approval, although in truth he had been troubled and depressed by this eager description of a flat, the grey horror of which he could so easily picture in his mind. As he grew older that craving for comfort and even luxury which had characterized him as a youth became, not weaker, but more and more strong. Squalor, such as he saw around him when he drove home, out into the country from the factory, induced in him what was almost a physical nausea. Looking back now to the years passed in Earl's Court, as he lay awake at night, he would shudder at the recollection of the cock-roaches that scuttled about the hall; of the sweet-sour odour of garbage from the basement; of the litter of milk-tops, squashed cigarette-packets and empty paper bags that collected about the steps outside, as though someone had intentionally swept them there. Often he nagged at Maureen or at the servants themselves if, running his finger over the burnished top of the grand piano, he found he could leave a streak; or if, when he went into the kitchen, he saw crumbs on the table or the floor—"The house will be infested!" he would shout out in rage.

Now, impelled both by this horror and by pity for his mother, condemned to spend her last days in this miserable "flatlet" of hers, he suddenly leant forward: "You know, darling, I've been thinking, I've been thinking about you a lot." It was a lie which he had so often told to her in the past, and always she had believed it.

"Yes?" she prompted eagerly.

"Well, I've been worried about you. Very worried about you. I know that you've been finding things difficult. Financially, I mean."

"Oh, it hasn't been so bad," she said: though it was bad, and was getting worse and worse, as prices rose higher and her little pension remained exactly where it had stood before the war. "You know that I'm not an extravagant person."

269

"Not extravagant! When you spend what you have on every Tom, Dick and Harry! You've virtually given away all your capital—haven't you? Well, haven't you?"

"Oh, if you put it like that. But these days, what's the good of clinging to one's money? Sooner or later they'll take it all away from us anyway.

"Anyway, I've decided to give you an allowance."

This was something which Rosemary had long ago said that Tim ought to do, and she and Christine had even wrangled about it. "But how can he, poor dear, with all the expenses he has to meet?" Christine had demanded. "That house needs a terrible amount of keeping up. And then there's the child—and Maureen who's used to having the best of everything." But secretly, in spite of this defence, it had rankled with Christine that neither he nor Gwyneth had ever thought of giving her any regular financial help.

"Of course it won't be much," he went on. "As you know, I have a lot of demands on me. But if things improve—as I hope they will—then, of course, I shall step it up. But for the moment the figure I had in mind was ten pounds a month."

Christine was overcome with gratitude and pleasure; and this in turn only intensified her son's pity and guilt. Ten pounds. . . . It was what they paid out to the German girl alone; less than what he himself would spend on a single pair of hand-sewn shoes; the cost of two of Jeremy's ten-minute visits to a doctor in Harley Street. Yet to her it would make the same difference as a hundred pounds to Maureen and himself.

"Now I can go in for one or two extravagances," she announced. "And do you know what the first one will be? You mustn't be shocked! . . . I'm going to hire myelf a T.V. set. Like that, it doesn't come terribly expensive; poor old 'Beddy' told me, they have one now, you know. And, of course, I shall save on what I spend on cinemas and bridge and things like that."

He wanted to cry out, as he and Gwyneth had so often wanted to cry out in the past. "Oh, stop, stop, stop, stop!" for the pathos of all this was terrible. But he controlled himself, as he leant forward, biting on his unlit pipe, and listening to her enthusiastic chatter.

". . . Of course, with that extra money, I could really afford to take the flatlet on the second floor—there's one vacant there.

But I don't see why I should. After all, in the summer, the basement will be much cooler, and you know how I hate the heat. And in the winter, there's a lovely stove, you know, a Cosy stove. . . . Yes, I think I shall be very happy, very happy and snug."

She went on to tell him how she had visited the furniture-depository to sort out the pieces she would need. What was left Larry could have when he and Louise and the children arrived back from India. "Unless, of course, you and Maureen would like anything, darling?" She had already given to them as wedding-presents most of the things of any value, and the rest were now with Gwyneth. So Tim shook his head.

"It's terribly sweet of you. But really we have all we need. This house is overcrowded as it is."

"I expect that Larry will be glad of anything that I can spare. I gather that the poor things will be very badly off."

After having to leave the Indian Army, Larry had put some money into a jute-factory owned by one of Louise's cousins, but soon that had failed. Later he became tutor to the son of a Maharajah: the boy had eventually gone to Harrow and his father had been deposed. There had been other and briefer, and less lucrative, jobs until he had come at last to the decision, which the doctors had already long ago made for him, that he ought to return to England. He was going to buy a farm, with what capital was left to him, and then at least—as he shocked Christine by writing in one of his letters—the State would educate his children and pay for his funeral.

Tim got up and sat on the arm of Christine's chair: he put his arm round her shoulders, and lowered his face so that his cheek touched hers. That touch of the stretched, grafted skin which had induced in Pat a feeling of animal panic only gave Christine a sense of contentment and love renewed and magnified. "Dear Tim," she murmured.

"I'm afraid things have been pretty tough for you," he said.

"No more than for anyone else of my age," she replied. She thought of all her old friends, living either in small flats and boarding-houses in Earl's Court or Kensington, or in cottages in the country, some of them bereaved, many of them lonely, most of them poor, and her pity, so often directed inwards to herself during these years, was now for them only. "But I feel the worst is over. When I met Sir Noël Hope-Ashburn the other day—it was quite by chance, you know, as I walked down St. James's—he told me that in their early sixties most people pass through a period when they feel low and unwanted and bitter about things. But if they can survive that, well, he says that then suddenly things improve. One *accepts*, yes, that's how he put it. One accepts. One learns to do without—yes, that was his other phrase." The facile optimism with which the great consultant had, from professional habit, attempted to cheer her up, had seemed to her genuine, considered, the fruit of a deep experience. It had heartened her, as it had heartened so many of his dying patients, who had not guessed they were dying.

"You're very brave," Tim said. "You know, I think you're rather a wonderful person."

Though he had said this to her often enough in the past, it was the first time he had ever really believed it.

V

"Really I've got to an age when going away has ceased to be any fun for me," Christine said to her neighbour in the flat above her, as she gave him her keys.

"Now you mustn't get set in your habits! That's the first sign of old age, you know."

"Yes, I suppose it is, Mr. Ferman. You know, yesterday, when I went down to buy a cake at the Apple-blossom, and found that it had been closed for redecoration, it really quite upset me to have to go to that other place up the road. Though the cake was much better."

"Well, there you are! You see! Now that's what you must guard against," the little Viennese furrier admonished her. "You should be looking forward to seeing your son and his wife and their children, and to having a change of scene."

"My stepson," Christine murmured.

"I'd give my bottom dollar to have a few days in the country!"

When Christine had been woken that morning by the tinny

rattling of the cheap alarm-clock by her bedside, she had experienced a sinking of her spirits. There was a mist, she noticed, as she peered upwards through the window, and a nasty chill in the air: other people's houses always seemed cold, and a farm house, only recently inhabited after months of being unoccupied, would be especially so. She did not want to leave her own gas fire, which she now got up to light, her television set, and all the innumerable little habits with which she now filled out her days. And there were other anxieties, about even more trivial things; for she had now reached that age when, for example, not to have the early morning cup of tea to which one has grown accustomed seems to be a major deprivation, and to have to use a strange lavatory or to sleep under three blankets instead of two blankets and an eiderdown a major discomfort. Probably the train would be crowded. Probably no one would meet her. Probably her knee would begin to be troublesome. . . .

Even the thought of seeing Larry, Louise, and the two children failed to console her. "It'll be lovely to have them back," she said to her friends, for that was what they expected her to say. But, when they actually arrived, she found herself as ill at ease with them as if they had been strangers. Dutifully, week after week, letters had passed between England and India; but, as so often, the personalities of those letters seemed only to be distant relatives of the personalities who now, in embarrassment, kissed each other and asked for each other's news. The crude vitality which had been the source of Larry's attraction for Christine as for others now seemed to have spent itself, like some torrent spreading out over mud-flats, in a sick and weary resignation. The vast frame remained: but he stooped, the right shoulder thrust further forward than the left, so that the impression of more than human stature was now wholly lost. The once red hair which sprouted at the opening of his shirt had turned a rusty grey; it had also receded away from his forehead which, having once seemed too narrow, now seemed to be unnaturally domed. Even his voice, its confident timbre faded, seemed to express an exhaustion which he could combat only by an effort of the will.

It upset Christine to look at him: for in her mind he had always remained as he had looked, shiny-faced, exultant and sturdy, on the day of his wedding.

Louise herself seemed to be as ill at ease and strained as when she and Larry had still not announced their engagement and Adrian was alive, answering Christine's questions in the off-hand, vaguely impatient manner which her defensiveness had always taken. "She thinks me silly and exasperating," Christine had decided. "I must take care not to seem to interfere where Larry or the children are concerned." For, already, on two occasions, when Christine had said something about Larry's health and made a suggestion about the children, Louise had snubbed her.

The children themselves had been the bitterest disappointment of all. They were quiet and undemonstrative, over-tall for their age, with spindly arms and legs and dark, peaked faces. The girl, who was eleven, was covered in hair. Each spoke with the same melancholy, sing-song accent, usually to each other, seldom to their parents, and never to Christine. Their names were Vivian and Violet. "What names!" Christine exclaimed to Gwyneth. "You'd have thought Larry would have objected." Like their colouring and their voices, unnoticeable to the majority of people round them, for Christine these names carried with them the unmistakable stigma "Eurasians". The truth was that, though she did not care to admit it, she felt ashamed of her grandchildren.

Larry was at the station to meet her, wearing a khaki shirt and pullover, some grease-stained corduroy trousers with a patch on the knee, and heavy boots, one of which, Christine noticed, was laced up with twine. He was leaning on a bicycle, talking to the Station Master, while he puffed at a pipe.

"Afraid I'm still tinkering with that bloody bus of mine," he explained. "Do you mind a short walk?"

"No, of course not," she said, although, cramped in a full third-class carriage, she had slowly become aware that her knee was beginning to throb. "I'd like to have some exercise."

"Good." He eased her suit-case on to the cross-bar of his bicycle, and, holding it with one hand, began to push it with the other. Although they then set off at a moderate pace, she noticed that soon he was breathless.

"How are you getting on?" she asked. "Have you settled in all right?"

"Still camping, I'm afraid. There's dry-rot in the dining-room, so for the moment we're eating in the kitchen. The place is in a terrible state."

"A lot to do?"

"I'll say there is! And no money to do it," he added gloomily. "Still, by next year when we've got the potato-crop, we hope to be on our feet. . . . Thank God for that furniture you let us have!" he added, pausing to wipe his forehead on the back of his sleeve. "Without that, we'd have been sunk."

"And how are you keeping?"

"Can't complain. I get my treatment on the Health Scheme. They jab away at me—emetine, horrible stuff—and my last test showed a great improvement. So they say. But this amoeba makes one feel so tired. And depressed. Suicidal."

"Yes, I know."

"And one never seems to reach the end of a day. You know what it's like on a farm. At it every bloody moment. Can't get help either, not easily. Had a boy, but he's just left us—gone into a factory. They all do that in the end."

They were making their way up what had once been the drive: nettles encroached on either side, dripping with the recent rain, and between them there was a zig-zag lane, now expanding and now narrowing, of bindweed and grass. Christine thought of the drive of Myra's farm which, even during the war, had been so carefully weeded and gravelled.

Suddenly there was a rustle from behind some straggly bushes, and the children emerged. They halted and peered intently at Christine while Violet stooped down and scratched at one of her hairy legs. "Here's Granny," Larry said.

Neither of the children answered.

"Hello, Violet. Hello, Vivian." Christine went forward to the girl; but at once, like some startled animal, she retreated, giggling, behind the dripping bushes.

"They're shy," Larry said. "But they don't stay like that for long. Unfortunately."

"I do believe they've grown even since I last saw them. How are they liking school?"

"Vivian came home with nits in his hair, and Mummy had to wash it in Dettol," Violet volunteered. Both of them let out a high-pitched spurt of laughter.

"I'm afraid that's the kind of thing they're likely to pick up with a liberal education," Larry said.

"The rabbits have got out," Violet suddenly announced, as the two children trailed up the drive at least two yards behind the grown-ups.

"What! Now who the hell was responsible for that? Which of you left the door open?" Larry turned, furious. "Well? Who was it? Own up! Come on, own up!"

"Vivian!"

"Vi!"

"I like that! I didn't!"

"You did!"

"*You* did! Little liar!"

"Liar yourself!"

Larry's anger passed as quickly as it had been aroused. Doggedly pushing the bicycle on, he muttered: "Christ! Another bloody job for this afternoon."

"I've brought you a present, children," Christine said. "I hope you like mint humbugs. They used to be Daddy's favourite sweet." She was hobbling now, the joint of her knee feeling as if a needle had lodged itself inside it.

The children said nothing.

"Well, where are your manners?" Larry demanded. "Vi, Vivian! What do you say, you dirty little rats?"

"Thank you, Granny."

"Thank you, Granny."

There was another wild squeal of laughter.

That night the boiler went out, and since both Larry and Louise, who had started a part-time job as assistant in a dress shop in the town, were obviously exhausted, Christine insisted that they should sit and listen to the wireless while she lit it again. It took her a long time, and the vast kitchen was icy. Draughts swept across the linoleum from the rickety back door to the door of the scullery as she knelt and grubbed with her frozen hands for clinkers; and meanwhile a long, thin cat with only one ear kept mewing piteously and rubbing itself against her. "Damn!" she said to herself. "Hell! Hell, hell, hell!" Spent matches were littered about her. Then she gasped: "Oh!" A mouse had suddenly scuttled across a rafter, unregarded by the cat, which continued to mew and to purr.

At last the task was finished; having put some milk in an aluminium saucer for the cat, Christine went back to the uncarpeted sitting-room, where she found Larry outstretched in one armchair, his eyes closed and his pipe between his teeth, and Louise in another, inexpertly darning socks as she talked. ". . . I don't know who they think they are. The airs they give themselves. 'Well, that might have been all right three years ago,' she said to me. And you could see how common she was, you could tell it from her voice. Her car was outside—a chauffeur, too, of course. . . ." The plaintive sing-song voice whined on and on, with Larry sometimes grunting, as if in response.

As Christine sat down, Louise broke off to ask: "All right?" and Larry opened his eyes.

"What? What?" he asked. Then, seeing his step-mother, he sat up, knocking his pipe out on the fender. "Well, is it going?"

"Yes. At last."

"You're a genius, Mummy!"

"But that kindling's all damp."

"I know. Shocking. That's how they sent it."

Suddenly Louise, who had previously been treating Christine as though she were an unwanted guest produced by a billeting officer, got heavily to her feet and urged her: "Come and sit here. Your hands are quite blue. Please!"

"No, really. I'm perfectly happy. Thank you, my dear. Perfectly happy."

"Don't be silly, Mummy." She retrieved a sock from the armchair, and cried: "Come! Come on!"

From that moment the constraint seemed to be loosened between them; and as Larry slept, breathing heavily, snuffling and grunting, they found themselves at last able to talk to each other. Louise had grown plainer with the years: no longer did she now bother to rouge her cheeks or to cover her arms, which were as brown and hairy as Vi's, with calamine lotion. She had a moustache along her upper lip, and she had developed a nervous tic which made it appear as if she were continually winking with her left eye. She was wearing slippers trodden down at the heels, which had probably belonged to Larry; an old camel-hair dressing-gown, beneath which a petticoat, grey with use, could be glimpsed; and two blue plastic clips, shaped as birds, to hold back her thick, greasy hair from the plumpening face.

She was talking to Christine about their life on the farm, with the same kind of weary, sardonic resignation with which

Larry himself would discuss it. Nothing had gone as they expected it; much had gone worse. She herself had had to take the job, for lack of money, and Larry's dysentery, instead of clearing up at once, as the doctors had promised, seemed to go on and on. She sighed, chewing on a piece of yarn to sever her darning-needle from the sock at which she had been working.

Then she leant forward.

"We were wondering how you would feel—whether you would like—whether you would care to make your home with us. Of course we've so little to offer in the way of amusement and comforts," she went on hurriedly as she saw the look of dismayed astonishment on Christine's face. "And, after all, you're very comfortably placed in your little flat, aren't you?"

Christine stared at Larry's slumped form: the once handsome, youthful face now, in the flicker of the firelight, looked old, old, old. He might have been her brother. "Well, yes," she agreed. "I'm really very comfy where I am." She thought of the bars of her gas fire; the milk bottle outside her front door, newly painted bright green; the photographs in silver frames of Adrian, Gwyneth and Tim—but not of poor Larry— the television set, and on it the vase in which she put the flowers which Mr. Fernam gave her from his garden. "Yes, very comfy," she said, conscious at the same time that her leg was again throbbing; that her back was icy, while her face smarted from the heat of the wood fire, and that outside the door the cat had again begun to mew. . . .

Larry sat up and rubbed his eyes, which were bleary under the jutting rusty-grey eyebrows. "Bed," he said. "Bed."

Christine's room contained nothing but a cupboard which creaked and tottered when she pulled at the knob, but stubbornly refused to open; a canvas chair and a folding bridge-table; and a bed which had once been Tim's. There were no curtains on the windows, one of the panes of which was broken.

She wandered about, slowly undressing; she did not know what to say in answer to Louise. "But I'm not strong enough," she told herself. "I'm too old for this life. I only want peace and quiet. Tim would be furious."

There was a knock at the door, and Louise came in with a steaming mug in one hand.

278

"I've brought you some Ovaltine. I hope you like it. Do you?"

Christine never liked to drink hot milk; but she took it from her, saying: "Thank you. How very thoughtful of you!"

Louise gazed down, as Christine placed herself on the bed and raised the mug to her lips with a funny, child-like sigh. "You know," she said, "I believe you're more beautiful now than when I first knew you. And I"—she looked at her reflection in the blotched glass of the cupboard, and her sing-song voice became more plaintive with a burden of suppressed tears—"I look a sight! Look at me! Look at me! A sight!"

VI

The next day Louise left the house early to catch the bus which would take her to her work. She had intended to walk the children to school first, but they had dawdled over their dressing and then over their breakfast, and she had had to go off without them. Larry had got up to milk their one cow and feed the pigs and hens, and had then gone back to bed, long before Christine herself had woken. He was having what Louise called "one of his bad days".

Christine went up to see him, where he lay, yellow-faced and shivering, under a number of grey army blankets, an overcoat, a dressing-gown, and a sheep-skin rug which had come off the floor.

"It'll pass, it'll pass," he said between chattering teeth. "It always does."

"Can I do nothing for you?"

"No, nothing. Thank you all the same. . . . Has poor Louise gone?"

"Yes. She had to race to catch the bus. The children are finishing breakfast."

"Haven't they gone to school?"

"No, I'm afraid not. Can they find their own way there?"

"They can. But will they? That's the question."

"Oh, I'll make them," she said. "I'll go with them myself, if need be."

"What a day! More mist—always mist."

"Poor Larry!" She put a hand down to his forehead, which was fiery and moist with sweat, and then ran her fingers back through his thinning hair. It was the first time she had caressed him since he had passed adolescence. "Well!" she shook herself. "I must deal with those children."

"Oh, leave them. It doesn't matter. Why should you bother?"

"But I must! I suppose that'll be one of my jobs, won't it? I must. They'll have to get used to me, if I'm going to live with you."

He showed no surprise; but, as he drew the coverings up to his chin, turning his body over, he grunted with contentment. "Very well," he said. "See what you can do with them." He shut his burning eyes, and then gave way, with what was almost a voluptuous pleasure, to the tremors that shook his whole frame.

The children were nowhere in the house. Christine wandered up and down it, calling their names: "Vi! Vi! Vivian! Vivian, dear! Vi!" Then, still calling, she went into the garden. "Children, where are you? Children! Children!" The mist entered her lungs and soon she was coughing. "Children! Vi! Vivian!" The cat appeared from nowhere and pressed against her legs, still mewing piteously.

Suddenly she heard a titter from behind the bushes. "Children!" she called. "No, this is very naughty. Come here at once!"

A stone flicked at her out of the mist, and stung her on the ankle. There was another high-pitched titter; and then another stone struck her, this time on the shoulder. But, undefeated, she continued to walk towards the bushes while the cat whisked and sidled behind her. "Children! Children! That's enough of that!"

Vaguely she discerned two shapes rising out of the bushes and coming towards her, reluctant, step by step.